THE QUIXOTE PACT

VICTORIA CARO

The Quixote Pact, while drawing largely on true historical events, is a work of fiction, and though some real locations and public figures are mentioned, all other characters and events described in this book are a creation of the author.

Unless otherwise specified, the source for the Founding Fathers' quotes is Founders Online, National Archives, https://founders.archives.gov. Original punctuation and grammar have been respected.

Cover Design: Nancy Caro/Funandesign.es
Illustrations in the novel: Victoria Caro

Discover other titles by Victoria Caro at:
www.victoriacaro.com[1]
TRAPPED IN A DREAM
ESSENCE
MARY'S APOSTLES

---

1. http://www.victoriacaro.com/

PART I

"Who shall write the History of the American Revolution? Who can write it? Who will ever be able to write it?"

—John Adams to Thomas Jefferson, 30 July 1815

"Nobody; except merely its external facts. all its councils, designs and discussions, having been conducted by Congress with closed doors, and no member, as far as I know, having even made notes of them. these, which are the life and soul of history must forever be unknown."

—Thomas Jefferson to John Adams, 10 August 1815

CHAPTER 1

"I would begin by informing the world and Posterity that the history of the United States never has been written, and never can be written."

—*John Adams, 2 November 1815*

Professor Antonio del Mar squinted into the beam of light to assess his audience. The obscure, immobile figures waited with expectation in dead silence. He felt encouraged.

He cleared his throat. "Much has been said about the American Revolution; about the great men who fought for a just cause; about the ragtag group of rebels heroically defeating the largest war machine of its day and the birth of an experiment that would change the world."

The professor paused. He took in a soft breath and sharpened his gaze. "All true. However, what you know is but half the story." He swept his pointed stare over his audience slowly. "I'd like you all to ponder the following: What exactly made the thirteen colonies think they could entertain a war against the largest war machine without a navy, artillery or basic gunpowder? Or think about this: The thirteen colonies were entirely surrounded by British territory on land. Why didn't the largest war machine simply strangle them with their mighty grip?"

Again, Professor del Mar paused, leaving the questions to hang for a few seconds.

Careful to pronounce each word clearly, he continued. "For over 200 years, a secret pact has been kept buried; a pact that ensured victory for the Americans and, more crucially, survival thereafter. Why buried? Unfavorable circumstances at the time required it. Today, I am compelled to lift its veil; the time has come for the whole story of the American Revolution to be told."

Hearing the shuffling of feet comforted the professor. He had captured the public's attention, and they were accommodating themselves in anticipation of the great revelation. They knew it was coming. He had made sure to publicize it well with hopes of achieving maximum attendance and diffusion.

A door in the back of the auditorium opened and the silhouette of a man backlit by the light in the hall, walked through. Professor del Mar observed how the shadowy figure remained standing in front of the entrance rather than taking a seat.

"Let me start by setting the stage," he went on to tease. "At the dawn of 1781, Washington was a weary man. His army had faced insurmountable challenges from the start and six years later they were at their greatest. When George Washington assumed command of the Continental Army in 1775, there was no such thing as an army, continental or otherwise. He found himself Commander-in-Chief of a haphazardly assembled band of militias and untrained citizen-soldiers, without a rudimentary infrastructure to transport supplies and equipment, or money to buy them. To make matters worse, a dangerous lack of widespread belief in the 'goodness of the cause' or, maybe more importantly, its viability, hardly helped sustain morale. Discontentment resulted in his forces leaving in droves as soon as their commission expired, while the threat of mutiny hovered ever-present. Against this backdrop, it should not come as a surprise that though some battles were won, most were lost. And, by 1778, Washington's Fabian approach, that is, hoping to wear out the larger opponent rather than to confront it, began to exasperate many, namely the generals who had indeed accomplished some of the few successes."

Del Mar's voice deepened. "If you are here, I imagine you have heard of the Conway Cabal, a handful of Washington's generals plotting to overthrow him; or the Newburgh Conspiracy, where officers of the Continental Army planned a coup on the Continental Congress. Did you know there was even a sinister scheme to assassinate Washington?"

Professor del Mar inserted a strategic pause, and then continued. "George Washington was a single man fighting several enemies at the same time. The last straw came with the betrayal of his brother-in-arms Benedict Arnold; it would throb in his chest permanently. The reality was that Washington could not trust anyone no matter which side of the enemy lines they were on."

The professor reached for his glass of water. As he took a sip, he sneaked a look at the brunette sitting in the front row. She was his prime target.

Her eyes were set firmly on him. He had her attention.

Del Mar placed the glass back on the stand and resumed. "In the midst of internal conspiracies and betrayals, and overwhelming challenges at the battlefront, the Commander-in-chief had to contend with some very ill-conceived priorities set by the Continental Congress. When the victory in Saratoga provided a window of hope by gaining the much-needed official endorsement of France, General Washington was despaired to learn that the Continental Congress had drafted delusional ambitions of invading Canada ... again. The idea had already been attempted at the start of the war with dismal results. Then, the general had supported it because carrying off with all the British territories in North America along with independence had been the initial plan. Years into the war, he was all the wiser. You see, it wasn't just that the struggling colonial army had proven to be in no position to accomplish such a feat; it was the foreboding consequence of it. France had lost Canada to Britain less than 20 years earlier. So, if by the Grace of God, the alliance between the Americans and France succeeded against Britain in Canada, France would reasonably claim its territory back, leaving the thirteen independent colonies engulfed between France in the north and Spain everywhere else, west and south."

Another door in the back opened, this time the one on the left side. Once again, the professor saw the likes of a man in a suit enter. He, too, stood squarely before the door when it closed.

Del Mar's words accelerated. "There is a long list of common-sense reasons why the free but war-battered independent sister colonies would find themselves at a survival disadvantage surrounded by their two much larger and seasoned neighbors, not the least important the fact that these two empires were united by family ties. France and Spain were ruled by the same Bourbon Royal house and had, for several decades, proven their mutual loyalty through secret family pacts." Del Mar narrowed his stare. "Let me underscore: These pacts were nothing to scoff at. A good example, very close to home for Washington, came to light in 1763. When France lost its North American territories to Britain—in a war that many would argue Washington triggered himself—the king of France, Louis XV, secretly ceded half of Louisiana to his cousin Charles III of Spain in compensation for his support. Now please keep in mind that Louisiana then comprised a third of today's United States. Let that sink in ..." The professor performed one slow sweep of the audience." Thanks to the family pact, Spain gained a territory that doubled the size of the thirteen colonies in addition to what she already held in the Americas. This extraordinary territorial expansion consolidated the Spanish empire's control over a huge portion of North America. By 1790, it extended from present-day Mexico north through 80% of US territory and over a large swath of western Canada into Alaska."

To make his point, Del Mar shared a slide with a map on the screen behind him.

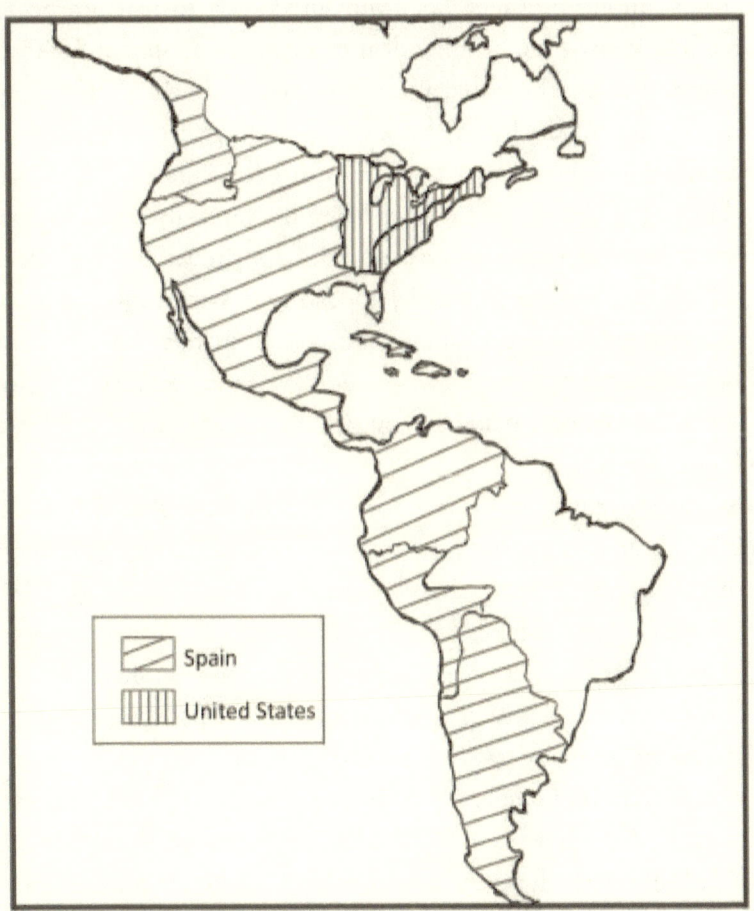

"I trust you understand Washington's qualms. Even with a hard-fought victory, the thirteen colonies stood little chance of true independence surrounded by these two family-linked empires. The only problem was that without their help there was little chance of winning independence altogether. In Alexander Hamilton's own words: *If we are saved, France and Spain must save us.*"

A cough in the front row and a couple of camera operators relaxing their arms signaled the public's slipping patience.

Professor del Mar rushed to dangle a piece of meat. "George Washington was a Freemason. He understood the benefits one reaped from secret pacts among brothers. So, confronted with dismal prospects and with the sole knowledge of a handful of men, the Commander-in-Chief saw only one way out: he sealed a secret pact of his own."

Del Mar stalled briefly to check on the two ghostly figures standing guard at the doors. He knew he was on borrowed time. He would have to hurry, but not at the expense of sacrificing his carefully crafted story. The professor knew that not everyone would be happy to learn the whole truth. His goal was to minimize impact by appealing to sympathy for a desperate man who resorted to desperate measures at a desperate time, and after all the shock and awe hope that what remained was the picture of a victorious president whose gamble paid off ... until now. After two hundred years, it was all in jeopardy.

A subtle movement to his right drew the professor's attention. Tucked discreetly behind a side panel, he recognized the scarred face watching him. Its stern gaze narrowed to a pointed glare.

His time *had* run out. He'd have to cut it short.

Del Mar rolled his eyes over the body of journalists sitting at his feet. He focused on the brunette. *If he could reel her interest in just enough ...*

"I'd like to jump forward in time and share with you a number of mysterious actions George Washington took as president in the construction of the new nation." The professor rushed through his slides and settled on one with several bullet points. "When establishing its new currency, he adopted for its symbol a crucial item burrowed from the

Spanish empire's coat of arms. Why? During his presidential inauguration, the privileged position of standing by his side was granted to a Spaniard no one has ever heard of. Why? On this same day, the only foreign warship welcomed to anchor in the harbor was Spanish. Why? And why was the layout for the new nation's capital copied from that of a Spanish town that few here have ever heard of?" Antonio inserted a purposeful pause. "Let me repeat: Washington D.C.'s layout is a copy of a certain Spanish town, and I assure you it is no coincidence."

Antonio could sense his audience was hanging onto every word.

"What about the White House, the ultimate symbol of the house of the people and executive branch? The great honor of laying its foundational stone was granted to a Spaniard no one has ever heard of. Why? And can it be mere coincidence that the date chosen for the symbolic event was the 300th anniversary of Spain's landing on the new world? Why not the date of the Mayflower's, which was a month away? The Capitol building, the ultimate symbol of the new nation's legislative power, was illustrated extensively with imagery and iconography common to Spain and the Americans under the words 'our history'. Why? And lastly, the establishment of the Supreme Court and ultimate symbol of the new nation's judiciary power was entrusted to the one person who spent a key period of the Revolutionary War in Spain."

The two men at the doors began to walk toward the stage.

"... Our history ...," repeated Antonio slowly as he refortified his gaze with unsettling intensity. "Every symbolic icon of the new republic is Spanish at its core. I cannot emphasize this enough, for the ultimate symbol of US sovereignty and identity, the Great Seal of the United States of America, derives its design from the coat of arms that distinguished the Spanish Empire when it dawned under Queen Isabella of Spain."

A comparative of the two seals was displayed on the screen. A quiet exhale of surprise filled the air.

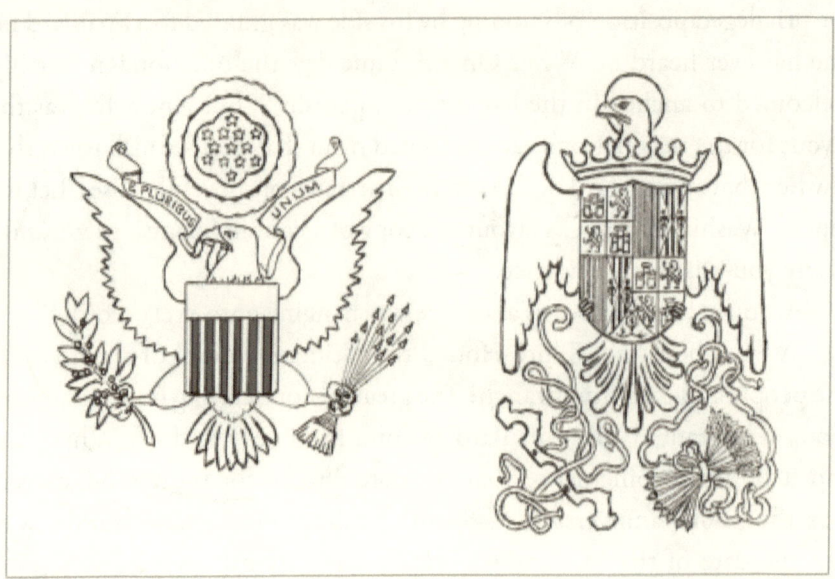

"Please notice the eagles, their halos, and the bundle of arrows," said Del Mar. He paused. "I have only mentioned a handful of examples. There are more. The question remains: why?"

The professor blinked at the sight of one of the approaching men reaching under his coat. He quickly turned his head to the side and observed Scarred-Face tense his muscles.

"Let me give you a hint," he rushed to say. "After signing the Constitution of the United States, the act that sealed the union of the new republic, and despite having spent several months in Philadelphia, Washington chose that day to stop at a bookstore on his way out. Of all the things he should have had on his mind as he prepared to return as the first president, it was the purchase of the Spanish novel 'Don Quixote' that occupied it. What was so special about this novel to warrant his attention in such a ceremonious manner? To further the mystery, upon George Washington's passing, this specific book was catalogued as found 'on the table'. He owned thousands of volumes. Why keep this one in hand's reach?"

A sudden altercation in one of the aisles was closely followed by the sound of a gunshot exploding in the air. A wave of panic washed over the audience aggravated by the overwhelming darkness.

Utter chaos ensued.

Del Mar reacted with extraordinary reflexes, throwing himself to the floor, purposely in the direction of the brunette.

She froze at his maneuver and stared at him with her large almond eyes. His handsome features were softly lit by the camera equipment nearby.

"On the table," he mouthed at her, and repeated: "On the table."

The TV cameras, broadcasting live, remained fixed on the empty podium as the technicians and press crouched down in their positions, nervously assessing their surroundings to see if it was safe to lift their heads.

Only the brunette saw the professor swiftly jump to his feet, launch one last forceful look at her, and disappear behind the curtains.

CHAPTER 2

"All the happy Effects of that Transaction [Spain's support] for America, are not generally known; I may sometime or other acquaint the World with some of them."

—*Benjamin Franklin to Horacio Gates, 2 June 1779*

What just happened? It took Sofia Auru-Soto a few seconds to react.

Abruptly, the auditorium lights switched on and all her colleagues leaped into action at the same time, running to their microphones and cameras as if a second shot had signaled them to do so.

Sofia had neither. She had come alone and was not even a real journalist. She was a psychologist who had made a name for herself grounding the human spiritual experience in physical neural activity or natural processes, meaning that she supplied a reasonable explanation for miracles and other unexplained religious phenomena. It was in this capacity that she occasionally consulted for an online magazine and had agreed to attend the event as a favor to the owner, who was also a friend. Business was slow and he was short on staff.

The strange thing was that this highly publicized presentation had little to do with the magazine's line of interest. "The Skeptic Warrior" focused on matters that pushed into the realm of superstition and the supernatural, yet they had received a frontline invitation to a highly coveted event unrelated to UFO abductions or voices from the afterlife. Dan, the owner-friend, accepted out of curiosity and the potential for business. He had planned to come himself, hoping to rub with some prominent elbows, but was held back at the last minute.

Sofia took a deep breath and methodically scanned her surroundings to get her bearings. Concluding that the danger was over, she stepped onto the stage to check where the professor had disappeared, while replaying the events in her mind. She had noticed he had been paying close attention to her. At first, Sofia thought he was checking her out, which she found flattering. Del Mar was attractive in a stereotypical kind of away: tall, dark, and handsome with a sexy Spanish cadence in his otherwise formal tone that made his speech enthralling no matter what he talked about. At

10

least, to her. Now, she felt a mixture of disappointment and confusion, wondering if his interest was different. Because why would he mouth the words "on the table" to her? What was that about? Had he mistaken her for another journalist?

She walked past the podium toward the broad gilded curtain that shortened the depth of the stage in half. It was massive. Sofia felt for an opening and located one, when she also saw a small fissure in the fabric. She poked at it. The hole was still hot. Sofia swallowed and slid through the break in the curtain. It didn't take her long to spot the lifted trapdoor on the floor, in the back. She approached it.

As she climbed down on the makeshift ladder, her phone vibrated. She reached for it. It was Dan.

"Sofia, are you alright?" she heard.

"Yes, I'm fine."

"Are you sure? I was following the event in my office, but your seat was outside the camera frame. It was difficult to judge how close it came to you. What happened?"

Sofia tucked her head under the floor planks and saw it led to an ample storage space where the usual backstage equipment was kept. It became apparent the trapdoor was a quick shortcut, since on the left, she saw the wider access to the side hall that led up to the stage. On the opposite side, there was a garage door, where the equipment for the auditorium was brought in, and beside it, the pedestrian access, or, in this case, exit. "I'm not sure. It was dark. I heard a commotion toward the other end of my row. I also heard the shot, but it happened so fast I can say what came first."

"Did anyone get hurt?"

"Not that I'm aware. By the time the lights came back on, the shooter had been tackled and removed." It just then hit her how speedily that had occurred.

"Where are you now?"

"Under the stage floor. I saw the professor run through the curtains. There is a trapdoor back here. It leads to an exit."

Sofia headed to it. Outside, she scouted the ramp. The professor was nowhere to be seen. She expected as much. She turned around and headed back in.

"Are you sure you're okay?" asked Dan.

"Yes, don't worry. Just a little shaken. I'll be fine."

"In that case, can you hang around and see what you can find out? Only if you feel up for it, that is."

"Dan, why do you think you were invited? It makes no sense. What does the Revolutionary War or George Washington have to do with unexplained phenomena?"

There was a brief silence.

Sofia heard Dan clear his throat.

"I wasn't invited," he finally said.

"What?"

"The invitation was for you and clearly marked non-transferable. The professor signed it himself. And before you ask, the envelope was addressed to me for the same reason I receive all your invites, so that I'll convince you to accept it."

She stopped at the bottom of the stairs that led back up to the stage. "I don't understand ..." Sofia trailed off as she thought about it. That meant it wasn't a case of mistaken identity. The professor was truly interested in her. She finished her sentence. "None of this has to do with my line of work, either."

"Maybe not, but the last time a strange guy showed up interested in you, it led to our bestselling series. It is still paying the bills. I don't turn down anything with your name on it."

Sofia reached out to hold onto one of the steep steps and proceeded to climb. "What do you know about him, the professor?"

Dan's voice came back with a little edge. "I would appreciate it if you read the briefs I prepare when I assign you a job. It's all in there."

"And I would appreciate it if you were honest with me when you assign them."

There was another split second of silence.

"Alright, here is what I have," started Dan. "Nothing. Other than some applauded academic publications, the background check I ran on Del Mar came back empty. Either he's a specter or he is hiding behind a very secure penname."

"Are you serious? You sent me out to report on a ghost who is claiming absurdities?"

"Read my briefs. That was part of the assignment, to find out who this man is. How does an anonymous scholar secure a presentation at a premium venue like the Smithsonian National Museum of American History and manage to attract half the cupula of the city press? If there ever was a strange phenomenon, this is it, wouldn't you say?"

Sofia stepped on the stage and sighed. "Dan, without much effort, two easy explanations come to mind. Either he has good contacts, which is how things are done in this town, or he is a very skilled hacker who snuck his way onto the museum's schedule and just as stealthily sent out invites. Any savvy 15-year-old can do it."

"Did he look like a hacker to you?"

"No, which leaves us with someone who just pulled off a publicity stunt for an upcoming book." Sofia nibbled at her lip as she looked askance at the bullet hole in the curtain.

"A book that would make for a very interesting read," stressed Dan, "if it were true, as he claims, that the secret pact was written on the back of the long-lost official Declaration of Independence; that he knows what happened to it, and that it has George Washington's signature on it. It would be the exclusive of a lifetime. Sofia, he literally handed you a front row seat to it."

"As I said: an absurdity. And not a very creative one. I saw the movie, Dan. Nicolas Cage walked out with it from the National Archives."

"Sofia, this is serious."

"If you want serious, how about George Washington never signed it? In July of 1776, he was in New York with his forces while the delegates of the Continental Congress did all the signing in Philadelphia."

"There's much confusion about that," started Dan. "What the delegates signed—later in August, not July—was the ceremonial engrossed copy. That's the one people see at the National Archives. The 'official' draft approved by Congress on the 4th of July went missing that same evening and has never been seen again."

"Still, Washington would not have been around to sign that one either."

"Sofia, I need you to get your head in the game." Dan's words came back with authority. "This is what we do. We investigate controversial claims. And let me remind you, someone is taking the professor very seriously."

The truth was Dan didn't have to beg. She was in from the moment Del Mar's large brown eyes came within inches of hers and whispered the three words.

"Fine," she surrendered.

"Wonderful. Here's what I need you to do: Head to the museum offices and find out what they know about Del Mar. What credentials did he supply to gain access? Does he come recommended or sponsored? You know the drill ... Meanwhile, I'm going to reach out to my contacts to see who knows what. Let's track this man down. I want his story."

"Fine," repeated Sofia absently, hatching a plan of her own. No, she wasn't going to waste time at the museum. Besides, it was probably better if she left right away. Police sirens could be heard blaring out front; she had to get out before the interrogations began. Sofia pivoted 180 degrees and headed straight back to the trapdoor. Professor Antonio del Mar, or whatever his real name was, had invited *her* specifically and had handed *her* the clue to follow. There was no need for her to track him down. She was confident he would track *her* down soon enough.

CHAPTER 3

"The Démarchés of Spain are mysterious..."

—John Adams, 25 July 1778

Back at her hotel room, Sofia collected her things in a rush, happy she had packed light. She changed out of her formal suit into a pair of comfortable jeans, a light blue sweater and black walking boots. Then she considered collecting her long wavy hair in a ponytail for comfort but decided against it. Since it was chilly outside, and she had not brought a scarf, leaving it down would help keep her neck warm.

A wise paranoia was fueling her urge. There was a good possibility someone witnessed the professor addressing her before he made a run for it. Maybe a camera captured it. Or, if anything else, her name was on the guest list. The authorities would want a word with her, eventually. She had to maximize whatever time she had to stay ahead.

The television was on and turned to the local news channel. Sofia stopped to listen when she heard the anchor cite the incident again. Perhaps this time they'd mention something about Del Mar. A few seconds into the report, she shook her head. No such luck. It was a repeat segment from moments earlier with no picture or background information on him. The emphasis of the piece was centered around the growing violence in the capital, and how it had reached the sanctity of its prestigious museums.

So strange, though Sofia. The media showed no curiosity for the professor despite the attack on him in front of their own crème. You'd think they'd be all over it if only because they were there to witness it.

Sofia picked up the remote and turned it off. She then walked over to the closet, reached for her navy-blue coat, and donned it. She returned for her backpack and phone, slipped the latter in a pocket at easy reach, and methodically swept the room with her keen eyes to make sure she wasn't leaving anything behind. Satisfied, Sofia walked out the door, closing it behind, and headed toward the elevators.

Her mind was running in several directions. It dawned on her that not only the police might want a word with her. What about whoever tried to stop the professor? What if *they* saw Del Mar whisper something to her? She felt a surge of dread and turned to check the hall. It was clear. As she sped up to reach the elevator and smacked the down-button, she took a deep breath to rein in her overactive mind. Her gift to envision an exceptional number of scenarios was a blessing for her line of work, but a headache any other time.

Just as her fears subsided, the phone rang, startling her. Sofia recovered it from the coat's front pocket and saw it was her sister.

"I'm fine," she answered. The elevator's door opened, she stepped in.

"Okay, good to know. Any reason why you shouldn't be?"

Sofia pressed for the ground floor. "I'm going to guess you are not in front of a TV."

"That hardly qualifies as a guess. You know I'm never in front of a TV."

"Right, your thing is reading and praying. What happened in your exciting life to prompt a call?"

"You're in a jolly good mood."

Sofia offered her sister a grunt as an apology, which Lily accepted with a giggle, their usual exchange.

"Anyway, for your information," continued Lily, "something pretty exciting indeed happened. Ready for it ... we've received a new sign from above."

Upon reaching the ground floor, the elevator door slid open. Sofia stepped out into the lobby and, distracted as she was, only then stopped sharp in a delayed reaction. "What did you just say?"

It had been over a year since the last time her sister had claimed to receive a sign from the heavens. The irony. While Sofia was a stern skeptic who questioned everything as a matter of course, her identical twin was a Catholic sister and historian who believed they were *chosen*. All because the mentioned "sign" had led Lily to discover a hidden message in one of Pope John Paul II's homilies; a message, which in turned contained a clue to finding Fatima's Third Secret. For those who believed in Marian apparitions—which Lily strongly did—Fatima's Third Secret was like the Holy Grail of lost prophesies. So, long story short, with Sofia's reluctant help, they set out to search for it—navigating coded miracles, obscure legends and lost sacred artifacts—only to unravel two mysterious straight lines that connected Europe and the Americas, and which did in fact lead them to the Secret in the end.

With Dan's enthusiastic blessing, their discovery was presented in his magazine as a double fold, metaphorically speaking. Her sister Lily narrated the search as the paving of a divine path, that led to a divine secret, guided by a divine hand. All very divine. People loved it. On the counter fold, Sofia provided her well-placed arguments to explain where possible their findings in strictly rational terms. This most people cared less about. Either way, their remarkable story combined to offer an inspiring message calling for world peace with much success on the printing front—including a book deal—but with very little impact on world affairs.

In conclusion, if they were truly chosen to save the world, they had failed miserably.

Lily answered Sofia's lingering question. "I said: We've received a new sign, a meteor."

"You mean as in an asteroid is coming our way? It's all over? The planet is going to blow up into smithereens because we dropped the ball?"

Sofia was being overtly sarcastic on purpose. She usually had a hard time taking her sister seriously, but now more so in her current situation. She was too busy feeling flustered while scouting the lobby for anyone hunting her down to think about celestial signals. Other than a family, an elderly couple, and someone reading an oversized newspaper, it was all clear.

Her eyes wandered back to the newspaper. *Who reads a real paper in D.C. anymore? No one.* She dashed for the exit.

"Don't get nervous. Let me finish," said Lily. "A meteor as bright as the moon lit up the night sky—"

"Lily, this is not a good time." Sofia stood outside the hotel looking up and down the street. She needed to think of a safe place to plan her next move. "Listen," she said into the phone as she randomly turned south toward Pennsylvania Ave. "Remember I told you last week that Dan asked me to attend a sketchy event in Washington?"

"Yes...?"

"Well, here I am. I was at the presentation this morning when someone took a shot at the speaker."

"Lord all mighty, is he okay?"

"He's fine, don't worry. It would appear that not only in action movies do bad guys have poor aim. The professor was on stage with all the light beams drawing a target on him. They missed."

"That's insane! Was the shooter apprehended?"

Sofia slowed her pace, remembering the commotion. "I think so." She wondered if someone had intercepted the attack, explaining the miss. She'd ask Dan about the police report later. She resumed her speed and recentered. "Lily, I need you to fly out to meet me here."

"Why?"

"I need your expertise and academia all-access card to archives and libraries."

"Sof, I'm in the middle of final exams."

"You won't want to miss this: The speaker claims to know what happened to the official copy of the Declaration of Independence. Apparently, it's lost. Before he was interrupted, he was insinuating something about George Washington agreeing to a secret pact, maybe with Spain, and somehow, the pact is spelled out on the back of the Declaration. I'm not sure how it all ties in. In any event, he referenced your beloved Queen Isabella ..."

Again, Sofia slowed down in reaction to her own words. Was that it? Spain had provided many of the historical clues during their previous quest. And in his speech, Professor del Mar shared a long list of items strongly related to that country. Was that why he sought her out? The thought made her flinch. What connection could there be between their mysterious lines and the lost Declaration? The two subjects were so far apart, she couldn't fathom one. Maybe there wasn't one. It was more likely this guy flapped his long eyelashes at her looking to piggyback off their recent success. The nerve. He would be disappointed, though. The magazine special had a nice run for a while, but interest was winding down fast. As things were going, they'd be lucky if their book deal didn't fall through.

"Okay," agreed Lily, oblivious to her sister's deliberations, "give me a couple of days to wrap things up and I'll be on my way."

"It can't wait. The speaker mouthed something to me before he disappeared, and Dan confessed the invitation was addressed to me, not him. I'm starting to suspect this has to do with our *lines*."

"If so, why hasn't the speaker simply picked up the phone and called you to discuss it?"

"Good question. Look, it's all a little dubious. Might not amount to anything. But Dan wants me to look into it and to be honest I'm curious myself."

"Well, it is getting interesting ... First the meteor and now this ..." muttered Lily. "Fine, I'll do what I can to get there as soon as possible. Where are you staying?"

"I don't know yet. I checked out of the hotel I had booked. It's the first place the police will go looking for me if they have questions. I'm trying to avoid them."

Lily chuckled. "I know a place no one will go looking for you: my friend Sister Genevieve's apartment. It's where I stay when I visit DC. I'll send you her contact information and let her know to expect your call."

Great, thought Sofia. She, the number one skeptic in the nation, was going to bunk beds with a group of devout nuns for the night.

CHAPTER 4

"Freedom, Sancho, is one of the most precious gifts bestowed upon man by the heavens; no treasure hidden on land or under the sea can equal it. For freedom, as for honor, life can and should be ventured."

—Don Quixote by Miguel de Cervantes Saavedra, 1605

It was cold and the day loomed dark under the thick clouds.

Sofia had rented a small non-descript sedan, picked Lily up at the airport, and was driving south on VA-286. Lily spent the initial stretch animatedly telling her about all the calls she made to find someone to cover for her along with anecdotes from each conversation.

Having run out of them, she switched subjects. "So, how was it last night?"

"Very nice," said Sofia. "Your friend Genevieve is a sweetheart. They all are. They went well out of their way to spoil me rotten. Do they have any idea what I think about their beliefs?"

"Of course. They love you all the more for it. Nothing like a good challenge. Did they convert you?"

"Sister Angelica's cinnamon rolls almost did this morning."

"Wow, they pulled out the heavy weaponry. If the rolls don't do the trick, you're definitely a lost cause. You ate them all?"

Sofia smiled. "Go ahead; the ones in the bag are for you."

Lily launched for it. "About time you offered. They smell delicious."

"I see you're leaving your hair long like mine," observed Sofia. Her sister had worn a jaw-length cut for as long as she could remember. Now, her hair was collected in a braid long enough to reach her shoulder blades. "It's going to get confusing."

Lily chuckled at that. Maybe on a genetic level they qualified as identical twins, but on the surface, the difference in their overall countenance could be detected a mile away. "Been too busy to worry about it."

"So, I spoke with Dan this morning," said Sofia. "He confirms there is someone in custody. The police are tight-lipped about it, though. His source told him the mystery has to do with the identity and motives of the shooter, not the professor. He checked out, which is odd, since Dan has been unable to find anything on him. It's all very strange. I tried looking him up myself. Nothing. That man is too elusive to be a scholar ..." Sofia drifted into her mind for a few seconds, but quickly resurfaced. "Anyway, the good news is that no one has asked about me."

"Let me give that professor a try. I'll reach out to my colleagues in Spain. What's his full name?"

"Antonio del Mar Valiente."

"Really? Are you sure? That translates to Antonio from the Valiant Sea ... Sounds more like the name of a dashing hero in a Spanish *telenovela*."

Looks like one, too, thought Sofia. "Likely an alias. It's all we have."

Lily took a bite of her roll. "So, what's the plan?" she asked with her mouth full.

"We are going to start by visiting The Washington Library at Mount Vernon."

"Why?"

"Del Mar shared a slide with a list of American icons he connected to Spain, implying they were related to the secret pact. I wrote them down." Sofia reached into her pocket, retrieved a folded piece of paper, and handed it over to her sister. "Then he said the key to understand why had to do with a book Washington bought the same day he signed the Constitution. The book is 'Don Quixote' and, according to the estate registry, it was found on a table when he passed away. And that's what the professor mouthed to me twice: on the table."

On the table ..., mused Lily to herself. She studied the list and whistled. "I didn't know Washington D.C.'s layout... Wait, the Great Seal was designed off Queen Isabella's armorial? No way."

"I saw a slide of them side-by-side. There are some common elements, but then most armorials look the same because of heraldic rules and symbolisms, so who knows."

"You don't buy anything he's saying, then?"

"To be honest, I'm starting to wonder. Last night I looked into some of the items. Only superficially. I didn't have time for much. There does seem to be a pervasive Spanish presence. At minimum, it would be a bizarre coincidence. At most, what's the reason and why don't we know about it?"

Lily's eyes ran over the list several times. "If any of this is true, what bothers me is that I'm a historian and I didn't know. I mean, obviously many place names and flags, especially in the south and southwest, are linked to Spain's historical presence in the area. That's to be expected. However, US founding icons ... that's a whole other level." Lily shook her head. "And somehow it ties in with the lost Declaration?"

"Apparently."

"Did the professor explain how?"

"He was going to but never got the chance. According to Dan, he asserts that the secret pact was written on the back and signed by Washington."

"On the back ... why on the back? To be clear, we are talking about the Declaration of Independence, not the Constitution, right? Because Washington was involved with the Constitution, not the Declaration."

"Yes, we are talking about the Declaration, and if true, can you imagine how valuable that lost copy would be?"

"Valuable? More like mind blowing." Lily narrowed her eyes. "You realize you're probably being played? It is true that the official copy of the Declaration is lost. That much I know. What's more, it's been labelled the American Holy Grail for its exceptional historical value. So, forget secret pacts, the document itself is priceless. If this professor has a lead on it, it's likely he read our articles and figures that if we were able to track down the impossible once, we can do it again. He wants you to find it for him."

Sofia nodded. "I suspect as much. As does Dan. But we are happy to play along. Either the professor is a fraud, and we get credit for uncovering it, or we find the Holy Grail. Win-win."

"Which one do you think it is?"

Sofia simply shrugged.

"That's it? Where's the enthusiasm? People would kill for the opportunity to hunt down the original Declaration."

Sofia scoffed. "You're right about that."

The road sign for the Fred W. Smith National Library came into view. Sofia turned off Mt. Vernon Memorial Highway onto the access road. They had arrived early and there were plenty of parking spaces. She chose one up close to the soft butter-colored building.

The entrance led to an ample reading room displaying the busts of six of the Founding Fathers with large windows overlooking a patio area. Ahead, next to the reception desk, was an engraved wall with the titles of Washington's sixteen most prized books. Among them, Sofia spotted *Don Quixote*.

As they approached the young lady at the desk, Lily took the lead.

"Let me do the talking. You're supposed to schedule an appointment when requesting access to valuable items."

The young lady, whose nametag read Mindy, smiled. "Good morning."

"Good morning, Mindy. I'd like to apologize for showing up like this. I'm Professor Lily Auru-Soto, a historian, and—"

"Yes, we were expecting you." She turned to Sofia, "Both of you. You must be Dr. Sofia Auru-Soto."

"That's right ... You were expecting us?"

"Certainly. Professor del Mar let us know you were coming. We have everything ready according to his instructions." She took her hand to her chest. "We were very concerned for him after what happened yesterday. What a relief to learn he is well." Mindy smiled again. "If you don't mind, I require some identification. A Mere formality."

The sisters exchanged surprised looks as they retrieved their respective IDs and showed them to her.

Satisfied, Mindy reached for the phone. "I'll let our onsite historian, Ms. Lederman, know you are here." She spoke a few quick words into the handset, replaced it, and stood up. "Please follow me. This way."

Sofia shared another wide look with her sister before asking: "Was the professor here in person to plan our visit? Is he here now?"

"No, unfortunately not. I was so hoping we'd see him again."

"You've met him before?"

Mindy's facial features lit up. "Yes, he is very charming. I met him a few years ago when he accompanied the king and queen of Spain during their visit to the library. He oversaw the arrangements. They were interested in the same books and manuscript we have prepared for you." Her gaze turned inquisitive. "It's the reason you are here, isn't it? To write a piece about them?"

"Yes, yes, of course."

Waiting in a mahogany paneled room stood Ms. Lederman with a pleasant smile. Her lively eyes couldn't help performing a double take on the twins. "Thank you," she said, dismissing Mindy with a polite nod. She signaled Sofia and Lily through a glass door to yet another room.

Once inside, she stood in the center and faced the sisters. "I'm Linsey Lederman, onsite Research Historian for the study of George Washington. Let me start by saying that I am familiar with your work and couldn't be more delighted to welcome you. I hope your visit to Washington D.C. is being enjoyable and productive."

"Most interesting so far, I would say," answered Lily with a slight tease in her tone.

"Ah, yes, I imagine you're alluding to what occurred yesterday. We are so happy Antonio is unharmed. There are crazy people out there."

"Antonio? You've worked closely with the professor?"

Lindsey grinned. "I had the pleasure to assist him during the Spanish royal visit."

"What do you know about him?" asked Sofia.

Ms. Lederman showed sudden confusion. "His work on Spain and the Revolutionary War is highly regarded."

"I meant privately. He is such a mystery."

"Antonio is a private man, for sure, but for us, here at the library, what matters is our mutually beneficial working relationship with him. We are very grateful for his generous gift and happy to attend to his requests."

"What do you mean by gift?"

"Spanish archives hold correspondence between the Founding Fathers and major Spanish players at the time of the founding. During the royal visit, Antonio donated a precious manuscript to our collection to strengthen our research collaboration." She opened her hands wide as if to say: *Thus, here I am.*

Sofia nodded her understanding. "You wouldn't have his number, would you? I've misplaced it and I'd like to thank him for all his trouble."

A hint of amused suspicion crossed her face. "Our communications with Antonio are conducted through his university in Madrid, *Universidad Carlos III*. He did not provide us with his private number." She winked.

Sofia blushed. "That's what I meant, the university, of course, but you know what? I can find it."

Lily raised an eyebrow as she watched the exchange.

"Wonderful," said Lederman. She brought her hands together. "May we begin? Antonio was insistent that I walk you through a couple of items we hold dear in this room."

CHAPTER 5

"Exitus acta probat."
(The outcome proves the deed)

—George Washington's motto.

Lederman swept her hand around the room. "You are standing in the Vault, as we like to call it. Here is where we keep Washington's collection securely protected with controlled temperature and other necessary measures."

Sofia studied the surrounding shelves. They were enclosed behind glass doors and reached from floor to ceiling. Straight ahead, on the wall, was what looked like a heavily embellished coat of arms presiding over the space, and two tables set in front, one on each side.

Ms. Lederman took Sofia's creased gaze as a cue to explain. "Antonio insisted that we placed the two tables flanking the arms." She pointed to the left one. On it was a single manuscript, it appeared weathered. "This is the original letter granting George Washington's older half-brother, Lawrence Washington, his commission in the provincial forces to fight alongside Britain against Spain." She then pointed to the two books on the right table. "And these are George Washington's Spanish and English copies of Cervantes's acclaimed *Don Quixote*. In reality, the two editions are comprised of four volumes each. What you see here is only the first volume for each language. We felt it was unnecessary to bring all eight out. They are very prized copies, especially the Spanish version. It's the 1780 illustrated edition. The Spanish king, Charles III, gave it to him personally as a gift." Ms. Lederman seemed to overflow with pride as if they belonged to her.

"The king's name was Charles III, as in the name of the professor's university?" observed Sofia.

"That's right," confirmed Lederman, without thinking much of it.

"Why would the king of Spain care to give Washington a gift?" asked Lily.

"A few nights before signing the Constitution, Washington met with the Spanish ambassador in Franklin's house. The novel came up in the conversation and Washington must have shown interest. Bear in mind that Franklin had long been corresponding with Prince Gabriel, the king's son, a very bright young man who had gifted Franklin a precious copy as well. Washington bought his English version the day of the signing, but the Spanish ambassador did not know this and arranged to get him the highly demanded Spanish edition on behalf of the king. That's how Washington ended up with two."

"What was the purpose of the meeting?" asked Sofia.

From Lederman's reaction, it was clear she had never been asked that question. "Well, it's hard to say. Though he was removed from the day-to-day governance in those days, Washington was very admired. Many called on him to appeal for his support for whatever they were pushing."

Lily sneaked a doubtful look at Sofia as she approached the wall to study the coat of arms.

"It's an enlarged reproduction of George Washington's bookplate," explained Lederman. "A bookplate was a stamp used to identify the owner of a book. Washington had his designed around his coat of arms."

Lily read its motto. "*Exitus acta probat*." And translated. "The outcome proves the deed."

"Excellent interpretation," celebrated Ms. Lederman. "You just saved me some work. Antonio wanted to make sure you were aware of its accurate translation. It is generally misunderstood to mean 'the end justifies the means'. Not the same thing. George Washington was a man of action and true to his motto believed that an action proved its worth when its outcome played out as the action intended, which is not the same as to say any action is justified. He had principals."

"Why is there a crown on the coat of arms?" ask Sofia. "He fought against the crown."

"The coat of arms has been traced in his family back to 1203, and the crown confers a nobility rank. Washington ordered the bookplate from England, in 1771, before the Revolution. You might be more familiar with the simplified version. Its two red bars and three red stars were adopted for the flag of the District of Columbia."

Sofia had not made the connection and acknowledged her surprise.

Lily moved onto the left table to examine the manuscript. "I imagine there is a story behind this?" said Lily.

"Indeed. That document is of great symbolic significance for Mount Vernon. It explains where the estate got its name from. You see, Lawrence Washington owned the estate before George Washington. In 1740, Lawrence was commissioned to join Vice-Admiral Vernon in a large-scale invasion of Spanish territory in the Caribbean. The port of Cartagena, in present-day Colombia, was a rich trading hub and for that reason of special interest to Britain. The attack to capture it turned out to be an embarrassing fiasco. The British forces were far greater than that of the Spanish. Vernon's numbered roughly 120 ships and 28,000 military personnel while the port of Cartagena was only protected by 5,000 defenders and 6 ships. Despite their considerable disadvantage, the Spaniards won under Admiral Don Blas de Lezo, who with this victory built upon his reputation for outstanding successes against unbelievable odds. He was a naval strategic genius."

"Are you saying George Washington's estate, Mount Vernon, was named after a British Admiral who lost like that?" asked Lily. She did not known that.

"Yes. It's quite ironic, really," explained Ms. Lederman. "George Washington grew up admiring his brother and wanting to follow in his footsteps. It was the reason he pursued a military career. Unfortunately—or maybe not so much for the rest of us—Washington was denied a royal commission. He craved one because he felt slighted for having to fight in the French and Indian war under lower ranking British officers. These experiences impressed on him that Americans were second-rate British subjects." Lederman drew a mischievous smile. "As Antonio would tell you, the irony is that while his brother named his estate after his British commander, Washington's front row seat to knowing the truth behind that commander's failure would become profoundly fateful. It brought to George Washington's attention that the British war machine was far from invincible as it boasted."

"Interesting," said Lily, truly impressed.

"How does it relate to Don Quixote?" asked Sofia, motioning at the books.

Lederman approached the English version. "Through another *interesting* coincidence. It just so happens that this English edition, the one Washington purchased the day he signed the Constitution, was translated by Tobias Smollett, a Scottish poet and author, who was at that battle of Cartagena precisely. As a firsthand witness, he was very critical of the Royal Navy's performance." Lederman paused and tapped the novel with her finger. "Are you familiar with the story of Don Quixote?"

Sofia nodded. "The character's delusion has come to define a psychological disorder. The book is considered the first modern novel and a masterpiece, among other reasons, because it can be many things to different people. It tells the story of an aging man who, driven insane by his obsession with books of chivalry, sets out to become a knight himself to serve his nation and the unfortunate in the name of his imaginary damsel. In his epic adventure, he is accompanied by a simple farmer, whose realism contrasts sharply with Quixote's idealism. So, while on the surface Quixote's quest is a compound of comedic foolish deeds—some tragic, some romantic, some endearing—a deeper analysis unveils a treasure trove for introspection and interpretation. In the end, the philosophical question is: was Quixote really crazy for trying to make the world a better place?"

Lily raised her eyebrows from behind Lederman to tease her sister for her unexpected literary insight.

Lederman nodded. "Quixote is a character generally mocked for his lofty ideals. Antonio believes Washington felt a kindred spirit with him. Today Washington may be admired beyond reproach, but back then, some of his worst critics were his closest peers who doubted his capabilities on two fronts: to win the war and to secure the union. Two idealistic quests that began the day he realized Britain was vincible, and, which later, against all odds, he completed the day he signed the Constitution."

"It would seem to me," started Lily, "that Washington felt closer to the Spanish underdog Admiral Blas de Lezo and the Spanish idealist Don Quixote than he did to the failed British commander who gave name to his estate."

Lily's observation had Sofia ponder on something the professor said. *Of all the things he should have had on his mind as he prepared to come back as the first president* .... She lowered her gaze and stared at the novel. "I think I am starting to understand. Washington's world view changed from English to Spanish."

Ms. Lederman seemed confused by that statement. "Washington was not the only Founder interested in this novel. I already mentioned Franklin, but so was Jefferson, Adams, Hamilton, and Madison. They all owned a copy. Some possessed several, gifted it often, and all quoted it extensively."

Sofia noticed that Linsey had mentioned the names of the six busts in the reading room. "Was the one he acquired in English the one found *on the table* according to the estate catalogue?"

"Yes, I believe so."

"Any special reason why he'd keep it there?"

"Washington's book collection exceeded 1,200 volumes. Not all fitted on his shelves, so he had several auxiliary tables with books in his study. Most were related to farming, agriculture, or state affairs. Literature was a rarity. Clearly this one story was special to him." Linsey shrugged. "Beyond that, I can't say."

Lily cocked her head as she recalled something. "Washington was known to use books to deliver secret messages. Has it been analyzed under that lens?"

Lederman appeared stumped. "Codes were necessary during the war, but I can't imagine what need Washington would have for them in retirement."

"Actually," started Lily, "retirement was never on his mind. Washington had a strong hunch he was coming back as the first president when he bought it."

"Still," insisted Lederman, "why would he need to communicate with secret codes? Not to mention that when he did, he used cheap, disposable books. These were valuable even then. He wouldn't think of parting with them."

"Right, but another method for coded communication was creating ciphers based on a book that all parties involved possessed," said Lily.

Sofia was impressed by her sister's suggestion. Since all the founders had the same book, they could use its pages and words as keys. "What would it take to have this novel tested for hidden ink or code marks?"

Lederman blinked. "A very good reason backed by very good evidence to justify it."

CHAPTER 6

"Dollars or units—each to be of the value of the Spanish milled dollar as the same is now current."

—Section 9, Coinage Act of 1792

Sofia and Lily sat in the car. It remained stationed in front of the library as they replayed their visit.

"That was intense ... weird ... weirdly intense," said Lily. "How did the professor know I was coming? I imagine he expected you to follow his breadcrumbs, but me?"

Sofia frowned. Was she really that predictable?

"So, what did we learn?" asked Lily, moving on.

Sofia reached back to the rear seat where she left her backpack. From the front pocket, she extracted her notepad and a pen. "Let's make a list."

"You know you can dictate things to your phone, right? Even I use mine as a personal secretary, and I'm a nun."

"Cute. For your information, it is demonstrated that the action of writing things down the old-fashioned way helps order, summarize and remember information better."

"Or someone is getting old," said Lily aware the joke was also on her. She turned her attention to the brown bag with the cinnamon rolls at her feet. There was one left. "As I see it ..." she began, pulling it out and waving it in front of Sofia. "You want half?"

"No, thanks."

Lily happily kept the whole thing and continued. "The professor wanted us to take away three ideas from his display: One, in relation to Washington's coat of arms, his motto tells us his actions should be judged in light of their outcome. Two, in relation to the manuscript, we now know Washington was uniquely poised to being aware independence was achievable ... which brings us to three, the books. I think you're right. They hint to Washington's changing world view in terms of steering away from

Britain and turning toward Spain. Now, what that means exactly is still to be determined. Because let's say he saw a regional ally in Spain, why the need to sneak around with secret book codes and secret plots after the war?"

Sofia dropped her pen in reaction to her sister's perfectly ordered summary. "Pact; not plot. Antonio mentioned something about a secret pact. And talking about breadcrumbs, he introduced the Spanish-American icons as *'mysterious actions Washington took as president'*. I'm going to guess those are the actions we should be careful not to judge until we understand their intended outcome."

"Antonio... so, you too are on a first name basis? From the reactions back in there, I gather *Antonio* is hot. You forgot to mention that little detail."

"Watch your tongue, Sister Lily." Sofia picked her pen up again and started writing to avoid her stare. "Don't forget to contact your colleagues for information on him. We know where he works now."

Lily grinned. "Already did. You'll be the first to get the scoop on him as soon as I hear back."

Sofia scribbled on her notepad:

1. *Prof. Del Mar > Universidad Carlos III > Who is he?*
2. *GW's actions > icons > story behind each one? Outcome?*
3. *GW's interest in Spain > pact? > purpose/terms?*
4. *Don Quixote > code key? + on the table?*

Sofia paused. "*On the table*," she murmured. "It's bugging me. What was he trying to tell me?" She turned to Lily. "Do you have the list I asked Lederman for; the one with the other books found on the table along with Don Quixote?"

Lily had it in her hand. "Looking at it."

"Check for anything else Spain-related besides Don Quixote. Maybe he was trying to bring my attention to something else on that same table."

As Lily ran her eyes down the list, she continued to torture her sister. "We can scrap fraud. Instead, I wonder if Antonio is an aristocrat. I mean, not just anyone accompanies royals on international trips. Maybe he even owns a castle. Lady Sofia ... it has such a lovely ring to it."

"Do you mind? I'm trying to think of our next move. How do we go about deciphering the secret code if there is one?" Sofia mulled over her own question. "Lederman said the Founding Fathers quoted the book extensively. Maybe if we analyze the quotes, the nature of the documents they were inserted in, and those who were involved in the communication, a pattern emerges ..." she paused to correct herself. "Six, we start by focusing on the six Founding Fathers she mentioned."

Lily raised her eyes from the book list with a thoughtful gaze. "You know, *on the table* could be a code itself, as in 'something to be considered."

Sofia froze in thought. Slowly, she turned to look at her sister. "You're a genius." Her brow quickly furrowed. "But what would Washington want *considered* upon death?"

"Come to think of it, the opposite can also be true. In parliamentary procedures, when a topic is *laid on the table*, it's meant to put it on hold or end its consideration."

"Right ... so, which one is it? Kill or go ahead?" Sofia gave it some more thought. "Maybe it wasn't Washington. If there was a pact, it strikes me as more likely that with his death someone placed the book on the table to signal its end."

She sighed at the increasing number of unknowns and added another item to her notes:

5. *On the table > Kill or go ahead with secret pact?*

Sofia tossed the notepad and pen onto the rear seat next to the backpack. "Let's head back to D.C. I want to visit the National Archives." She started the engine and slowly steered the vehicle out of the parking spot toward the exit. "Anything on the book list?"

"It's long. I tell you what; Washington must have been the world's leading expert on farming and agriculture if he truly read all these books. I did find one other Spanish related item, though. I kid you not, the following is its title: *A Discourse, Intended to Commemorate the Discovery of America by Christopher Columbus; Delivered at the Request of the Historical Society in Massachusetts, on the 23rd Day of October, 1792, being the Completion of the Third Century since that Memorable Event.*"

"Third century since the discovery of America ... Antonio mentioned that anniversary in relation to the White House. He said the cornerstone was laid by a Spaniard precisely on the 300th anniversary of the discovery." Sofia tapped the steering wheel as they reached the exit of the library grounds. She stopped the vehicle and dug in her pocket for her phone. "I'm going to ask Lederman to send us a digital copy of that *Discourse*. It being on the table as well is too much of a coincidence." When she was done texting, she placed her phone on the center console tray and maneuvered the car east toward George Washington Memorial Parkway. "Why don't you get started on the icons. The first one is the dollar sign. The professor said it had something to do with the Spanish coat of arms."

Half an hour later, they were crossing the second bridge over the Potomac River on 695 into D.C. They were minutes from turning north on 7th St. to cut through the National Mall. The Archives were located on the other side. They were almost there, yet Lily had not produced anything.

Sofia assessed her sister and couldn't tell if the furrow between her brows meant she was concentrated or concerned. "What's taking you so long? How difficult can it be to find out about the dollar sign for a historian?"

"Oddly, very difficult. I haven't been able to find a single reliable and comprehensive timeline of its history in one place. The official sites are the worst. Their takes on it are either vague, lacking or *M.I.A* altogether. What information I was able to find was scattered and I had to stitch it together myself to draw the complete picture."

"Okay, and what is it?"

"To sum it up: the US dollar sign is simply the Spanish dollar sign. It came as part of the package when the US adopted the Spanish dollar as US currency. So, yes, indeed it has everything to do with Spain's coat of arms."

Sofia showed her surprise. "We adopted the Spanish dollar? I didn't even know there was a Spanish dollar."

"Not anymore. Its closest survivor is the Peso."

"And that's it? What's Washington's involvement?"

"He formalized the package."

Sofia took her eyes off the road briefly to give her sister a chiding glance. "You sound like those sites you're complaining about. Could you explain yourself a little better?"

Lily drew an impish grin. "You asked ..."

"I beg you, just a summary."

"Sure ... So, it goes back to the start of the 16th century."

"Oh boy, here we go."

"Just listen. It's interesting, because did you know *dollar* comes from the German word 'thaler', which means *valley*?"

"No, but we've almost arrived. Could you skip forward a couple of centuries, please?"

"Seriously, let me explain. Antonio is onto something here. The dollar and its sign give us our first glimpse into the secret dealings between Spain and the colonies."

"Fine."

"Alright then. As I was saying, 'thaler' means *valley* and, naturally, formed part of the names of towns located in valleys. One such town was *Joachimisthal* or St. Joachim of the Valley. Today, it is in the Czech Republic, but in 1518 it was under the Holy Roman Empire umbrella. Silver was mined in this town and its coins were named *Joachimthalers* or *thaler* for short. Then, in 1525, Charles V, the Holy Roman Emperor, standardized the currency system, giving the thaler a standard value. Therefore, the term *thaler*, or *dollar* in English, went on to refer to silver coins of a certain weight or size rather than a coin linked to a certain place or mint." Lily paused. "Following me so far?"

Sofia nodded. "Yes, *dollar* went from meaning 'valley' to naming a specific type of silver coin."

"Good. Well, it just so happens that Charles V was also the king of Spain where his grandmother Queen Isabella had undertaken the standardization of Spanish currency twenty-eight years earlier. Since her 'Piece of Eight' was equivalent to the *thaler*, or vice versa, it became known as the Spanish dollar in English. Around the same time, also under Charles V, the silver mines in the kingdoms of New Spain and Peru were discovered, and their mints established. And, as the Spanish empire went on to dominate global trade the next three hundred years, its coins became the most stable and least debased in the world, establishing the Spanish dollar as the world's dominant currency. Even today's Chinese Yuan derives from it."

"Really? The dollar was a global currency for hundreds of years before the US was even the US?

"Pretty much. And for this reason, as soon as the US became the US in 1776, the British pound was abandoned, and the Spanish dollar was adopted as the US monetary unit instead."

Sofia shook her head amazed. "Okay, so Washington adopted the dominant currency, and the outcome is that the dollar continues to be the strongest in the world. He did good. What's the mystery in *mysterious action* then?"

"That's where the dollar sign comes in. Let me explain: When Charles V, the Holy Roman Emperor, ascended to the throne of Spain as Charles I, he added the Columns of Hercules to his coat of arms. The columns had been associated with the Iberian Peninsula since classical Greek times, because they represented the promontories on each side of the Strait of Gibraltar, placing Spain, and Portugal, at the limit of the known world to those within the Mediterranean. In fact, until the discovery of America, the legend associated with the columns was "NON PLUS ULTRA", meaning *No More Beyond*. With the discovery of America, it changed to "PLUS ULTRA", *More Beyond*. Today, it continues to be Spain's motto, and you can see it on a ribbon wrapped around the columns on their coat of arms and flag, forming what looks like an 'S' crossed vertically by the column. So, going back to the 16th century, when the Spanish dollar began to be minted in America, the columns were added to the reverse of the coins, becoming their signature feature. From there, the *S* with two strokes—for the two columns—became shorthand in international ledgers for Spanish dollar. It was so widely used as such that when minting of the Spanish silver coins began later in Potosi, in current Bolivia, its mint mark was designed on purpose to look like the Spanish dollar sign by placing the letters PTSI over each other. In this case, it resulted in one stroke, explaining the one-two stroke interchangeability."

Sofia slowed down. She was driving in the vicinity of the National Archives and was on the lookout for a parking spot. The streetlight turned red. Lily took the opportunity to show her the phone screen with an enlarged image of a coin.

"Look." Lily pointed to the right column and traced the ribbon to draw an S. Then, she brought Sofia's attention to one of two mint marks seen on the sides of the coin between two flowers.

"Okay, I see it. I knew about the Columns of Hercules but not how they were behind the dollar sign. Interesting."

"Now get this: This particular coin," continued Lily, "was the one circulating in the colonies at the time of the Revolution. It was known as the Pillar Dollar because the columns were enhanced to flank two overlapping globes, representing the old and new worlds. The words ULTRAQUE UNUM were added to mean *Both are One* under Spain's rule across the ocean."

The streetlight turned green, and the car started to roll again. "Why does it sound familiar?" asked Sofia.

"Because it was the basis for Benjamin Franklin's design on the 1776 Continental paper money. The paper money worked as bills of credit payable in Spanish dollars, so he took the overlapping globe idea and linked thirteen overlapping circles with the names of the colonies. In the center he added WE ARE ONE. This design was later adopted for the Continental dollar coin."

Lily showed her.

Sofia glanced at it quickly. "Wait, so you're saying Franklin had already adopted Spanish iconography for the continental currency. That would mean the changing world view from British to Spanish had begun during the war."

"That's right, and there's a good reason for it. Spain was secretly supplying the Continental Army with large amounts of money in addition to gunpowder, medicines and other items via the Mississippi and Ohio Rivers, and Oliver Pollok kept detailed records of the transactions."

"Never heard of him. Who is he?"

"He was a wealthy Irish merchant who settled in Spanish New Orleans at the outbreak of the Revolutionary War and became the secret mediator between Luis de Unzaga, the Governor of Spanish Louisiana, and the Continental Army, aka George Washington. I mention Pollok, because his ledgers are among the oldest to show the use of the dollar sign in the colonies, though still attached to the Spanish dollar."

Sofia spotted a parking space and quickly maneuvered to take it.

"In sum," said Lily to wrap up, "since the Spanish dollar had become the currency in use during the war, the Continental Congress resolved in 1785 *'that the money unit of the United States of America be one dollar'.*"

"But you said it was George Washington who formalized both the dollar and the sign."

"Yes, while President, he formalized the US dollar on par with the Spanish dollar under the Coinage Act of 1792, then he, personally, signed the first federal bond that contained—for the first time—the Spanish dollar sign as attached to the US dollar."

Sofia turned the ignition off and sat quietly for a few seconds. She was trying to register how the dollar symbol had checked out in such a big way. Beyond it revealing that Washington had adopted Spanish currency and iconography, it also revealed that behind it was Spain's secret help during the Revolution. So, if this much was true for the unassuming dollar sign, what could it mean for the Great Seal of the United States?

CHAPTER 7

"Thus, to the generous decision of a female mind, we owe the discovery of America."

—*Reverend Jeremy Belknap, cofounder of the Historical Society of Massachusetts,*
1792

The National Archives Building enjoyed a privileged location within the Federal Triangle. Halfway between the White House and the Capitol, its monumental design was the work of John Russell Pope, who envisioned a temple rather than a vault to preserve the History of the United States. He succeeded. Its grand staircase and massive bronze doors on Constitution Ave, its seventy-two colossal Corinthian columns that hugged the body, and its over seventy feet tall dome crowning the Rotunda for the Charters of Freedom impressed awe upon the visitor. Unfortunately, built in 1933, it also belied the tragedy that it had taken over 150 years, several fires in government buildings, and the invaluable loss of records to neglect before it dawned on someone that the memory of the United States had to be conserved in a secure location.

For Lily, a Catholic Historian of all things, Pope's vision could not have been more fitting. While Sofia attended to a call, she admired the two large sculptures flanking the researcher's entrance on Pennsylvania Avenue. They represented *Future* on the left and *Past* on the right. Future was embodied by a young, confident woman with an open book on her lap, its empty pages yet to be written. Her motto, WHAT IS PAST IS PROLOGUE, was an invitation to learn about the past to get a glimpse of the future, and when Lily walked over to study the aged male who embodied Past, his motto, STUDY THE PAST, would appear to confirm this. However, the closed book he guarded tightly on his lap made Lily wonder how much of it would ever truly be accessible.

Sofia put her phone away. "Okay, let's head inside." As they approached the entrance, she briefed her sister. "Dan's freaking out. When I asked him for a team to work on decoding *Don Quixote*, he said there was no way in Hell he was delegating that on anyone. He wants to keep it between us and has taken up the task himself."

Lily chuckled. "You really thought he was going to risk someone leaking an exclusive like that? And I'm supposed to be the naive one?"

"I'm not convinced there is anything worth leaking yet," said Sofia. Her expression was tense. "The Great Seal will determine if we are wasting our time or not. For now, the adoption of the Spanish dollar and its sign can be explained by historical circumstances; it was the strongest currency at the time. But the Great Seal is a whole different story. Think about it, it's the symbol of the United States' sovereignty and identity. Within hours of approving the Declaration of Independence, Franklin, Jefferson, and Adams were tasked with its design. Their proposals would not prosper, and it would take six years, three different committees and a total of four proposals to get it right. I mean, they really thought it through. So, if, as Antonio claims, it truly derived from the Spanish Empire's coat of arms in the end, the implication is ... I don't know ...."

"You're right," agreed Lily. "It's hard to imagine there is any purposeful relation, otherwise, what could the reason possibly be?"

Sofia noticed a man standing in the distance toward the edge of the building preoccupied with his cellphone. He was tall and lean, dressed in dark gray cargo pants and a taupe bomber jacket that hinted to an active lifestyle. His confident posture, as he relaxed his shoulder against the wall, gave her a distinct sense of déjà vu; someone she thought she'd never see again. Sofia tried to see his face, but it was slightly turned away and hidden under a baseball cap and sunglasses.

"What is it?" asked Lily.

Sofia slowed down to let someone walk in through the entrance door ahead of her. When she turned to look again, he was gone. "I thought I saw someone."

"The professor?"

"No, not him." Sofia took a quick look around, but didn't see him. She chose to shrug it off. "Anyway, even if the Great Seal turns out to be a false flag, we still have to find out what Antonio's agenda is. Have you heard from your contacts in Spain?"

"Not yet. I'm also waiting for information on Queen Isabella's coat of arms to compare. I should be getting something shortly. In the meantime, we can look up the description for the US Seal to get an idea what the thinking was behind its design."

They stepped into the reception area and pulled out their IDs.

"You get started on that," said Sofia. "I have some reading to do. Lederman sent me an online link to the *Discourse*, you know, the one with the long title celebrating the discovery of America."

Lily nodded.

Quietly, just outside the entrance, the man with the baseball cap waited for them to clear security. A pronounced scar running across his left cheek came into full view as he removed his cap and raised his face to examine his surroundings. Slowly, his eyes wandered around, probing parked vehicles, building corners, and passersby with suspicion. Once he completed the scouting to his satisfaction, he stepped inside.

A little while later, the twins jumped to their feet at the same time as if synced through Wi-Fi. They had taken up seats at separate tables facing each other in the research room under one of the large windows. The elegance of the space, with its high wood-paneled ceilings and crossbeams, inspired the due respect expected for the historical memories cuddled in the Archives. The sisters, in their excitement, forgot the code of silence.

"You need to look at this," said Lily.

"And you need to listen to this: I think I know why George Washington switched his world view from British to Spanish," said Sofia.

"Okay, you go first."

"Wait." Sofia looked confused. "You found something? Does that mean the US Great Seal and the Spanish empire's coat of arms are related?"

"Are they ever."

"Oh ..." Sofia let it register. It took her a second. "Well, there may be a good reason for it." She pointed to her laptop, which sat on the table. "It's laid out in the *Discourse*. As the title indicates, it commemorates the 300th year anniversary of the discovery of America, but with a particular focus. It credits the discovery with the scientific and intellectual revolution that followed, believing it was orchestrated by the hand of Providence. In fact, it goes a step further. The *Discourse* is the work of Reverend Jeremy Belknap, founder of the Historical Society of Massachusetts and honorary Doctor of Divinity from Harvard College. He treats the discovery as the fulfillment of a prophecy."

"Are you telling me we are on the hunt for another lost prophecy?"

"No need to hunt this one down. He quotes it from the Bible." Sofia checked her notes. "Daniel, Chapter 12. *Many shall run to and fro and knowledge shall be increased.*"

Lily wrinkled her forehead. "I don't understand. In this chapter, Daniel, a prophet, is handed the *Book of Truth* by an angel, presumably Gabriel, on condition that he'll keep it sealed until people are ready to deal with its content. So, that verse is thought to imply that once people actively seek the truth—*run to and fro* searching for it—that's when they'll be receptive to it and *knowledge shall be increased.*"

"Does the chapter reveal what that ominous truth is?" asked Sofia.

"Yes. The End Times. It prophesies the rise of Michael, the Archangel, at the time of the end, because he comes to deliver God's people, that is, the wise and good who seek and understand the Truth." Lily shook her head. "Not sure how it applies to the discovery of America."

Sofia offered her best skeptical grin. "As with most verses from the Bible, people interpret them as best suits them."

Lily let her sister enjoy her moment with grace, if only because she was right.

"In the case of Reverent Belknap," explained Sofia, "he applies the verse to the voyages *to and fro* through the Columns of Hercules, which were seen as the gateway to Enlightenment. Following the discovery of America, Spain undertook a wide range of exploratory expeditions, bringing about great advancements in science and technology. I did some research, and it turns out this thinking about the columns being a gateway to the *new* was quite popular. Take Francis Bacon, for instance. He adopted the Spanish motto PLUS ULTRA for himself. And for his book, Novum Organun of 1620, where he details the new logic that must replace the old, he chose for his cover two Spanish galleons sailing through the Columns of Hercules into the horizon. He copied it from the book cover of a Spanish cosmographer, cartographer, mathematician and astronomer, Andres

Garcia de Cespedes, who was making great scientific advances in all these areas in late 16th and early 17th centuries, particularly in navigation."

Lily understood. "The Founders saw the discovery as the launch of a new enlightened era and America as the chosen land to run with it."

"*And*" emphasized Sofia, "the Freemasons saw themselves as the flag bearers. I've studied them. They were all about the Enlightenment; their spiritual purpose was, in fact, the pursuit of the *enlightened truth* through the exercise of wisdom and virtue."

"They fancied themselves *the chosen wise and good* from the prophecy," translated Lily.

"It all ties in. Remember the two Columns of Hercules and the two globes on the Spanish Dollar?" said Sofia. "Many Freemason lodges adopted them for their logo and added the overseeing Eye of Providence to it. Notable among them was the Grand Lodge of the District of Columbia, which governs the lodges in Washington D.C., still today. George Washington belonged to one of them. That symbolism might explain why he personally formalized the Spanish dollar sign as that of the US dollar. I think that in breaking away from Britain, there was a need to forge a new identity. And by turning to Spain, they rooted it in the discovery to bask in that ideal of the New World chosen for greatness."

"It makes sense." Lily brandished the prints she held in her hand. "Does the *Discourse* make any reference to Queen Isabella specifically?"

"Actually, it does. I was going to mention it. Much like you believe, Reverend Belknap identifies her, not Columbus, as God-chosen for the discovery. He implies that Providence placed obstacles in Columbus' way to guide him to Queen Isabella, evidenced by the fact that he had pitched the Atlantic crossing to the kings of Portugal, Britain, and France, and they all systematically turned him down. Not even King Ferdinand, Isabella's husband, showed any enthusiasm for it. Only she saw the potential in Columbus' vision and invested in him." Sofia looked down at her laptop screen. "The reverend writes: *Thus, to the generous decision of a female mind, we owe the discovery of America*." She glanced at her sister. "Queen Isabella receives all the credit."

"More than you think," said Lily. "Check this out." She laid two similar sketches side-by-side on the table.

Lily started by pointing to the image on the left. "This is Charles Thomson's proposal for the Great Seal. He was the secretary of the Continental Congress, and it was his proposal, this one, that was finally approved in 1782." Lily slid her finger to the other image. "And this image is from 1473. It's Queen Isabella's personal seal. She designed it herself while still a teenager."

Sofia examined both and then shook her head. "At first glance they may look similar, but all they really have in common is the eagle."

"True, but bear with me." Lily laid a third image on the table below the first two.

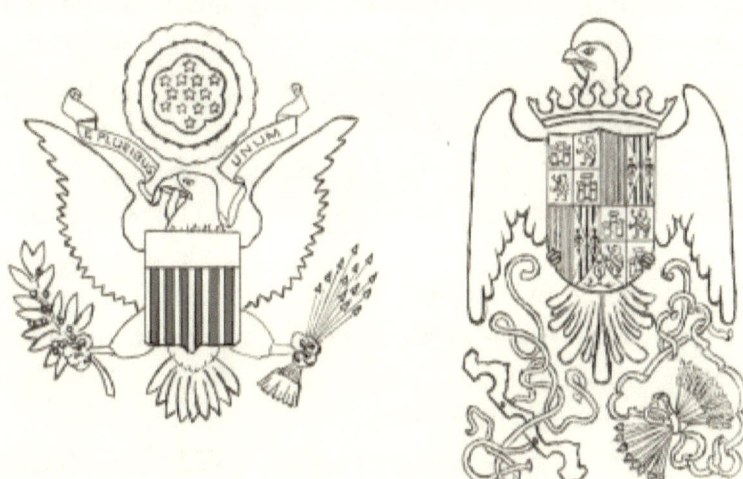

Sofia recognized it. "That's the slide the professor shared during his presentation."

"I know. I found it online. It's going viral with a lot of creepy conspiracy nonsense attached." Lily pointed to the Spanish image on the right. "When Isabella married Ferdinand, her eagle went on to become the support for their shared coat of arms. By the time Columbus set sail in 1492, their arms displayed a shield with five kingdoms united under the crown. The equivalent description applies to the US seal: it displays a shield with thirteen colonies—the white and red strips—united under congress—the blue horizontal bar—supported by an eagle."

Sofia studied the images as Lily continued.

"Up to here, the case can be made that it's simply a coincidence due to heraldry rules. The thing is Queen Isabella had the habit of personalizing standard symbols to make them her own. In her lifetime, she adopted only two personal emblems, both carried her unique mark, and ..." Lily paused with a twinkle in her eye, "... both are found in the US seal."

"Meaning they cannot be reduced to heraldry standardization or a coincidence," said Sofia.

"Exactly." Lily pointed back to the first top right image. "As I mentioned, this was Isabella's personal seal while still the princess-heir. The shield displays a castle and a rampant lion, doubled up in four quadrants. They represent the kingdoms of Castile and Leon she was heiress to. That's standard. To support the shield, she chose an eagle, which was widespread in Europe as a legacy of the Roman Empire. It symbolizes strength and power. But here's the twist: rather than the Roman royal eagle, she chose instead St. John the Evangelist's eagle as denoted by the halo. In addition to strength and power, it also symbolizes protection." Lily swung the tip of her finger to the US seal. "I think St. John's eagle was customized in the form of the American eagle and its halo made to portray the Glory breaking through the clouds, revealing a constellation of thirteen stars as the birth of a new nation."

Lily paused to check with her sister, who appeared pensive.

"I think you're right. It would be consistent," said Sofia. "The reverse of the Great Seal is replete with Freemason symbolism, and St. John the Evangelist just happens to be one of their two patron saints. They would have been all too happy to adopt her eagle on the front, especially if they are trying to make that connection back to her and the discovery."

"Well, that's not all." Lily turned her attention to the Spanish arms. "Since her eagle went on to support the united kingdoms of Spain, Isabella had to come up with a new emblem for herself. Ferdinand had chosen the yoke in reference to a legend honoring Alexander the Great's ingenuity in resolving challenges." Lily showed Sofia by pointing to the bottom right and continued. "Queen Isabella chose the bundle of arrows. It was her personal take on the Roman fascia, which consisted of rods, not arrows. It signifies strength in union. The idea is that one rod is easily broken, while several bundled up together resist much better." Lily swung her finger back to the US seal and pointed to the bundle of arrows in the eagle's right grip. "On the US seal it symbolizes Unity and strength in war."

Sofia was impressed. "To recap, Queen Isabella adopted two Roman Empire symbols, the eagle and the fascia, giving them her personal touch. And both appear on the US seal in the same position, with equivalent function and meaning."

"That's right. But if in doubt, look at this." Lily slammed her last print on top of the other two. It displayed a coin on the left and the stamp of a continental bill on the right.

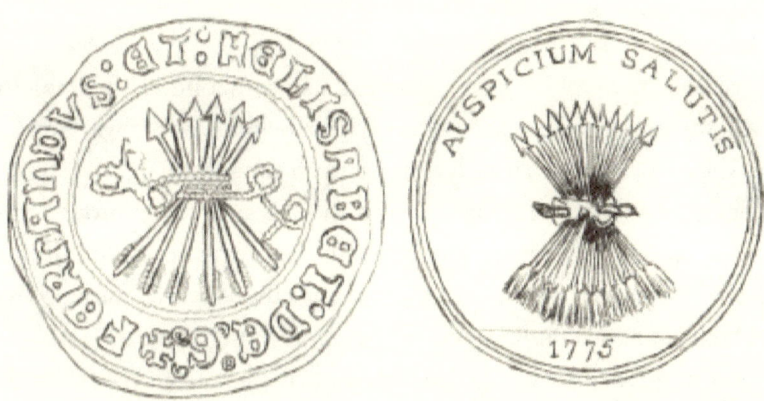

"You might recall when I told you the history of the dollar that, when it was standardized back in the early 1500s, it equated to Queen Isabella's Piece of Eight. That's how the Spanish coin came to be known in English as the Spanish dollar."

"Yes, I remember."

Lily tapped the image of the coin on the left. "This is it. This is a Piece of Eight from 1474. It carried her bundle of arrows on one side and her husband's yoke on the other." She then pointed to the image on the right. "In 1775, during the Revolutionary War, South Carolina dug up that 300-year-old image and replicated it on their five-pound note as if a lucky charm of sorts. Look at the words above it. AUSPICIUM SALUTIS. It means, *An Omen for Good*."

Sofia took a moment to think about it. "I don't get it," she started. "Even if they believed she had been chosen by Providence, it's a little much. Why the obsession?"

Lily shrugged. "It's hard to say, but they were obsessed alright. She was also the first woman to appear on a US stamp, which is significant considering that the Stamp Act of 1765 was the spark that contributed to the formation of the Continental Congress."

"Lily, this opens a whole new can of worms," said Sofia, reflecting concern.

"Why do you say that?"

"Because in heraldry you can't just use someone else's emblem for yourself without permission, especially if it belongs to a royal house or a country. It's a privilege that only the monarch can grant."

That gave Lily pause. "Right ... and the US seal was approved in time for the peace treaties. Spain was party to those treaties as an ally to the US. Rebels or not, in that crucial moment, it's unlikely the Founders would adopt Spanish royal emblems without their ally's permission."

Sofia nodded. "Meaning that there must have been a pact and that the Great Seal aligned with it in some way. Otherwise, why would the king of Spain grant the US the privilege to adopt Queen Isabella's personal emblems?"

"But that would imply an alliance of a deeply intimate nature. I mean, you don't do that for a trade deal."

Sofia bit her lip. "I don't know, Lily. I'm starting to wonder if it's prudent to meddle with this. If it was kept secret all this time, there must be a very good reason for it."

CHAPTER 8

"It is unreasonable to suppose, that France or Spain will give us any kind of assistance, if we mean only, to make use of that assistance for the purpose of repairing the breach, and strengthening the connection between Britain and America."

—Thomas Paine, Common Sense, 1776

The Auru-Soto sisters suddenly felt overwhelmed. What were they getting themselves into?

Sofia took a deep breath to steel herself. "Alright, let's not get carried away. We still have no evidence of a secret pact, much less to presume anything about it. As for the Great Seal, there may be a perfectly reasonable explanation for it. We just don't know it yet."

Lily agreed and waved the concern away as if it were a pesky fly. "The reality is that a pact, secret or not, shouldn't surprise us, anyway. In a war, allies are sought. It was the whole reason for the Declaration of Independence in the first place."

"It was?" said Sofia surprised.

"Come with me," said Lily.

They collected their things and headed to the Rotunda for the Charters of Freedom. As they walked through the bronze gates, their eyes were drawn up to the towering half-dome that stood seventy-five feet above the room's focal point: the Constitution of the United States flanked by two massive columns crowned with guardian eagles.

On the right, a group of school students piled on each other eager to get a glimpse at the Bill of Rights. Lily was interested in the document displayed on the left and went straight to it.

Sofia followed. Upon reaching the Declaration of Independence, she squinted, finding it hard to read. Its words were slowly fading away and that troubled her for what it meant symbolically.

As a Native American, she naturally had mixed feelings about the Declaration. To start, one of its sentences was particularly insulting to her and her people, but beyond that, the concepts of equality, life, liberty, and the pursuit of happiness did not apply to over 70% of the population for quite some time. Far from it. However, the fact that those words were included—akin to a sacred promise—allowed them to slowly, but stealthily, seep through the country's conscious over time, extending gradually to be all-embracing. Some would argue it wasn't perfect yet, but there was no denying their impact had come a very long way and inspired a large portion of the world.

Consequently, to see the ink of these vital words vanishing was deeply unsettling.

Lily pressed her index finger against the display's glass. "What you see here is the engrossed copy, that is, the final copy written up pretty for the ceremonial signing, which happened later in August," she started. "As you can see from its layout, the Declaration consisted of a list of grievances that justified the colonies' emancipation from the British Crown. But it was not intended for the British Crown. The Revolutionary War had been going on for over a year, and the colonies had already been declared in rebellion. The Declaration was a statement for the rest of the world whereby the thirteen colonies asserted themselves as a confederacy of sovereign nations with full powers to seek alliances." Lily pointed to the last paragraph and read. "*We, therefore, the representatives of the United States of America ... have full Power to levy war, conclude peace, contract alliances, establish commerce, and to do all other acts and things which independent states may of right do.*"

Lily looked up. "France and Spain had been helping the war efforts secretly from the beginning. As the natural enemies of Britain, they saw it as an opportunity to weaken Britain. What they could not afford was to back the rebels officially in an all-out war just for the sake of a temporary family feud. Many here were still hoping for reconciliation. If there was any hope of France and Spain committing to a war, the colonies understood they had to assert their own commitment to Independence." Lily then pointed to the last sentence. "*And for the support of this Declaration, with a firm reliance on the protection of divine Providence, we mutually pledge to each other our lives, our fortunes and our sacred honor.*" Lily turned back to her sister. "By affixing their signatures to the Declaration, these 56 signers were assuring potential allies they were all in, come what may."

"I never thought to look at it that way," admired Sofia.

"That's because Abraham Lincoln emphasized the spirit of the Declaration's second sentence during his Gettysburg address as what set the United States apart. Since then, it has been viewed as a Declaration of American Values, rather than a call for help."

"Okay, so, since allies were being sought for the war, it's feasible some kind of pact was agreed to and that it was kept secret for whatever reason, but here is the problem: most of the actions Washington took in relation to the icons occurred while he was President, long after the Revolutionary War was over. What need was there to continue keeping the alliance secret then, and even today, seeing we still don't know about it?"

"Good question."

The two sisters looked at the weathered document as if it could offer the answer. It prompted another question, instead.

"The lost copy," said Sofia. "What do you know about what happened to it?"

"Not much, since no one does. As I said, the Declaration was simply that, the instrument informing the world that the colonies had unanimously voted for their independence and therefore were sovereign to agree to whatever alliances, treaties, or pacts they wanted to. Otherwise, no one cared for it until Thomas Jefferson ran for office in 1800. It's all he had to show for his contribution to Independence."

"What's the big deal with it then?"

"Oh, it's a big deal, alright. Look, the action of declaring independence was a three-step process. First, in June of 1776, Richard H. Lee introduced a three-prong proposal. It included a vote for the *dissolution of the political connection* with Great Britain, measures to form foreign alliances, and a plan of confederation. Already there you can see the intent was to find allies. While his proposal was debated, and foreseeing it would pass, Congress tasked a committee of five with writing up its public pronouncement, that is, the Declaration. Thomas Jefferson led the task and produced several drafts. When, on July 2nd, Lee's Resolution passed, meaning independence was officially approved, according to Jefferson himself, he had a four-page clean draft ready, otherwise known as a fair copy. This is where it starts to get fuzzy because, with independence sanctioned, everyone went into panic mode to make it public as soon as possible. Still, Congress made some last-minute changes, which were annotated on the fair copy itself and then authorized it *as is* on the 4th of July for immediate printing. That fair copy is, therefore, the *official* copy of the Declaration of Independence. Now, bear in mind that no other drafts or manuscripts produced before or soon after were word-for-word alike." Lily tapped the glass again. "Even this engrossed copy was marked up with slight changes for the signing. Hence, the value of the fair copy: Not only is it the *official* and *original* hardcopy, so to speak, but in its uniqueness, it's also the only *true* one. It went missing that same night."

No wonder it's been labelled the American Holy Grail, thought Sofia. She assessed the one-page oversized parchment in front of her. "Leaving aside its remarkable value, what we are really looking for then is a four-page document. Who supervised the printing?" she asked.

"Again, fuzzy. The same committee charged with writing the Declaration was tasked with its printing and distribution. Apparently, Jefferson was out shopping for gloves at the time, so through a process of elimination, it has been concluded that John Adams must have taken care of the printing with the aid of Charles Thomson."

"Charles Thomson? Wasn't he the designer of the US seal?"

"Yes, he would have acted in his role as the secretary of the Continental Congress. In fact, his signature as secretary bore witness to John Hancock's as President in approving the Declaration. Their two signatures were sufficient to authenticate the fair copy."

"Are you saying this guy, Charles Thomson, who I had not heard of before today, is the designer of the Great Seal of the United States and one of only two signers of the real Declaration of Independence?"

Lily nodded. "I can only imagine what that man saw, heard and knew. He was the proverbial fly on the wall during the fifteen years the Continental Congress existed. Think about it. He was the secretary through the war, the Constitution and George Washington's election. During all that time, everything went through him as the attester of resolutions, recorder of minutes, and keeper of journals. I believe he even kept the secret codes for the Committee of Secret Correspondence. No one else, not even the Founders were as thoroughly privy to what went on as Thomson was."

"In that case, if there ever was a secret pact, he would have known about it. Where are his papers kept? We should take a look at them."

Lily froze. "Actually, Thomson did something shocking with them." She paused briefly as if trying to straighten her thoughts. "Here's the thing: while in Paris preparing for the peace treaty with Britain, John Jay, who was the diplomat sent for that purpose, mailed Thomson a strange note. Jay asked Thomson to write the true *political* story of the Revolution, stating it was *highly important to the Cause of Truth with posterity*. And not only that, Jay also suggested that Thomson do it discreetly and wait to have it published after his death. Thomson heeded Jay's advice and wrote it all down in the form of a memoire ... I think." Lily narrowed her eyes trying to remember the details. "The point is that years later, shortly before dying, Thomson suddenly burnt all his papers, along with the memoire. When asked why he'd do such a thing, he said something about not wanting to offend future generations with the truth."

"Offend ...? About what?" Sofia was stunned. "And how bad could it be to warrant burning the truth about it?"

"I don't know, but ..." Lily was visibly stressed making more connections, "one of the items on the list you gave me this morning is the Supreme Court; something about the person who established it. That person was precisely John Jay. He was the first Supreme Court Justice. And get this: during the war, he was also the President of the Continental Congress when he was chosen to go to Spain on a diplomatic mission as the highest representative of the colonies. It was from there that he went to Paris to prepare for the peace treaty."

Lily's inference was clear. John Jay was a major player in the political side of the Revolution and personally involved with Spain at the highest level. His request to Thomson, asking him to write the true political story of the Revolution, was not to be taken lightly.

The sisters exchanged a prolonged look. It was becoming increasingly difficult to deny something secret went on with Spain.

A young child ran up to the display, squeezing in between them. Sofia and Lily stepped aside realizing they had been hogging it. Then, through the corner of her eye, Sofia saw the familiar man again. He was standing behind the bronze gate. This time, he made no effort to hide his face or its conspicuous scar. Instead, he winked at her and signaled with his chin toward the exit. Swiftly, he moved that way.

Sofia drew a suspicious frown as her eyes trailed him. "Lily. Have you been in touch with Michael?"

"Yes, I was planning to tell you about it. Why?"

"Was part of your plan to let me know he'd be joining us?"

"What?" Lily looked around genuinely surprised. "I swear we did not conspire behind your back this time."

Sofia rolled her eyes. "Text him. Tell him we'll meet him in five at the Café."

She sighed.

Michael in the picture was bad news.

CHAPTER 9

"At 22:25 local (Spanish) time, a rock [...] impacted the atmosphere at 76,000 km/hr. [...] giving rise to a fireball [...] it's luminosity equivalent to a full moon [...] extinguishing over La Albuera."

—*J.M. Madiedo, Astrophysics Institute of Andalucia, 15 September 2021*

Lily squeezed Michael with a joyful hug. As they separated, she smacked him on the shoulder. "Why didn't you tell me you were coming?"

He raised his hands, palms out. "You know how it is."

"You're here on official business?"

"Something like that."

He slid an intense glance toward Sofia. Their relationship was not as cozy. He tried smoothing things with his sugarcoated smile.

Sofia relented and offered her hand. "I'm going to say it is nice to see you again, because it is, but I am concerned for the reason."

Michael happily settled for the handshake. "We have to talk." He invited them to sit down on two of three chairs, reserving the one against the wall for himself. He had chosen a table with a good panoramic view of all access points.

Sofia studied him. His age-defying baby face, damaged with unsettling scars, had succumbed to developing maturity around the edges; his curly hair was cut shorter than she remembered; and his deep thunderous voice still surprised her for clashing with the serene aura he radiated. Michael was a man of contrasts, which extended from his looks to their relationship.

In terms of his intentions, Sofia knew she could trust Michael, but he was a brick wall for information, and that was the source of their uneasy rapport. Presumably, he worked for the NSA. Though Lily had known him for years, Sofia only met Michael during their search for Fatima's Third Secret. Apparently, a very dangerous someone, somewhere codenamed Red Dragon, got wind of it and moved to keep it buried. The NSA, always according to Michael, had been keeping an eye on Red Dragon and hand-picked him to protect them under the cover of his friendship with Lily. It wasn't totally altruistic, of course. The NSA sought first access to the prophecy and the remarkable relic associated with it. Michael brought on his cousin Gabriel as additional muscle, and, in the end, played it straight with them. However, they never received clarity regarding Red Dragon's identity or what came of him.

So, yes, Michael was bad news.

"When did you two reconnect?" she asked him.

"A couple of months ago."

Sofia looked at her sister, demanding a better explanation.

"He called me to alert me about the meteor," explained Lily. "I wanted to look into it before informing you about it."

"So much for not conspiring."

"Hey, you're the one that demands evidence."

Michael intervened. "This past year, I chose to keep my distance from both of you for your own sake. Unfortunately, recent events signal something is brewing, and it involves the two of you again."

"Red Dragon?" asked Lily.

"I wouldn't completely discount he is behind it."

Sofia was getting anxious. "Can we please start from the beginning? What's the deal with the meteor?"

"I tried to tell you yesterday when I called," said Lily. "On September 15th, a fireball that shone the size of the moon lit up the night sky in Spain. It appeared in the south of the province of Badajoz and disappeared over a small village called La Albuera."

"So? Meteors light up the night sky every night all over the world. What is so special about this one?"

Lily reached into her pocket for her phone and navigated its apps looking for a file. When she had it on screen, she showed Sofia. It was a map displaying their two "divine" lines as they crossed the Iberian Peninsula. One, they called the Spanish Line because that was pretty much its geographical extension, and the other they named Mary's Line, since it started by connecting several major Marian shrines in Europe. But, as they continued their search for the prophecy, Mary's Line grew to become a lot more. Eventually, it extended across the Atlantic connecting an unfathomable number of locations through wild coincidences that Sofia was still trying to explain. Lily was about to add another one to her plate.

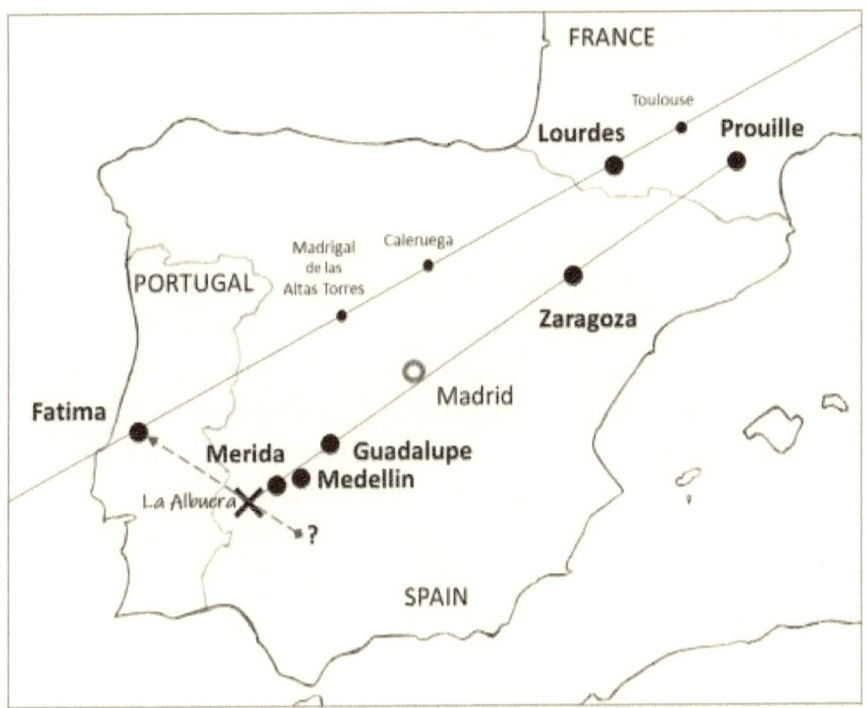

Lily pointed to the X mark on the map. "As I said, the meteor disappeared over this little town, La Albuera, which is located at the end of the Spanish Line as it extends southwest beyond the city of Merida. This little town happens to be the birthplace of the founder of one of the other Meridas, the one in Venezuela, which, as you know, is on Mary's Line."

Sofia's eyebrows rose slowly. "Okay, so the two lines, along with two of the Meridas are linked through La Albuera. Interesting. Still ...?"

"It doesn't end there." Lily briefly glanced over at Michael as she explained. "The only church in La Albuera is named Our Lady of the Way. This Marian advocation was crucial in helping us build Mary's Line. Now, get this, its feast day is celebrated precisely on September 15th, the same day the meteor disappeared right over it. What are the odds? And last, but not least," Lily pointed to the arrow on the screen, "According to the trajectory outlined by the Astrophysics Institute that tracked it, the meteor pointed straight to Fatima. Sof, if those are not signs intended for us, you tell me what is."

Sofia released a cautious sigh. Too many coincidences to brush off as a coincidence, and there laid the problem. "Lily, if meteors were a rare occurrence, I'd be the first to get excited about this one, but enough space rocks make it into our atmosphere to warrant one meeting a number of coincidences. It is too easy to disregard the hundreds of meteors that don't, while latching onto the one that does because it satisfies a personal belief."

Lily insisted. "Meteors this large are by no means frequent. It could be seen over 372 miles away. It must be a sign, Sof. It has to be. All the crucial elements of our lines are referenced in this single sighting as if it were a summary of our search for Fatima's secret. It clearly wanted to capture our attention. And you know that our Hopi prophecies, as those of Fatima, talk of a sign in the sky that will signal in the End Times."

"Lily, I don't think you realize what you are implying. In order for all those coincidences to come together as a sign, someone had to arrange for them to concur in that one town over hundreds of years, and then hang a fireball above it just so that you and I could sit here today to see it as such. Do you grasp the enormity of it?"

She did, but not in the way Sofia intended.

"Exactly. It's trying to tell us something, because I happen to know that even Queen Isabella is connected to that town. Her most loyal commander, the Great Captain, proved his military brilliance for the first time there, fighting in the battle that secured the throne for her."

Sofia exasperated. "What are you talking about? Did you listen to a word I just said?"

"Yes, for a little town in the middle of nowhere with little else to boast about, all these events must have happened there for a reason." Lily pointed up to the ceiling. "Someone up there is trying to tell us something."

Sofia took a slow deep breath. During their quest to find Fatima's Secret, she had come to accept that their brains followed the laws of two different universes. She turned to Michael, interested in what he had to say.

He surprised her.

"I agree with you on this one, at least in part."

"Wait, what?" said Lily. "You called me about the meteor."

"I was hoping you'd use your special talent to identify an angle we might have missed. That meteor has caught the attention of a dangerous domestic terrorist group, who has latched onto it," he said, using Sofia's words, "because it suits their devious plans. That's why I'm here."

"I don't understand," said Lily. "Why would a terrorist group care about a meteor?"

Michael shifted in his seat. "It has to do with your published story; the way your search for Fatima's Third Secret unfolded. You might not realize this, but for the members of secret societies, it looks a lot like the *symbolic* journey an initiate undertakes as they rise through several levels of revelations toward the ultimate final Truth."

"I'm sorry, Michael," said Sofia, "I find that a stretch."

"It's not a stretch for those who thrive on symbolism. Take the Freemasons, for instance. You've written extensively about them. You know, that one of the symbolic secrets they strive to glean along their journey of growth is God's secret name. So, imagine the upheaval you caused when you went beyond symbolism and cracked God's secret name for real. You two have become icons. You have a cult-following."

"How can that be?" said Lily. "I haven't heard anything?"

Michael was right, thought Sofia. She had studied secret societies and was starting to understand. She answered Lily's question. "The whole point of a secret society is to keep what they do secret," she explained. "Not because of any nefarious intent necessarily, but because that's the appeal. There was a time when their secrecy provided a safe space for members to practice a persecuted faith or exchange political ideas. Today, they function more like weekend clubs that pander to the ego through exclusive memberships and the alure of mystery. And though secular in general, most seek a spiritual journey of growth in pursuit of some ultimate wisdom. I can see how groups like these may consider our search for Fatima's lost message as the quintessential esoteric journey, even if we didn't intend it to be that way."

Lily's shoulders slumped. "And if they are anything like me, they saw in the meteor what I saw: a sign related to our 'journey.'"

"That's right," said Michael. "Following the sighting, a burst of online chatter spread among the secret societies that are tuned into your story. Unfortunately, a nationalist group saw the opportunity to exploit it as a recruiting tool. They call themselves the Knights of Destiny and the NSA has been monitoring them for a while. Since everything related to you falls under my purview, I was called in when the Knights joined the excitement to toss their net."

Sofia was about to protest, but Michael quickly showed his palm. "I know; how can a hostile political group benefit from harmless social clubs or you? The Knights of Destiny are a paramilitary group that believes the discovery of America was divinely orchestrated to create a new utopian Atlantis based on their supremacist ideals. Nothing new. Groups like this have been around since Independence. Unfortunately, this one has found new fertile ground thanks to your lines, which they are conveniently mangling to support their delusion. Since Mary's Line points to America, they exalt it as proof that Providence chose America."

"They sound loony," said Lily, "and you don't do looney. What gives?"

"However crazy it may sound, groups like these are no joke. Some have come very close to creating real havoc. Take John Wilkes Booth. It's suspected he belonged to the Knights of the Golden Circle when he assassinated Lincoln. The Golden Circle wanted to invade Mexico and the Caribbean, enslave their population, and form a new country with its center in Havanna and its radius reaching Washington D.C. If the name is any indication, the Knights of Destiny follow in their footsteps." Michael paused to give them a strange stare and added: "It gets weirder. The chatter was not picked up by us, but rather by our counterparts in Spain. Given that the meteor was sighted there, the chatter caught their attention, and they brought it to ours when they decoded the Knights boasting they had a lead on the lost Declaration of Independence. Spain takes the traffic of national treasures very seriously and had the courtesy to alert us to it."

"Michael, I love you," started Lily, "but the more you talk the less sense you make. What does the Declaration have to do with any of this?"

Michael laughed. "I know, very confusing. Let's backtrack. According to the Knights, they trace their roots, through the Golden Circle, all the way back to a handful of generals who conspired against George

Washington during the Revolutionary War known as the Conway Cabal. The Knights sustain that the Cabal righteously formed because one of its members learned of a secret pact according to which Washington had handed the thirteen colonies over to Spain. And, as if a cruel joke, he had the pact written up on the back of the original Declaration."

Lily was aghast: "That's absurd. Why would Washington do such a thing?"

"To save his neck. Per the Knights' propaganda, he was a coward and an incompetent commander. In view of his dismal results, the prospect of execution for treason was becoming all too real, so he turned to Spain for help."

"The Commander-in-Chief, who personally fought on the front during eight years in grueling conditions, was a coward, they say?"

"Forget logic. They wouldn't be called extremists if they bothered to think sensibly," said Michael. "The point is that groups like these find strength in political division. The Knights are on the hunt for the Declaration to prove Washington's treason, because by delegitimizing Washington, they tumble his greatest legacy: The Constitution."

While a shiver ran through Lily's body, Antonio flashed in Sofia's mind.

"Yesterday, I attended a presentation by a Spanish professor who referenced the secret pact," she said. "I recall him mentioning the Cabal and he, too, claims that the pact was written on the back of the Declaration. Dan asked me to check into it. That's why we are here at the Archives."

"I know. I followed you there yesterday, and it's a good thing I did."

Sofia was taken aback. "That was you who tackled the shooter?"

Michael nodded.

"It can't be a coincidence. The professor invited me personally."

"It isn't."

"What do you know about him?"

"It's classified."

Sofia blinked. *Here we go*, she thought. "Why?"

"I'm sorry, I can't say."

She tensed her jaw. "Was the attacker a member of the Knights?"

"Yes."

"Why did they go after him?"

"To get rid of the competition," started Michael, "which puts you in the same spotlight. The Knights are well organized, funded, and run by powerful interests. They can and will move fast to eliminate obstacles in their way. Please, don't be alarmed, though. We've been keeping an eye out and haven't noticed anyone on your trail; that's not to say you are in the clear."

Sofia reined in her long-standing frustration with him and sighed. "So, what happens now?"

"That is up to you. You can go home and let us handle it, or we work together to counter the Knights' efforts. Our intel tells us they are not bluffing about their lead on the Declaration. Either way, you can trust we will do our best to keep you safe."

"How serious is the danger?" she asked.

"Considerable. As I mentioned, you are both stuff of cult, now. The Knights may decide you are an asset and attempt to coerce you into publicly supporting their claims, or worse, prevent you from contradicting them."

Sofia turned to Lily. "I see no other option. We have to collaborate."

Lily shrugged. "I didn't doubt that for a second."

Michael drew a broad smile as he adjusted his earpiece. "Someone is very happy to hear that."

He gestured with his head across the common area. A younger version of him leaned against a column with an oversized newspaper in one hand and waving with the other. It was Gabriel.

CHAPTER 10

"I can only express my gratitude for your polite offer of service by entreating you to afford me opportunities of testifying my readiness to execute any commands with which you shall be pleased to honor me."

—*George Washington to Diego Jose Navarro, Spain's Commander for the Gulf of Mexico and Louisiana, 4 March 1779*

They were back together, but matters were going to be conducted a little differently this time, if Sofia could help it.

"Here's the deal," she began. "You are NSA and there is only so much you will share. Fine. I'll flow with that for now. But, if we are going to team up to search for the lost Declaration, I want to know everything you have on *that* up front this time."

Michael considered her for a moment.

Sofia felt a slight shiver. His penetrating eyes, the color of smoky quartz crystals, had a way of reaching under her skin.

He spoke slowly. "I'm not here as NSA. I'm here as a concerned friend."

Lily didn't like the sound of that. "Why? What's going on, Mike?"

"The Knights of Destiny are not your run-of-the-mill paramilitary group. Not that any are, but when I said that they are ruled by powerful interests, I meant their tentacles reach out from within the government. Not the other way round. The NSA must focus on the bigger picture, and if they feel they need to use you two as bait to flush the head out, they will."

"So, when you said you'd protect us," understood Lily, "you meant you and Gabriel alone from both, the Knights and the NSA."

"Don't forget Raphael." He tapped his earpiece. "He says 'hi' by the way."

"Can you get into trouble for this?" asked Lily.

"No need to worry about us."

Sofia observed he exuded excessive confidence; more than stood to reason for someone defiantly juggling the country's top security agency and a formidable threat.

A waitress approached with four coffees on a tray and placed three on the table. "Anything else I can get you?" she asked.

The sisters showed their surprise.

"I thought I'd go ahead and order while I waited," explained Michael. "I trust I got your beverages correctly?"

Sofia studied hers. Coffee. Black. No sugar. Exactly what she wanted and how she liked it. She had forgotten how much he knew about them, and it still bothered her deeply. She resorted to a terse nod. A word out of her mouth at that instant would have sounded like an unpleasant grunt.

Lily approved by taking a generous sip out of her pumpkin spice latte.

The waitress left in Gabriel's direction.

"How much do you know about what happened to the fair copy?" proceeded Michael.

"I told Sofia what little is known," said Lily, licking her lips. "Basically, nothing."

"Then you know what I know."

Was he pushing her buttons on purpose? Sofia, slowly and deliberately, put her cup down and gave him a piercing stare. "By your own admission, a terrorist group, which your people are tracking, has a lead on it. And a Spanish professor, who you refuse to talk about, seems to have a great deal of knowledge about it. So, how about you drop the shy act and let us in on the intel you have."

Michael surrendered with a grin. "Okay, maybe a certain working theory has reached my ears."

Lily leaned in. "Please, do tell."

"During the war, Washington had a direct secret channel with Spain. Consequently, if a secret pact was agreed to on the back of the Declaration, it was most likely routed that way."

"Really?" said Lily. "I knew Spain helped more than is generally known, but a direct channel with Washington?"

Sofia felt left behind. "I'm going to need some background. I belong to the 'generally known' camp."

Lily shifted to look straight at her. "The Revolutionary War was not an isolated affair between the colonies and Britain. It was part of a global war between France and Britain. Some even say it was the real First World War. Their battle over North America was only one of three theatres. The other two were Europe and Asia. Incidentally, it all started when the French royal House of Bourbon ascended to the throne of Spain at the turn of the century, because it tilted the balance of power in France's favor. This did not sit well with Britain, leading to the confrontation between the two powers for most of the 18th century. As for Spain, since she shared the same royal house with France, they became a common front through their family pacts, meaning roughly that an attack on one was an attack on both."

Sofia nodded, recalling Antonio mentioning it.

"The problem was," continued Lily, "that Spain found herself dragged into France's global conflicts all too often with the disastrous result that she partook in the loss of the French and Indian War. Land shifted hands in Europe and Central America, but particularly here in North America, Britain gained Canada and the eastern part of Louisiana up to the Mississippi from France, while Spain had to hand over Florida. In compensation, France gave Spain the rest of Louisiana."

"Quite the consolation prize," remarked Sofia.

"You'd think, but from a strategic point of view, it hardly compensated for loosing Florida, because until then, Spain had had full control of the Caribbean. In any case, with France out, control over North America was now divided between Britain and Spain with great gains for both, which led Britain to make a couple of decisions she'd soon regret. She raised taxes on her colonies to cover military expenses in the region and barred them from extending into the newly acquired territory, preferring to leave it in the hands of the Natives to serve as a buffer zone with Spain. As we all know, the colonies did not take either measure well."

Lily glanced over at Michael to signal he could take it from there.

Michael put his coffee down. "Which brings us to the Revolutionary War," he said. "France might have been out of North America, but she was still battling Britain in Europe and Asia. Spain, on her part, saw with deep concern Britain's growing presence in America. Therefore, both, quietly, sent observers to gauge the rising temperature in the colonies with great interest."

That reminded Sofia of something else Antonio had said: *What exactly made the thirteen colonies think they could entertain a war against the world's largest war machine without a navy, artillery or basic gunpowder?* "Seeking to debilitate Britain, is it possible they gave the colonies a nudge by promising their support?" she asked Michael.

He responded with a non-committal shrug. "France, maybe, even likely. Spain, no, for what I'll explain in a minute. Either way, there's no doubt the colonies took full advantage of the rivalry between the Bourbons and Britain. France and Spain immediately set up a secret supply network through Paris, while the Continental Congress established two Secret Committees. One was the Secret Committee of Trade in charge of acquiring the supplies, and the other was the Secret Committee of Correspondence to channel communications."

Michael leaned in. "Now, with regards to the Declaration, what matters is that Spain's physical presence in North America enabled her to establish her own private distribution and communication channel through New Orleans separate from France. This is important, because having supported France for most part of the century with less than satisfactory results, Spain was as ready as the colonies to emancipate, which may explain their secret pact."

At this, the two sisters leaned in, as well.

"It's important to understand that the Revolutionary War posed a serious challenge for Spain: It was happening on her doorstep with a bleak outcome whichever way it went. Spain was already stretched thin in the Americas as it was and dealing with internal tensions of her own. If the Revolution was successful, her American territories were at risk of following suit. If it wasn't, she'd have her worst enemy getting stronger and stronger in her traditional turf.

"So, while France jumped at the opportunity to join the Revolutionary War with nothing to lose in North America and much to gain elsewhere, the king of Spain, Charles III, acted with extreme caution and sought, instead, to leverage Spain's weight as a peace mediator. He offered Britain to stay out of the war with two conditions: One, that Britain agreed to give Spain back the territories lost in the previous war and, two, this part is critical, that Britain would commit to withdrawing from the Thirteen Colonies."

Sofia arched an eyebrow. "Wasn't that the whole point of the Revolutionary War?"

"Yes, but the peace proposal gave Britain the option to withdraw over a period of 25 to 30 years. In the meantime, Spain volunteered to take the colonies on as a protectorate to prevent abuses and violations from Britain while she withdrew."

Sofia was surprised. "What happened?"

"By early 1779, it was painfully clear to the Thirteen Colonies that Spain had no appetite for another war and that France alone could not deliver victory. With this in mind, Britain rejected Spain's proposal and sent a delegation to the colonies, trusting they'd agree to put their arms down if offered forgiveness. It's at this point that the Knights claim Washington sold his soul and the colonies to Spain on the back of the Declaration, because that June, Spain did a U-turn and entered the war."

"Are you inferring that the secret pact may contain the terms of a protectorate?"

"To be clear, the NSA has no evidence there was a pact to start with, much less what it contained," clarified Michael. "That said, there are sufficient signs to suspect that something like that went down."

Lily shared her thoughts out loud. "Okay, I get why it was written on the back of the Declaration. It was the one document that asserted the colonies' sovereignty to seek an agreement. It would have made a solid statement that the colonies were serious about committing to whatever they were committing to, considering they were rebels. The puzzle piece is Washington's leading role in it. He was the commander of the army, not the President of the Continental Congress. That would have been ..." she drifted off "... John Jay at the time." Lily wondered if that was the political truth that Jay had asked Charles Thomson to write about.

"There is a very powerful reason why Washington would have had a prominent role," said Michael. "As I mentioned, Spain had created her own private distribution and communication channel through New Orleans, whereby her commander in the region, Diego Jose Navarro, coordinated directly with Washington. Their letters are upstairs. Furthermore, Navarro sent a secret agent to act as their liaison on the ground and asked Washington to take care of him. Juan de Miralles arrived under the ruse of a private merchant forced to make a landing due to bad weather."

"Did Congress know about this secret agent?" asked Sofia.

"Indeed. He was welcomed wholeheartedly because he came bearing gifts, namely intelligence. Miralles settled in Philadelphia to be treated *de facto* as a diplomatic envoy, until that is, tragedy struck, and the Cabal showed their face for the first time."

Michael abruptly paused to check on Gabriel, leaving the sisters hanging.

Gabriel gave him a thumbs up.

Michael then picked up his cup, while the twins held their frozen stares on him.

"Okay, here's what happened," he said, feeling urged. He put the cup back down. "In 1778, on his way to Morristown to meet with Washington, Miralles fell ill. He was attended to by Washington's doctor and wife in his own residence. Nevertheless, he died. Washington arranged a funeral with the military honors of a patriot and took part as chief mourner. Congress followed by attending a Catholic mass in Philadelphia in his honor. Unfortunately, since his true role had been kept secret, from the public's point of view, the level of respect dispensed to a mysterious Catholic Spaniard by the Commander in Chief and Congress was difficult to understand and played right into Benedict Arnold's hands. At the time, Arnold had already opened channels with Britain and happened to be in Philadelphia seeking command of West Point when the Catholic mass took place. Britain had long been stirring up anti-Catholic prejudices to undermine France's and Spain's support. Arnold followed suit by denouncing Congress as a devious entity that cuddled with *the anti-Christian corrupted Catholic Church* and added: *'the pious ancestors of the colonies would have witnessed* it *with their blood'.*"

"Someone has a flair for the dramatic," commented Lily.

"I thought Arnold was a lone wolf, so to speak," said Sofia. "I didn't realize he belonged to a cabal."

"The term 'cabal' should be used loosely. They weren't well organized. More like a pack of disgruntled lone wolves who came very close to overthrowing Washington. Aside from Arnold, prominent among them were also General Charles Lee, who was second to Washington in the Continental Army; Horatio Gates, who won the battle of Saratoga, and a younger soldier by the name of James Wilkinson, who'd eventually become the most dangerous of them all."

Sofia shook her head amazed at what she was learning. "That is some high-level disloyalty. I'm familiar with Arnold and Gates, but how have I never heard of Lee or Wilkinson?"

"Because their activities are related to Spain and, as with everything related to Spain, it is shrouded in mystery." Michael injected intensity into his stare. "Have you ever wondered how the name *The United States of America* came about?"

The question caught Sofia of guard. It stumped her. She always assumed it was Jefferson who came up with it when he titled the Declaration. Given the question, she was guessing it wasn't. She shook her head.

"The word 'colony' was a British concept, not Spanish. Spain had viceroyalties that functioned like states, so defaulted to refer to the colonies as such. This is evident in the earliest written record known for the use of *The United States of America*. Stephen Molan, an Irish immigrant who had spent time in Portugal and Spain, was Washington's secretary and Spanish translator. In January of 1776, Molan applied for the job of ambassador *'with full and ample powers from the United States of America to Spain'*."

"That was six whole months before the Declaration of Independence," noted Sofia. She looked at Lily who appeared just as shocked, if not more.

Lily was feeling distressed by the widening gap in her knowledge of American history. "So, what is going on? How do we not know any of this? Does this mean there are grounds to suspect the US became a protectorate?"

"Again, I suggest we tread with caution. Spain's secret dealings do not imply something nefarious was going on. But it does give us a glimpse at what the Knights can do with it as heirs to the Cabal. I told you about Arnold's misguiding propaganda. Let's discuss Charles Lee. He wasn't just second to Washington in the Continental Army, he also happened to run the Southern Department. As such, he personally coordinated supplies with the Spanish Governor of Louisiana, Luis de Unzaga, through Oliver Pollack in the early stages of the war."

Sofia recognized that name. She checked with Lily, nonetheless. "Wasn't Pollack who used the Spanish dollar sign in his ledgers?"

Lily confirmed with a nod.

Sofia turned back to Michael. "Sorry, go ahead."

"No, that's fine. In fact, it reinforces the point I want to make. General Lee knew better than anyone the nature of Spain's involvement and relationship with Washington, that is, Spain was helping with supplies and intelligence. Regrettably, Lee ruffled feathers with Washington. Their relationship got so bad, he was court martialed and suspended, and his loyalties thereafter became questionable. True to the Cabal playbook, just as Spain officially entered the war, Lee published an anonymous article in a Philadelphia newspaper to whip up unrest. In it he questioned Spain's love for Washington, insinuating a treasonous relationship." Michael paused. "We suspect the Knights of Destiny have inherited that same playbook."

CHAPTER 11

"Mr. Gardoqui I hope will be in America & treating with Congress before this can reach you. I beg your Countenance to this Gentleman, who Mr. Jay will inform you, has had ever the most Liberal Sentiments with respect to America. I am informed the English wish to blow the flame of Discord between us & Spain in America on acct of the Navigation of the Mississippi. I can assure you that the Same Endeavors are employed here—The Minister of G.B. [Great Britain] has just left me, holding the Same Language, while I know he holds the Contrary to the Ministers of this Country."

—William Carmichael, US ambassador to Spain, to George Washington, 25 March 1785

Michael cocked his head as he paid attention to his earpiece. He then looked at the twins. "Gabriel says we have been here too long. Suggests we get moving."

Sofia got up, stretched her legs, and looked around. "Just curiosity, if there was someone trailing us, what difference would it make if we moved or not?"

"It is easier to spot a tail when you move. And if there isn't one, it makes it harder to gain one."

"Fair enough. How do you want to proceed?"

"Finding lost objects is your superpower. I'll leave that up to you."

Sofia took a minute to recalibrate and reasoned out loud. "If there was a secret pact, and if it was marked up on the back of the fair copy, and if Washington personally signed off on it—" She pursed her lips. "If-if-if, I hate so many ifs ... Anyway, it does make sense the Declaration would have been delivered to Spanish hands through the New Orleans route, as your working theory suggests."

"Which raises the question," wondered Lily, "how are we going to find it in Spain?"

Sofia thought about it. "What we should be asking is why the Knights of Destiny think *they* can find it. What do they know that we don't? And why now?" Sofia looked at Michael. "You said the Knights claim to descend from the Cabal, right?" It wasn't a real question. She was just thinking out loud.

He nodded, nonetheless.

She continued. "The Cabal was made up of senior officers, so it is reasonable they'd be associated with someone knowledgeable about the pact. We also know that at least one member of the Cabal, General Lee, was personally familiar with the New Orleans route. So, again, it's reasonable the Knights would know the fair copy was delivered that way. Let's say they lost track of it when it reached Spain. My question again: Why would they have a lead on the fair copy now? What has changed? That's the key." And once more she addressed Michael. This time for real. "I'm going to guess the Knights have been infiltrated with poor results?"

"You guess correctly. The reason the Knights are structured like a secret society is because it favors lack of transparency. The base-tier members agree to obey without questioning as they wait to escalate grades. It's part of the deal. What they don't know is that the higher levels are reserved for a tight-knit family circle."

"What about the Spanish professor," suggested Lily. "The Knights went after him. He must be onto something. I say we don't neglect his clues."

Her sister's words reminded Sofia that she had not heard from Antonio. She expected he would have reached out by now.

Michael read her mind. "Has he contacted you?"

She arched an eyebrow. "I'm surprised you haven't bugged my phone to know for yourself."

"Sofia, this is important. We must collaborate."

"I appreciate that, Mike, but my problem with you is that there is no *quid pro quo*. You know everything about us, while we get scraps from you. Why can't you tell us about Antonio? It could help us advance."

"It's his wish to remain classified. We honor his privacy as we honor yours."

She didn't expect that. It left her unarmed.

"As for *quid pro quo*," he added, "Rafael fed the novel Don Quixote to our state-of-the-art decryption system and found no sign it was used as a code key by the Founders in their communications."

Just when she was ready to be forgiving. "You see what I mean? When were you planing to tell us?"

"I just did."

"Only because you felt compelled to."

"Please," said Lily. "We are on the same team here. Can we please focus? We know the US dollar and its sign are rooted in the Spanish dollar. And we know the Great Seal contains Queen Isabella's personal emblems. Antonio's clues are holding up. So, if Don Quixote is not a key to a communication code, then it represents something else. We keep searching."

"What's left on the list?" asked Sofia.

Lily retrieved it from her pocket and read: "The mystery guy and the warship at Washington's presidential inauguration. Washington D.C.'s layout. The Whitehouse cornerstone. And the Capitol Rotunda. We can cross out the Supreme Court. We already know it was John Jay who Washington appointed as first Chief Justice and that he spent time in Spain during the war. Actually, scratch that, maybe we should find out more about his mission in Spain."

"It's a lot," said Sofia.

"I can help with the inauguration," offered Michael. "The Spanish guest and the warship go back to the Revolutionary War."

"Thank you," said Sofia. "You can tell us about it as we head over to the White House Visitor Center to learn about the cornerstone. In the meantime, is there any chance Rafael can dig up old maps of D.C. with that fabulous technology of yours?"

"Sure."

"Great. According to Professor del Mar, D.C.'s layout is based on a Spanish town. It would be interesting to find out which one and why."

Michael just stood there nodding.

"Could you ask him? Now would be a good time."

"He heard you." Michael taunted her with a grin.

Sofia's jaw tensed.

Lily stepped in between them and grabbed their arms. "Come on you two, let's go."

The distance to the White House Visitor Center was roughly a fifteen-minute walk from the National Archives. Before leaving, the group ordered sandwiches to go and were now on Constitution Avenue heading west.

It was a pity they were on a mission, lamented Sofia. The day had warmed up and the large fountain in the sculpture garden across the street looked like an ideal spot to take a break for a late lunch. As her eyes yearned in its direction, a motorbike waiting at the red light caught her eye. It was an exotic beast. She loved motorcycles and owned one herself. She noticed this one had been debadged, modified and customized all in black for a clean look. She approved, and briefly imagined herself hitting the open road on it. The rider, dressed in black like his bike, turned his head toward her, possibly perceiving her stare. She couldn't see his eyes behind the helmet's visor, but quickly averted them anyway, and sighed. She had planned a trip that weekend. She'd have to cancel.

Having lost her appetite, she slipped her sandwich untouched in the side meshed pocket of her backpack and checked on Gabriel. He was doing a good job of camouflaging into the background, now that he had gotten rid of the newspaper, that was.

For their part, the group of three failed miserably to go unnoticed. Michael stood between the twins, a full head and neck taller. His handsome frame flanked by two identical attractive brunettes turned male and female heads alike.

While Lily attacked her chicken wrap, Sofia chose to dive back in. "So, Michael, tell us who that mysterious Spaniard was at Washington's inauguration."

Michael had not ordered anything to eat; only a small bottle of water, which he had just finished. He crushed it effortlessly in his grip and tossed it into a nearby sidewalk bin with impeccable aim. "He's not really all that mysterious, or shouldn't be," he said. "Both, the French and Spanish ambassadors to the United States were invited as guests of honor for their countries' contributions. Both men participated in the parade to Federal Hall alongside the committees from the House and Senate, and stood next to Washington on the balcony when he was sworn in."

"That's it? Why the mystery?"

"That's the mystery. Why is he a mystery? To begin with, he wasn't just any diplomatic envoy. Diego de Gardoqui was the first foreign contact to answer a call from the colonies for money and weapons."

"Did he have a personal relationship with Washington like that other Spanish agent ... What was his name ... Miralles?"

"Not during the war. Gardoqui worked via his company's distribution routes to the East Coast. One of its trading ports was in Marblehead, Massachusetts. It was there where Jeremiah Lee, a member of the Massachusetts Congress, reached out to him asking for supplies. Gardoqui answered the call by braving the British privateers and navy, not to mention risking his own business with Britain. But he didn't do it alone. He did it with the Spanish crown's blessing and in harmony with his cousin, Luis de Unzaga, the Governor of Louisiana, who ran the New Orlean's route. Soon enough, Charles III made him the official financial intermediary between Spain and the colonies, using his company in Bilbao as cover. The amount of money and supplies he funneled added into the hundreds of millions in today's dollars. Gardoqui coordinated most of it with Benjamin Franklin and Arthur Lee."

Sofia was impressed. "Leaving aside his contributions, call me a cynic, but with all the more seasoned diplomats at the king's disposal, I doubt Gardoqui—a businessman—was made ambassador for his diplomatic skills."

"Let's call you perceptive. Thanks to his good name in the US, we suspect Charles III chose Gardoqui for a secret mission, if only because his curious relationship with Washington gives it away. Take his arrival, for instance. It was preceded by the announcement of a prized gift for Washington from the king: a jackass."

"That *is* odd," said Lily, with a full mouth. "Who gives an ass?"

Michael chuckled. "Now, now, Sister."

Lily just then realized how her question sounded and elbowed him with a giggle. She swallowed. "What I meant was that a donkey doesn't come across as the type of fancy gift a king would offer."

"You'd be surprised. That donkey was extremely valuable. Spanish jackasses were considered the best in the world for their size and strength, so the crown established tight restrictions on the export of studs.

Washington had tried to procure one for breeding through Juan de Miralles during the war, but Miralles died before being able to deliver it. Gardoqui took the opportunity to do it on behalf of the king as his presentation card. Washington named it 'Royal Gift' and that one Spanish stud went on to become the father of today's American mule, the backbone of American farming and, maybe not incidentally, the mascot of the US army."

Something was not adding up for Lily. "The historian at Mount Vernon told us that one of Washington's copies of Don Quixote was also a gift from Charles III."

"Yes, the Spanish version. That was Gardoqui's doing, as well. Washington and Gardoqui dined at Franklin's house in Philadelphia a few days before the signing of the Constitution. The novel was discussed, and Washington showed interest. Gardoqui informed the king, who arranged to send him a highly valuable special edition, though Washington had already procured his own English version the day he signed the Constitution."

"Yes, that's what she told us. Which means, Washington received two exclusive gifts from the king of Spain ..." murmured Lily, thoughtfully.

"There is one more as far as we know. Merino wool fabric; it, too, very prized."

Lily shook her head. "George Washington was a private civilian at the time. Why was the King of Spain courting him so generously?"

"That's the curious part in their curious relationship," said Michael. He paused to look up at the street sign. They had reached 14th Street, they turned north. Their destination was at the end of the long block on the left. He continued. "When Gardoqui arrived in 1785, his purported mission was to close a delicate trade deal involving the Mississippi. However, we have reason to believe his true mission was to help thwart a plot involving the Cabal, who was behind the problems hindering the trade deal negotiations." Michael lingered briefly to straighten his thoughts and proceeded slowly. "Let's see, the period between the end of the war and the signing of the Constitution was particularly delicate because the infighting between the states almost ended the union before it took its first free step. Cracks were opening everywhere for a number of different reasons, but

two became critical. One was slavery, as we all know, which divided the north and south. But there was another one that came dangerously close to severing the new incorporated west from the original thirteen eastern colonies."

"The navigation of the Mississippi," interjected Lily. "It could be argued it defined the terms of the Constitution." Lily knew this episode well. She looked at Michael. "May I?"

"By all means."

Lily had finished her sandwich. She folded the paper wrapping and put it away in her pocket until she found a bin. "As part of the peace treaty between the United States and Britain, the US gained East Louisiana, which extended the thirteen original colonies to the Mississippi. And that opened the proverbial Pandoras box."

"Let me guess: land rush and speculation," said Sofia.

"If only it stayed at that. Everyone wanted a piece of the cake: States that did not border the western lands claimed rights equal to those that did; veterans who had been promised land grants in lieu of pay during the war found their rights tramped on by competing powerful landowners; clashes between the local tribes and the settlers who encroached in their lands turned horrific. To top it all off, most of the Founding Fathers were large investors in land, Washington first among them. This led many in the west to question the neutrality of Congress, decrying the potential abuse of centralized Federal power."

"Right, but what does the Mississippi have to do with any of this?"

"Simple. During the war, Spain recovered Florida, which at that time extended to the Mississippi, as well. Actually, it was two Floridas, East and West. Anyway, since Spain also controlled West Louisiana, that meant that the two banks of the Mississippi south of latitude thirty-one were Spanish territory, giving her full control of the river beyond that point and its access to the Gulf of Mexico. This upset many in the west, because during the war, Spain had opened her ports along the river and in the Gulf as part of her aid, providing American ships with safe passage and harbor for repairs and reloading. But once the peace treaties were signed, it was back to business as usual and trade controls on the Spanish border and ports were reestablished. For the westerners, this was a disadvantage since the easterners had full—free—access to the Atlantic Ocean. And land speculators feared its repercussion on the value of their holdings. So, while the easterners wanted to move on with peace and start trading with Spain, the westerners refused to sign any trade deal that did not include free navigation of the Mississippi with free access to a port in New Orleans."

Michael took over. "This would have fallen within the usual give and take between neighboring countries. The problem for Spain and the US was that Britain was still staked north up the river flaming tensions, resorting to the usual trick: demonizing Catholic Spain. Rumors spread, claiming that Spain, not content with controlling the mouth of the river, had intentions of extending north into the eastern shore to take over the whole river. It wasn't true, but the growing unrest had many frontiersmen pushing for the preemptive invasion of Spanish Louisiana, while others like the Cabal saw the opportunity to make money."

Michael paused as they reached Pennsylvania Avenue. The group checked the traffic to cross left. It was safe, so they proceeded, and Michael resumed, ready to finish up since they had almost arrived. "Long story short: the Cabal resurfaced in the person of James Wilkinson. Wilkinson had fought with Benedict Arnold in the failed attempt to invade Canada in 1775, and shortly after became aide to Horatio Gates, fighting alongside General Charles Lee. It was Wilkinson who, drunk one night, spilled the beans about the Cabal plotting to overthrow Washington, thwarting the whole thing. Fast-forward to 1783, Wilkinson reappears in Kentucky, which at the time was still a district of Virginia, during the Mississippi agitation, and decides to cash in on it. He started by further inflaming tensions and pushing for the independence of Kentucky, not only from Virginia, but from the Union itself. Meanwhile, he secretly reached out to the Governor of Louisiana, declared his allegiance to the Spanish crown, and offered to hand Kentucky over in exchange for the monopoly of the Mississippi with the promise that the rest of the new west would follow."

"Am I understanding this correctly?" started Sofia. "He was plotting to hand the west over to Spain in exchange for the exclusive rights to the Mississippi?"

"Yes."

"He could hardly have done that alone."

"No. He had powerful contacts in Virginia and Tennessee plotting with him. Luckily, Wilkinson's brain was as sharp as his sense of loyalty. He committed the mistake of threatening Spain with going to Britain if she didn't accept. Spain and Britain were receiving offers like this left and right from an unfortunate high number of characters looking to becoming kings of their own kingdoms in the new frontier. It was a serious problem for the stability of the region. As we know, Spain had no appetite for more conflicts, so, while the Governor of Louisiana played along and put Wilkinson on the payroll for the intelligence he was volunteering, King Charles III rejected his offer and sent Diego de Gardoqui to Philadelphia to help tame matters."

The group came to a stop under a dark blue awning.

Michael continued. "Congress welcomed Gardoqui with open arms. They knew well of his contributions during the war and wanted stability as much as Spain. As for Washington, leaving aside his personal grievances against Wilkinson, he favored paving roads and opening waterways between the west and east to strengthen internal unity and trade. Letting merchandise in the west drain down the Mississippi was not high on his priority list. In fact, to this end, Washington was personally mediating in another river dispute, the control over the Potomac between Virginia and Maryland in what would be known as the Mount Vernon Pact. It led to the founding of the Potomac Company and the massive undertaking of roads and canals."

Sofia was stunned by the implication. "So, basically, the US and Spain were reunited once again against a common foe and Gardoqui was sent to coordinate efforts with Washington discreetly. It sounds a lot like those Bourbon Family Pacts where an attack on one was an attack on both," she insinuated. "How was it resolved?"

"This might shock you: It's shrouded in mystery," teased Michael. "All we know is that one of Wilkinson's allies was John Brown, a representative for Virginia in Congress. They had called the seventh convention in Kentucky to vote for complete separation. But then something enigmatic happened. Following Gardoqui's meeting with Washington in Franklin's house—the one where Don Quixote was discussed—Gardoqui met with John Brown. Brown never disclosed what was said, but suddenly changed his tune and reversed his support of Wilkinson during the convention. It tacitly killed Wilkinson's momentum, saving the Union. Gardoqui stayed around for Washington's inauguration, then moved back to Spain, and was awarded knighthood in Charles III's order, the highest civil recognition. He proudly shared the news with Washington in their last known communication."

CHAPTER 12

"The ships at anchor in the harbor, dressed in colors, fired salvos as it passed. One alone, the Galveston, a Spanish man-of-war, displayed no signs of gratulation, until the barge of the general [George Washington] was nearly abreast; when suddenly as if by magic, the yards were manned, the ship burst forth, as it were, into a full array of flags and signals, and thundered a salute of thirteen guns."

—Washington Irving, Life of George Washington, 1855

Sofia's phone signaled a call. She checked the screen. It was Dan. "I need to take this," she announced, and addressed Lily. "Why don't you go ahead and see if they have a historian onsite that can inform us about the cornerstone. I'll be right in."

"Sure." Lily invited Michael to follow with a tilt of her head.

He wavered. "I'll stand by the entrance to keep a lookout."

Sofia stepped away and took her call. "Dan?"

"Hey, how's it going?" she heard.

"Complicated. I suggest you watch what you say."

Dan's tone came back concerned. "Are you okay?"

"Yes, just being cautious. Our guardian angels have shown up."

There was a moment of silence. "Why do you need *those* guardian angels again?" Dan's unease was almost tangible through the phone.

"As I said, complicated."

"Their agency isn't in the business of handing out bodyguards, much less without a good reason," he insisted.

"It's okay. When I get the chance, I'll explain. You wouldn't believe me over the phone, anyway. Just don't worry, okay?"

"Of course I worry. I worry very much. My sources tell me that the people involved in yesterday's shooting are messed up; really, really, messed up."

"I know."

"Then I don't need to remind you what people like them think of people like you?"

"People like them think the same about everyone. Not even you are safe, Dan. They don't stop at skin color. It's also gender, religion, politics, orientation, you name it. No one that is not their clone is safe, and even then, only one fits at the top. You can bet they are comparing their penises to see whose is more alpha, as we speak."

Dan sighed loudly. "You are not taking this seriously enough."

"I assure you I do."

She heard a grunt.

"What about you-know-who? Any contact?" he asked.

"No, but his leads are valid so far ... they are drawing an interesting picture." She decided to throw him a bone to make him feel better. "This case is shaping up to be the real deal. It could be huge for your magazine."

It backfired.

"Forget my magazine, Sofia. You are not a trained investigative journalist. You have no business risking—"

"Dan, I've got this. And look on the bright side, my back is well covered by the best." She switched subjects, again. "Talking about the best, they told me you can give up on your reading. It's a dead end."

Another grunt. "Whatever ... Just promise you'll text me regularly, so I know you're okay."

"You're worse than my father. You know I have one, right? I don't need two."

Sofia saw Lily come out and head her way.

Michael's eyes followed her as he remained by the entrance on a call of his own.

"Dan, have to go. I'll text. Promise." She hung up.

Lily was holding something in her hand. She leaned into Sofia and whispered. "They were expecting us here as well. The lady at the counter had instructions to direct us to the White House Historical Association. She said someone there has the answers we are looking for. Then she gave me this."

Sofia noticed Lily was blocking the handover from Michael. It was a small envelope. She questioned her sister with a puzzled look.

"I love Michael, but you were right the first time. I've learned my lesson. He has too many secrets. Maybe we should keep some of our own. For whatever it's worth, he doesn't need to know about your *boyfriend* helping us."

Sofia couldn't believe it. Her trusting, transparent sister was being surreptitious. Sofia could handle evil Knights, but if it came down to her saintly sister having to connive, it confirmed the End Times were truly at hand.

Michael could be heard finishing up his call.

Sofia gestured with her chin his way. "Do you believe he is NSA? I'm starting to have serious doubts. Dan is right, that agency doesn't hand out bodyguards. And it makes no sense that he, Gabriel, and Raphael, can get away with being rogue—*again*—for our sake. He's concealing something."

Lily shrugged. "Whatever it is, I do believe he cares about us."

"If that's the case, how did we end up involved with domestic terrorism? He's not exactly insisting we go home to stay safe, is he? And, really, a meteor?"

Lily simply shrugged again. For her, not to be able to fully trust Michael was wrenching.

Sofia drew her attention to the envelope. Inside, there was a card. She slid it halfway out to take a quick peek at it. It read: *"The cornerstone points to the Heart of Columbia. Who is Columbia?"* She quickly slid it back in and tucked the envelope in her pocket.

Michael finished his call, checked on Gabriel with a nod, and joined them.

"I was telling Sofia they don't know anything about the cornerstone in there," said Lily. "The receptionist suggested we ask someone from the White House Historic Association. Their offices are in the Decatur House around the corner on the other side of Lafayette Square. She kindly set up an appointment for us."

"Sounds good," approved Michael. "Let's go then."

Sofia was shocked. Her sister used to be a lousy liar. No more. Definitely the End Times.

"Everything alright with you?" asked Michael.

"Ah, yes, it's nothing. Dan heard about the Knights and is worried. He suggested I drop it." Sofia released a nervous chuckle. "You know you are way in over your head when your own boss is willing to give up the exclusive of the century."

Michael lingered his stare on her. It was penetrating as usual, although this time it carried a hint of softness.

"So, what about that warship?" said Lily, turning north.

Michael politely signaled Sofia to go first and then repositioned himself between the sisters. "It was named *Galveztown*," he started, "and it was at the inauguration to honor its namesake as much as George Washington."

"Galveztown as in Galveston, Texas?" asked Sofia.

"Yes, or Galvez in Louisiana. Bernardo de Galvez was assigned Governor of Louisiana in 1777 to replace his brother-in-law, Luis de Unzaga, who in turn was promoted to Captain General of Venezuela to oversee the Caribbean. It was Spain moving her pieces on the chessboard, preparing for war in case the peace negotiations with Britain fell through."

"I've noticed they all seem to be related one way or another. Wasn't Gardoqui, Unzaga's cousin?"

"The intricate network of secret agents Spain set up in America and Europe would be the envy of the CIA today. Much of its success relied on the agents having family and business ties that helped disguise their operations, while linking them directly back to the king. It's no coincidence that Galvez's uncle, Jose de Galvez, was the Minister of the Indies, meaning spy master; he dealt with no one but the king. The family affair made it an efficient safeguard against leakage."

"I see," said Sofia. "So, you were saying about Galvez, the one who named the ship?"

"Bernardo de Galvez was an accomplished military leader sent by the Spanish crown to lay the groundwork for Spain's potential entry into the war. While Galvez prepared, he continued to provide a massive amount of aid through Oliver Pollock to support, among others, General George Rogers Clark's campaign in the Ohio country. Initially, the Revolutionary War had been conscribed mostly to the Atlantic because Britain was taking advantage of her navy to move forces up and down the coast. Washington's army was not as nimble on land. But then, seeing the war was dragging on, Britain set her sights on taking Spanish New Orleans hoping to control the Mississippi, block supplies, and enforce her pinch around the colonies.

Spain intercepted British correspondence revealing their intentions, which was the king's salvo to let Galvez loose.

"His mission was to recapture the Floridas for Spain, and this way regain control over the Gulf of Mexico, while protecting the backside of the colonies by removing the British threat from the Mississippi valley. Galvez delivered with a streak of immediate successes, until a couple of hurricanes complicated efforts. It took him a little longer than planned, but in the end, he was able to complete his mission in early 1781 when he captured the crown jewel, Pensacola. Galvez did it with a heroic action that has become legendary."

Michael checked on the sisters to see if they cared to hear about it. Lily was all ears and wide-eyed. Good enough. He focused on her. "The entrance to the bay of Pensacola was shallow and, due to an odd visual effect, it also appeared narrower than it really was. The navy commander working with Galvez had his doubts that his fleet could clear the depth of the channel or steer free from the range of fire coming from land. Galvez assessed his chances and was confident passage could be achieved if they unloaded the boats to make them float higher. The navy captain still resisted, so Galvez set out to prove it himself, leading the way on his ship, the *Galveztown*. The British fire from land was brutal, but once the smoke settled, the Galveztown emerged triumphant with negligible damage. His bold act awarded Galvez the motto *I alone* for his coat of arms.

Michael recentered on Sofia. "Now, remember, this happened in early 1781. With Pensacola taken, Britain was left with no bases in the Gulf and forced to divert some of her forces to protect what possessions she still held in the Caribbean, because Spain and France were building up to take Jamaica and the Bahamas. With Britain's forces syphoned to other fronts, a crucial window of opportunity opened up for the colonies: Yorktown."

Lily jumped in. "And it couldn't have come at a better time. After six years of war, the Continental Army was on the verge of collapse, dangerously teetering on a massive desertion. In Washington's own words," she quoted, "*We are at the end of our tether, and that now or never our deliverance must come.*" Her eidetic memory was as sharp as ever.

Michael nodded. "Deliverance indeed came, thanks to the people of Havana, who contributed the money for the offensive. Spain, through

Galvez's most trusted man there, Francisco Saavedra, collected the funds necessary to move Washington's forces and Rochambeau's fleet south to Virginia. He also sent Spanish ships to guard France's interests in the Caribbean to free up Commander de Grasse so he could add his boats to Rochambeau's fleet. The rest is well-known history: General Cornwallis found himself outnumbered on land and at sea. He still put up a good fight for three weeks, but the end of the Revolutionary War had been sentenced."

"Was Galvez at the inauguration with his boat?" asked Sofia.

"No, he died victim to a typhoid epidemic a few years earlier. He was only forty. His boat, the *Galveztown,* did the honors. Upon Washington's arrival in New York on his barge, the *Galveztown* received him with 13 salvos, and when Washington was hailed President on the balcony of Federal Hall—Gardoqui by his side—it was Galvez's ship that shot the celebratory cannons."

No French ships, thought Sofia, just a Spanish one. And not just any Spanish one, one highly symbolic of Spain's victorious intervention. And, again, not only present but granted the lead role in the celebrations for George Washington's inauguration as the first president of the United States.

For Sofia, a clear pattern was starting to form.

* * *

Dan stared at his screen. He was awash in dread. It was one thing to send Sofia on a questionable quest to find a lost American treasure; it was another to involve her in an ugly supremacy conspiracy. And to learn that Michael had reappeared, it unnerved him further. Why were the twins involved in this?

A year ago, he had considered their role in discovering the enigmatic lines quaint, endearing even. Their story, the fulfillment of a Hopi prophecy, had provided a human touch to his skeptical magazine. But he had never fully believed that there was an obscure hand lurking in the shadows. Much less named Red Dragon.

Maybe he should have.

Dan completed the task he was working on by choosing the SAVE option that popped up. He was storing a copy of what little he had had time to research on the novel Don Quixote to his pen drive. He wasn't ready to get rid of it in case things changed again and it turned out there was something there after all. But the truth was he felt a guilty relief when Sofia told him not to bother with it. The task was monumental for one man with no time.

As he prepared to step out for a bit, he heard a muffled sound behind him.

Dan turned and froze.

A man was standing in the middle of the room clutching a gun. He was squarely built, hair shaved military-style, and displayed a tattoo on his neck.

Dan's heart sank. That was no ordinary tattoo. It identified an affiliation, and Dan had become familiar with it over the last twenty-four hours. Dan immediately realized that this man's brazen neglect to cover his face or tattoo augured a dreadful fate for himself.

"What do you want?" he asked.

"Give me everything you have on the Quixote code."

"There's nothing there—"

The man pointed to Dan's knee. "Everything."

"I swear, I don't have much, and what I do may not mean anything—"

The man pulled the trigger.

Dan screamed in pain as he reached for his leg.

"Now!"

A wave of cold sweat seized Dan. He swiveled the best he could in his chair and reached for the thumb drive still connected to his computer. His hand was shaking. Clumsily, he retrieved it as his other hand sketched the man's tattoo on the underside of the table with his own blood.

"Throw it to me."

Dan turned, barely able to endure the excruciating pain in his knee as it crept up his spine. With great effort he threw the pen drive at the man hoping his shaky hand would not fumble it. It was his primal instincts grasping at any chance of survival by doing exactly as he was told.

The dark figure caught it effortlessly in his black glove. He set his lifeless eyes on Dan. "I know where your daughter and grandson live. I'll ask one last time. Is this everything?"

A tear rolled down Dan's cheek. "That is everything."

The man took aim and shot.

CHAPTER 13

"The ceremony was performed by brother Casanave, master of the lodge, who delivered an oration well adapted to the occasion. Under the stone was laid a plate of polished brass, with the following inscription: "This stone of the President's House was laid the 13th day of October, 1792, and in the 17th year of the Independence of the United States of America."

—Charleston Gazette, 15 November 1792

The austere red brick building, once the residence of secretaries of state, members of Congress, and a vice president, stood two hundred years proud in its 21st century environment. The Decatur House was named after its original owner who envisioned it as a social gathering spot conveniently located up the street from the White House. Today it could be booked for just that, while also holding a museum and the headquarters for the White House Historical Association. Founded by Lady Jacqueline Kennedy, the association's mission was to preserve and provide public access to the history of America's executive mansion.

It would seem Sofia and Lily were in the right place.

The twins headed straight for the front door. Michael followed but, upon receiving an urgent alert on his phone, motioned the sisters to go in without him.

Waiting for them in the entrance hall was a pleasant looking man dressed in a dark blue suit accessorized with a bright red bowtie. His white radiant smile denoted he knew without a hint of doubt they were the special guests he was expecting.

"Welcome, my name is Ben Dhruv, Senior Historian, and I'm delighted to receive you." Suddenly, he hesitated whose hand to shake first.

Lily reached out. "Thank you, I'm Lily Auru-Soto, History Professor, and this is my sister Sofia. She's just the writer in the family."

After welcoming Lily, he moved to greet Sofia with a polite chuckle. "I'm familiar with your academic work, Dr. Auru-Soto."

He gestured toward a sitting room adjoining the entry hall. It displayed 19th century décor in soft red, white and blue colors, presided by a round wood mirror crowned with an American eagle over the fireplace. The sisters accommodated on one of two striped sofas, while Dhruv sat across on its replica. He had prepared. Between them was a rectangular coffee table with an old map of the city laid open on top, some other papers underneath, and a few picture books piled on the floor.

"I thought we'd be more comfortable here than in my cramped office," he explained.

"Thank you for receiving us with such short notice," said Sofia.

"My absolute pleasure. Professor Del Mar informed me you were interested in the laying of the White House cornerstone." He paused to share an amused grin. As with his bowtie, it contrasted sharply with his otherwise formal composure. "I'm not accustomed to professionals of your tier interested in such a subject. May I ask why *you* are?"

"I'm not sure what you mean by *such a subject*," said Lily.

"Please, don't take me wrong, the aura of mystery that surrounds Freemasonry has been a blessing to maintain mainstream interest in our work; a large percentage of our visitors are lured by it to our museum and database." He bounced his gaze between the sisters. "You are aware the cornerstone isn't really lost as urban legend would have you believe? Well, sort of ..."

"To be candid," said Lily, "I didn't even know it was claimed to be lost."

Dhruv showed his surprise. "Maybe I misunderstood the purpose of your visit."

"When did Professor Del Mar contact you?" asked Sofia.

"Early this afternoon."

"What were his instructions, exactly?"

"I was to inform you of the cornerstone's true location and about the Freemason master who laid it. I jumped to the wrong conclusion on my own." He looked at Sofia. "Your occasional work on the side threw me off balance. I truly apologize."

His over-the-top reverence was making Sofia uncomfortable. What was it about Antonio that had this effect on everyone? For a ghost, he surely inspired admiration, and other things. "Have you met the professor in person?"

"No, I've never had that honor."

"Why do you hold him in such high regard?"

Dhruv froze mouth-agape at her question. "Professor Del Mar's reputation precedes him and his private archive of early American correspondence with Spain is priceless. We are very grateful to him for granting us access."

"Private archive?" repeated Sofia. "As in family inherited or privately collected?"

"I'm sure you are aware the professor is somewhat eccentric, especially when it comes to his personal life, so I can't answer that question. I don't think anyone can. Regardless, his research papers on the matter—derived from his archive—are much valued in the field."

"I'm sorry, I struggle to understand how his work is admired if so little is known about him," countered Sofia. "Do you even have any proof of his qualifications?"

Dhruv delayed his reply. It was difficult to tell if he was still confused or just being cautious. "The professor informed me that your current project overlaps with his, and following what happened to him yesterday, he is convinced it can help uncover the perpetrator. For that reason, he expressed how personally important it was to him that I collaborated with you." Dhruv said this last part looking at Sofia with deep suspicion. "Therefore, I thought you would be better acquainted with him and his work."

Sofia drew a conciliatory smile. "You said it yourself; he is somewhat eccentric in terms of his extreme privacy, meaning he is an enigma. Familiar as you are with my work on the side, I'm sure you understand that makes the professor as interesting to me as tracking down who tried to harm him." She saw Dhruv's facial features relax. "So, let's say our collaboration with the professor is strictly on a need-to-know basis and only through his university. Is it the same for you, or have you been granted special access to his archive in person?"

Visibly put at ease, Dhruv chuckled. "I'd wish. No, same here, through his university; a very respectful institution, I must add. I trust they did their due diligence in confirming his credentials."

"May I ask," started Lily, "what information drew you to his archives in relation to the White House?"

Dhruv's gaze turned shy. "I'll get to that in a moment. It's another reason the professor asked me to receive you. He believes it might help. But allow me first to provide some background. It contains information he also considers important for you."

While Dhruv reached forward to reposition the map of Washington D.C, Lily leaned closer to Sofia and whispered in her ear. "Your boyfriend is quite the micromanager."

Sofia shushed her. "Stop calling him my boyfriend."

Dhruv looked up wondering if they were talking to him. Seeing they weren't, he returned his attention to the map, which he had turned upright for the twins, upside down for him.

The sisters slid forward for a closer look.

Dhruv ran his finger around the perimeter of the District of Columbia to outline a diamond shape as it was originally envisioned. He explained. "George Washington, as president, was given free rein with regards to the planning of the new capital with only one condition: that its size did not exceed ten miles per side. Washington rotated the perfect square into a diamond when he chose 'Jones Point' in Alexandria as its most southern corner and installed the relevant marker in a masonic ceremony there. He then assigned the task of locating building sites to Pierre Charles L'Enfant, a French military engineer, who had fought in the Continental Army. L'Enfant had trained as an artist in Paris. Driven by his enthusiasm, he did more than merely suggest locations; he went all out and designed a detailed master plan for the entire city."

Dhruv swept his hand over the map. "This is it. It was quite ambitious for the resources available at the time. Many of his recommendations had to be cut back or put on hold, but Washington was stern about retaining the overall vision. The White House was the first public building constructed in the District. A national competition was held for its design and the Irish-born James Hoban's won."

Dhruv paused briefly to assess the map and pointed alternatively to two spots.

Sofia and Lily stretched their necks to follow.

"You can see L'Enfant placed the White House and the Capitol Building at each end of an unusual L-shaped design. It was delimited by the Tiber Creek, which he foresaw converted into a navigational canal." Dhruv outlined the canal as he drew a wry grin. "Sadly, instead, it became a sewer, but that's another story." He continued. "Basically, the White House looked down the north-south leg of the L, while the Capitol presided over the longer east-west leg, as they stand today."

Antonio's note drifted into Sofia's thoughts. *The cornerstone points to the Heart of Columbia.* She narrowed her eyes while placing the tip of her index finger on the vertex of the L-shape. "Would you say this is the center of the District? I can't quite tell."

"If you're referring to the intersection of the city's four quadrants, that would be the Capitol Building. There is a marble compass in the Crypt under the Rotunda that marks it. The city streets, and their numbering, radiate out from there like twelve spokes of a wheel. At least, according to its original design. It's been slightly modified since."

Sofia looked at the location of the Capitol Building and assessed it wasn't even close to the center of the diamond. "No, I mean the center of the District's rhombus shape." She drew a circle around the approximate spot, which roughly included the vertex of the L-alignment."

"Hmm, good question. L'Enfant suggested placing George Washington's equestrian monument on the convergence of the two legs. Instead, the Obelisk eventually took its place. But to be honest, I'm not sure if it's also the center of the District. If not," he said, pausing to judge for himself, "I imagine it should be thereabouts."

That stroke Sofia as odd. She studied Dhruv on the sly for a moment. How did he not know where the center of his perfect square capital was? Especially when Washington D.C. was spotted with heavily promoted historical markers of every type and size for the delight of tourists. There were boundary stone markers, meridian markers, zero milestone markers, and a wide range of miscellaneous memorial markers everywhere. And whole guided tours designed around them. Surely the exact center would have been reserved for a singular commemorative marker of some sort, especially if the Freemasons had a say in it. Yet this man, who was particularly well informed about the District's history, didn't know about it. And if he didn't, no one did, meaning there was no interest in promoting it. Why?

She was about to ask for a ruler when another thought took over: Freemason's systematically placed cornerstones in the northeast corner of buildings. In the case of the White House, that would *point* in the opposite direction away from the rough area that in her judgement framed the *Heart of Columbia*. It contradicted Antonio's note. She looked up at Dhruv. "What's the mystery with the cornerstone?" she asked. "You mentioned something about its true location?"

Dhruv searched under the map, extracted a sheet of paper, and handed it to Sofia as he explained. "For all the detailed documentation we have on the designing of the capital and its buildings, there is only one source of information in relation to the White House's foundational ceremony." He gestured at the sheet of paper. "It's an article published in Charleston, South Carolina, a month after the ceremony, of which only one copy has survived. To make it further obscure, the article reproduces an extract from a letter of an anonymous witness to the event. So, as you see, it's a miracle we have any notion of it at all."

Sofia skimmed through it while Dhruv continued to explain. "According to the anonymous witness, the Freemasons of Georgetown were in charge of the ceremony. If accurate, that would have been Maryland Lodge No. 9. The article states that the lodge master, brother Casanave, performed the ceremony. Washington was not present. He was in Philadelphia for his fourth annual address to Congress."

"That's strange," remarked Lily, "why would he skip it? He was present for Jones Point and the Capitol building. Why not the White House?"

Dhruv did not know what to answer.

"What about the lodge's records," asked Sofia. "For the Freemasons, the whole point of the foundation ceremony is to stress the importance of starting with a strong foundation for what the building will symbolically represent. In this case, the executive power. They would have been particularly interested in recording the historic moment. Why do they not have records of it?"

"All their records prior to 1795 mysteriously disappeared. In fact, the lodge itself disappeared for a while. It was later reestablished as Potomac Lodge No. 5."

"Really ...?" Sofia turned her attention to the miraculous survivor. "I see the article dates the ceremony to October 13 of 1792. I was under the impression it took place on the 12th, the 300th anniversary of Columbus' arrival."

"There has been much confusion about that. Bear in mind that the article was not rediscovered until the 1940s. Until then, little to nothing was known about the ceremony. Since Casanave, the master, was Spanish, some assumed the 12th for the reason you just stated. On the other hand, Freemason enthusiasts pointed to the 13th because it's the date of the Knight Templar's persecution. When this piece reappeared, the matter was settled in favor of the latter. However, I should add there are those who suggest the ceremony was extended over a 24-hour period to accommodate both anniversaries."

"Wait!" Sofia bristled. "It says here the cornerstone was laid on the southwest corner of the White House." She looked up. "That is contrary to Freemason tradition."

Dhruv nodded. "And that is the reason it was believed lost. Several attempts had been made to locate it in the northeast corner without success. That piece," he said, signaling the article, "appeared around the time President Truman undertook the reconstruction of the White House. Since it states that a brass plate was laid under the stone, Truman's architect took the opportunity to borrow a mine detector from the army engineers and scanned the perimeter. The most distinct response was obtained near the southwest corner, confirming the article correct. Surprisingly, Truman refused to dig it up, which only added to the legend because the White House was literally gutted. If there ever was a time to confirm the cornerstone's location, it was then."

"That makes no sense," noted Lily. "Truman was a Freemason; a very active one. In fact, he was Grand Master, receiving the highest 33rd degree while in office as the 33rd President. Quite a meaningful coincidence for someone deeply moved by symbolism. If all this was happening under his watch, why would he let that opportunity pass? The contents of its time capsule would have been of extreme historical significance for him and the brotherhood."

"Maybe he didn't let it pass," whispered Sofia, retreating into deep thought. She quickly resurfaced to ask: "What can you tell us about the lodge master who conducted the ceremony, Casanave?"

"He is yet another peculiar case," said Dhruv. "Very little is known despite his close relationship with George Washington and relevance in Georgetown. His name was Pedro Casanave, and he was born in Navarra, Spain. He moved to the States in 1785 when he was only nineteen with nothing but a letter of recommendation for Washington. It would appear Pedro Casanave was the nephew of Juan de Miralles, a Spanish agent stationed in Philadelphia during the Revolutionary War."

Sofia bristled again. "You said Juan de Miralles? Casanave was a nephew?"

"Yes, that's right."

Her eyes began to flicker.

That told Lily her sister's brain was making connections beyond recognizing the name.

Unaware, Dhruv continued. "Miralles and Washington must have been close because Washington took Casanave under his wing and Casanave prospered fast. He settled in Georgetown and successfully tried his hand at a variety of ventures. The man was creative. One was a night dancing school for gentlemen who were too busy during the day." Dhruv chuckled at that. "After taking on real estate as well, he married into a distinguished local family, the Notley's. It was on their lands that the Capitol Building was built. At the same time, Casanave also handled the student finances for the Georgetown College boarding school and ..." Dhruv paused to think. He shook his head. " I know I'm missing something. Anyway, Casanave died very young, twenty-nine or thirty, though nothing is known about the circumstances ... Wait, how could I forget?" Dhruv smacked his forehead. "Casanave was also mayor of Georgetown."

Lily pantomimed a whistle. "Plus, master of the masonic lodge ... And all that before turning thirty."

The fact that Casanave died so young under unknown circumstances caught Sofia's attention. She did the math. Her calculations established his death around the time the lodge and its records disappeared. Could it be connected?

She added it to her *Suspicious Loose Ends* mental file and looked at Dhruv. "Please tell us about your research. You said the professor believed it might help us."

Dhruv shifted in his seat as a blush of shyness reappeared. "Some of its driving elements are, how should I put it, delicate."

Lily's professional empathy recognized the discomfort. "You mean, controversial?"

Dhruv cleared his throat. "Pedro Casanave was not the first Spaniard to lay a cornerstone for an emblematic building. Seven years earlier, the first ambassador of Spain to the United States, Diego de Gardoqui, laid the cornerstone for St. Peter's Church. It was the first Catholic Church in New York City, the capital at the time. The king of Spain, Charles III, had donated a generous amount for the project."

Lily widened her gaze. Yet another generous gift from the king, only this time with a more serious implication. "You suspect the king might have had a monetary hand in the building of the White House, as well."

Dhruv nodded and braved his reasoning. "How else do you explain that Washington would grant the great honor of laying the foundational stone for the new executive residence and first public building in the new capital of the new nation to an otherwise unknown Spaniard?"

And not just any Spaniard, thought Sofia. The pattern repeated itself. Casanave symbolized, once again, Spain's involvement in the Revolutionary War through his uncle, and performed the leading role in a prime ceremony.

Little by little the pieces were coming together, although the larger picture remained blurry. Regardless, one thing did render clear in Sofia's mind, and she was eager to confirm it.

She jumped to her feet. "Mr. Dhruv, you've been extremely helpful, but we must leave now. Do you mind if we take this?" she asked, referring to the map and newspaper article.

"Please do. I made those copies for you."

Dhruv guided them to the door, somewhat surprised by the sudden rush. He reached under his suit, feeling for his shirt pocket. "If I can be of any further assistance, please do not hesitate to contact me. Any time." He handed them his business card.

"Thank you," said Lily, accepting it. "Good luck with your research."

Outside, they found Gabriel standing alone on the sidewalk.

"Where is Michael?" asked Lily.

Gabriel's young face seemed unsettled. "He's following up on something. He asked me to take you to our safe house as soon as you were finished here. It's not far. He'll meet us there."

"Has something happened?" asked Sofia.

"I don't know all the details. It's better if Michael informs you."

She paled. "It's the professor, isn't it? The Knights got to him?"

Gabriel shook his head. "No, the professor is fine. Please, come with me, we should go." He gestured with his hand south.

Sofia exhaled relieved. "Okay, but there is something I want to see first." She pulled her phone out to perform a coordinate search for the center of the District on a modern map. As Antonio's note indicated, it was southwest from the White House cornerstone. No more than half a mile."

Lily looked over her sister's shoulder. "The Heart of Columbia?"

"Yes, it's just down the street. Let's go."

Gabriel hesitated. "Michael's orders were to head straight to the safe house."

"We're not going far. It shouldn't take us long," said Sofia.

"But ... Michael said ..." It was futile. The twins were already on their way before he could finish his sentence. Gabriel followed behind with eyes vigilant and relaying matters through his earpiece.

Lily struggled to keep pace. "What is it, Sof? What did you figure out?"

Sofia began by shaking her head. "I don't think the secret pact was a mere war arrangement. I think it was something much bigger."

"What makes you think that?"

"All the pageantry around it. Everything we've seen has Spanish and Freemason elements intertwined, either symbolically or ceremoniously."

"Right, but to an extent, it's normal to be grateful to an ally and invite them to relevant ceremonies as the guest of honor, especially if they are footing the bill.

"It's more than that. Think about it. Pedro Casanave had his hands in everything that was going on with the new capital. But why? Why would a young Spaniard looking to prosper in the Americas choose Georgetown? In 1785, when he arrived, Georgetown was no more than marshlands, and the District of Columbia barely a thought. The kid had a powerful family in Cuba. In those days, Havana was one of the most prosperous cities in the world. Yet he settled in Georgetown under Washington's wing and surprise-surprise just happens to go on to have an integral role in the development of the nation's capital. Even his youth signals to a long-term project. But a decade later something changed and with Casanave's early death, all trace of what he was up to was erased."

Lily was stunned. "What kind of long-term project?"

"The one and only. It's plainly proclaimed on the back of the Great Seal."

Lily tried to visualize it in her mind. *The All-seeing eye ... the unfinished pyramid ... and, of course ....* "The New Order!" She looked at her sister amazed. "The Great Seal was telling us all along."

"Yes, and it establishes the general pattern. I noticed that Spain was repeatedly leading the foundation-related icons and ceremonies, just like Queen Isabella's emblems are on the front of the seal akin to the foundational stone of the unfinished pyramid in the back, the New Order."

They had arrived at their destination. Sofia slowed to a stop and grabbed the newspaper article she was carrying in her other hand with the map. She handed it to Lily. "It clicked when I read this." She pointed at the paragraph. "It says here that after the cornerstone ceremony they all went back to Sutter's Fountain Inn in Georgetown, had dinner, and then toasted sixteen times. Check out toast number four."

Lily read it as Sofia assessed what stood behind her. "*District of Columbia: may it flourish as the center of the political and commercial interests of America.*" Lily looked puzzled again. "The District was being built as the capital of the United States. It makes sense they wished it to flourish as its center."

Sofia drew a satisfied grin. "They weren't referring to the United States. Lily, it's no coincidence they named the District *Columbia* and then, contrary to tradition, placed the cornerstone on the southwest corner of the White House pointing to its *Heart*." She signaled behind her sister. "Turn around. Look what is located in the center of the District and who stands in front."

Lily was so engrossed by the conversation she had not even realized they had stopped. She quickly turned and saw an attractive building, Beaux Arts style. Above the three arched glass entrances that dominated the facade, Lily read:

ORGANIZATION OF AMERICAN STATES

Then, she turned her attention to the solemn six-foot bronze sculpture that greeted visitors at the foot of the access stairway *in front* of the building. Her jaw literally dropped when she read who it was on the pedestal. "You have to be kidding me ..." Slowly, Lily raised her eyes up the length of the regal figure until she reached the face. "... Queen Isabella."

CHAPTER 14

"Until death, it is all life."
—Don Quixote by Miguel de Cervantes Saavedra, 1605

Michael paced back and forth, listening intently into his earpiece. At the same time, he repeatedly checked on the entrance door. He expected it to open any moment. He could hear their steps approaching.

He wasn't happy.

The door opened; in came Sofia and Lily, followed by Gabriel.

Michael halted in the middle of the room. Sofia instantly picked up on his rigid body, while Lily studied the small apartment. The immediate area was a common space shared by the living and dining rooms, and a small kitchenette to one side, all painted from a palette of earth colors. She surmised the three closed doors on the other side led to a couple of bedrooms and a bathroom.

"Nice," she said. "And great location; so convenient."

"Next time I instruct you to move to safety, I expect you to listen," said Michael, tightly.

His authoritative tone magnified by his bass voice smacked Lily into realizing the tense situation.

Sofia, on alert, had started revving on the defense the moment she entered. "Excuse me?!"

"I left you with Gabriel trusting you'd follow my instructions. You were to come here as soon as you finished at the Decatur House."

Gabriel moved silently toward the far window, hoping to vanish from the conversation.

"With due respect, *we'll* go where *we* consider *we* have to go," said Sofia. "And I have no intention of asking permission to do it."

"Do you have any idea what goes into keeping you safe?"

"No. I'd love to hear about it. And while you're at it, why don't you tell us why you do it."

Michael opened his mouth to say something but caught himself. He took a long breath. "Please sit down. I have something to tell you." He pointed to a small couch.

Lily had never seen him like this. "Mike, what is it? What's happened?"

"Lily, just, please, sit down. I'll explain." His tone had moderated, still he turned a moment to recompose.

Sofia initially resisted. Her pride refused to follow his instructions.

Her sister nudged her.

She reluctantly moved toward the sofa but spoke her mind, nonetheless. "I realize there are dangers out there and that you are trying to help, but that gives you no right to—"

Michael pivoted with a raised hand. "I apologize." His words came across more like a demand to end the matter than an expression of regret, but sincere enough.

As the sisters sat on the couch, he grabbed a chair from the small dining table and placed it in front of them. He too sat, and leaning forward, forearms on thighs, he set his gaze squarely on Sofia. They had softened to a degree that made her quiver. It became apparent he was bearer of really bad news.

"What I'm going to tell you is not yet public and won't be for a while. It must stay between us."

She offered a subtle nod.

"Earlier today, someone ... Sofia, Dan is dead. He was found dead in his office. He was shot ... twice."

Sofia narrowed her eyes trying to make sense of the words: *Dan, dead,* and *shot.*

Lily took her hands to her mouth in shock. She had met Dan only occasionally despite her recent collaboration with his magazine, but her impression of him had been very positive: a nice man who couldn't help treating Sofia like a teenage daughter rather than a professional consultant. It was cute to watch. Lily slid closer to Sofia, reached for her hand, and held it tight.

Sofia didn't notice. She was focused on Michael. "I just spoke to him a little while ago. He was fine."

"The afternoon cleaning service found him—sitting in his chair—and called it in approximately two hours ago." Michael paused. Sofia's eyes were begging for more information, and he hated what he had to offer. "Dan received one shot to the knee and one to the head. The police think the knee was first to force him into complying, and when they got what they wanted, they killed him. There's no doubt it was a professional hit job."

"Who? The Knights ...?"

Michael's stare regained its usual intensity, as he offered a firm nod. "Dan left us ... you a message. He drew a circle with an eye in its center under his desk. It's their symbol. They've repurposed the Eye of Providence and inserted it in a circle as homage to the former Knights of the Golden Circle."

A million thoughts pelted Sofia's mind. "Nelly, I have to talk to Nelly."

"The police are already with Dan's daughter. They immediately deployed a team to her house. Nelly and her son are okay. They'll stay under surveillance until more is known."

"What about our parents? Could they be in danger?" asked Lily.

Michael drew a soft smile. "I have them covered."

Sofia slowly lowered her forehead to rest it on the palms of her hands. She wasn't breaking down; she just needed to catch her breath. Her lungs felt constricted.

Knowing her sister, Lily gave her the moment she needed and simply rubbed her arm gently without saying a word.

Somewhat settled, Sofia looked up at Michael. Her eyes were moist. "Why him? Do you know why he was targeted?"

For Michael, this was going to be the hardest part. Once again, he took a deep breath. "Dan was asking a lot of questions and these people have eyes and ears everywhere. His laptop was transferred to the forensic lab. A preliminary diagnosis indicates that the removal of a thumb drive was the last action taken on it. None was found in the office, so it is presumed they took it."

"I don't understand," said Lily. "What information did they think he had? And if it was information they were after, why only take the thumb drive and risk leaving information behind on the laptop?"

Michael shook his head. "Forensics is still trying to determine what was transferred to the external drive. In any event, the fact they left the computer or that his office was not ransacked suggests information was not what they were really after." He focused somberly on Sofia. "I'm sorry, Sofia, it's likely they killed Dan just to send *you* a warning."

* * *

Several hours later, Ben Dhruv collected his things, ready to leave. He had stayed in late to finish a report. Contrary to most people, he was rarely in a hurry to leave work. He cherished the quiet hours in his office after everyone else was gone for the day.

Satisfied he had been productive, he stepped out onto the front landing, closed the door, and locked it. The evening had clouded, but the temperature remained pleasant. Dhruv was looking forward to his walk home. Maybe he'd stop by his favorite joint for a quick drink.

Just as soon as he turned the corner on H St., heading west, an imposing figure holding a gun blocked his advance. The man wore a wide brimmed hat and dark sunglasses despite the absence of sun or much electric light, for that matter. Dhruv froze, confused. He worked in a safe part of town, a few yards from the White House. A brazen armed robbery like this was unheard of, if only because there were half a dozen Secret Service cameras focused on them right now.

The odd disguise suddenly made sense. Still, neither fight nor flight kicked in. The strangeness of the situation and a false sense of security was making Dhruv's reflexes sluggish.

"My wallet is in my pocket," he said. He had roughly $50 in it. He wasn't about to resist over that ridiculous amount.

"Today, the Auru-Soto sisters visited you," said the attacker with unnerving calm. "I am familiar with your work, Mr. Dhruv. Therefore, I want you to focus on telling me anything else the twins showed interest in or commented on."

The reality of what was happening clicked in his head like the detonator of a bomb. Dhruv was a smart man and instantly realized there was only one reason anyone would know or care for the Auto-Soto's visit and that would be someone connected to the attempt on the professor. A blast of fright surged through his chest as he found himself wishing it had been a robbery. He stuttered his response. "They asked ... were curious about Professor Del Mar ... told them about my access to his archives—"

Dhruv observed with horror as the man raised the gun to his forehead.

"Let's try again. I need you to focus. What did they want to know that's not related to your work?"

"Casanave ... the cornerstone ceremony—"

The man reached out with his free gloved hand, grabbed Dhruv's red bowtie, and twisted it to chocking point. "Was anything said by you or them that isn't public knowledge about either one?"

Instinctively, Dhruv reached with his hands to remove the attacker's hold. It was ironclad. He was having a hard time concentrating. "The writer ... she seemed interested in the stone's placement, orientation ... asked where the center of the district was ..." he coughed, "she appeared to doubt Truman would pass on digging up the cornerstone during the renovation."

"That's much better."

But rather than providing relief, Dhruv felt the iron grip twist the bowtie even further. He could not breathe and desperately clawed at what he could, sensing he was going to pass out.

Abruptly, the roar of a motorcycle filled the air. It came flying from across the street, producing an explosive noise as if it had just broken the sound barrier. Through the corner of his eyes, Dhruv saw the machine lunge directly for them.

His attacker released him and jumped into action a split-second too late. The biker whipped the back tire with such accuracy it swept the legs from under the assailant.

Dhruv watched in shock as his attacker bounced right back up onto his feet with the gun sturdy in his hand, but rather than stopping to use it, ran for his vehicle.

The biker did not chase after him. He calmly straightened his motorcycle up, stabilized it, and stood guard making sure the attacker left. Then he turned his head slowly to look in Dhruv's way.

All Dhruv could see were his own panicked eyes reflected on the helmet's visor. The rider was dressed completely in black, looking like an extension of his impressive machine. This was no ordinary Samaritan.

The rider lifted an inquiring thumb at him.

Dhruv responded in kind with a shaky okay.

The mysterious biker then took off.

CHAPTER 15

The rest of the evening had been a blur and the night a procession of grieving thoughts mixed with warm memories turned painful. The hours were creeping into the early morning, and the traffic could be heard slowly waking up outside.

Sofia had given up on sleep. She poured herself another cup of coffee and reached for her phone to cancel the *Do Not Disturb* setting. The screen lit up to deliver a single message from an unknown number.

I'm so sorry. AdM.

It was him, Antonio. She stared at it for a few seconds, but the flutter of surprise was quickly overridden by the boiling frustration she felt since learning of Dan's senseless death. She could have asked herself how Antonio knew or why he'd care. Instead, she debated whether to throw her phone out the window, scream at it or respond to the message with a couple of unsavory words. Why didn't he call and talk? Why the coded messages? Who was he? What did he want from her? ... Why did he send the stupid invitation? Maybe if he hadn't, Dan would still be alive.

Michael's voice broke her silent struggle. "How are you holding up?"

Sofia swiftly darkened the screen and turned as she tucked the phone in the back pocket of her jeans. She responded with a shrug as she studied him. He had removed his sweater and only wore an untucked t-shirt. He had been working out. "Would you like one?" she asked, lifting her cup.

"No, thanks. I'm fine." He came over and leaned against the kitchenette counter next to her. "Can't sleep or don't want to?"

"A little of both." Sofia lost her gaze in the darkness of her coffee. "I can't help thinking about how unfair Dan's death is. To think he was worried about me. He was planning on retiring soon, you know. He wanted to move closer to his grandson. When his wife passed away a few years ago he had buried himself in his work. Then his grandson came along and infused him with new life. He was excited to spend time with him; had so many plans."

Sofia started walking toward the dining table where she had set up her laptop. "I know it's not my fault. I know I can't change anything. And I know Dan would prefer that I stayed safe rather than pursue this story." She turned slightly to share her defiant look. "But right now, what I really want to do is go after those rotten—" Sofia tightened her lips not willing to stoop to their level even with words. "I want to help bring them down."

"Remember when we met?"

Michael's question surprised her.

"You asked me why I stayed in my line of work. I told you I did it because I wanted to bring change to my ancestor's land."

The memory made her feel guilty. "You said it was human nature to see war as the solution. You were tired of it and wanted to do your part to bring peace."

"Yes; unfortunately, I often find it is necessary to remove the *rot* that stands in the way first." He deployed his sweet smile. "Let's bring them down together, Sof."

For all his secretive ways, in that instant she felt a warm wave of gratitude for having him on her side.

"Let's do it!" they heard Lily say. She was standing in the door frame to her bedroom. "I'll prepare more coffee."

"I'll scramble the eggs," volunteered Gabriel from his.

A sudden rattling noise startled everyone. It came from the corner of the room by the window. It was the printer. It had been activated.

Michael grinned as he approached it. "It's Rafael. Says less talk; we are wasting precious time. He found the map you wanted and is sending it."

Following breakfast, they all sat around the table except for Gabriel. This mission had little to do with his area of expertise, so he kept himself preoccupied with his phone and an eye out the window.

Day had broken.

Michael shuffled through his allotted prints. Rafael had sent more than just a map and the three were taking turns, reading through the stack of pages. While he skimmed the one in his hand, he asked: "By the way, what did you find out yesterday?"

Sofia was on her laptop following up on a couple of strong hunches. She paused to hand him the Charleston news clip about the White House cornerstone ceremony. "We think Washington and Charles III teamed up to foster the New Order together."

Michael raised an eyebrow as he accepted the article.

"The White House cornerstone was laid by a Spaniard," she started to explain. "He was Georgetown's lodge master. After the ceremony, the Freemasons headed to Sutter's Fountain Inn and toasted several times. You'll see the toasts listed in the article; they are quite telling. Take a look at number four. It's dedicated to the District of Columbia, hoping it will flourish as the center of the political and commercial interests of America, meaning, all America, as in the Americas. There can be no doubt about this, the toasts are specific when referring to the United States. See one, two and six."

Michael read: "*1. The fifteen United States. 2. The President of the United States. 6. Constitutional liberties of the people of the United States of America.*"

"If still in doubt," she said, "the last one, toast sixteen, reads: *May peace, liberty and order extend from pole to pole.* They don't say around the world in the usual horizontal sense, but vertically as in the American continent."

Michael observed: "The United States is toasted to several times, as is France and even Lafayette, but I don't see Spain mentioned once."

"That's because Spain was leading the ceremony. Pedro Casanave, the lodge master, was the nephew of Juan de Miralles, the Spanish secret agent you told us about."

"Miralles. Interesting."

"Interesting doesn't come close to describing it," said Lily. "Casanave arrived in 1785 when he was nineteen and only seven years later, he's laying the cornerstone for the United States' executive mansion."

"If that is your way of insinuating it looks suspicious, I agree," teased Michael. "The White House ceremony is a huge honor for an unknown foreigner who just arrived on scene."

"That's the point," said Sofia. "There is a whole lot of honorary pageantry going on with Spain's fingerprints all over it. And that ceremonial aspect hints to a transcendental commitment, something grand and ambitious beyond a mere political alliance. In fact, I'm starting to wonder if Casanave buried the pact itself in the White House cornerstone to cement that transcendency."

"You think the lost Declaration is buried there?" asked Lily.

"Not anymore. I think Truman found it." Sofia took L'Enfant's plan for Washington D.C., the one Dhruv had given them, and put it in front of Michael. She started by bringing him up to speed. "Pierre Charles L'Enfant was the designer of the capital's layout, and he was very detailed in assigning a purpose to every lot in the city. Yet he left this one," she tapped it with her finger, "as an undefined green space. That lot happens to be located in the exact center of the District."

"Meaning that, symbolically speaking, it's prime real estate," said Michael, confirming his understanding.

"Exactly," said Sofia. "Washington was personally involved in the District's planning, so knowing what is there now, it's clear he reserved it with the secret pact in mind."

"Why? What's there now?"

"The Organization of American States, the oldest regional organization in the world."

"*From pole to pole*," he acknowledged. Michael took a moment to review the information in his head. "How do you make the connection to the pact, though?"

"Because it is coded in the Great Seal," explained Lily. "The seal was approved in time for the peace treaties. On the front is Queen Isabella through her personal emblems, St. John's eagle and the bundle of arrows, and that's only possible if Charles III, a crucial partner in the peace treaties, had consented to it. Then on the reverse is the Eye of Providence approving the construction of the New Order." Lily paused to look at Michael. "That same coded symbolism is replicated in the center of the District. Guess who stands in front of the Organization of American States?"

Michael listened knowing the answer.

"The statue of Queen Isabella," she continued. "And she is holding a pomegranate in her hands with a dove carved into it. Today the dove is the symbol of peace, but until the Renaissance, it symbolized Providence, while pomegranates symbolized prosperity."

Michael nodded impressed.

"So, going back to Truman," started Sofia, "Check out what Article 1 of the organization's charter says: *The organization was established in order to achieve among its member states an order of peace and justice, to promote their solidarity, to strengthen their collaboration, and to defend their sovereignty, their territorial integrity, and their independence.*" Sofia looked up. "Exactly what toast sixteen called for: *May peace, liberty and order extend from pole to pole.*" She grinned. "Can it be coincidence that the organization's charter was signed under the Truman administration?"

"He must have found the pact and felt it was his fate to finish the pyramid," said Lily. She explained the thinking to Michael. "We learned yesterday that the White House was gutted for renovation under Truman. A lot of effort was put into locating the cornerstone, but when it was found, he refused to dig it up. Truman was a Freemason and awarded 33rd degree while 33rd President. We can't imagine him passing up the opportunity to recover a Freemason time capsule."

Michael looked at the sisters for a long second. "Everything you've said is compelling, but it doesn't add up. Why would the king of Spain agree to a New Order with its capital in the US and contingent on his territories becoming *sovereign* and *independent,* if he was running the show? And, if he was indeed running the show, as it would appear, that can be a big problem, because it proves the Knights right: Washington catered to the Spanish king."

Sofia shook her head adamantly. "I agree we still have some wrinkles to iron out, and I don't deny that when the pact was signed, Charles III was in the position of strength, but he died in 1788. All of Washington's actions, in terms of adopting Spanish related icons, took place afterwards."

She searched in the pile of papers for the map of the Spanish town Rafael had sent. When she found it, she placed it next to L'Enfant's design of D.C. and patted it. "What I see here is the action of a grateful man, not a subservient traitor."

CHAPTER 16

"The Cristian king [Louis XVI of France] per his strict execution of his commitments with the United States of Northern America, has proposed and requested that his Catholic Majesty [Charles III of Spain], from the day he declares war on England, recognize the sovereign independence of the mentioned states and offer not to lay down arms until said independence is recognized by the king of Great Britain, making this point the essential base for all peace negotiations that may be undertaken thereafter. The Catholic king [Charles III of Spain] has desired and desires to please his Christian nephew [Louise XVI of France] and procure the United States all the advantages they aspire to and may obtain."

—*Article No. 4, Treaty of Aranjuez, 12 April 1779*

Lily came around to Michael's side to examine the two maps side-by-side.

"Bear with me, I'm still trying to put it together," said Sofia, getting ready to parse her thoughts. "Look, believing one is blessed with Providence's favor is nothing new. Every nation, religious group, pharaoh, king, president, or general that is or ever was, believes themselves chosen and blessed in their undertaking by the divine." She pressed her palm against her chest. "Our Hopi tribe believes it was chosen to secure peace in the world.

"Additionally, the discovery of America shook the foundations of the Old World to its core. Everything Europe knew or thought it knew was shattered, in a good way. New horizons to a new world, new knowledge, new riches, and extraordinary potential were opened. So, it's natural for a new country in America like the United States to see itself chosen and to embrace it as part of its identity. This explains the queen and the icons. But it's not only about rooting the identity. It's also about building the country going forward. That's where the coded seal and the ceremonies come in, suggesting the construction of a New Order across the continent." She paused. "Which brings us to the matter of who had the upper hand. I suspect neither, given all the pageantry in the first place. But this confirms it." Sofia pointed to the Spanish map.

Lily and Michael looked at it with anticipation.

Gabriel's curiosity was piqued as well. He approached the table.

"This is a 1775 map of the Royal Site of Aranjuez, a town south of Madrid, where the royal court spent time each year for hunting and entertainment." Sofia picked up several pages from a stack in front of her and handed them out. "And this is a case study by professors of Cartographic Engineering from the Polytechnic and Almeria Universities in Spain, published by the American Society of Civil Engineers. According to it, crucial sections of Washington D.C.'s layout were mirrored from Aranjuez's design, chiefly the rare L-shape between the White House and the Capitol, the 12-roads-radiating out from the Capitol, or the trapezoid street combination north of the White House and the Capitol. Even the navigational canal was replicated."

The similarities were uncanny, still Lily asked the question. "Could it be a coincidence? I mean, there is only so much you can do with streets. City maps are bound to look similar. Besides, L'Enfant was French. What would he have known about Spanish towns?"

Michael reached for two of the prints he had been reading and handed them to Lily. "It's explained here. The Spanish royal engraver of the map of Aranjuez worked twelve years alongside L'Enfant's father in the same academy in Paris that L'Enfant himself attended. It's also known that two copies of Aranjuez's map had reached Paris the year before L'Enfant left to join the Continental Army. He would have seen them."

"Why were the copies sent to Paris?"

"For promotional purposes," said Michael. "Copies were sent to several European cities. Charles III had undertaken a massive infrastructure renovation project in Spain. Aranjuez was his favorite royal site and chose it to showcase how a refined urban design could coexist with agricultural sustainability in harmony with natural landscapes. Today, that vision has been awarded a spot on the UNESCO's World Heritage list."

Lily widened her gaze impressed.

"So, the question then becomes," continued Sofia, "did L'Enfant copy it of his own accord because it was the latest European fad in city design, or was he explicitly instructed to?"

"Knowing of Washington's interest in agriculture, I wouldn't be surprised that alone was his appeal to adopt Aranjuez's map, but I'm going to guess the answer is different," said Lily.

Sofia switched windows on her laptop screen and read. "On April 12th, 1779, Spain renewed her Family Pact with France by which she formally committed to entering the war on the side of France and the United States. At that moment, the Spanish court resided in Aranjuez, thus its name: the Treaty of Aranjuez." She set her gaze on her sister. "Coincidence?"

"I would say very unlikely."

"That's right," agreed Sofia. "What I'm seeing here is Washington commemorating Spain's crucial backing by designing the new capital in honor of the town where it was sealed. In this case, it's not about the discovery of the New World or satisfying Freemason symbolism with regards to the New Order. There is none of that. This is a simple and clear gesture of gratitude."

Lily spoke with a thoughtful gaze. "I'm going to play the devil's advocate. Charles III funded Catholic churches; he sent agents to foil disruption in the land and lay historical cornerstones here and there as if the place was his. And from every aspect, the capital couldn't be more Spanish if Picasso designed it himself, while a Spaniard had his hands in everything that was going on there. Washington could have agreed to, let's say a protectorate, and when Charles III died, his son inherited the agreement, keeping Washington bound to observe it."

"I have no doubt that is the perspective the Knights will push, probably worse," said Sofia. "But here's the thing: We know the United States and Spain had a common enemy interested in creating disruption in the region: Britain. Spain had been fending Britain's incursions in her American territories for centuries. Now Washington was confronted with the same prospect, as we saw in the conflict over the Mississippi. I'm not guessing here; he said as much in his Farewell Address. He also said that further turmoil on the American continent, before the United States had a chance to build muscle, was the last thing the young country needed. He was adamant about staying out of conflict, as was Spain.

"Their pact was one of Strength and Prosperity in Union: The New Order. What worked for the 13 colonies, could work for the continent."

Sofia then repeated Pedro Casanave's closing toast. *"May peace, liberty and order extend from pole to pole.* If there ever was a secret pact, that was the spirit of it. And now we must find the fair copy, before the Knights do, to prove it."

* * *

The old man steadied himself with his cane. His rheumy eyes inspected the equestrian statue as the corner of his lips curled with derision. It was the only monument of a woman on a horse in the city and, in his opinion, a joke. Men were rendered confident with a strong grip on the reins and an authoritative composure regardless of the horse being on all four or rampant. Here, Joan of Arc looked like she was barely keeping her balance with her legs stiff off to the sides despite her horse's gentle trot. Her features were gracious, those of a lovely young lady looking up to the heavens, but she held the sword high in her hand with her arm set back in such an awkward position it seemed she had dislocated her shoulder under its weight. It could not portray his personal sentiment any more accurately. As far as he was concerned, everyone had a god-designated place, and that of women was certainly not brandishing a weapon on a horse.

The mid-morning air was crisp, and the leaves showed every autumn hue to their fullest intensity. The old man with the cane chose Meridian Hill Park to meet because it was just under a 10-minute walk north from the Temple, and the steps along its 13-basin cascading fountain provided a reasonable climb to exercise his knee. He was now on the top mall, leaning heavily on his cane, and waiting as he recovered his breath, looking around disapprovingly. In his opinion, the park had seen better days.

Still, he preferred it to the House of the Temple. He never conceded to meeting there. He refused to enter that dreadful building as a matter of principle. What were the fools thinking when they designed it. Surely King Solomon would turn in his grave if he knew the Freemasons had modeled their headquarters after the tomb of Mausolus. Hailed one of the Seven Wonders of the Ancient World, what few people knew was that the tomb was also a monument to an incestuous relationship. Artemisia II of Caria built the tomb around 350 B.C. for her husband-brother, sparing no expense to enshrine her extraordinary grief for his death. It was said she mixed his ashes in her drink for the next two years until letting go of life to join him. Disgusting.

The old man with the cane spat a sigh. Yes, the fools knew well what they were doing, for what was also little known was that incestuous sibling love was an integral part, in its origins, of the utopian concept of *brotherly love*. In designing the ideal state, Plato suggested in "The Republic" to pick out the strongest and brightest boys and girls from among the population and isolate them from the rest to receive a rounded education aimed at tailoring the ideal statesmen and women. They would mate only among themselves, and their children would be removed from their mothers as soon as born so no parent knew which child was theirs. This way, all parents raised all the children as their own, no favoritism. It also meant the children never knew who their blood-siblings were, thus joining in oblivion; one big happy family, ruling the several Greek states in peace. What a misguided understanding of a superior race, lamented the old man. In the end, it all came back to Egypt where the daughter of the Pharaoh carried the legitimacy of the crown. It was the reason Pharaohs married their sisters. Yes, it was no coincidence the Temple was also decorated inside with ostentatious Egyptian and Greek adornments. Disgraceful.

The old man felt deep contempt for anything related to Freemasonry yet bemoaned with nostalgia the good-old-days when—at least—they represented a robust selection of white, cultivated men who met to exchange impressions on how to best run their towns and government. But then Albert Pike came along to instill the 33 degrees with pagan practices, each with a ridiculous ritual and pompous title, converting the Scottish Rite into no more than a pseudo-cult-club of grown-up men hiding from their wives to dress-up and make-believe they were knights in some delusional play. Pathetic.

Unfortunately, at this moment, he had important business to conduct with them.

The old man drew his best friendly smile as he spotted his appointment approaching with a rolled-up package in his grip. "Rowen, thank you for agreeing to meet me here."

"My pleasure, Aaron."

They shook hands.

"Mind if we talk on our way back down to my car?" suggested Aaron.

"Of course." Rowen politely signaled the old man to lead the way. "I'm happy to see you are up and about."

"Doctor's orders, though my knee disapproves." Aaron tilted his head toward the package. "I see you found it."

"It was exactly where you suggested looking; among Truman's papers in the library."

"Wonderful. Will it be missed?"

"I trust not. To be honest, I doubt my brethren would even care. Believe it or not, it was registered as a poor forgery. In its place, I slipped in an unpublished private letter where Truman comments on his reservations about the atomic bomb."

"I commend you. That is a very elegant touch."

"Thank you, but not all is good news. The reason it was thought to be fake is because the fair copy is incomplete. Of the four pages, the two first ones are missing. It would appear the White House time capsule only contained the last two."

The old man grinned. "As it should."

"I don't understand."

Aaron enhanced his lopsided grin. "The pact between Washington and Charles III was written up in both languages. The Spanish version was expressed on the back of the two front pages, while the English version was transcribed to the back of the second half. Each party to the pact then took custody of their pertinent half. Given that the Declaration itself was of historical significance, both parties held it close to the chest as if a gemmed key to a jewelry box."

"Sorry to insist on bad news, Aaron, but the text is barely visible. Time has eroded the ink, making it unreadable."

"Nothing a good chemical analysis can't solve."

"Also, the whole text is conscribed to one page. The other one holds an image difficult to discern. If one page contains the whole agreement, it would seem too scant for a comprehensive pact."

Aaron's chest swelled with the thrill of the challenge. "The text is merely a digest of its spirit."

"What's the point of a written pact if you are not going to lay out the terms clearly?"

"Honor was the point. This was not a treaty between two nations, but a private commitment between two men of the Enlightenment guided by their shared motto of *Virtue and Merit*. Neither one ever crossed the Atlantic. In the absence of a physical handshake, the symbolism of sharing a document like the Declaration was the next best thing." Aaron stopped at the bottom of the fountain to rest his knee. "Why do you think the American half was preserved in the cornerstone of the President's House?" The rhetorical question came slightly condescending.

Aaron reinitiated his slow pace. Having reached the south end of the park, he stopped momentarily before James Buchanan's Memorial to dwell in the irony. While conversing about the most admired president of the United States—whose idealism made him a weak man in Aaron's opinion—their stroll had led them to one of the most disdained for failing to prevent the Civil War. He swallowed to rid his mouth of the unsavory taste of injustice. Never had they been so close to succeeding.

With a subtle tilt of his head in reverence, Aaron tightened his grip on his cane to continue toward the corner exit arduously disguising his painful limp. His car waited at the end of the short ramp with his personal driver holding the door open; a tall square man, with a military cut and the glimpse of a tattoo on his neck peeking out from under his shirt's collar.

Aaron paused and turned to Rowan. "Your contribution to the cause is invaluable and will be duly acknowledged".

"Thank you," responded Rowan visibly pleased while handing over the package.

Aaron signaled his driver to take it.

"I look forward to the chemical analysis revealing the truth," continued Rowan, "Our great country will be forever in your debt."

Aaron accepted the grateful remark with a gentle nod. "Please say hello to your lovely wife for me."

"Will do."

The old man got in the car, cherishing the repose.

His driver closed the door and walked around the back to the other side and took his place in the driver's seat. He unrolled the package with care and slid it inside a black art suitcase lying flat on the passenger seat. He then inclined his head slightly back. "Where to, sir?"

"Drop me off at the office and then come back to take care of him."

"Yes, sir."

CHAPTER 17

"...Spanish is most important to an American. Our connection with Spain is already important, and will become daily more so. Besides this, the ancient part of American history is written chiefly in Spanish."

—*Thomas Jefferson to future son-in-law Thomas M. Randolph, Jr., 6 July 1787*

Sofia returned to the dining table with a glass of water. Lily was busy on her laptop and Michael had left after taking the latest foreboding call. He didn't say where he was going but made them swear on their mother's future grave they would not move or breathe until he got back.

Out of curiosity, Sofia looked up the address for the NSA headquarters. They were over forty minutes away in Maryland. Last time he stepped out, he wasn't gone long enough for the trip there and back, much less to include a meeting. Maybe they had a D.C. office.

She checked on Gabriel. He was sitting by the window, next to the printer, chuckling at something on his smartphone. Like Michael, he too was perplexing for his contrasting qualities: a lethal bodyguard and a solid Jewish scholar wrapped in the looks of an angelic beardless young man. It made her wonder about Rafael; what kind of odd mixture was he?

Sofia shook her head to refocus. *One mystery at a time*, she told herself and picked up her notepad.

1. Prof. Del Mar > Universidad Carlos III > Who is he?
2. GW's actions > icons > story behind each one? Outcome?
3. GW's interest in Spain > pact? > purpose/terms?
4. Don Quixote > code key? + on the table?
5. On the table > Kill or go ahead with secret pact?

It was a little discouraging to go through the list. Nothing definite had been accomplished on any point. She still knew nothing about Antonio. The Capitol and the Supreme Court remained pending items on the list of Washington's actions. Though she felt comfortable about the intended benevolence of the alliance, its terms were still elusive. The novel had become an item she avoided because it reminded her of Dan. And the answer to point five would likely reveal itself on its own when the other four were resolved.

Alright then, she decided. The best thing to do was to revisit each point starting from the beginning.

"Lily," she whispered. "Did you ever hear back from your colleagues in Spain regarding the professor?"

"Yes, but nothing of note. They rehashed his great reputation and clarified that his relationship with the university is more honorary than anything. He doesn't teach there, more like hosts well-attended lectures. To add to his mystic, though, he only publishes in Spanish, which is strange since he is fluent in several languages."

"Why would he do that?" asked Sofia.

"All I can think is that he's not looking for international acclaim despite his international acclaim, which makes him your perfect match: you're both a little weird ... And talking about that, I found out one more thing."

"What?"

"He's single." Lily winked. "Got your back. I asked."

"Well, thank you."

"You're welcome."

"Seriously, how does he do it? How does he get away with anonymity while inspiring admiration in the academic world?"

"I find it all very bizarre," said Lily. "I can't get over how little I knew about what we're learning." She motioned at her laptop screen. "I feel like I'm researching American history in an alternate universe."

"Why? What are you working on now?"

"Okay, so," Lily shifted in her seat, "it occurred to me that after the war, the usual suspects—Franklin, Jefferson and Adams—spent extensive periods of time abroad as diplomats stationed in Paris and London. Therefore, their only way to communicate was in writing and, considering their line of work, I figured the occasional reference to the secret pact would have been inevitable. Since the National Archives have their communications online, I thought I'd scan their letters for traces of it."

"Good thinking."

"I started by skimming Benjamin Franklin's letters but nothing relevant popped out, probably because it was his waning years. I did come across this one letter from 1779, in which he tells Horacio Gates—of all people—how he intended on telling the world about Spain's positive involvement in the war, but it doesn't look like he ever got around to doing it. In any case, we know that Washington met Gardoqui at his house a few days before signing the Constitution, so clearly Franklin was privy to something." She shrugged. "Finding nothing there, I moved on to Thomas Jefferson, and he's a whole other story in an unexpected way." Lily shared a wide-eyed expression to emphasize her point. "He displays this odd obsession with telling his family members to learn Spanish. And get this: In the case of his daughters, he repeatedly checked in on their education making sure they read ten pages a day of Don Quixote. But it's how he pushes the subject with the males in the family where it really gets interesting. As early as 1785, Jefferson recommends they learn Spanish to further their careers on the basis of an *important connection* between the United States and Spain." Lily gestured with her hands. "What connection? As far as I'm aware, the first official treaty ever signed between Spain and the US was in late 1795, ten whole years later."

"*Important connection.* Sounds like code for secret pact right there," acknowledged Sofia.

"Exactly what I thought. He refers to it several times through the years. Here, I'll read some examples." Lily turned to her computer screen. "For instance, in a letter sent to his nephew Peter Carr in 1785, to which he attached a Spanish dictionary, a grammar book, and other unspecified material, he explains:

> '*Our future connection with Spain renders that the most necessary of the modern languages, after the French. When you become a public man you may have occasion for it, and the circumstance of your possessing that language may give you a preference over other candidates.*'"

Sofia frowned. "I don't know. It doesn't sound all that suspicious in this passage. He's talking of a *future* connection. Spain controlled a large chuck of the Americas. A trade treaty would have been in the pipeline; it makes sense he'd tell his nephew to learn the language if he planned on being involved in business with the rest of the continent."

"Agreed, however, what's strange is that Jefferson never diverted from employing the word 'connection' in his letters, never clarifying what it meant."

"Right, but foreign affairs are a delicate matter and 'connection' is conveniently vague."

"That's the point," Lily persisted, "the fact that Jefferson obsessively insists on referring to it in light of its delicacy. Look, here's another letter to the same nephew two years later:

> *Spanish. Bestow great attention on this, and endeavor to acquire an accurate knowledge of it. Our future connections with Spain and Spanish America will render that language a valuable acquisition. The ancient history of a great part of America too is written in that language.*

"You see what I mean? He is stern in ensuring that his nephew understands the importance of learning Spanish and then out of the blue brings up the common history. What's that got to do with anything, much less with a future trade deal?"

Sofia nodded thoughtfully.

"And how about this," continued Lily. "It turns out Jefferson misplaced that letter. When he came across it a year later, he sent it with a one-paragraph cover apologizing as follows:

> *'I'm sorry for it on account of the article relative to the Spanish language only. Apply to that with all the assiduity you can. That language and the English, covering nearly the whole face of America, they should be well known to every inhabitant who means to look beyond the limits of his farm.'*

"That letter," explained Lily, "contained Jefferson's thoughts and recommendations on a wide variety of subjects from Philosophy and Religion to languages and travelling. Yet, when he realizes he never sent it, his one regret is that he could not remind his nephew how important Spanish was. Don't you think it's a little much if it's just about an uncle giving business career advice to his nephew?"

Sofia didn't say anything. It was apparent she was considering Lily's suspicions seriously.

"While you think about it, let me also point out that Jefferson is all over the place regarding the timing of the mysterious connection. While in these letters he refers to it as a future event, in another letter to his future son-in-law a month prior to the misplaced one, Jefferson states that the *important connection* already exists and that it will become more so daily. It makes sense if you think about it. Building a New United Order would have several preliminary stages before announcing it to the world, right?"

"Okay, fine," said Sofia. "I see what you mean."

Lily grinned proud of herself. "You are one hard nut to crack, girl. I was prepared though. I had left the best for last. Want to hear about it anyway?"

Sofia raised an eyebrow. "Please."

"In 1788, Jefferson mentions the mysterious *connection* to someone outside the family. John Rutledge Jr. is touring Europe and Jefferson tells him to forget about Northern Europe and to focus on visiting Madrid and Lisbon instead:

> *'Our connections with the Spaniards and Portuguese must become every day more and more interesting, and I should think, the knowledge of their language, manners, and situation, might eventually and even probably become more useful to yourself and country than that of any other place you will have seen.'*

Lily lifted her index finger. "Attention to this part:

> *'The womb of time is big with events to take place between us and them, and a little knowledge of them will give you great advantages over those who have none at all'.*"

"*The womb of time is big with events ...*" repeated Sofia. "Well, that's ominous." She pondered on it briefly. "He includes the Portuguese this time. I imagine it's in reference to Brazil, which reinforces the *pole-to-pole* theme."

"About that ..."

"What?"

"There is this other letter; an early one from 1786. Jefferson addresses it to Archibald Stuart, a member of the Virginia House around the time Kentucky was thinking of separating from the Union. Jefferson says:

> *'Our confederacy must be viewed as the nest from which all America, North and South is to be peopled. We should take care too not to think it for the interest of that great continent to press too soon on the Spaniards. Those countries cannot be in better hands. My fear is that they are too feeble to hold them till our population can be sufficiently advanced to gain it from them piece by piece.'"*

"Ouch!" said Sofia. "That is cold."

"I know, right? Those Spaniards are awesome, but we're going to chew away at their territory, anyway."

"I don't get it." Sofia shook her head. "If that was the plan, why the Seal of the United States, the layout of the capital, the White House cornerstone, the US dollar sign ...? These are permanent tattoos displayed prominently on the forehead, not a ring you can give back when you break up. Why display that level of symbiosis with Spain in all your identity symbols if you are scheming to turn around and stab her in the back?"

"I think it just means that Jefferson's long-term lookout differed from Washington's. Jefferson was devious that way. While working in Washington's administration, Jefferson had no qualms about brutally criticizing his policies behind *his* back. When Washington found out, they had a bitter fallout. If Jefferson could do that to Washington, forget about any loyalty to Spain."

Sofia sighed. "The truth is who knows what they were thinking; all we have is speculation. We won't know anything for sure until we find the pact." She tapped the table with her fingers. "At least, we have a lead now. Where would Truman put it after recovering it from the cornerstone?"

"Most likely in a masonic lodge."

In that moment, they heard the entry door open. Michael walked in looking deeply troubled and making no effort to disguise it. Sofia's memory muscle clasped her chest, while Lily stopped blinking, and Gabriel rose from his seat to come closer.

Michael didn't beat around the bush. He addressed the sisters. "Ben Dhruv, the gentleman you met yesterday, was stopped at gunpoint later in the evening and questioned about your visit."

"Oh, no," exclaimed Lily. "Please tell me he's alright. He seemed like such a nice man."

"Yes, he's alright. It would appear a good Samaritan stepped in." Michael said this sharing a loaded glance with Gabriel who arched a message-received eyebrow. "Unfortunately," continued Michael. "Rowen McIntyre, a prominent D.C. lobbyist, wasn't so lucky. He was found dead in his car a couple of hours ago."

The sisters displayed identical puzzled looks.

"The name isn't familiar. How does he relate?" asked Sofia.

"He died of a clean shot to the head. Same style and bullet as Dan. We are still trying to determine his involvement. He was found parked near the House of the Temple, the Scottish Rite's headquarters. He held a high degree there."

Sofia turned to meet Lily's gaze, who said: "We're late. They have it."

CHAPTER 18

"No People can be bound to acknowledge and adore the Invisible Hand which conducts the Affairs of men more than the People of the United States. Every step, by which they have advanced to the character of an independent nation, seems to have been distinguished by some token of providential agency."

— *George Washington, Inaugural Address, 30 April 1789*

The small apartment fell into a tense silence. Then, during a brief exercise of denial, different scenarios for the lobbyist's death were thrown around, but in the end, the simplest explanation prevailed: he had found the Declaration, and the Knights had captured it. And if that were the case, the search was over. The sisters had little else to offer. It was up to the FBI, the NSA and whatever other alphabet agency to recover it or deal with the potential fallout.

It didn't matter. Sofia wasn't ready to give up. For her, the underwhelming defeat clashed with her need to seek justice for Dan. "We don't know for certain that the Knights have it. I say we stay on course until we do."

"Stay on course for what?" asked Lily. "Even if they don't have the fair copy, we can't simply walk into the Freemasons' headquarters to recover it ourselves. It's up to them," she said, waving her hand at Michael and Gabriel. "Besides, it's getting awfully dangerous. Two men are dead. We need to rethink this."

Michael agreed. The Knights were proving more ruthless than he felt comfortable with for the sisters' sake. "I suggest we take a step back and reassess. Let my people find out more about McIntyre and gather intelligence on the Knights' movements. Changes in their behavioral pattern will tell us what the situation is."

"That's all fine, but I'm not going to sit here and wait," said Sofia. "Look, if the Knights have the fair copy, we've become irrelevant. If they don't, all the more reason to stay on task. We only have two items left on our list. While your people do whatever it is they do," she said to Michael, "I don't

130

see the harm in us following up on the Capitol and the Supreme Court," she concluded, looking at Lily.

To everyone's surprise, Gabriel spoke. "There is one aspect we have not considered. In those days, travel by sea was unreliable. It was routine practice to produce two or three copies of important correspondence and send it by various routes to ensure one made it to its destination. The Declaration, for its intrinsic value, is our priority, but we shouldn't neglect the value in locating a copy of the pact to know what the terms stipulate. It's imperative we don't let the Knights control the narrative."

Sofia felt stifled by awe. As he had done in the past, Gabriel displayed enigmatic wisdom and maturity when least expected. And he was right. There had to be copies.

Lily was unfazed. She protested. "If a copy exists, it would reasonably be in Spain. And even if we knew where to find it—which we don't—we'd be faced with the same dilemma. We can't go there, grab it, and casually walk away with it."

"We might not have to," said Sofia. "Antonio. He's been several steps ahead of us at every turn. I bet you anything he has a copy in that precious archive of his. We need to track him down and get some answers."

"What do you mean he has been ahead at every turn?" asked Michael.

"Let's say he's been sending tips our way."

"You should have told me."

"I just did." Sofia saw his jaw tense and immediately regretted slinging his own words back at him. It didn't feel as good as she thought it would. Her shoulders slouched. "Listen, we're losing here. The fair copy and the memory of what it contains is in danger. You said the professor was classified because that was his will, but the moment he dragged me into this, he waived his right to privacy."

From Michael's reaction, it was obvious Antonio made him uncomfortable. For an NSA agent, he had some serious tells.

Even Lily noticed. "Is Antonio dangerous?" she asked.

"Not to you." Michael roamed a few steps back and forth like a cornered animal. He abruptly stopped, released a heavy sigh, and faced the sisters. "Conspiracy junkies have long held that well-known clubs like the Freemasons or the Bilderberg attendees control world events. I'm not going to deny that powerful people commune in their circle and may have some influence, but their overall impact on global affairs is as consequential as that of a handful of golfers talking politics over drinks at the club."

Michael paused to signal a change in his discourse. "However. There is a certain ... shall we call it *association,* that truly does have that kind of power. This association doesn't care for colorful initiation rituals or weekend gatherings. They are the real deal, and their mission is to keep humanity on the right track in terms of the survival of the whole. They do not get involved in day-to-day concerns or, at least, shouldn't. For them, it is about the bigger picture. In essence, they are literally the Hand of Providence."

Lily and Sofia stared at him, motionless.

For Sofia, the struggle to react was greater. It was a side effect of having an analytical mind. Information could not be processed until it fitted in the proper node, and she did not know where to start fitting what she had just heard. "Are you suggesting Antonio belongs to a group of people who rule the world? Like, for real?" She couldn't believe she was even asking that question.

"They don't rule anything; they believe in free will. They merely influence events at crucial junctions if they fear matters are barreling toward catastrophe. Think of it as a train. These people do not seek to conduct the train, choose the destination, or determine what its passengers will do once they arrive. Their intervention is limited to switching tracks at a railroad junction if the train is headed to a cliff."

Sofia was incredulous. "How is that even possible? Who has the bird's eye view to see there is a cliff ahead? Or the wherewithal to determine it's time to switch tracks? Or the means to coordinate it ...?"

"That, I can't say."

Sofia stared at him feeling unsettled. She wasn't sure what was scarier, to discover that the Hand of Providence was real or that it was human. "Are Lily and I pawns in their chess game?"

Michael's countenance suddenly developed a strange aura. "Sofia, if I'm revealing this to you, it's because you should have gleaned by now how special you are. No, you are not the pawns; you and Lily are the King piece. The rest of us work to protect you and your message."

"You are one of them?"

"Not exactly." From his softened gaze she could tell there were a million things he wanted to tell her but wouldn't.

Lily's take was much different. For her, Michael's allegory only came to confirm what she had always believed, which incidentally reenergized her. She took a solemn step toward her sister. "Sof, I know you struggle with the notion of being chosen. That's alright. In fact, it's more than alright, it's expected of you. Your need for evidence and to ground everything in reason is your gift, and it is pretty apparent that whoever holds the reins respects you for it. But at some point, you're going to have to accept that we've been chosen for a higher purpose."

"With due respect for higher purposes, I'd like to be consulted if I want to be chosen for it. Doesn't it bother you that this *association*, whoever they are, gets to decide that for you?"

"Not if they are guided by above."

"You don't know that. How do you even get there?" Sofia felt aggravated. "Lily, we don't know anything about what is going on, who these people are, their intentions, or who is pulling their strings. Nothing. Yet somehow, you and me, two little nobodies, are in the middle of it."

"You're right, we might not know anything about this so-called *association*, but *I* do know one thing: no human hand can light up the sky over Spain with a meteor to capture our attention. I'm telling you, it's all related and a higher hand is behind it. That's my gift, Sof. To see beyond reason. And that's why we, little you and me, are chosen, because as a wise woman once said: *we complement each other*. I now appeal to that wise woman to trust me on this one. The meteor was loaded with too many coincidences directly related to us and our message, and it's trying to tell us that the pact is connected somehow. So, forget what I said about things getting dangerous. What's next on the list? The Capitol? Let's go."

* * *

Dr. Wang ran her eyes randomly over her monitor screen blinking repeatedly as if she had a tic that impeded her from focusing on any section. The reality was that her years of experience allowed her to scan swaths of data and accurately pick out the minimum amount of information she required to compose an impeccable preliminary conclusion.

In this instance, her blood was rushing through her arteries in response to what she was seeing.

Wang was a world leading expert in codicology and her job was to determine the period and provenance of the document entrusted to her. To that effect, the paper had been carefully subjected to a series of sophisticated material analyses.

Her excitement was not for the paper's material worth. A lifetime of working with ancient parchments thousands of years older had this youthful 18th century paper pale in comparison.

It wasn't for its art, for it didn't display any.

It wasn't for its prose since its genre did not welcome creative articulations.

And it wasn't for its aesthetics, because the document was a rough messy draft full of rushed corrections and notes on the margins with large portions crossed out.

The document wasn't even complete. Its two front pages were missing.

It was for its exceptional historical significance.

Dr. Wang had immediately recognized the invaluable piece of American history, and the data she had in front of her, though preliminary, confirmed its authenticity. She couldn't wait to inform her generous patron.

Standing vigilant by the door was his personal bodyguard. She took a quick look at him through the corner of her eye. At first, his intimidating presence made her uncomfortable. Now she understood why he was there supervising her every move.

She was not ready to announce her results, though. One, because her professionalism required her to retest and reconfirm her preliminary hunch; and two, because she had also been tasked with recovering the faded patches on the document's reverse. That had been an exhilarating surprise, and a cursory examination had told her it was possible. All she had to do was employ light to determine the spectral signature of the ink and then trace its residue in the faded sections to recreate its digital image.

However simple, the process would be nerve-racking for a diligent professional like her. The preservation of the document's integrity was paramount.

Dr. Wang quivered at the thought with equal parts of thrill and dread. She was about to become the first person in a very long time to read a previously unknown text left behind by the Founding Fathers.

CHAPTER 19

"However unimportant America may be considered at present [...] there will assuredly come a day, when this country will have some weight in the scale of Empires."

—*George Washington to Marquis de Lafayette, 15 August 1786*

It was invigorating to be out of the apartment. Once the wild revelation had settled, and despite the lurking dangers, doing something to advance in their search conjured a comforting sense of control. Sofia had decided to muffle her concerns over shadowy world-rulers to focus on something more prosaic like fighting bad guys in memory of a good one.

It was mid-to-late afternoon and temperatures had plateaued at a pleasant level. Sofia and Lily, with Michael and Gabriel not too happily in tow, rushed down the steps to the Capitol Visitor Center, knowing they were pushing their luck. It closed in thirty minutes. They weren't sure what they were looking for, but if experience was any guide, there would be a historian waiting for them, displaying a broad friendly smile, and delighted to stay late to please Antonio and share something extraordinary.

Security screening was a breeze since they had left their backpacks in the apartment.

Lily and Sofia headed for the visitor's desk, not without inevitably stopping to raise their eyes up the 19.5-feet-tall Statue of Freedom that presided over Emancipation Hall. Commissioned under Jefferson Davis while he was Secretary of War, it was the plaster cast of the 15,000-pound bronze monument that stood atop the Capitol dome, depicting a goddess in military regalia to represent *Freedom Triumphant in War and Peace*. The sisters rejoiced in the irony. Davis had rejected the initial design because it had been conceived wearing a Liberty Cap, the symbol of freed slaves in Ancient Rome. Providence would rebuke Davis by having the bronze statue cast at the hands of Philip Reid, a slave freed while working on it during the Civil War, and then installed on top of the dome just in time to witness the Thirteenth Amendment of the United States Constitution pass.

Sofia and Lily proceeded to check in.

"Good afternoon," said Lily. "I'm Professor Auru-Soto."

The senior volunteer at the desk looked at her computer. "I'm sorry, what was your name again? Auru-Soto?"

"Yes." Lily spelled it out.

"I do not see you registered for the last tour of the day." Ms. Martinez—according to her name tag—looked up from the screen. "It left several minutes ago. I'm afraid you're late. Did you reserve, dear?"

"Actually, I was hoping that my colleague Professor Antonio del Mar had made special arrangements ... maybe?"

The senior volunteer furrowed pensively. "I'm not aware of anyone who works here with that name. Do you know what department?"

Lily slumped as she looked at her sister, and then turned back to Ms. Martinez. "That's okay. Any chance you have a private guide available who can walk us through the art of the Rotunda?"

Ms. Martinez perked up. She was an attractive woman in her late sixties with a wealth of long hair gracefully pinned up on the sides allowing for the rest to cascade down her back in an elegant scale of greys. "You are specifically interested in the art?"

"Yes."

The volunteer's features lit up. "It's your lucky day. That is my area of expertise, and I wasn't supposed to be here today." She looked at her silver vintage watch. "How about that? My shift at the desk just ended."

Lily shared a mischievous grin with Sofia. "How about that?"

Sofia surprised herself seriously wondering if this was the act of Antonio or a higher power. It felt creepy to her. So much for free will if either one had truly had a hand in this nice lady's schedule so that she would be available for them.

A man porting the same volunteer blazer that Ms. Martinez donned, approached the counter. "Elena, thank you for stepping in at the last minute like this. I'll take it from here."

"My pleasure. I know we are nearing closing time, but if you don't mind, I'd like to take these two young ladies to the Rotunda for a short expose on its art."

The man smiled. "Well, that's Karma for you; your reward for kindly helping us out on your day off. By all means, please do."

Reward ..., thought Sofia. *Still, it wasn't her choice.*

Ms. Martinez coyly explained. "I'm a retired art historian. I volunteer hoping to share the nuanced story behind the building's architecture and art, but so few visitors are interested in the finer details. I simply cannot pass this opportunity."

Fine.

The austere doorway to the Rotunda deceived expectations. As they walked into the circular space, the sisters' breath was siphoned by its monumentality. Despite several trips to D.C., generally work related, they had never had the time to visit it.

Gabriel lingered by the south entry, while Michael drifted ahead closer to the northern exit. Being in one of the best guarded buildings in the world did not seem to give them any confidence.

Ms. Martinez approached the center of the room and swung her hands wide as if opening a giant fan. "The Rotunda," she announced. "George Washington personally selected its design. What's more, he was very vocal about what he wanted, and Dr. William Thornton, an amateur architect with a keen eye for grandeur and symbolism, succeeded in satisfying his vision. At one point, lack of funds and structural challenges called for scrapping the whole idea. Luckily for us today, Washington would not hear of it."

Lily and Sofia took a moment to appraise the 96-feet-wide space encircled by 48-feet-high Seneca sandstone walls adorned with pilasters and relief panels above the doors depicting scenes from colonial history. They found it a challenge to keep their eyes down at floor level. As if imbued with a will of their own, they pulled up beyond the two drums that sustained the dome to the fresco 180 feet above.

"Magnificent, isn't it?" remarked Martinez. "Throughout most of the building, Dr. Thornton respected the neoclassical style in vogue at the time, but here, with the Rotunda, the ambition was to reproduce the Pantheon of Rome." Martinez let it float in the air as if that were self-explanatory. The sisters' blank faces gave her the cue it wasn't, which appeared to delight her. She cheerfully explained. "Through the ages, public and private buildings alike have functioned as propaganda billboards. Their architecture and art are coded windows into the hearts of their patrons. If we analyze the Capitol Building under that light, a fascinating story unravels. With this in mind, know that the building you see today was built in two general phases. The first one took thirty-six years, beginning in 1793. Its expansion, which doubled its original length and raised the dome, took another fifteen, ending in 1866. Therefore, as I guide you through its architecture and art, proceeding from the ground up to the cupula, you'll be able to appreciate the changing times and attitudes of our leaders through that troubled period."

"Just curiosity," interrupted Sofia, "do we know where its cornerstone lays?"

"Oh ... well," Martinez toyed with the top button of her white blouse as she thought about it, "there are three, in fact. The first one was laid by Washington, personally, in 1793; the second one was laid on the northeast corner of the new House by President Millard Fillmore as part of the expansion; and Dwight D. Eisenhower laid the third one for the East Front extension on its northern corner. Unfortunately, the location of Washington's stone is unknown."

"Why would that be?"

"I believe there is only one eyewitness account, which places it on the southeast corner of the original building. Oddly, a search conducted in 1991 was unable to locate it there. As far as I know, to this day, nobody knows where it is."

Southeast? wondered Sofia. She consulted her mental map. The other two were placed according to Freemason tradition, but, once again, Washington's stone wasn't. If the intent was to follow the White House pattern, that is, have it point to the heart of the District, then the cornerstone would have been placed on the northwest corner, not the southeast. Maybe that's why it wasn't located.

Martinez shrugged. "It's a pity, really. What I'd give to peek inside its time capsule. At least, I hope there's one if they ever find the cornerstone. Washington was a strong believer in Providence and symbolism; it would be fascinating to see what he thought appropriate for the occasion."

Abruptly, she paused and giggled. "On second thought, this space spells it out quite clearly."

"You seem fascinated with the psychology behind the art more than the art itself," observed Sofia.

"They are inextricably intertwined, my dear." Martinez grinned. "My major was in Political Science. Art was my minor and secret tool to pry under the surface to get a glimpse of the true soul of our founding leaders."

"You think the Rotunda hints to Washington's vision for the United States?" asked Lily.

"Most certainly, as do his own words. Washington saw the United States as a *rising Empire*. All the Founding Fathers did. Thus, the Pantheon of Rome," she said twirling one hand in the air. "It's no coincidence the building and its grounds are named after the Capitoline Hill in Rome. Intimately, they were hoping to replicate the greatness of the Roman Republic."

Pressed for time, Sofia felt she had to redirect the conversation. "Ms. Martinez, you wouldn't happen to know if there is any underlying Spanish contribution to the building, its art or symbolism, would you? Other than that painting there," she clarified, gesturing toward the *Landing of Columbus,* in which he was depicted claiming the land for Queen Isabella. She briefly wondered if that was what Antonio had brought them here for. But it seemed too simple and obvious.

"Interesting you ask." Martinez tilted her head slightly. "When Washington laid the Capitol cornerstone, the Spanish Empire was at its peak extension, and her American cities, such as Mexico City, Potosi, Havana or Cartagena, to name but a few, were the wealthiest in the world. That reality at the time is reflected in all three, the Rotunda, its art and symbolism."

Sofia raised her eyebrows not expecting the all-rounded confirmation.

"Let's take the Rotunda, for instance," continued Martinez. "Why the Pantheon? Leaving aside it is an architectural wonder—reason enough to model it—its construction was started by Emperor Trajan who raised the Roman Empire to its peak extension, and it was finished by his successor Hadrian, who focused on strengthening the empire by raising it to the peak of its political and economic power. Trajan and Hadrian thus ruled the Empire at the apex of its greatness and prosperity, and their Pantheon is symbolic of that." Martinez fixed her eyes on Sofia. "Both Trajan and Hadrian were born in the part of Hispania that corresponds to present-day Spain."

* * *

Dr. Wang felt sick to her stomach.

Keep your eyes on the screen, she ordered herself, fighting the instinct to check on the bodyguard.

Everything was going so well. The spectral analysis had identified the fading ink's signature with ease, and she had been able to retrace its residue swiftly. So, in possession of a juicy historical secret, Wang had awarded herself the guilty pleasure of reading the long-lost message quietly before announcing her success.

What followed was utter shock.

She wasn't sure why she had assumed the text would contain inspirational advice from the Founders for future generations. Instead, the back of one of the pages charted an astonishing agreement. But it was the image on the back of the other page that had Wang hypnotized. It consisted of five coats-of-arms, all still in use, that when brought together formed an unfathomable picture with the potential to shake the historical pillars the country had been founded on.

How had no historian ever noticed?

And just as she had reined in her stupor, something else happened.

The temperature, humidity and lighting in her lab had been adjusted to ensure optimal conditions for the preservation of the brittle document. What was optimal for weathered paper, was uncomfortable for the bodyguard. He had pulled on his collar several times until resolving to unbutton it and loosen his tie, which revealed his tattoo.

She recognized it instantly. The FBI approached her that same day asking her to be on the lookout for an image like it. Curiously, she had been told it might appear on a ring, maybe cuffs, or a number of other arrangements, but a tattoo had never been mentioned. She was explained little else, other than the carrier could be very dangerous and to report it immediately.

Dr. Wang had not given it much thought since she was often alerted to be vigilant for illegally obtained manuscripts. It was amazing how many reputable museums unsuspectingly acquired historical artifacts listed on international contraband watch lists and innocently brought them to her for authentication. Private individuals with the resources to obtain pieces of such pedigree rarely made that mistake. They were hardly innocent and thus savvy enough to retain the services of a shadowy expert.

She was not one of the latter, and as for her patron, Wang would never have guessed he was one of the former. Now she found herself in a serious bind. Wang was aware that if a man of her patron's status and impeccable reputation had brazenly brought this historical document to her and left behind a guard associated with the image of that tattoo, things did not bode well for her.

Wang tapped on the keyboard and switched analysis screens to feign she was contrasting results. In truth, she was devising a way out. She had always been accused of displaying a stoic demeanor to a fault. Who knew it might save her life.

She had assessed her options carefully. Her mobile was restricted to her office, and her lab was so darn modern it no longer contained a landline; not that she would have been able to use it unseen anyway. As for the internet, the connection had been deactivated for the same reason no communication devices were allowed: no one was to know about the Declaration's authenticity or content before her patron, which she thought sensible at the time. He was a high-ranking government servant, and her lab had collaborated in sensitive projects before.

Dr. Wang took in a slow deep breath. She had an idea.

CHAPTER 20

"[...] it will be well to say that the mouth and navigation of a certain river will be shut against all Americans [...] You may inflame the minds of the people; in a certain way, so as not to let out any of our plan, and yet put things in such a situation as will make our plan, when it takes place, appear as the salvation of the people, [...]"

—*Annals of Congress, Senator William Blount's impeachment, 1797*

Closing time was fast approaching and a couple of Capitol personnel were ushering the last of the visitors toward the exit. One was about to address Michael, when Martinez signaled that he was with her, extending the gesture to all four. The man tilted his head and left.

They were alone.

Michael and Gabriel relaxed and came closer.

Pleased her audience had grown in number, Martinez continued. She appeared in no hurry. "Spain's imprint is everywhere, and our country's inception and growth can't be understood without her." Martinez's jovial eyes embarked on a journey around the room to reaffirm it was written on its walls. "As we've seen, the Rotunda itself reveals that the Founding Fathers had strong imperial ambitions from the very beginning and weren't shy about it. The reason is simple. To this day, power requires strength and strength equates to size. But they didn't all agree on how to go about growing. That is revealed to us in the Rotunda's art."

Martinez teased them with a summary. She started by gesturing toward the east wall. "For Jefferson, it was about secretly supporting private armed expeditions into Spanish territory." Her eyes crossed over to the west wall. "For Hamilton it was about sympathizing with revolutionary enterprises in Spanish America." Slowly, her gaze elevated to the frieze that circumnavigated the base of the dome. "For Madison, Monroe and those who came later, waving the flag of Manifest Destiny and name-sake doctrines justified everything." Lastly, all eyes converged on the cupula. Martinez's voice acquired an enigmatic tone. "Washington defied them all. He was obstinately opposed to aggression." She redirected gazes down to ground level and posed an intriguing question. "Therefore, if you are opposed to aggression, how do you grow an empire?"

The New Order crossed everyone's mind, but Lily narrowed her stare to protest the characterization. "With due respect, Ms. Martinez, George Washington was no Angel of Peace. He had no problem triggering the French and Indian War; fighting the British; attempting the invasion of Canada or clamping down on Native Americans."

Martinez grinned. "Exactly."

Lily recoiled, confused.

"We can debate all afternoon if he was an angel or not, but one thing he was not was a coward. Yet, under his watch, he blocked every attempt of hostility toward Spain and her territory to the extent that he unilaterally resorted to proclaiming his two Neutrality Acts to assert his position on the matter."

"Wait," said Sofia. "I was under the impression the Neutrality Acts were meant to keep the United States out of the perpetual war between Britain and France."

"On the surface, indeed they were." Martinez drew a grin. "At their core, however, it was all about Spain." Martinez brought their attention to the painting that hung adjacent to the one depicting Columbus' landing. "That painting is the *Discovery of the Mississippi by De Soto* and should be an enigma to all who see it."

Lily tilted her head as she analyzed it. "Why an enigma?"

"I invite you to take a moment to think about this: There are eight monumental paintings hanging on the curved walls of this room, and I trust you agree with me that this is no ordinary room in no ordinary building. The eight were chosen carefully in the 19th century to depict seminal instances in the birth of the nation. The four on the west wall center around the Revolutionary War, which I will come back to in a minute. The four on the east wall go back to the Spanish discovery and English colonization. In that sense, the *Landing of Columbus*, The *Baptism of Pocahontas,* and the *Embarkation of the Pilgrims* fit with the traditional picture. However, why would the exploration of the Mississippi by a Spaniard take the last privileged spot?"

Unbeknownst to Martinez her audience had a strong hunch.

Lily disclosed it. "Spain's control over the Mississippi mouth is easily the one source of conflict that could have dismembered the Union before the Civil War. Politicians, powerful speculators, and foreign agendas relentlessly weaponized it. Consequently, taking control of it with the Louisiana purchase symbolized inevitability and kickstarted the westward expansion that was underway at the time a topic was being decided for that spot."

Martinez brought her hand to her chest, pleasantly impressed. "So refreshing. You know your history."

Not as well as I had believed, though Lily. "I'm a historian like yourself; though my expertise is World Religions, more specifically Catholicism."

"Oh, in that case, I apologize. Here I am babbling about troubled times, and you probably came for the Apotheosis." Martinez pointed up to the cupula. "You should have said something."

"No," interjected Sofia, "Please, the troubled times. I'm very interested."

Martinez paused to eye her with curiosity. "Are you a historian?"

"No, a writer. My sister and I are researching Spain's influence in the early years of formation.

"Wonderful," celebrated Martinez. "In that case, you've come to the right place. Where were we ... yes, the Neutrality Acts. Indeed, the Mississippi was a great source of conflict until one day Washington had enough. Under his administration, global affairs turned particularly ugly with the French Revolution. The execution of the French king in January of 1793 had it spiral out of control, antagonizing France against half of Europe. Here, while Jefferson sympathized with their attempt to spread Republicanism, Washington was horrified by the brutality and chaos, steering the United States clear of it. But then, France declared war on Spain, aiming for control of her territories in America. One of their early targets was Louisiana thinking they could take advantage of the Mississippi unrest to enroll the United States help by offering Washington West Florida with access to the Mississippi's east shore.

"The thing is that Britain had attempted the same strategy only a few months earlier. Washington had rejected it then and would again. He wasn't about to let Britain form a pinch around the US again or allow France to move in next door after the hot mess they were creating in Europe. Either scenario spelled out doom for the young United States. He much preferred the amicable status quo with Spain, any day."

Reaffirming the need for the New Order, thought Sofia.

Martinez lowered her voice almost to a whisper. "France did not accept his *no* for an answer. They sent Edmond Charles Genet as new French minister to the US to coordinate the invasion of Spanish Louisiana. With Jefferson's underhanded blessing, as soon as Genet disembarked, he began to further inflame discontent among the already disgruntled westerners, but in doing so committed a dreadful mistake. He also tried to sully Washington and his stance in the process, and this did not fly in most quarters. When Washington heard that Genet had ignored his wishes and was recruiting American citizens to invade Spanish territory, it infuriated him so, that he proclaimed the Neutrality Act of 1793. Then, he demanded France to recall Genet and forcefully asked the Governor of Kentucky to thwart any attack expedition on Spain. It fell on deaf ears. The Kentuckians had long been conditioned to care little for Federal mandates. Tensions boiled for over a year, forcing Washington to threaten sending in the army and issuing a second Neutrality Act in 1794, this time to make it illegal for an American to wage war against a country at peace with the US. Jefferson resigned as Secretary of State shortly after and his relationship with Washington only went downhill from there."

Michael's deep voice startled Martinez. "This is pertinent to our research," he started, addressing the sisters, "because William Blount, the Governor of Tennessee and soon-to-be Senator, took up where Genet left off, hoping to cash in on the fuming emotions. Blount spread the rumor that France's true intent in taking Spanish Louisiana was to close off the Mississippi completely and then argued it was best for Britain to have it instead because they would guarantee its free navigation."

"Unbelievable," said Lily. "It's never ending."

Sofia shook her head. "That's because it is the oldest trick in the book, and it works every time: Feed fear and hatred, present yourself as the savior, and you got yourself an army of ravenous foot soldiers happy to do your bidding. It's no wonder the country barreled toward a civil war," she added. "The same people were continuously ignited for decades."

Martinez cocked her head as she regarded Michael inquisitively. "Historian or writer?"

"Journalist. My expertise is warfare. I'm helping on a consulting basis." He flashed a smile and rushed to continue before she asked more questions. "Senator Blount would become the first government official impeached in the United States. Jefferson, who was vice-president at the time, was accused of being in the know for this one, as well. And when he became President, his vice-president, Aaron Burr, would end up on trial for attempting the same maneuver, only this time, Louisiana already belonged to the United States. Yet, regardless of who controlled the territory, these conspiracies continued because they all shared the same instigator."

"The Cabal," said Sofia.

Michael nodded. "Their face throughout this period was James Wilkinson. The same guy who attempted to break Kentucky away from the Union. He was involved in every case, failed every time, but never paid for any of them. Instead, Jefferson made Wilkinson Senior Officer of the United States Army, and when Louisiana finally fell in his hands, Jefferson awarded Wilkinson the Governorship."

Martinez was in heaven discussing deep history with worthy peers. "Wilkinson is quite the enigma. Despite decades of scheming against both, Spain and the United States, while holding the highest posts in the military and government, if you check historical records, he is mostly dismissed incorrectly as a second-rate Spanish spy." Martinez paused. "Yet, I'd like to bring your attention to an even greater mystery."

Here it is, thought Sofia, *the big revelation.*

"Senator Blount's impeachment trial took place during John Adams's presidency. When recalling it years later, Adams wrote something very strange." Martinez quoted from memory. "*A conspiracy was fully proved, to dismember the Empire and carry off an immense portion of it, to a foreign dominion.*"

"That *is* odd," agreed Lily. "Blount wasn't impeached for trying to dismember the US, he was impeached for attempting to invade Spain in defiance of the Neutrality Acts. Louisiana still belonged to her."

"Maybe it did, maybe it didn't, maybe both can be true," said Martinez. "My question again: How do you grow an Empire without aggression?"

* * *

Dr. Wang took a deep breath as she summoned all the courage she could muster. She had rehearsed her idea in her mind enough times to get dizzy and knew she could not delay it any longer.

She turned to the bodyguard. "Excuse me." Her voice almost cracked. "I need to order more adhesive."

The bodyguard narrowed his stare.

She swallowed. "I'm sorry, I thought I had enough. Unfortunately, the document is very brittle. I must attend to it in short order, or it could end up irrevocably damaged." She avoided technical vocabulary, hoping it would deter him from asking for clarification. She feared too much explaining would let her nerves give her lie away.

"Who supplies it and how long can it take to receive it?"

"Not long at all. LabWork is just down the street ... They can send someone over quickly ... They are good about that...." *Stop talking*, she ordered herself.

The tattooed bodyguard retrieved his phone.

"Their number is 202-LabWork," she rushed to say.

He dialed and listened. "Is this LabWork?"

Wang could see the bodyguard's jaw tighten.

"I said LabWork ... Do you supply Dr. Wang, yes or no?"

Wang sensed her heart stop.

"Hold on," she heard him say. The tattooed man approached her seeming to grow into a terrifying gorilla as he came closer. He handed her the phone.

She took it barely concealing the tremor in her hand and placed the order. Then she concluded. "Please hurry with it. It's quite urgent. I'm in a little bind with a precious manuscript." She listened. "Thanks, I appreciate it—"

The bodyguard yanked the phone from her ear and went back to his spot in front of the door.

Wang swallowed so hard it hurt her throat.

CHAPTER 21

"I hope to have the Happiness of seeing the Evening of your Life more useful and more glorious than its Noon, and of saluting you, my Dear Sir, not merely as the Father of the United States, but of the United Empires of America."

—*John Trumbull to George Washington, 24 March 1799*

Martinez approached the west wall and stood under the *Declaration of Independence*. She dwarfed in contrast. The painting was truly impressive.

"Strength in Unity," she said. "It's no secret that was Washington's North Star. But what if I told you that it was not limited to the states, that he contemplated a Union of Empires in America?"

Sofia and Lily exchanged glances wondering how their discovery about the New "United" Order had suddenly become general knowledge.

Martinez smiled. "Washington's Neutrality Acts are a good indication of his deep concern for hostile actors meddling with the region's stability. Unity among the states was not going to be sufficient. America at large, too, had to unite. And don't think the thought extravagant." She swept her open hand across the wall behind her. "Let's take John Trumbull, for instance. He was the artist of these four Revolutionary War paintings. He once hailed Washington the Father of the United Empires of America. At the time, Spanish America was organized as four large viceroyalties that functioned liked empires in their own right."

Lily exhaled a breath of exasperation. "The painter? Where was I when they taught that in history class?"

"Wrong class, my dear. I wasn't exaggerating when I said Art was my secret tool. You see, Trumbull was an interesting character. He belonged to a family of statesmen from Connecticut and, during the war, fought under George Washington. Thus, his inclination for battle scenes and the Revolutionary War." Martinez pointed to the *Surrender of General Burgoyne*, the *Surrender of Lord Cornwallis*, and *General George Washington Resigning His Commission*. "The discomforts of war were not his cup of tea, and, after only a year, he moved to London to train as a painter. While still there in the mid 1780's, Jefferson invited him to Paris, and it was during that stay when he began sketching the first draft of this one," Martinez pointed above her head, "his most famous piece, the *Declaration of Independence*. However, contrary to what most people think, it does not depict the signing of the Declaration. It depicts the presentation of its fair copy to the Continental Congress."

This sounded off all the alarms for Sofia and Lily. Both stepped closer with probing eyes.

Sofia instantly started to run through a host of questions in her mind: Could it be coincidence that the painter who hailed Washington the Father of the United Empires had also focused his iconic painting on the lost fair copy? Could it contain a cryptic message about the pact? About its content? About its whereabouts?"

Lily must have been thinking the same thing. She elbowed Sofia to bring her attention to the document itself.

Sofia understood. The painting displayed the four pages lying *on the table*. Too much of a coincidence. She eagerly addressed Martinez. "How accurate is the scene?"

"So-so. It was Jefferson's idea, and he provided Trumball with the details, so it is generally presumed historically faithful. However, some liberties were taken. Not all the members of Congress depicted in the painting later signed it, nor all who later signed it are in the painting."

On the table ... The three words churned in Sofia's head. If Jefferson had Trumbull place the fair copy on the table for the painting, what if it was also Jefferson who arranged to have Don Quixote placed on the table following Washington's death? Knowing of his preference for taking Spanish territory rather than teaming up with Spain, the message was clear: Kill the pact that is outlined on its reverse. But why express it in this dramatic fashion?

As if in on the secret, Martinez unknowingly supplied the answer: "As I said, Trumble was an interesting character. While in London, he performed odd jobs—among them, spy—but he also cultivated a special friendship with the South American revolutionary Francisco de Miranda." She paused. "Are you aware of Spain's role in the Revolutionary War?"

"Yes, and about their need to keep it quiet so it wouldn't catch on," answered Lily, recognizing the name.

"Well, their fears were well founded. No sooner were the peace treaties signed, some in Spanish America began to harbor revolutionary ideas of their own. Francisco de Miranda was first among them. He was born in current day Venezuela and fought in some of the Spanish battles during the war, but following a legal fallout with his superiors, fled to the US in 1783 where he began his one-man quest to rally help for Spanish-America's independence. He found many sympathizers, like Hamilton, but little substantive backing, so he moved along to Britain, where he developed a close friendship with John Trumbull and William S. Smith. Smith was John Adam's secretary and soon to be son-in-law.

"Britain was all ears but not reckless, having just come out of a war, so Miranda undertook a European tour to gain support. William Smith accompanied him for a few months. On his way back to London, Smith stopped in Paris to visit Jefferson, and presumably informed him of Miranda's lack of success. Smith would stay entangled with Miranda, thereafter. In fact, it was Smith who acted as Frances' middleman to inform Washington of their intention to invade Louisiana during the Genet affair. Miranda had been chosen to lead that campaign. If you recall, Washington refused, proclaiming the first Neutrality Act."

Sofia and Lily didn't know if to nod that they remembered or shake their heads at the tangled web.

"In any case," continued Martinez, "Miranda spent a decade touring Europe with little success and in the end almost got himself guillotined in France. However, by this point, geopolitics had changed, and Miranda returned to London to a much warmer reception and began to design a plan to invade his own country. John Trumbull formed part of his cozy circle and kept Hamilton and Jefferson abreast of the details. Eventually, in 1806, with the help of Smith, Miranda indeed attempted a failed invasion. Smith was put on trial for defying the Neutrality Acts, and claimed on his defense that Jefferson, President at the time, and Madison, his Secretary of State, were behind the plot. Smith walked free, but it was revealed during the trial that the mission had failed because Miranda's fellow compatriots were not as enthusiastic about independence as Miranda had sold them to be and had fought back."

Martinez reflected in her saddened gesture the tragedy that followed. "Here we have an unfortunate example of Washington's worst fear: How internal divisions and instability, aggravated by the destructive intervention of foreign actors, doomed Spanish America. The four prosperous viceroyalties sunk into a string of bitter civil wars and crumbled."

She sighed. "All this to say that for over a decade everyone was in the know of Miranda's plan except for George Washington."

"Wait," said Lily. "Miranda toured Europe for a decade. Even Spain must have known of his plans. How would Washington not?"

"Let me rephrase. What Washington didn't know was that some as close to him as Hamilton had been tiptoeing around him in contact with Miranda, cuddling the plot."

"I'm sorry to insist," pressed Lily, "but how do you know they tiptoed?"

"Easy, because in 1799, John Trumbull—our painter—laid out Miranda's plan as his own in a letter to Washington. This can only be understood if Washington had been kept in the dark about it. You see, in 1799, Napoleon was a rising figure, and he too, as everyone else, had his eyes set on Spain and her empire. Hamilton had always favored breaking Spanish America away from Spain but had never trusted Miranda to be the right man for the job. Now, however, dreading Napolean more, he was willing to back Miranda with one condition: that Washington was onboard. But, knowing of Washington's resistance to act against Spain's interests, he had Trumbull make the case that it was preferable for Washington to take charge of America than Napoleon. Thus, Father of the United Empires."

"How did Washington react?"

"Jaded. Global affairs were indeed bad, and this was the type of plotting he had resisted tirelessly knowing of its dire consequences. Distressed, Washington came out of retirement and took on the role of Commander-in-Chief once again in preparation for a potential war with France. Misfortune would have him pass away within days of Napoleon taking absolute power and Thomas Jefferson throwing in his hat for President."

And that was that ... thought Sofia. With Washington dead, the New Order was laid *on the table* and a dark period for the Americas followed.

CHAPTER 22

"The gradual progress of the continent from the depths of barbarism to the heights of civilization; the rude and barbarous civilization of some of the Ante-Columbian tribes; the contest of the Aztecs with their less civilized predecessors; their own conquest by the Spanish race; the wilder state of the hunter tribes of our own regions; the discovery, settlement, wars, treaties; the gradual advance of the white, and retreat of the red races, our own revolutionary and other struggles, with the illustration of the higher achievements of our present civilization, [...]"

—*Description of concept for the Rotunda frieze, Architect of the Capitol, 1855*

A sad aura enveloped Martinez. "With Washington's death, any hope of a peaceful and prosperous union of empires in America died with him," she explained, "and an unbridled craving for expansion took its place. The problem was that Natives and Spaniards stood in the way. So, once more, aggression was fueled on the frontier. Manifest Destiny vilified Natives as savages and the Monroe Doctrine vilified Catholic Spaniards as tyrannical brutes; both had to be removed to spread civilization." Martinez pointed across the room. "We begin to see a glimpse of this dark spirit in those four paintings on the east side. Notice how in the paintings of Columbus and De Soto the Spaniards are depicted as weapon-loaded conquerors intimidating naked natives. And now contrast that with the other two paintings."

The Hopi sisters turned to examine them. In one, a *civilized* Pocahontas was dressed in a white, long, silky gown receiving baptism, while in the other, harmless pious pilgrims prayed on their knees as they departed for America.

"It becomes more explicit up there." Martinez motioned upward to the frieze that decorated the first drum of the dome. "Conceived under Jefferson Davis, the nineteen scenes around the frieze narrate *the gradual progress of the continent from the depths of barbarism to the heights of civilization.*" Martinez appraised the twins. "I'll leave it there. I'm sure you get the idea." She motioned further up, switching to a pleased grin.

"Brumidi, the artist who painted the frieze, took graceful revenge for the distasteful commission."

Curious about the remark, all eyes ended their ascent on the 4,664 square-foot fresco visible through the eye of the dome.

"The *Apotheosis of Washington* was Brumidi's idea. Painted in 1865, at the end of the Civil War, it depicts George Washington ascending to the heavens surrounded by female figures symbolic of the original thirteen colonies. In hoping to put the nation back on track, Washington was chosen as the reunifying icon. Now look below him."

They all did. A woman, holding a shield reminiscent of the US coat of arms in one hand while brandishing a sword in the other, towered threatening over six individuals.

"It's Columbia vanquishing division from the land," said Martinez. She chuckled. "One of the disagreeable characters at her feet—the one holding two torches fueling discord—was depicted with the likeness of Jefferson Davis."

Sofia studied the scene. Helping Columbia was a conspicuous angry American eagle gripping a bundle of arrows tightly with both talons. Discord out, unity back in. The painting's message was praiseworthy, but was it truthful to Washington?

She asked: "For a man who voluntarily surrendered his military commission, stepped down as President, rejected a crown, and maybe even a lordship over empires, what do you think he would have felt about his godlike apotheosis?" asked Sofia.

"Satisfaction, my dear."

The answer surprised Sofia.

Martinez drew a smile, aware it would. "The symbolism of the apotheosis is misunderstood. It is not meant to depict Washington as a god, but rather to come full circle with the Pantheon. Constantino Brumidi was born and raised in Rome. He knew the Pantheon was built on the site—not by chance—where according to their local tradition, Romulus, the founder of Rome, was raised to the heavens in an apotheosis. But more than his divinization, the apotheosis of Romulus represented the approval of the gods for his vision, that is, the resulting Empire. Here, the six allegorical scenes that surround Washington's center piece represent the gods doing just that, protecting and guiding US prosperity. I think George Washington would have been very pleased to be portrayed in *his* Rotunda receiving Providence's approval for *his* vision of strength and prosperity in unity."

* * *

A knock on the door almost provoked a heart attack in Dr. Wang. The tension build-up that followed the phone call had been insufferable. She had tried to feign busy work, but she could only stretch the gambit so long and the tremor in her hands had intensified beyond her control.

The tattooed bodyguard sent Wang a warning stare instructing her to remain quiet. A bullet would not have been more effective. She obeyed by burying her face in the monitor screen, remaining alert and ready.

The bodyguard turned around and opened the door just wide enough for his hand to take the delivery or grab the delivery boy by the neck if needed.

Instead, an iron fist smashed him squarely in the face, sending him reeling backward.

The assailant thrust the door open and lunged for him.

Dr. Wang leaped to her feet with relief. It was the FBI agent who warned her about the tattoo symbol. Her idea had worked.

She had made up the company name LabWork to fit the phone number the agent had given her. Fortunately, she had left his business card in the drawer of her desk in the lab and had been able to look it up. Luckier still, the guard was old enough to be familiar with vanity telephone numbers and used it, rather than asking his smart phone assistant to call the non-existent lab for him. That had been her greatest concern.

Wang saw the agent throw another sickening punch targeted at the bodyguard's jaw just above his tattoo. The crushing sound made her want to find a bucket but froze short. The bodyguard had regained his ground rapidly as if slapped by a feather and reacted with a closed fist of his own. The agent ducked with impressive agility and lunged for the bodyguard's waist, throwing his arms around it with his full weight and wrestling him to the ground.

Weapons were not allowed in the building. The lab was one of several entities headquartered on its premises that collaborated with law enforcement and other governmental agencies, making security screening a high priority. All weapons were surrendered at check-in. No exceptions. So, it was encouraging to Wang to see this agent had been trained well for a fist fight. Nonetheless, she searched anxiously for something, anything, that she could use to help. The thought of pulling the fire alarm had just crossed her mind when shock paralyzed her again. She noticed the bodyguard struggling to his feet with his eyes set on the two pages of the Declaration. They rested on a worktable in transparent protective sleeves.

He made a run for them.

She had to stop him.

Wang reached for the wheeled cart she had close by and swung it around smashing it into his abdomen. As the bodyguard folded over, the FBI agent caught up, grabbed his shirt's collar, and strangled him away from the Declaration toward the door.

The bodyguard sprung around, freeing himself, and slowly rose to straighten his body to its full six feet five inches preparing to attack. He heaved a few times, gaging the special agent, who matched him in size and was clenching his fists ready to receive him.

It all came down to a split second. That was the amount of time the bodyguard had to choose between being captured and played with to help bring his boss down or abandoning the document and recovering it later. He took one step back, turned, and ran out the door.

The agent made no attempt to go after him.

Wang had picked up a tray after swinging the cart. She let it sag in her hand. "He's getting away. Aren't you going to chase him?"

The brown-eyed special agent relaxed his fists, adjusted his black jacket and, lastly, ran his fingers through his wavy hair. Satisfied he was presentable, he replied. "My priority was to ensure your safety. I can take care of him at another time, if his master doesn't first."

Wang blinked puzzled.

"He failed here," explained the agent. "That's an unforgivable mistake in his world."

Wang felt her adrenaline drop. It was so stark she had to sit down. Without meaning to, her hand let go of the tray and it bounced on the floor making a raucous sound.

The agent approached her. "Are you okay?"

"Yes ... it's just that ... I was so scared. When I saw his tattoo ... knowing what I had in my hands ..." she rubbed her face.

"Dr. Wang, you were very brave today. And your presence of mind to sneak in that call to me the way you did was brilliant. It is a tribute to your outstanding intelligence. You can be very proud."

First, he saves her life, now these kind words. Wang was grateful. "I'm sorry; my intelligent mind seems to be in a fog. What was your name again ...?"

The agent drew the most gorgeous smile. "Just call me Antonio." Slowly, his face turned serious. "Dr. Wang, I apologize for reverting so quickly to business, but this is important. Is that document on the table everything this man brought you?"

"Yes, two pages. Both are there."

Antonio walked over to it.

"It is very delicate. Please don't touch it," asked Wang, as she joined him. "You won't believe what it is."

"I know very well what it is. I will need to take it with me. Do you have a way I can transport it safely?"

Wang wavered with evident apprehension.

Antonio locked eyes with hers. His semblance was severe. "I see you were able to retrieve the text on its back. I imagine you read it?"

She nodded slowly. There was no point in denying it.

"Then you understand how sensitive it is. Your patron has long tentacles and ill intentions. I must secure it." Antonio paused. "I don't wish to alarm you, but I think it would be prudent if you found a safe place to stay for a while. Do you have one?"

"Yes," she responded quickly. It was the first thing she had planned to do if she made it out alive. "You're not an FBI agent, are you?"

He raised a coy eyebrow. "I never said I was. I merely stated I was a special agent, which I am. You must have assumed the rest. But I promise you I mean no harm to the document. I am tasked with delivering it to the people who can best safeguard it."

Wang appraised Antonio briefly.

Maybe it was his hypnotic, deep-set eyes; maybe it was because he had saved her life; maybe because her patron was truly of concern, or maybe because this mysterious agent could have easily walked out with it instead of asking so kindly, she believed him. Wang proceeded to place the two sleeves between protective layers of refortified cloth and slid the pack carefully into a tight, solid case.

"I scanned it and saved it on the server," she said.

"That's alright," said Antonio. "We'll leave it there. I prefer they have access to the information on the server than go after you for it. Besides, it's time for the truth to come out. Unfortunately, as these things go, some will attempt to twist it beyond recognition. The original hard copy must be protected to preserve it." With that, Antonio tilted his head in the way of a polite nod and left.

CHAPTER 23

"In one of the English papers I have the honor to enclose, is a copy of the Family Compact between the Branches of the House of Bourbon, as it explains the political connection between France & Spain. I think it interesting."

—*John Jay to George Washington, 2 March 1779*

Sofia, Lily, Michael, and Gabriel all squinted as they emerged from the Visitor Center despite the sun being low at a forty-five-degree angle behind them. They proceeded up the ramp, which led toward *First St.*

"That was fascinating," said Lily, "though I'm not sure we learned anything useful from it."

"Yes, we did," sentenced Sofia. "Martinez gave us the answer to *on the table.* I think we can safely conclude Jefferson did not approve of the pact and, when Washington passed, called it off."

"I could have told you that after reading about his intentions to take Spanish territory piece by piece."

"Right, but we also learned that John Adams saw William Blount's conspiracy to *piece* Louisiana away from Spain as a personal affront to the United States. That made me think of the secret family pact between France and Spain that awarded Spain the possession of Louisiana in the first place. Thirty years later, France and Britain are still at each other's throats, only this time aiming to destabilize the boarder between Spain and the US as they vie for control of the Caribbean. So, what if, as part of their united front against this type of toxic meddling, Washington and Charles III promised each other first dibs on adjacent territories to secure each other's loyalty and neutrality? It would explain Gardoqui's collaboration with Washington to diffuse Kentucky's separation, Washington's stern resistance to go against Spain's interests, and Adams' odd recollection."

Sofia then proceeded thoughtfully. "Jefferson didn't care for a union, but was fond of the *important connection* at first, most likely because it gave the US breathing room until it got strong enough to take control. But while in France, aware of Miranda's revolutionary intentions, he became concerned that Spanish America would slip away and had Trumbull signal the need to end the secret pact. Washington resisted, so Jefferson resorted to secretly supporting every private expedition that came his way. Washington's Neutrality Acts foiled them all, until eventually, with his death, Jefferson was able to formalize the pact's termination, collaborate with Napoleon and, lo and behold, Louisiana falls on his lap. I read somewhere once that when Washington died, his secretary, Tobias Lear, conveniently lost correspondence between Washington and Jefferson that was unfavorable to Jefferson and that Jefferson rewarded Tobias with a government position for it. So, it is conceivable that Tobias took care of ensuring the novel was registered as *on the table* for the estate audit."

Lily arched one eyebrow. "For a skeptic who won't take a breath without evidence of there being oxygen in the air, you sure drew a creative picture with nothing solid to go on."

"As solid as your meteor," responded Sofia with an angled grin. "Now you know how I feel. It's that easy to conjure up a conspiracy or see signs where there aren't any."

"Are you serious? You just made all that up to make a point?"

"I didn't make it up. It's what we are being led to believe. And that's the problem. It's too easy. We are told where to go. Once there, someone is conveniently waiting for us with exactly the right information to compose a very convenient picture. I'm done."

"So that's it? We pack and go home?"

"No, we take charge. We investigate for ourselves, and contrast all data points, not just the ones cherry-picked for us."

"Good," said Michael. "We head back to the apartment and reassess, as I suggested earlier." He started to turn north.

Sofia instead headed for the crossing. "Let's stop by the Supreme Court first."

Everyone exchanged confounded looks.

Lily skipped after her. "You just said you didn't want to follow the professor's clues anymore."

"No, I was suggesting we don't depend solely on them. He has been right, but right doesn't mean full picture. We need to widen our scope and contrast everything. I don't want us so sucked in that we lose sight of the horizon."

"You are not making any sense. A break would do us all good."

"Later. The Supreme Court closes in a few minutes. Let's find out want Antonio wants us to know about John Jay. He's our last clue. I looked him up earlier. Jay was like the treaty negotiator-in-chief. He was present with Washington in his meetings with Spanish envoys early in the war. He was the President of Congress when Spain joined the war. He resigned as President so he could personally go to Spain to secure a treaty and loans during the war. Yet, after two crucial years there, Jay apparently left for Paris to negotiate the peace treaty with Britain, failing to sign anything with Spain, which is highly suspect. I came across a letter from Gouverneur Morris to him in January 1781, asking Jay not to notify Congress of the loans Spain granted. He was asked to channel them through Havanna quietly. So, what else were they keeping secret?"

"Got it," sighed Lily, more out of fatigue than anything. "If anyone negotiated the secret pact, or wrote it up, that was Jay."

Michael's phone beeped the kind of beep that carried bad news. He closed his eyes, swore under his breath, and reached for it. "Excuse me," he said as he stepped away to answer it.

Just then, Sofia's phone buzzed as well. She fished in her coat pocket to retrieve it. The screen was lit up with a notification:

Forget John Jay. No time.
Focus on John Adams' Catholic pilgrimage.

Sofia stiffened her neck and whipped her head in every direction. Behind them was the wide pedestrian avenue that led to the Capitol, flanked by the two ramps that led back down to the Visitors Center. They were lined with symmetrical treed spaces. Opposite them, across the street, the Supreme Court stood solemnly to the left and the Library of Congress to the right, both preceded by more trees, guardhouses, monumental stairways, and a fountain. Antonio could be watching discreetly from anywhere.

"What is it?" asked Lily.

Sofia showed her the screen.

Lily's jaw dropped. "You have his personal number? No one has his personal number."

"I'd wish. It's one of those No Caller IDs."

"Still, you've been texting with him. No one gets to do that, either."

"Again, it's only a one-way communication. I've tried texting back; no answer."

Lily pointed at the screen. "What does his message mean, anyway? John Adams was a Congregationalist. Everyone knows he had contempt for the Catholic Church. There is no way he would have made a Catholic pilgrimage."

Sofia shrugged as she typed.

MAN UP AND SHOW YOUR FACE!

"Unbelievable," said Lily. "You're flipping off the most coveted guy in the academia universe. You better get used to being single."

Sofia ignored her. Before tapping SEND, she double-checked her spelling and wondered if to add more exclamation marks.

"Just SEND already," said Lily. "Let's see if he responds this time."

"Fine." She *sent*.

Suddenly, the screeching sound of wheels breaking on the pavement startled them.

They heard Gabriel shout: "Run!".

Sofia looked up and saw him waving at Lily and her as he dashed for a dark van that had come to an awkward stop by the curb.

Michael reacted immediately, dropping his phone and sprinting toward the van as well. He too yelled their way. "Run! Now!"

She felt a hand grip her arm. It was Lily pulling her. "Let's go."

Sofia turned and followed. They retraced their steps back to the Capitol, away from the van. A barrier of iron posts prevented it from reaching them.

Sofia glanced back. She saw Michael slam the passenger door on a guy who was attempting to get out. Meanwhile, Gabriel had reached the back doors. They had swung open, and two men had jumped out porting machine guns. To Sofia's amazement, angel-faced Gabriel skillfully tripped one of them while knocking the other one out with his own weapon.

Unfortunately, the driver of the van had slipped through and was racing her way with a handgun as more scary-looking men flowed out the back of the van.

"The trees," shouted Lily.

Sofia climbed over the railing. Lily hid behind a tree trunk and signaled Sofia to do the same. They could not outrun the athletic-looking mercenary, much less his bullets. They waited. As he approached scanning the area, Lily dashed for another tree, revealing herself. He briefly halted his advance and grinned.

Not for long.

Sofia snuck up behind him and swung a dead branch over his head. The man stumbled forward and collapsed to the ground. Sofia immediately grabbed his gun and ran, as a couple of puzzled bystanders jumped out of her way.

Lily was ahead leading back down the ramp to the Visitor Center hoping officers from the Capitol police were still there guarding the doors.

To her relief, they were.

Sofia was coming around when another armed man, looking even more threatening, if possible, blocked her advance and trained his weapon on her.

She recoiled uncertain which way to go.

"Drop it," he ordered, signaling the gun she held.

Sofia's gut reaction was to tighten her grip on it, instead.

Out of nowhere, a roaring sound sprung on them followed closely by a spectacular motorbike, capturing the man's attention. He quickly shifted his gun in the driver's direction. The biker held a weapon of his own and pointed as he maintained the bike steady with the other hand. His shot was impeccable. It ripped the gun out of the mercenary's hand.

Sofia recognized the motorbike from the day before, realizing it must have been following her. Could it be ...?

The biker headed her way without losing a beat and skidded to a sharp stop, uncomfortably close.

Everything was happening too fast. Her reflexes were tangled. What to do? She rapidly trained her weapon on him. She had no assurance he was friendly.

He gestured calm with his gloved hand, tucked his gun into a special compartment in his black jacket with the other, and then lifted his visor. His eyes set intensely on her. "Come with me."

It *was* him.

Sofia took a small step back. She didn't know what to do and found herself seeking out Michael, who had just elbowed a guy in the ribs and was ready to take on another. Despite their impressive defense, Michael and Gabriel looked overpowered.

Michael halted as if he could perceive her gaze. When he saw Antonio, his nostrils flared, yet he surprised her. "Go!"

She then noticed that several of the attackers who surrounded Gabriel turned their heads to look at her. They clearly weren't a random bunch of ragtag miscreants. This was one ugly militia group. And they did not seem happy.

Sofia jumped on the motorbike.

PART II

"There is no Court [Spain] in Europe at which Secrecy will so much recommend a Negociator as that to which you are destind. [...] You are to negotiate with a People of honor & a Ministry of wisdom. They will propose fairly & perform faithfully. You will not be embarrassd by intrigue, at least none of Spanish origin, nor will it be advantageous to employ any.

These considerations together with the good sense & great abilities for which you are distinguishd make one hope, Sir, that you will accomplish with facility the important purposes of your mission to the advantage of our Country & to your own honor.

The House of Gardoqui has executed what was entrusted to them with diligence, & as far as I can judge with fidelity. They therefore deserve your confidence."

—Arthur Lee, US envoy in Paris, to John Jay, 17 March 1780

CHAPTER 24

"'I do not insist,' answered Don Quixote, 'that this is a full adventure, but it is the beginning of one, for this is the way adventures begin.'"

—*Don Quixote by Miguel de Cervantes Saavedra, 1605*

They had not gotten far when two motorbikes tracked them down on hot pursuit. Sofia knew that her best contribution as a passenger was to become one with the pilot by aligning her body with Antonio's to minimize counterweight distractions. Antonio proved to be skilled at dancing with the traffic, and, for a moment, it looked like they had succeeded in losing their tail. They hastily stopped to toss her phone and the borrowed gun into a dumpster, lest one be tagged. Antonio retrieved a helmet for Sofia, but she had barely buckled the chin strap when they were intercepted again. The chase that followed included driving the wrong way on several side streets, navigating the debris of a bridge closed off for repairs, and a zigzagging escape between two buses that still had her heart reeling.

Finally, or at least for now, it appeared they were in the clear. Sofia tentatively looked around. The area was unfamiliar. They had left the District southbound and were currently meandering at a reduced speed through a cute, quiet neighborhood. As the stress of the chase melted away, she noticed her arms aching from the tension of girthing Antonio's waist. Sofia relaxed her strangle, which she got the distinct impression he appreciated.

Antonio slowed down further upon reaching a dead-end for vehicles but didn't stop. A few yards ahead, the start of a walking trail was marked by a post warning against trespassing. Beyond it, little was visible since it disappeared into a thick wooded area. Undeterred by the sign, the lack of asphalt or the encroaching greenery, Antonio took it.

Sofia was surprised to find the path led to a golf course and was even more surprised when she saw a modest sign for Joint Base Andrews posted next to a sand trap. Behind it, a gated chain link fence led to a runway.

Antonio drove the motorcycle up to the gate, which opened automatically as they approached. A guard, standing to one side, tipped his head and Antonio responded likewise. No check-in was demanded.

This stunned Sofia. How were they not asked for identification? Heck, they weren't even required to show their faces. She straightened up and looked around trying to understand. Maybe the check point was somewhere else.

Antonio must have sensed her unease. He pointed to the lone plane parked ahead.

A plane? They were going to board a plane? Her active brain went straight to thinking the worst: no one knew she was there. Not even the guard knew who she was. She could disappear without leaving a trace. Mounting distress set in as she examined the aircraft. She had never seen one like it. To her it looked like a hybrid between a small military tactical airlifter and a luxury business jet. What that said about Antonio, she had no idea.

The ramp in the back was down. Antonio climbed it.

As soon as they came to a steady stop in the cargo area, Sofia jumped off and retreated to the opening. She nervously removed her helmet and dithered at the top of the ramp unsure if to disembark or stay onboard. The last thirty minutes had been a blur, and she felt overwhelmed.

Antonio dismounted, removed his helmet, and looked at her. As he ran his fingers through his hair, he said in a calm voice: "You are free to leave if that is what you wish. I can arrange for Michael to pick you up. You'll be safe here at the base until he arrives."

Sofia's large, brown eyes flickered between the hatch opening and Antonio. She couldn't decide. "Why are we here, on the plane?"

"I was hoping you'd come with me to Spain."

"Why?"

"To continue the search for the truth about the secret pact."

Her gaze lingered reflectively on him. "Why do you need me?"

"I've been following your work closely for some time. Your analytical skills are unique. I believe we can be very productive if we work together."

"Can't we search for the truth from here?"

"Not if you want the complete picture. It's a long story. Unfortunately, we are pressed for time. Our window of opportunity to leave safely is closing fast. The same technology used to intercept us on the road back there," he said, motioning in the direction they came, "can be used to intercept us in the air. The sooner we gain distance, the better."

Sofia reacted very slowly on purpose to his urging. She turned to look through the hatch at the gate and took a moment to think. If he had truly been following her closely, he should know that rushing her to make a blind decision only elicited the equivalent amount of caution from her. She pondered her situation and options as rapidly as a few seconds allowed, and then, just as slowly, turned her attention back to him. "Since time is of the essence, I suggest you hurry up and craft a convincing summary," she demanded. She looked determined to take the ramp.

Antonio patted the air. "Okay. How about this: In 1779, when Spain joined the war, the Continental Congress sent John Jay and John Adams to Paris on different missions. Officially, Jay was to procure a formal alliance with Spain, while Adams was to prepare for peace with Britain. Despite departing around the same time with the same destination, they travelled separately and something very curious occurred. While on route, both their boats suffered untimely damage that forced them to divert from their planned routes."

"Paris? I don't know about Adams, but Jay was sent to Madrid, not Paris."

"John Jay did not hold an open invitation to Spain—purportedly. The plan was to arrange for one from Paris, that's why on the trip with him was the French minister, Gerard, who was supposed to intercede for him. However, within days of departure from Philadelphia, a storm damaged their ship, forcing them to veer south all the way to Martinique in the Caribbean, which delayed their crossing a month. Gerard protested the nonsensical detour, claiming—correctly—that they would have been ahead staying on course and crossing the Atlantic. When they did finally cross, the first stop was in Cadiz, in the south of Spain and—coincidently—her main trading hub for her territories in America. Alleging it was too dangerous to continue to France due to pirate activity, Jay stayed put, leaving Gerard to continue to Paris on his own."

Sofia listened attentively. He had captured her interest.

"In the meantime," he continued, "John Adams's boat sprung a leak, having no other option, apparently, but to safe dock in Ferrol, in the north of Spain, and—coincidently—her main military port, where joint Spanish and French navy preparations against Britain were underway. Adams spent three weeks there and then undertook a very unnecessary land trip across the north that eventually led him to Bilbao before crossing over to France. In Bilboa, he was hosted by Diego de Gardoqui for several unreported days.

Sofia recognized the name Gardoqui. That guy seemed to be omnipresent.

"To conclude," said Antonio, "Adams then continued to Paris while John Jay waited in Cadiz until Gardoqui reached Madrid, and only then did Jay proceed to the capital himself. A few weeks later, Arthur Lee, who was stationed in Paris and had been until then the US's secret liaison with Spain, sent a letter to Jay, in which he officially transferred his duties to him, informing him that Gardoqui had diligently executed what had been entrusted to him. What that was is not explained."

Sofia was in disbelief. "You're inferring Jay orchestrated the sham detour to Martinique to distract Gerard while Adams carried out a secret mission." She thought through it out loud. "John Jay was the official high-ranking negotiator; all eyes would have been on him. So, while he played decoy, John Adams delivered the paperwork for a secret alliance to Gardoqui that not even France could know about." For Sofia, it made sense. It explained Gardoqui's appointment later as first ambassador and his role in helping to calm matters with the Mississippi. He belonged to the small group in the know.

Antonio's shrug was non-committal. "There is only one way to know. Adams kept a diary. I would like you to retrace his journey with me to work out where the delivery took place."

"You just said Adams spent a number of unreported days with Gardoqui in Bilbao. Wouldn't that be the logical drop-off site?"

"Bilbao is on the coast and has a splendid port. Why take an extremely uncomfortable month-long journey through rugged territory in the dead of winter if that was the plan all along?" Antonio then stood calm, giving her the moment she needed.

Damn, he was good, she thought. Not only did he learn quickly to back off from rushing her, but he had also made a hell of an intriguing case. She wanted in badly, so badly she was now the one anxious to proceed.

She played it cool, though.

Sofia took a few steps toward him. "I witnessed how you were allowed into a major US military base with a nod. I'm pretty certain even the President of the United States is subjected to tighter scrutiny when boarding Air Force One here. There must be a mighty good reason to give you such latitude, which means that, if you need me, I must be mighty important myself. And I don't buy it's only for my analytical skills. So, let's lay some ground rules: No more games. No more cryptic messaging. Understood? You will tell me straight what this is all about." She then showed herself deeper into the plane. "Where's the secure phone? I want to see if my sister is alright."

Antonio followed her through the corner of his eye with a devilish grin as she passed him by. He quickly secured the motorcycle and headed to the cockpit to give instructions.

CHAPTER 25

"Providence has favoured me, with a very unexpected Visit to Spain [...] If the Business of my Commission is not retarded by my accidental Journey, through Spain, I shall have no Reason to regret it. I have been treated with as much Civility, and with a more studied Attention and Respect, in this Country, than I ever was in any other."

—John Adams to James Lovell, Committee of Foreign Affairs, 16 December 1779

Lily's grip on the phone was tight. "You are going where?" she said, and shot a look at Michael. "She's on her way to Spain!"

They were back in the apartment. When Sofia fled with Antonio, two mercenaries on motorcycles, who were stationed up the street protecting the rear, set out on their pursuit, while Michael and Gabriel subdued the rest with the help of the Capitol police. That was the easy part. The challenge had been to come up with a reasonable excuse to explain the attack. Gabriel dealt with the officers, buying time, as Michael worked the phone to have someone call their chief.

All the while, Lily was a nervous wreck wondering if her sister was alright.

"I think the plan is to track down a copy of the pact, but I don't know the details yet," she heard Sofia say. "We just took off. I wanted to see if you were okay, first."

"No need to worry about me. A couple of brutes made a half-hearted attempt at grabbing me before a kind officer and Gabriel jumped on them. It would appear you were their grand prize."

"I don't get it. Why the interest in me? You're the historian."

"I know, right? So rude. But enough about me. It's so exciting, you're on his private plane. No one gets to do that. Is it nice?"

"Not bad."

"Is he?"

"I guess."

"I swear ..." mumbled Lily under her breath.

"Are you allowed to do that?"

"You're not going to get off that easily."

"Not the time, sis."

"I'll take it as you can't talk right now."

"Let's go with that."

"You know what? You need an intervention."

"I'm ready to hang up."

"Fine. Subject dropped. I'm backing up slowly, hands up. Happy?"

"Very much. Thank you."

"So, now what?"

"While I find out more, why don't you take a look at John Adams' diary. Read the part about his trip across Spain in the winter of 1779-1780. See if something jumps out at you; a suspicious stop along the way; a strange encounter ..."

"John Adams was in Spain during the war? I didn't know that. It's no wonder no one's interested in me. I'm a lousy historian."

"You're not supposed to know or care. His trip was disguised as accidental, slipping through history as irrelevant."

"If it wasn't accidental, what was it? A secret mission?"

"Most likely; probably to deliver the signed pact. The idea is to follow in his footsteps to identify the potential drop off site and track it down from there."

"Who knew? Grouchy Adams a secret agent on a secret mission. Fascinating. That explains why the poor fella felt unappreciated. Did you know he doesn't have a memorial in D.C. and that he knew he'd never get one? I wonder if this has anything to do with it?"

"While you think about that, can you pass the phone to Michael?" asked Sofia. "I'd like to talk to him."

Michael was standing within arm's reach of Lily, looking eager. She offered it to him; he snatched it out of her hand. "Hey, I'm glad to hear you're alright."

Lily observed him for a long minute. It was not like Michael to be so jittery. She had known him for years and seen him exhibit much more control in tighter situations. On this mission, he displayed an uncharacteristic air of vulnerability.

She stepped over to confer with Gabriel. "Your cousin is exceedingly concerned for Sofia and don't you dare deny it. What's the deal with Antonio? Should I be worried about something?"

"It's not that. Sofia couldn't be in better hands."

"Then what is it?"

"Nothing. Antonio has his own way of doing things and it makes Michael nervous."

"Please, Gabriel. I know Michael. I'm certain it's more serious than a procedural disagreement."

Gabriel hesitated. "I don't want to scare you, Lily, but the world is in a really bad place right now, and Michael is stressed out about it. Everything you've been learning about cabal forces fueling fear, anger, and division is happening on a global scale at levels not seen since World War II. If the Knights get their way in the United States—the leading power—it could be the tipping point that pushes everyone else into free fall. We can't fail, Lily. The stakes are too high. We have to neutralize the Knights and Michael demands laser focus."

Lily felt a shiver.

Michael could be heard finishing up. "You can trust him," she heard him say. "Please, do what he tells you and stay safe. We'll coordinate from here."

Sofia placed the phone on the table and took a moment to run her eyes around the plush space. It was a tangible way to get her bearings in her new situation. The front part of the plane was closed off from the cargo area and decked out with basic comforts she wished for her condo. Her eye-tour ended on Antonio. He was sitting across from her on the other side of a small, wall-anchored table reading something on the screen of his laptop.

Her eyes lingered on him. She found it difficult to judge his age. His looks placed him in his late thirties, but she was inclined to increase it to his mid-forties due to the well-balanced confidence he exuded, the type that combined a solid degree of life experience with a good amount of vigor still left. The one thing she had no doubt about was his penchant for fine things in view of the cashmere grey sweater that smartly outfitted his toned body and the glass of top-shelf sherry he gingerly swirled in his hand.

She was holding one, as well. If her sister saw her now, she would never hear the end of it.

"Are we good?" he asked.

"We're good. Michael vouches for you." Sofia sharpened her gaze. "What's the deal with you two?"

"What do you mean?"

"I get the impression there is some friction."

Antonio seemed amused by her observation. "We have philosophical disagreements on how to do things. Nothing you need to worry about."

"I do worry. I worry very much. I'm in your hands. So, tell me, what is it exactly that you do?" She pointed around the cabin with her finger. "You're obviously not a professor."

"I'm many things, a professor among them. For now, I can't tell you more than that."

"Please, let's not get started. The deal was you'd tell me everything."

"I'll happily comply with regards to the pact. With regards to me, I ask that you respect my privacy." His words were polite, though firm.

"It doesn't help with trust," she said.

Antonio glanced at her. "You've made it clear you are not a woman who gives your trust freely. If I'm going to earn it, I'm certain it will be with my actions, not with anything I say about myself."

He got her there. She curled a smile. She liked men who paid attention. "Okay, and—clearly—you are talented, resourceful, and well ahead of me, while I'm miles out of my comfort zone and heading further away. I'm not sure how I can contribute."

"You will." Antonio leaned forward, stretching his glass toward her as an invitation to toast with him. His deep-set hypnotic eyes pulled her in. "My grandmother used to say: *when the time is right, the magic will happen.*"

* * *

Aaron lounged out on the patio. The unexpected evening storm had moved on, and the low sun filtered its last rays over the horizon through a handful of straggling clouds. The day had been marginally warm for the season and the red sunset forecasted an auspicious amount of delight for the next day.

Aaron's attention was absorbed by the two-sided scanned prints his bodyguard had delivered moments earlier. "I assume you eliminated the file from the lab computers and servers?"

"Yes, sir."

"What about Wang?"

"She's in hiding. Not for long. I'll find her."

"No, don't waste resources on her. There will be time. We have more pressing matters to contend with." Aaron said this restraining the profound disdain he had developed for his enforcer. Necessity made Aaron trust the more delicate side of his business to this man, who until then had performed reasonably well. But then the mysterious agent appeared, outdoing his enforcer twice already. Unfortunately, considering where things stood and the level of extreme confidentiality that he required, it wasn't that simple to replace him. Not rashly, anyway.

Aaron redirected his frustrations to the text in his hand. It was not what he had expected. He knew of the secret covenant thanks to his father, who had known from his father, and so on back to the time of the Founding Fathers. But that was it. All he knew was that it existed with the mandate to find it and destroy it. The finer details of its content had been lost to memory on purpose, for an abhorrent secret could not leak if not known.

The scant information he had inherited talked of two documents: One, the original draft of the Declaration of Independence on the back of which the pact had been written. And two, a simple copy of the pact itself. But then to complicate it, since each document contained the terms expressed in two languages, the documents themselves were split in two, meaning there were four parts in total. And if that were not overdramatic enough, each party to the alliance took custody of the two halves in their language and then deposited them in highly symbolic sites as though they were sacred objects.

Aaron saw in the ceremonial waltz a show of pathetic self-importance by two leaders arrogantly believing themselves chosen for greatness. Instead, the only thing the two fools had accomplished with their superstitious nonsense was to leave clues behind conducive to finding the sites.

The two American halves were located with relative ease. In the early 1800s, one of Aarons' great ancestors tracked one part to the cornerstone of Saint Peter's Church in New York. Then, conveniently, the church's ceiling caved in, pushing plans to rebuild a new and larger structure, allowing for the document's recovery. A similar tactic had been attempted with the White House, but Truman outwitted Aaron's father, making him believe the secret would remain sealed in its tomb forever.

The sister's visit to Mr. Dhruv revealed the deception; an unexpected gift, that his enforcer botched. Aaron's knee throbbed at the thought. He reclined his patio chair hoping the elevation of his leg would subdue the discomfort. It helped with the pain but not his ire.

Regardless, Aaron was confident he'd recover the American original half in due time, for he had seen the sign. *He* was the true chosen one; chosen to protect America from it. And as he studied the image on the second page of the printed copy, he came to understand why. For all the dread and speculation about the terms of the alliance, it was the image that he found terrifying.

There was no time to waste. They had to hunt down the two Spanish halves before Del Mar did.

Aaron addressed his bodyguard. "Anything on the meteor?"

"Yes, sir. Your suspicions were correct. The analyst confirms that the clues provided by the sighting point to a specific location in Spain. I have the details. It looks promising. He also insisted he could locate the second site if he knew what you were looking for."

Aaron's patience had reached its zenith. Fishing for information was one grave error too many on a day of one too many grave errors. "Terminate his services. Then pick one of your best men. I want you to go personally."

"Yes, sir."

Aaron's eyes trailed his bodyguard as he walked away. A man like him did not survive forgiving errors from anyone.

CHAPTER 26

"I was afraid to keep any Journal at all: For I had reason to believe, that the house was full of Spies, some of whom were among my own Servants, and if my Journal should fall into the hands of the Police, full of free remarks as it must be, to be of any value, it might do more Injury to my Country than mischief to me."

—*John Adams' diary, France, 27 April 1778*

Dinner was a serving of lemon salmon with vegetable rice and a side of salad. Simple, light, and satisfying. To accompany it, the conversation had been an entertaining battle of wits. Sofia attempted every professional maneuver she knew to inquire about Antonio's personal life, while he deftly shifted to commenting on her work, particularly the successful magazine supplement she had written with her sister. In the end, Antonio appeared to believe, like everyone else, that she had a divine gift to find what fate reserved for a few anointed ones. Sofia tried to explain how a simple exercise of well-informed reasoning could get the job done, no miracle or divine anointment required.

To this, Antonio answered with a teasing compliment: "A person exercising well-informed reasoning is the miracle."

Now, as she savored her espresso, he laid open a map on the table between them.

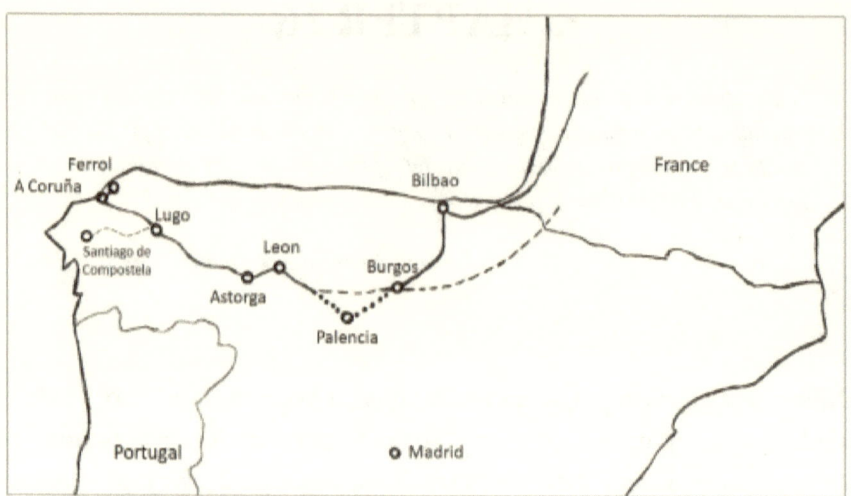

It depicted the north of Spain. On it, Antonio had outlined a route with several stops. Sofia surmised it was the one John Adams had followed.

He confirmed it. "The solid black line tracks Adams' journey according to his diary. It starts here in Ferrol on the west coast," he pointed, "and proceeds eastward, ending up here on the northern coast in Bilbao. From there, he continued into France."

"Why is this middle section to Palencia dotted?" asked Sofia.

"According to his diary, Adams travelled along the St. James Pilgrim Trail between Lugo and Burgos. However, we know from his son's diary that they departed from it to go to Palencia—no reason given. Adams does not mention it." Antonio looked up. "Adams' sons, John Quincy and Charles, were both on the trip."

Sofia looked down at it. "Interesting ... I assume the dashed line is the part of the pilgrim trail he diverted from."

"That's correct, though to be exact, it's one of many trails. The Way of St. James is a network of trails that cross the Iberian Peninsula to converge in the city of Santiago of Compostela where the Apostle St. James is buried. John Adams followed the more trotted one. It's named the French Way for obvious reasons. However, in Burgos, he diverted from it again by turning north to Bilbao."

"That is quite the detour if he was headed to Paris."

"Yes, especially if time was of the essence. Adams justified his overland trip by claiming it would be faster than waiting for his boat to be repaired in Ferrol. This, itself, is debatable. Regardless, if he was in such a hurry, why divert to Bilbao and spend a week there?"

"Yet you're not convinced that's where he delivered the pact?"

"It is hard to justify a difficult trip like this, especially when traveling with children, if the destination was a major port city. Why not make Bilbao your accidental stop?"

Sofia grew reflexive. "You said Ferrol was a military port, right?"

"Yes. It was designated the royal shipyard in the 18th century and housed the Maritime Department, becoming the leading naval center for the defense of the Spanish empire under Charles III."

"Maybe Adams wanted to maximize his accidental visit. You know, dock in Ferrol to spy what was going on there before heading over to Bilbao."

"There was no need for spying. When he landed, he was treated like royalty. Adams stayed for three weeks. Every night he was entertained by the highest-ranking authorities and during the day he was toured through navy installations and other governmental institutions in the area, all the while receiving comprehensive reports on war preparations and operations."

"Meaning he was expected and treated like an allied diplomat."

Antonio nodded. "It would appear so. And according to his diary, it was the local authorities who suggested that he proceed by land, to which he *reluctantly* agreed in the name of haste." Antonio reached for a file he had laid on the side of the table and pushed it toward Sofia. "In here you'll find a copy of his journal as it pertains to his trip across Spain. It won't take you long to read. You'll observe it is basically a narration of his discomforts along the way, while underrating most of what he sees. I'll point out some glaring examples on the ground. But perhaps most glaring is the absence of any meaningful political or business commentary."

Sofia understood. "You think his entries are crafted to depict a reluctant traveler, encrypting the truth."

"I do. Adams had learned to guard what he wrote in his diary during an earlier trip to France."

"Which raises the question: Why keep a diary at all if you can't be honest in it? It defies the purpose of a journal, which reinforces your suspicion it had an alternate purpose."

Antonio nodded once more. "Adams included this trip in his autobiography twenty-five years later with a few changes. I attach a copy in case you wish to analyze the differences. And lastly," he said, tapping the file with his index finger, "I also include the trip report he prepared for Congress once the trip was over, and he felt secure. You'll appreciate the stark contrast. It is very positive and full of productive observations."

"In sum," acknowledged Sofia, "the only reason to keep a guarded, nagging diary would be to encode a treasure map."

Antonio confirmed with a smile.

She examined the map for a quick review of what she had learned so far. "We can discard Ferrol as a drop-off, since why undertake the journey over land afterwards? Bilbao is unlikely, as well, since why not simply dock there from the beginning? And ..." she looked up at Antonio, "I'm going to guess you have your doubts about Palencia, since you haven't settled for it despite how conspicuously suspicious it is that he wouldn't mention the detour."

Antonio chuckled. "No, I haven't discounted Palencia or any city for that matter. There are good reasons to keep them all in play. But it is a lot of information to throw at you all at once. I thought it might be more productive to address the particulars as we visit each city. To give you an idea, let's take Burgos, for instance. This is the city where Arthur Lee and Diego de Gardoqui met secretly for the first time as early as 1776. Madrid was avoided due to the presence of British spies. Following that meeting, an extraordinary amount of Spanish support and supplies was agreed to for Washington's troops. Lee was a close friend of Adams; in fact, Adams was on this trip because of Lee, so he was aware of the encounter and its outcome. Yet Adams' entry in the diary for Burgos makes no mention of it. Instead, he goes on a rant about the hardships endured during the trip and the incompetence of his staff."

"Diversion," conceded Sofia immediately. Then, just as swiftly another possibility came to mind. "What if he was truly annoyed? It's also here in Burgos where he diverts from the pilgrim trail to turn north. Perhaps Adams and Gardoqui were meant to meet in Burgos, as Gardoqui had done with Lee, but someone in his staff messed up and they were forced to reschedule in Bilbao. The mission could have been jeopardized and the arduous trip rendered unnecessary."

"Perhaps ...." Antonio leaned back in his seat. "As I said, there is still a lot you don't know."

Sofia's chest swelled with excitement. She was in the presence of a genuine treasure map and embarked on a true treasure hunt. What remained of a child in her was thrilled to bits with the challenge. "Okay then," she settled. She reached for the file with one hand and the espresso with the other. "I'll get to work."

CHAPTER 27

"I have always regretted that We could not find time to make a Pilgrimage to Saint Iago [Saint James] de Compostella."

—*John Adams, entry for 28 December 1779, Autobiography*

The breeze coming in from the ocean was icy cold. Sofia took a deep breath; it was invigorating. She felt good. She had enjoyed several hours of restful sleep on the plane and woke up to the smell of warm pastries, fresh orange juice and a large cup of coffee; all prepared and served by Antonio. Shortly after, they landed in A Coruña, the capital of the region, located just across the bay from Ferrol. Their first order of business had been to shop for a couple of clothing changes for Sofia and equip her with the proper gear for their motorcycle road trip. The second had been to test it on a short visit to the Atlantic coastline before heading east. Antonio assured her it was the best antidote for jetlag. And he was right. If the beautiful mesh of meadows and green forests lined with alternating robust shores and white sandy beaches didn't wake you up, the crisp fall air certainly did.

It was bittersweet, though. Sofia was getting her road trip after all, and while improved with the company of an attractive man through a gorgeous countryside in search of a buried treasure, Dan's death hovered too recent to enjoy it carefree.

At this precise moment she was parsing her emotions atop the Tower of Hercules, an ancient lighthouse rebuilt entirely in stone during the time of the Roman Emperor Trajan on the site of an earlier Phoenician or Celtic structure. A World Heritage Site for being the oldest lighthouse still in use.

Adams had mentioned visiting it in his diary but oddly referred to it by its French name, *Tour de Fer*. For Antonio, this minor detail was illustrative of the diary's deceptive nature. He pointed out that Adams was a big fan of Hercules and even proposed one of his parables as the theme for the Great Seal of the United States when he was member of the first committee assigned to design it. Yet in his journal he failed to mention the lighthouse's

or city's pervasive link to the legendary hero. A true diary is an intimate narrative. Some indication of a personal association like that would have been expected.

Sofia agreed and made a mental note, planning to share everything she learned and saw with Lily.

The breeze played with her hair as her eyes drifted north, out over the water to scrutinize the distant horizon. Legends abounded on this rugged coast. Curiously, one was Irish. According to the Lebor Gabála Érenn, a medieval Irish book, it was from this site where the son of Breogan, a Celtic warrior and leader, saw the shores of Ireland and set out to conquer her, becoming the ancestor of the Irish people. It was an obvious exaggeration since Ireland was impossible to see from Spain, but no dutiful tourist could resist trying for fun.

Beyond mythical lore, the region was seeded with ancient megaliths that told the true story of seafarers who braved the waves up and down the European Atlantic coast as far back as 7,000 years. Seeing the ocean's immense vastness from the perspective of those who endeavored one day to lose sight of the coastline and sail west, was awe-inspiring, intimidating, and foreboding all at once. Sofia had a whole new appreciation for the motto *Nothing Beyond*. And it was hard to fathom the degree of valor, faith, and large dose of adventurous spirit seafarers would have required to sail into that unknown without the guarantee of reaching something *Further Beyond*.

Antonio was by her side providing more precious contextual information to Adams' diary. It was astounding to Sofia how without it, nothing she had read in it would have ever garnered a second look.

"Prior to becoming a Christian pilgrimage," he was explaining, "the Way of Saint James was long travelled by peoples from all over Europe, who pilgrimed here believing this was the End of the World. The area was well-trotted and provided shorter trails options for Adams to choose from if time was truly of the essence. For instance, he could have taken the northern coastal route to avoid the interior mountain crossing." Suddenly, Antonio paused to glance at her. "The coastal route is dotted with quaint fishing villages on the skirts of lush green valleys and picturesque ports where he would have enjoyed outstanding seafood and cider, while cutting down on his travel time considerably."

"Put that way, the mystery is why he didn't move there," teased Sofia. "It sounds amazing."

A hint of mischief sparkled in his gaze. "It is. Maybe I can take you some time."

Sofia felt her cheeks blush. Quickly, she looked away into the horizon.

"Luckily for us," he continued, "we know why he chose the interior route. Adams had considered going to Madrid, which once again, contradicts his urgency to get to Paris. In a letter to Foreign Affairs, in which he reports his accidental landing, he indicates it might be a polite thing to do. And it looks like that was the plan until he reached Astorga, where he decided against it according to his son John Quincy. I'm inclined to think he didn't fully discard the idea until Palencia, explaining the silent detour."

"Spain had just joined the war giving everyone hope that it would wrap up fast," reasoned Sofia. "That's why Adams was sent to Paris as early as 1779 to prepare for a peace treaty. It makes sense he'd want to be polite and stop by the court to say hello."

"It doesn't fly. Spain joined the war as partner to France, avoiding any direct link to the colonies to shield her territories. All her support continued to be supplied secretly, and that's why John Jay didn't have an open invitation. So, for Adams to suggest it would be 'polite' to stop by Madrid to present his respects is clearly a red herring."

Sofia shook her head. To her it was mind blowing to think of John Adams, 2nd president of the United States, and John Jay, the first Supreme Court justice, faking to be stranded in Spain in a game of international deception.

"Ready?" Antonio turned to head back down. "We will follow his route faithfully and drive through the sites he mentions, but I'd like to suggest Lugo as our first stop, unless you determine otherwise."

Sofia furrowed as she tried to refresh her memory. "I don't recall much about Lugo other than Adams liked the Cathedral ... Wait, wasn't it in Lugo where he encountered a Bostonian boy who he chastised for becoming a British privateer?" She abruptly paused. "Come to think of it, what was a

Bostonian privateer doing in Lugo? Lugo is inland. Could it be code for informant?"

"I'll save you the headache. In this case, it really doesn't matter if he was an informant or not. What Adams doesn't say is sometimes more valuable than what he does. Lugo is a neat city. It was founded by the Romans on a prior Celtic site as a center for their gold-mining operations. And fun fact, it is also the only Roman city to preserve its entire Roman city wall." They reached the ground floor and headed for the tower's exit. "For the purpose of our search, the key point is that the older Primitive Way and the French Way converge there. If Lugo had been Adams' destination, once the drop-off was completed, he could have proceeded north along the Primitive Way as a shortcut to connect with the Northern Coastal route. I must insist, the coast route would have been preferable to the mountain crossing. As we travel east, try to imagine doing it on mule in winter."

Sofia could picture the discomfort already, grateful to be wearing the latest in thermal gear. And it was only fall. "Okay, so if we can discard Lugo as a drop off site, why are we stopping there?"

Antonio gave her a sneaky grin. "They serve outstanding *tapas* for an early lunch."

She laughed. "You should have started there. An absolute must then."

They reached the motorcycle and Antonio saddled it. He reached for Sofia's helmet, which was hanging from one of the handlebars, and offered it to her.

She took it and put it on as he readied the bike for her to mount. "How did the French trail become the popular one if it was so challenging?" she asked.

"There are many reasons, but chiefly necessity. It has to do with the Christian *Reconquista*. Tradition has it that the Apostle St. James developed affection for Spain while preaching here, so after being martyred in Judea, he was brought back to be buried. His tomb site went forgotten until—miraculously—it was rediscovered in the 9th century as the Christian kingdoms became strong and pushed south."

"I detect a touch of skepticism in your tone."

"I have great respect for the traditions of my country, but there is no denying that the heavy pilgrim traffic that followed and all the infrastructure build up around the trail served as a convenient buffer between Christian and Muslim Spain. Large commercial centers like Astorga, Leon and Burgos popped up along it, connecting the Mediterranean and France with the west Atlantic coast. And military orders like the Order of Santiago—or St. James in English—were founded to protect the pilgrims, much like the Templars protected those who went to Jerusalem. Over the next six centuries, the Christian forces, led by the Order of Santiago, reconquered the Iberian Peninsula with the symbolic protection of the Apostle; a process culminated by Queen Isabella and her husband when they took Granada. As a result, St. James became the patron saint of Spain, and his *Camino* one of three leading pilgrimages in Christianity. As for the French route, it retained its status as a major causeway, and it's scenic mountains today are sought out by nature lovers."

Sofia adjusted her helmet. "Just curious: Do people still believe the apostle is buried in Santiago?"

Antonio stared at her with his bottomless gaze. "The more devout do, the rest of us happily make-believe. The true appeal of the *Camino* is not the destination but the journey. The pilgrim, or tourist if you prefer, is invited to slow down from their hectic lives by trekking through a culturally rich environment in commune with nature, while befriending kindred strangers who come from all over the world. The crown jewel at its end, after visiting the apostle's shrine, is this, the End of the World," he said, swiping his hand across the vast ocean. "Leaving aside one's personal beliefs, an unforgettable spiritual experience is guaranteed."

He started the motorcycle.

"Do you always do that?" observed Sofia.

"Do what?"

"Talk like a guidebook. Not that I'm complaining."

He drew his heart-throbbing smile. "Occupational hazard, I guess. I practice English traveling."

Sofia settled in behind Antonio. As she embraced his waist, it occurred to her she could use some slowing-down.

Seafood and cider ... Maybe she'd take him up on it.

CHAPTER 28

"The Vicinity of this Power [Spain], her Forces, her Resources, ought to make Us, attentive to her Conduct. But if We may judge of the future by the Past, I should hope, that We have nothing from it, to fear. The Genius and the Interest of the Nation, inclines it to repose. She cannot determine upon War, but in the last Extremity, and even then, she Sighs, for Peace. She is not possessed of the Spirit of Conquest, and We have Reason to congratulate ourselves that We have her, for the nearest, and the principal Neighbour."

—John Adams to the President of Congress, 4 August 1779

Lily stifled her excitement as she read through the journal a third time to be sure she had not missed something. As usual, she applied such diligence only to appease her sister, for she had no doubts about her conclusion.

Lily had figured it out. She had identified the city where the pact was delivered and had good reason to suspect it was still there. It was almost scary how easy it had been.

She had spent the morning studying Adams' diary, tracing his journey on an online map, and carefully contrasting his observations against historical records. It was the best she could do from a safe house in Washington D.C.

Her professional know-how had served her well with regards to the cold data. But, in terms of introspection, Adams' diary provided little. For a man aware of his place in history, the narrative of his adventure at the time of make or break for the colonies through the country all hopes were centered on, was lacking. His commentary swung from acknowledging the kind treatment received to excoriating remarks about the lodging and the difficult journey, the more bitter, the longer the trip. John Adams was known for his caustic character, but it did appear to be a little over the top even for him at times. So, Lily, too, reached the conclusion there was an element of masking his mission in that of a disgruntled traveler. The problem with this was that it made every observation come across as suspicious ... until she recognized one of the stops.

It was thanks to the meteor.

Even she struggled to believe it at first.

But it was true.

When Michael called her up about the meteor sighting, she examined it by applying the same method she had used to unravel the lines during her previous quest. This approach had produced two unequivocal clues, and both pointed to a certain city, which now just so happened to be on Adams' route. As far as Lily was concerned, if the heavens wanted her to know this, it could only be because the secret pact was still there.

She reveled in the idea of sharing her findings with Sofia in a video conference. She couldn't wait to see her sister's face when she told her.

* * *

Sofia felt tired; delighted with the trip and enamored with the company, but nonetheless tired. Antonio's words floated back. *Imagine travelling by mule.* He was right, yet again. Retracing Adam's steps in person provided an invaluable perspective. It took Adam's party nine days to cover the distance she had travelled in less than one. It was no wonder the poor guy was so grumpy. Maybe he wasn't all that deceptive.

After Lugo, Sofia requested a stop in Ponferrada. The town was not highlighted on Antonio's map but was mentioned in the diary. What piqued Sofia's interest was that Adams had casually commented on churches, monasteries, roads, rivers, bridges, and steep cultivated mountain slopes along the way, yet neglected to mention Ponferrada's impressive Templars Castle. Now, if Adams had been a Freemason, that castle right there would have made a meaningful setting. But he wasn't. Sofia thought it wise to be thorough anyway and check it out. Other than that, no other place along the route so far had given off vibrations of being a transcendental drop-off site, because that was what she was looking for: a glimpse of suppressed emotion filtering through the guarded narrative.

From a psychologist's perspective, the experience was interesting. On the plane, her look at the diary had been cursory to gain a rough idea of what to expect. Now, at every stop, she'd pull out the pertinent entry and applied surgical attention, sensitive to the emotional weight a mission of this caliber would have borne on Adams.

She was learning a lot about the man. No doubt he had written the journal cautiously with an audience in mind. Despite this, to her trained eye, he exposed much. There was the occasional spout of frustration with the discomforts of the trip, considerable religious animosity, and a good dose of cultural arrogance. Yet Sofia knew that behind his haughty air, Adams was the real deal. He was one of the few who genuinely supported the cause of independence exclusively out of belief in its values versus so many who saw in it the opportunity for personal gain. His heart would have been one hundred percent in the mission. Ironically, that meant she identified more of Quixote's idealism in Adams than Sancho Panza's realism, which she was certain he would have strongly protested. And that Quixote in him set out proud in the face of the older European traditions, unsuspecting of the personal growth ahead.

Adams liked the Spanish people. He complemented their *Gaiety, Vivacity and Loquacity*. He praised their generous hospitality. And often celebrated their peaceful temperament as neighbors and good predisposition toward the cause. Yet, he also pitied the superstition that symbolically shackled them to the tyranny of the Catholic clergy, ignoring the crucial services that men and women of the cloth rendered to the community. He'd list the 'ridiculous' number of religious institutions and despised their wealth in contrast to that of the people, in denial of the appalling gap between the aristocratic landowner and the literally shackled population back home. So, it was interesting to read Adams' reaction while visiting the city of Leon when finding out that it was the lay Spaniard who, along with their *wicked* clergy, was actively and voluntarily funding the American cause. Sofia observed in his begrudging admittance that it was a painful realization, for back home the greatest challenge Congress struggled with was the collection of funds from adverse taxpayers for Washington's bereft army.

Begrudgingly or not, to Adams' credit, Sofia had noted several instances where he came to recognize his intransigence. One case summarized his growth beautifully. It, too, occurred during his stay in Leon on January 6th, the Feast of the Three Kings Day. It was cute how the Puritan in him justified his curiosity for the Catholic high mass by brushing off his presence stating: "*we happened to be there*". He then went on to describe how the bishop gestured heaven's blessing on the worshipers, who kneeled in gratitude as he passed. Adams interpreted the kneeling as a sign of subservience to the bishop's persona, contenting himself, as he put it, with a bow when the bishop reached him. The episode must have gnawed at him thereafter, because twenty-five years later, when revisiting the episode for his autobiography, he explained his error—albeit in third person: "*His eyes followed me so long that I thought I saw in his countenance a reproof like this 'you are not only a heretic but you are not a gentleman, for a gentleman would have respected the religion of the country and its usages so far as to have conformed externally to a ceremony that cost so little'.*"

Emotional load like this was the type of giveaway Sofia sought, and, from this angle, all the sites visited so far could be crossed out, leaving the city of Leon top on her radar.

For now, Sofia and Antonio had arrived in Astorga and planned to spend the night. The sun was setting as they stood before one of the city's pride and joys, the 19th century Episcopal Palace. Reminiscent of a fairytale castle, it was designed by architect Antoni Gaudi in the neo-medieval style to complement the 15th century cathedral. Adams would not have seen the palace, but one could not walk by it indifferently. As with all of Gaudi's masterpieces, the structure was a feast for the eyes.

They turned toward the cathedral, which Adam's claimed was the most magnificent he had seen in Spain. As they did, Sofia noticed a sign indicating the way to the Chocolate Museum. Was she in heaven? "I think we should take a look at it," she said facetiously, pointing to the sign. "Spanish chocolate impressed Adams. Said it was the best thing ever under the sun, or something like that. We would be derelict in our research if we didn't confirm it."

"You make an excellent point," said Antonio. "In that case, let's cover all our bases: I suggest *churros con chocolate* for breakfast, and since he also loved Spanish *jamon*, we should check that out for dinner."

"I can settle for that." Sofia felt like a spoilt kid in a candy store. She was having the time of her life. Despite all his mystique, Antonio had been very easy-going when not amazingly attentive. But there was also a dangerous side to him. She had identified a touch of restrained mischief that made her crave to set it free. She could see it becoming intoxicating and repeatedly reminded herself she knew nothing about him and to focus on the mission.

The streets were buzzing with life. Sofia felt its vitality reenergizing. They were touring the city because Adams had displayed unusual enthusiasm for Astorga, and Antonio considered it warranted special attention.

Sofia wasn't so sure. As she saw it, Adams' enthusiasm made sense. At the time, Astorga was the first major center with improved conveniences for the traveler built around the pilgrim hospital located in the cathedral complex. It would have been a welcome reprieve after the mountain crossing.

Antonio insisted. Nothing in the diary entry with regards to Astorga was extraneous and he carefully explained the nuanced cues as they followed in Adams footsteps.

They had started at the ancient city walls from which Adams wrote, *"We saw the Road to Leon and Bayonne, and the road to Madrid."* Thanks to his son's diary, they knew this harmless remark carried an ulterior missive. Adams had been considering going to Madrid, and it was here in Astorga that he decided against it, proceeding to Leon instead. Antonio suspected that Adams's reason for hanging around a day was waiting to receive instructions and that they arrived by way of a newspaper; one precisely from Madrid delivered to him by an anonymous messenger. Later in the entry, Adams admitted to being in contact with an American agent through a *genteel Spaniard.*

Sofia understood what Antonio was implying. Adams was not flying solo or randomly. But why the newspaper? It would have been just as easy for the *genteel Spaniard* to simply tell him to stay away from Madrid. "If I recall correctly," she said, "the newspaper contained an article reporting on his arrival to Spain. How do you conclude it carried instructions? It appeared innocent enough when I read it."

"Innocent if not for one no-small detail," said Antonio. "The reporter erroneously claimed that Adams was accompanied on the trip by Mr. Deane, when in reality he was accompanied by his secretary, Mr. Dana."

Sofia was struck by the detail. Adams had included the article in his biography. When she read it, she didn't think anything of it. "The names are similar. It could have been an honest mistake for a Spanish reporter."

"That would be true for a spelling mistake, not an identity one. In order for the Spanish reporter to confuse Dana with Deane, he would have had to know about Silas Deane, and if you know about Silas Deane, you do not make that mistake."

"Who is Silas Deane?"

"You see? My point," grinned Antonio. "You would never have made that *innocent* mistake." They strolled to a stop in front of the cathedral's Baroque facade as Antonio explained. "The reason why Adams and Jay were the ones chosen for their diplomatic assignments went back to a bitter controversy surrounding Silas Deane, precisely. Deane was the first US envoy sent to Paris secretly—weeks before declaring independence—to obtain financial help and military supplies. Which, by the way, he successfully brokered from France and Spain with the help of Beaumarchais, the author of the Figaro plays."

"Wait," said Sofia, showing surprise. "The author of *The Barber of Seville* and *The Marriage of Figaro*? He was the broker helping secure supplies for the Revolution?"

"Yes, a man of many hats. Investing in the American cause was one. In the end, it didn't pay well for him or Deane, who was accused of mishandling funds and other dubious dealings. When Benjamin Franklin and Arthur Lee later joined Deane in Paris, it was Lee who sounded the alarm. Additionally, Lee was very suspicious of Deane's assistant, Edward Bancroft, who time would prove was indeed a British spy. Congress initially took a hands-off approach, which pushed the dispute into the public arena, jeopardizing international monetary aid and coming back to divide Congress." Antonio waved it off with a hand gesture. "It's all very complicated because, as these things go, the Deane corruption scandal was only the tip of the iceberg. There were an endless number of disputes pitting one faction in Congress against the other."

"Ah yes, the inception of our two political parties," recognized Sofia. "It doesn't look like they've changed much."

Antonio wisely stuck to history. "Right, well, in order to appease the two sides, both Lee and Deane were recalled. John Adams, who favored Arthur Lee, was chosen to replace Deane in Paris, and John Jay, leader of the Deane faction, was selected for the Spanish embassy, the job Arthur Lee had wanted for himself."

Sofia was bewildered. "You're saying that Adams and Jay were on different teams, so to speak."

"Something like that."

"I'm very confused. We've been looking at Adams' trip as a secret mission to deliver a secret pact, but it could just as well have been his attempt to get a foothold in Spain for his side in competition with Jay."

Antonio shook his head. "Their accidental trips were well coordinated. Something greater than home politics was at hand. Besides, for Adams it wasn't about politics. Siding with Lee was a question of principle. Adams found it embarrassing for the reputation of the colonies to have their international envoys messing with international aid."

Sofia stared at Antonio slack jawed by the convoluted chess game hidden behind a simple name-mix-up. She shook her head to refocus. "In sum, what all this means is that for Adams to have his name associated with Deane in the newspaper article was a bad thing. That's how you conclude that Deane's name was inserted as a warning of sorts."

Antonio nodded pleased. "A warning that kept Adams on route to his next stop: Leon."

CHAPTER 29

"There is a School of Saint Mark, here as it is called, an Institution for the Education of noble Youths here in Mathematicks and Philosophy."

—John Adams' diary, 6 January 1780

What's taking her so long? Lily paced the room impatiently. Sofia had promised to call as soon as she checked into a hotel for the night, which Lily judged should have happened at least an hour ago. She was in the safe house alone with Gabriel, who seemed carefree, nibbling on pizza leftovers. Michael had left earlier in the day after receiving news about increased activity at the Knights' headquarters and he too was taking his sweet time to get back.

Lily wondered why he did that. The apartment was well-equipped with all the necessary communication devices, and she needed him. She had done more research and not only was she confident about the city, but she was also convinced she knew the exact site within the city and yet here she was pacing back and forth unable to run it by anyone.

"You seem uneasy," she heard Gabriel say. "Can I help you with something?"

Lily stopped sharp, almost surprised he was there. What was she thinking? "Actually, yes. I think I know—"

Just then, the front door opened. Michael walked in. The first thing he did was ask about Sofia. "Did she call yet?"

"No."

He frowned.

"How about you?" she asked in return. "What did you find out?"

"The Knight's leadership has been called in from out of town for an emergency meeting."

"Is that bad?"

"It's never happened before."

"That bad, huh? Any idea why?"

"There is only one reason to take an unprecedented risk like that. They are planning a big move, and it must be imminent."

The room's state-of-the art secure communication system, which looked like a standard all-in-one desktop computer to Lily, alerted to an incoming call.

She jolted. "It must be Sofia."

Gabriel confirmed by waving them over as he activated the camera.

Sofia came into view rosy-cheeked and smiley. "Hi, Gabriel."

He barely had time to correspond.

Lily jumped in front. "About time," she complained. "Where have you been?"

"Sorry, long day. We had a late dinner. It's a thing here. We just checked in. I'm exhausted."

"Tough trip?"

"Oh, no, it's been wonderful."

Lily raised one eyebrow. "Really? How so?"

"Oh, well, one minute I'm transported back to the Roman Empire; the next I'm riding through stunning landscapes, when not walking on cobbled streets from the Middle Ages or assessing a real-life Knights Templar Castle. And the cathedrals are just crazy."

Lily's eyebrow rose further. "Something is wrong with the universe if I'm the one stuck in an apartment researching while you're the one enjoying a pilgrimage trail."

"Who says you can't have some fun while you work, right?"

"You *kinda* used to."

Sofia giggled.

That was unlike her sister. Lily grew suspicious. "What exactly did you have for dinner?"

"A lot. I'm sure I've added several pounds since I arrived. We went to this place in the old quarter and sampled their specialties." Sofia gestured animatedly with her hands. "Each serving came with a taste of wine. I'm becoming quite a sommelier."

Oh my, she is tipsy, thought Lily. She shared a wide-open stare with Michael, who stood to the side out of frame. She noticed his muscles tensing around the jaw. Was this the type of distraction he was concerned about? Lily quickly turned back to Sofia. She inadvertently lowered her tone to a whisper: "Where is Antonio?"

"Taking a call."

"Are you sharing a room?"

"Of course, not ... well, sort of. Antonio suggested we book a suite with two rooms, you know, so he can stay close for my safety."

"Did he, now?"

"Oh, shut up," said Sofia with a guilty grin. "He's been nothing but a gentleman."

Michael stepped into the camera frame.

Sofia stiffened. "Michael. Hi."

"Sofia," he said with a grave tone, which coming from him sounded like a thunderstorm, "I'm happy to hear you are having fun. You should know there are indications the Knights are getting ready to strike. Have you noticed anything strange on your end?"

Sofia cleared her throat. "To be honest, I haven't given the Knights much thought since we've arrived. Antonio hasn't mentioned anything, either."

"They are showing unusual agitation. Their ground members have been notified to be on standby. Groups like this feed off anger and disruption, so whatever they are planning, it will be media explosive and intended to elicit a violent reaction, if not preceded or accompanied by violence. Normally, we'd suspect their activity to be contained within the US borders, but we've also pinned two of their top security agents on a flight to Madrid. In what city are you now?"

"Astorga. You suspect they've tracked me down?"

"Either that or they have a lead of their own. Maybe both. Have you come up with anything?"

"Not yet. We still have half the route to cover, and then I must review my notes, do some research, perhaps revisit some spots ... We're looking for a secret document delivered more than two hundred years ago in a country I'm not at all familiar with. I'm going to need some time ..." Something gave Sofia pause. "Hold on, why would the Knights care to track down a copy here if they already have the original?"

"I think we need to reconsider our assumptions," said Lily. "I'm pretty certain they are still after the original and I know where it is."

There was instant silence.

Michael stared at her inquisitively.

"I figured it out while you were gone," she said. "And, by the way, you need to stop disappearing like that."

"How do you know and so quick?" asked Sofia.

Lily drew a proud grin. "With a little help from a shooting star."

"You're kidding? The meteor?"

Lily couldn't help herself. "I told you it was trying to tell us something." She broadened her grin to a full smile and wagged a finger at the screen. "You know the drill, sis. You must listen to the end. No interruptions. No buts. No eyerolls."

"Just get on with it," said Sofia with a teasing eyeroll.

"Cute. Now, get ready, I'm going to blow your mind. If you recall, the meteor appeared the 15th of September over an unspecified location in the southeast of the province of Extremadura and followed a northwest trajectory, pointing straight to Fatima, while disappearing over the small town of La Albuera. This town and the meteor accumulate all the defining elements of our two lines, indicating it was intended for us."

Sofia interrupted. "Yes, yes, yes, the gods of Olympus lit up the sky with fireworks in the south of Spain to capture our attention, *but,*" she emphasized, "how does that help us find a location in the north of Spain connected with this mission?"

Lily could barely contain her excitement. "I'll explain it in a language you can understand," she said with a taunting grin. "John Adams' route through the north of Spain did not cross either one of our two lines, therefore, fireworks over his drop-off site would have been meaningless to us. In their infinite wisdom, the gods of Olympus did the next best thing: they displayed the firework show where they knew they would secure *my* attention, and then threw in a couple of conspicuous clues pointing to the drop-off site." Lily could see that Sofia, the sommelier, was amused instead of losing her patience as usual, which was spoiling half the fun of shocking her.

Lily continued savoring the moment, anyway. "One of the clues is the date. It's no coincidence the meteor hung over the church of Our Lady of the Way on the day of her feast. Clearly, it's a sign that she is important. And two, the local astrophysics institute that reported on the sighting, provided every possible detail about the meteor except for one glaring omission: the name of the place over which it entered our atmosphere." Lily took a deep breath of anticipation. "I looked into both clues, Sof. Both point to the same location on Adams' route, as if an arrowhead on a map."

Sofia stayed silent but showing interest.

"I'll start with Our Lady of the Way," said Lily. "For us, this advocation was central to unraveling Mary's Line, but when I looked her up, it turns out this particular version in La Albuera doesn't get her name from her Byzantine counterpart. Instead, she gets her name from the Way of St. James, because that's where her worship began in 1505 when she performed a miracle on *The Way*, particularly in the city of ... Leon."

Leon, thought Sofia quite surprised. That was the city at the top of her list. Adams' entry about his visit to Leon filtered the type of emotional tension she expected from a man undertaking a fateful mission. But it wasn't only that. She had also picked up on several narrative oddities in his entry for Leon that had all the markings of being serious clues. She had planned on addressing them when they got there.

"Leon was the capital of the kingdom," continued Lily, "so this Virgen of the Way became the Patron Saint of the kingdom." Lily's smile turned enigmatic. "Now ask me how the patron saint of a northern kingdom ended up naming a church in the south." She was really going to play this up.

Luckily for Lily, Sofia was in a great mood. "How? I'm dying to know."

"During the Reconquista, the Kingdom of Leon extended that far south thanks to the Order of Santiago." Lily paused.

"And this is important because ...?"

"Because that knight's order also began in Leon to protect *The Way*. And while their foundational headquarters in the north were in Leon, guess where their southern headquarters were as they conquered the south?"

"The nameless place over which the meteor appeared," said Sofia.

Lily nodded energetically. "Llerena. I was able to figure it out thanks to a virtual recreation the astrophysics institute published on their website. What are the chances, Sof? Two clues. One provided by the place where the meteor appeared and the other by the place where it disappeared, both having to do with foundational events, and both in Leon."

The fact that she was in a good mood made it all the tougher for Sofia to spoil her sister's fun. "Lily, I realize it's awfully compelling, especially the date coincidence, but here's the thing: Precisely because the Kingdom of Leon expanded south, if you dig enough, you'll find that most towns and cities that fell under its influence at the time are liable to have a connection with its capital. It's the nature of sharing a common history. What's more, thanks to the *Six Degrees of Separation Principal*, you don't even need a common history. Give me any location in the world and I bet you a bag-full of Angelica's cinnamon rolls that I can connect it to Leon in six steps or less."

Lily smiled smugly. It was time to deliver the shocker. "There's more."

Sofia should've known better. Her sister always retained a power punch up her sleeve. She shrugged with a chuckle. "Hit me."

"The headquarters for the Order of Santiago in Leon was housed since the 12th century in the Convent of Saint Mark. During the building's enlargement and renovation in the 16th century, a row of 24 architectural medallions were added to its facade. Each medallion carried a portrait of a renowned historical or legendary figure alongside that of Charles I, the Spanish king at the time, otherwise known as Charles V, the Holy Roman Emperor." Lily clarified: "You know, the one who added the Columns of Hercules and Plus Ultra to the Spanish coat of arms, the Spanish Dollar, etc, etc, etc." Lily rolled her hand in front of the screen's camera.

Sofia nodded.

"The idea behind the medallions was to legitimize his universal imperial reign by depicting him among universal figures, some historical like Alexander the Great or Emperor Augustus, some mythological like Hercules, and some biblical like David or ... Judith."

Judith ...? This piece of data hit Sofia in the right spot. It showed on her face.

Lily broadened her smile. "Odd one out, wouldn't you say?"

"Yes, I would say. How is she universal? Jews didn't think her universal enough to include her book in their bible, and half the Christians don't even know she has a book in their bible. Why include her among prominent figures on the facade of the headquarters of a knighthood?"

"Exactly. Yet there she is. But get this: she's not there alone. She is placed to the right of none-other than Queen Isabella. Sof, think about it. Judith was the clue that revealed Mary's Line to me in the same way that Queen Isabella was the clue that revealed the Spanish Line to me. Now, I find them side-by-side on a building in Leon, drawn there by a meteor that contains all the chief elements of both lines. I'd like to see you do that with any location in the world."

"And that is a problem," announced Michael. "If you made that connection, the Knights may have as well."

"They certainly have," came Antonio's voice off-screen. "May I join?"

Sofia waved him over.

Antonio stepped into the frame, sliding a chair next to Sofia. He smiled. "Sister Lily, it's a pleasure to meet you. Your findings on the meteor are truly impressive."

Her face lit up. "Hi, the pleasure is mine. I've heard a lot about you. You're pretty impressive yourself."

"Do you have intelligence you'd like to share?" interrupted Michael.

Antonio fixed a pointed stare on him. "Hello Michael, it's been a while. It's nice to see you, again." He waited.

Michael's lips tightened. "Nice to see you, too."

Antonio offered a slight nod, and then proceeded to answer the pending question. "Two members of the Knight's security arm landed in Madrid this morning. They rented a vehicle and are heading this way as we speak. They come with an all-access authorization to the Convent of Saint Mark in Leon, which they requested and obtained through diplomatic channels. I have arranged to have the file forwarded to you with the details."

Sofia spoke. "That confirms they're looking for the original in Leon. Truman must have found a copy in the White House cornerstone. You don't pull diplomatic levers for a secondary copy if you already have the original, right?"

Michael answered. "What it means is that Leon has become too dangerous. You must stay away."

"You can't be serious. We're so close. We were heading there tomorrow."

"I can't protect you from here."

Surprise flashed in Antonio's eyes. "I can," he said with an inflection that showed his puzzle for having to state the obvious.

"You don't need her there. It is an unnecessary risk," said Michael.

"It's the only way. The clues in the diary only go so far."

Lily observed the exchange between the two men greatly amused. *You go, sis.*

Sofia, however, protested. "Do I have a say in this?" She started with Michael. "I appreciate your concern, Mike, but it would appear the Knights are very capable of figuring things out on their own. They don't need me." She then turned to Antonio. "And quite frankly, I still don't understand why you do. All I've done so far is play catch-up with you and I have the gut feeling I'm still far behind."

"The Knights are headed to the Convent of St. Mark because a meteor pointed them to it. Do you settle for that?" he asked.

"Of course not. I'm not ready to settle for anything."

"That's why I need you," said Antonio, "You don't settle or get easily distracted." Antonio broke away to look at Lily. "No disrespect intended."

"Actually, I think I agree with you," said Lily. "I wouldn't settle for the convent, either."

"Why?" asked Sofia.

"Until a few minutes ago, I was convinced the convent was the site, as well. Judith and Queen Isabella are together on its facade. That must mean something. But learning that the Knights are on their way there makes me think it's too easy. Anyone capable of shooting stars for my sake can't be so sloppy as to give away the exact location to the likes of the Knights. We are the chosen ones for a reason, Sof. The meteor helped me get us to Leon promptly, so, I guess now it's your turn to find the true site."

Sofia shook her head with a soft laugh. "Your logic is overwhelming." She slid her attention toward Michael. "Look, I have my own reasons to think Leon is a good candidate and might even have some ideas how to go about looking for the site. I must go there and find the fair copy before the Knights do. I can't allow Dan's death to be senseless."

Strangely, Michael looked pleased. "In that case, we'll go to Leon together." He addressed Antonio. "Don't move from Astorga until we get there. We're heading out right now." He didn't wait for a reply and disconnected.

Back in the hotel suite, as the screen went abruptly dark, Sofia noticed Antonio transfixed in deep thought.

CHAPTER 30

"I am I and my circumstance."

—*José Ortega y Gasset, philosopher, Meditations about Quixote*

Dawn was breaking.

In front of Sofia was a cup of hot chocolate with a plate of churros. Her attention drifted absently out the window. In the distance, the first rays of sun brushed over the treetops, bringing the full range of fall ochres and reds to life.

Her mood had been souring since the previous night. Whatever the contention between Michael and Antonio, it resulted in Antonio lifting a thick wall between them following the call. He was still polite, still attentive, still obliging, and darn gorgeous, but from a considerably greater distance.

"You don't like them?" she heard him ask.

Sofia peeled her eyes from the window. He was sitting across from her, dressed in a black sweater and tailored chinos to match, with his hair combed back, and mildly wet from his morning shower. A model selling smart casual attire for the businessman would not have looked sharper. As she wondered if he was real, her attention was lured by a strand of hair that had curled dry and dropped on his forehead. For a fleeting second, she was inebriated by the temptation to comb it back in place with her fingers.

Antonio, inadvertently, got to it first and took care of it himself.

She blinked and looked down at her plate. "They're delicious."

"If you think about it," he said, "Michael was right. I was walking you into the lion's den." He smiled at his own play on words, trying to make light of the tension he sensed from her.

Sofia looked at him seriously.

"Lion—Leon? Get it?" he said.

"I get it."

He released a soft breath. "While we wait, I'll give you some background on the city."

Sofia leaned back in her chair. "What's changed, Antonio?"

He closed his eyes.

"Your demeanor towards me changed last night. Why?" she insisted.

Antonio lingered, shifting in his chair. "I relaxed. I was enjoying our time together, neglecting the challenges we are faced with. I was reminded of it. I'm not going to let that happen again."

"You're making up excuses. Please don't insult my intelligence."

Antonio suddenly fixed his deep-set eyes on her. "There are forces at play you don't understand."

"Maybe if you explained them to me, I would."

"I can't."

"I'm tired of that answer. It's all I get from you and Michael as you both toss me back and forth like a volleyball." Sofia got up and took a few random steps, mirroring her own words. She stopped. "Why are you deferring to Michael? Is he your boss?"

"He thinks he is sometimes, but no, we move in different spheres. I do have great respect for him, though."

"Regardless, he does not get to choose how you and I relate."

"It's not about that. I've never seen him personally invested like he is with you and your sister. I can't ignore it."

"My sister and Michael have been friends for years. He helped us with our previous search. It's what he does."

"No, it's not. That's the point. It's not his job to protect or help up close and personal. Or mine for that matter. It's one of the reasons we clash. He is very strict on that front and I'm not. So, for him to do it ... Look, it's clear you are important to him on a level I was unaware of. I am now. I must honor it."

"What does that even mean? Is it some kind of brotherhood code from that mysterious association of yours?"

His eyes widened with surprise for a fraction of a second, before reverting to his stern front. "I don't expect you to understand."

"That's it?"

"I'm afraid so."

Sofia growled under her breath. This conversation was ridiculously frustrating. She walked away from him to the window in the adjacent sitting area. She didn't know if she felt angry, sad, offended ... disappointed.

That was it; the prevailing sentiment was disappointment, but with herself. There were always secrets with these two. What did she expect? And if anything, both had been honest about one thing: to them, she served a mission.

Her gut reaction was to abandon, or at least threaten to, unless he explained things. It was getting old to be kept in the dark while told she was front and center to success.

When the time is right, the magic will happen.

You are special, the king on the chessboard.

What. The. Heck?

Then, just as fast as her frustration had swollen, her body deflated. It was tempting to use herself as leverage, but they had also been honest about one other thing: she was free to walk. And she did not want to walk. They were on the cusp of finding a historic treasure with only-God-knew the secret written on it. No one in their right mind would walk away from that alone, much less if it could thwart a national threat and bring justice to Dan.

Sofia inhaled a deep slow breath.

In the end, what remained of her emotional roller-coaster was the sting of rejection wrapped in a thick coat of pride, because hell if she was going to let Antonio see her sulk.

She composed herself and returned to the table. "Got it. This is bigger than us and there is much at stake," she said, taking her seat calmly. She picked up her cup of thick, hot chocolate, determined to enjoy it despite the tight grip in her chest. "Tell me what you know about Leon."

* * *

Thirty-three miles away, tattooed man pulled on his turtleneck. He hated covering his neck as much as wearing fake reading glasses, but it was a minor sacrifice for the sake of invisibility.

He and his second had arrived in Leon late the previous evening. They scratched a few hours of sleep and rose early, having secured special access to the Convent of St. Mark's Museum and archives before opening hours. Without delay, they first tackled the curated and classified sections.

Tattooed man was under no illusion he'd find anything in plain sight or sitting on a shelf nicely labelled. Starting there was a matter of extreme diligence.

The real work started next. He and his second headed down the stairs to the basement guided by Elvira Conde Luna, the lovely green-eyed city archivist sent to attend to them. He was grateful for the drop in temperature as they descended. He appraised Ms. Conde Luna, drawn to the small tattoo on the inside of her wrist. He studied it while she worked on the rudimentary lock to the storage room. Like his, it resembled a logo: a simple black semicircle, flat side looking up, with a candle centered on top, it too in black, leaving the red sword that floated inside the semicircle to stand out. He didn't know about the rest, but the sword was clearly a homage to the Order of Santiago. Their emblematic red cross in the form of a sword was carved on its facade. He grinned. Again, like he, this woman wasn't shy of expressing her loyalties. He leisurely toured her tall slim body with his eyes concluding on her nose piercing, a small diamond stud on her left nostril. Elvira didn't look like any bookworm he had ever seen, and her edgy style made him feel pathetic in his stereotyped nerdy disguise. He'd ditch his stupid elbow patch blazer at the first opportunity.

Elvira led the two men in and showed them around the dusty stacked shelves, while explaining the challenges of scanning a thousand years-worth of historical records. For tattooed man, the ancient knack in Spain to record absolutely everything played in his favor. He could see how the two missing pages of the Declaration could get lost in a country swamped with unimaginable documents waiting to be rediscovered. In this basement alone, he could see needing several days just to complete a cursory search. With a little luck, it wouldn't be necessary. Elvira guided them to the section that contained the materials dated within the timeframe he had expressed interest in.

Once again, Elvira offered to help, as she had done insistingly all morning, proving to be annoyingly protective of her precious archive. Tattooed man started to lose his patience. The sooner she got her pretty little ass out of there, the sooner he could get to work. He knew his neck was on the cutting board and had no intention of delivering the two pages. They were his life insurance.

"Ms. Conde Luna, we'll let you know if we need anything," he said sharply.

She did not seem impressed by his size or tone. Her metallic violet lips curved a smile, while her large green eyes narrowed just enough to deliver a subliminal warning. "I don't need to remind you how delicate these materials are. Please handle with care." With a flick of her head, she whipped her long, dark blond hair back and turned toward the storage exit. On her way out, she pointed to a phone on the wall. "If you need anything, you can reach me on number 2."

The moment Elvira closed the door behind her, tattooed man signaled his second to get to work. He was certain they were in the right place. The Convent of St. Mark met all the requirements worked out by Aaron's family over their two-hundred-year search. When the Spanish ambassador laid the cornerstone for St. Peter's in New York City and then another Spaniard did it for the White House, in a young country with a limited number of landmarks at its inception, it was akin to publishing the secret sites on the front page of a newspaper. And the two chosen deposit locations didn't surprise them at all. They were consistent with the two men who had selected them: one, a religious zealot who carried his religion as a title, and the other a man who saw himself as the enlightened messiah of a New Experiment.

From there, logic dictated that in Spain the equivalent would be true. They were looking for two iconic sites, one varnished in Enlightenment and the other obviously Catholic, and both accessible to the two prominent Americans who visited Spain during the Revolutionary War.

In Madrid, where John Jay had spent two years, the king had invested heavily in the name of the Enlightenment, raising some of the capital's most emblematic palaces, museums, monuments, fountains, and boulevards. Even a botanical garden that grew free medicinal plants for the people. Any one of them would have pleased messiah Washington. However, in sticking with equivalencies, the best match for the White House was undoubtedly the Royal Palace, which, coincidentally, was also completed under Charles III's supervision. Unfortunately, this posed an insurmountable challenge. If one of the halves was truly there—presumably the Spanish-original—it was as good as buried for eternity. The Jackson family had no way of getting their hands on it. Hopefully, nor would anyone else.

That left the fourth and last site: a Catholic building located somewhere along the route followed by John Adams. And, in this respect, the pilgrimage trail was the proverbial haystack. It was another insurmountable challenge that had Aaron's family stumped until Providence gave Aaron a sign: the meteor. His analyst concluded it pointed to the Convent of St. Mark and when Aaron learned the Catholic convent had been built to house a prominent knight's order, it was settled, it had to be there. The Order was initially created to protect the pilgrims going to Santiago much like the Templars had been created fifty years earlier to protect those going to Jerusalem. But unlike the Templars, the Spanish knights were never thrown to the fire. They had performed exceptionally well in conquering the south, so Queen Isabella incorporated the order into the Crown, and entrusted its members with the conquest of America, meaning that Charles III was its Grand Master through inheritance. Ultimately, the Convent of St. Mark had the pedigree to please an enlightened Freemason and a Catholic king alike.

It was almost too easy.

Which it was.

Aaron Jackson and, subsequently, his enforcer were making a very common mistake, that of judging others through the lazy lens of personal bias. They had not bothered to look beyond the surface to understand what truly moved Washington, much less Charles III.

CHAPTER 31

"God knows I have not desired, nor desire, anything from anyone, but wish only to protect that which, by his infinite kindness, he has given me and that no one disturb it or take it."

—King Charles III of Spain, re. protecting his territories, 1760

As Antonio went to his room to retrieve something, Sofia reviewed the notes she had taken on the city of Leon, a crude summary of a long, intense history:

29 BC: Founded by Romans as a military encampment.

-Permanent legion > Hispania's military capital for @400 years.

-Name: Legion > Leon

5c. AD: Visigoths (Arian Christians) invade peninsula from north > Convert to Catholicism

8c. AD: Islamic Moors invade peninsula from south > Leon buffer-town for 200 years.

10c. AD: Leon made lead-capital for Christian side and springboard to continue the retake "Reconquista" of the peninsula > Kingdom of Leon born.

-Next 500 years new Christian kingdoms develop as peninsula "retaken".

1492: Reconquista completed + Most of Iberian Peninsula united under Queen Isabella & King Ferdinand + Columbus sets sail.

-No fixed capital for a while > political center moved around with the court.

-Leon remained an important crossroad & stop along pilgrim trail.

1808: Leon among first cities to uprise against Napoleon.

Present: Capital of namesake province and flourishing hub for information, communication, and biotechnologies.

From what little she knew of Spain's history, Leon's seemed to be a micro representation of her last two-thousand-years. As such, its identity was largely rooted in the Roman Empire followed by a considerable amount of frontier-battling between two worlds defined by their religions, a Christian north confronted with a Muslim south, and a strong Jewish presence in both. Interestingly, while Christianity prevailed at the end of the 800-year tug of war, the country today proudly embraced her Moorish and Jewish cultural, artistic, and intellectual inheritance for their invaluable contribution to her finely embroidered character.

According to Antonio, Leon thrived during the Middle Ages between the 10th and 13th centuries while one of the principal Christian capitals of the Reconquista. The sites visited by John Adams during his stay in the city were all founded during this period.

Sofia sat back in her chair shifting through these historical pieces of information to see if she could couple any of them to Adam's notes. Nothing productive came of it. The general historical overview was fine to place her in the right frame, but to an analytical thinker like her, and more so as an expert in human behavior, nuance was everything. If she was to identify a specific location chosen to guard an 18th century secret alliance, she first had to dive into the hearts of the two leading men to grasp their personal motivators in combination with their place and time. Only then would the deposit site reveal itself.

When she expressed as much to Antonio moments earlier, he suddenly stood up and stepped away to collect something from his room.

It didn't take him long. She saw him return with an oversized sheet of paper. It was folded.

"I think this is a good time to share something important with you," he announced.

Sofia perked up.

Antonio placed the folded paper on his chair and started to clear the table. She eagerly jumped to help by removing what remained.

With the table cleared, they stood around it as Antonio laid the sheet open to reveal another map. Sofia recognized it since it was an enlarged print of one of the maps she and Lily had included in their published essay;

the one that framed their lines as they ran through Spain. She noticed two cross marks had been added to Mary's Line.

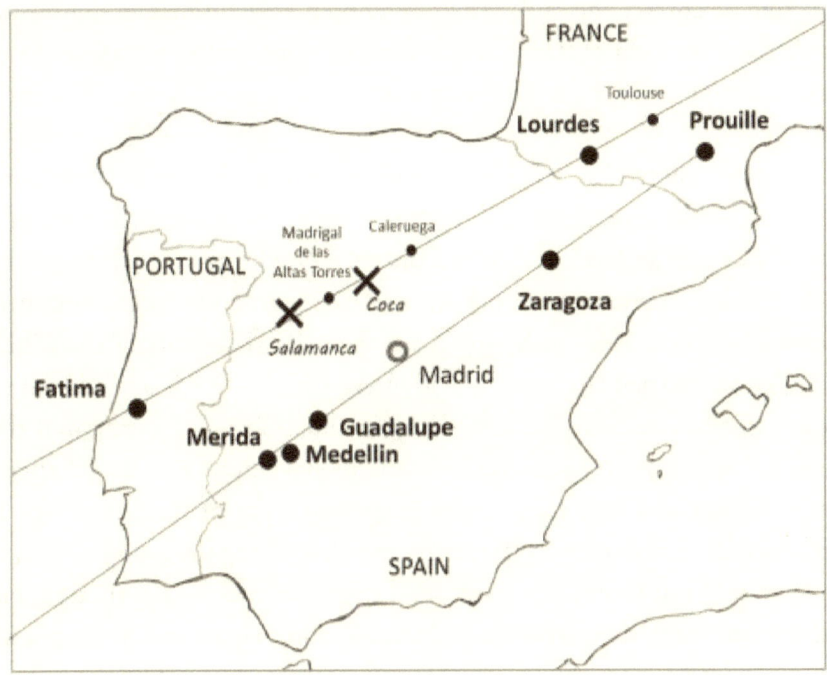

Sofia examined them unsure how they—or the lines—could possibly tie in with Washington's or Charles III's motives and choices.

The lines were amazing in many ways. She did not deny that. Afterall, she had helped her sister uncover them and knew better than anyone of the remarkable *coincidences* that went into building them; not to mention the astonishing picture they drew in the end. But, at the same time, she was all too aware that one could draw a random straight line anywhere in the world and find historical commonalities between neighboring locations to create the illusion that the line had a purpose. So, true to herself, Sofia was still working on rationalizing her own "miraculous" lines. For this reason, when Antonio showed interest in them during their flight over, she thought it was because they were the target of her current work. It would appear, however, that the lines themselves were the focus of his interest, which raised the inevitable question: why? What in the world did he see in the lines that made him think they were linked in any way to the secret pact?

He began to explain as she listened intrigued.

"You are correct," he said. "The sites chosen were intimately significant for the men who chose them. You've had the opportunity to take a closer look at Washington. Now I'd like you to get to know Charles III a little better."

Antonio invited her to sit back down as he took his chair. "Both men were much alike on a personal level," he started. "Both were children of a second marriage and would inherit from their childless older half-brothers. Both were loyal family men. Both were relatively grounded regarding their personal interests. And both would see their life change in 1759. While Washington married the wealthy widow Martha D. Curtis and moved to Mount Vernon, becoming a respected socialite, Charles III inherited the Crown of Spain, a three-hundred-year-old global empire that had changed the world but was starting to show dangerous signs of slowing down. It foreboded decline and her contenders circled, smelling the blood.

"It would not intimidate a seasoned ruler like Charles III, though. He had reigned quite successfully as Charles VII in Naples and Sicily for 25 years, standing out as a European leader in the progressive Enlightenment movement. To give you an idea, and leaving aside his effective administration, under his sponsorship, the archeological sites of Pompeii and Herculaneum were excavated, giving rise to the neoclassical movement that swept Europe and America, inspiring, for instance, the design of Washington D.C. and its buildings. Further, his patronage of the arts ushered in the golden age of Naples, securing her key position on the Grand Tour of Europe, an educational rite of passage for upper-class men.

"With this experience under his belt, Charles III set out to do the same with Spain, keeping a laser-focus on protecting her territorial integrity. He encouraged national reforms, from governmental restructuring to public and welfare modernization, but particularly undertook an important reorganization of his overseas territories to improve the efficiency of their administration and military defense. All that said," emphasized Antonio, "what matters for the purpose of our search is that Charles III, who was born and raised in Spain, never lost sight of his fundamental duty toward the Crown's Roman-Catholic legacy, which is greatly misunderstood."

Sofia shook her head. "No, I think I get it. Seven hundred years under Roman rule followed by a thousand years of religious wars leaves a mark. He was wise not to neglect it. It would have alienated him from his subjects."

"And there is the misunderstanding," he gently pointed out. "First, it's not that we were ruled by the Romans. After seven centuries, you become Roman. Hispania was the first territory outside of Italy incorporated to the Roman Republic and stayed Roman until the collapse of the Empire. It shows in our languages, laws, religion, culture, and chiefly, in the notable rulers and sages we gave the Empire. But beyond this, what few people know is that the Spanish Crown itself carries the legal title to the Roman Empire, and with it, the mandate to protect the Catholic Faith."

"Woah, time out," said Sofia, gesturing with her hands as if a referee, "*Legal* heirs to the Roman Empire? A *mandate* to protect the Catholic Faith?"

Antonio seemed amused by her skepticism. "I realize I am talking about bizarre foreign notions from bygone years, but please bear with me. Remember, we are trying to understand a man who unexpectedly inherited an empire in dire straits, while at the same time recipient of a legacy that he was bound to uphold and protect. Understanding that legacy is key to understanding and finding the pact."

Antonio's hand drifted across the map to rest on the two cross marks he had added. "Let me explain," he continued, "It goes back to the year 380 A.D. when Theodosius I ruled the Roman Empire. The empire was besieged by the Goths and a wide range of internal divisions. In order to unite against the Goths, he resorted to a very common tactic: he galvanized his population around one religion in opposition to the religion of the enemy. In this case, the two sides in conflict were both Christian with one defining difference, the belief or not in the Trinity. Theodosius favored the predominant version in Rome, which believed in the Trinity, contrary to the Goths who didn't. He then decreed that the followers of the Trinity were to adopt the title Catholic, meaning *universal,* and declared

Catholicism the official religion of the Empire." Antonio tapped the map with his finger. "Remember his name. It's important."

Sofia shot a quick glance at the map, confused but expectant. "Okay, so Theodosius defined Catholicism as the universal faith and declared it the official religion of the state. I imagine that means the state was thereafter obliged to protect it, thus the mandate."

"To be more accurate, as head of the empire, the emperor was also head of the Church, linking the mandate to the imperial title. Back then, the pope reported to him. In sum, as of Theodosius, the imperial crown and the protection of the Catholic Faith went hand in hand, and consequently the bearers fashioned themselves universal rulers."

"Right, but their *universal* empire split. So, what happened to the mandate and how did Spain end up with it?"

Antonio grinned. "It gets tricky."

"No kidding."

"The western half of the Roman Empire collapsed in the 5th century, overtaken by the Goths, while the eastern half survived another thousand years until overtaken by the Ottomans. Today, we refer to the eastern half as the Byzantine Empire because its capital was Byzantine, no longer Rome. They, however, saw themselves as the natural continuation of the Roman Empire and referred to themselves as such; a situation the pope—based in Rome—was not particularly happy about. So, when the 8th century saw the rise of the Frank Charlemagne in the west, who was a friendly figure to Rome, the pope saw the opportunity to detach himself from Byzantine and revive the western half by crowning Charlemagne the rightful Roman Emperor. A little later, when it passed to German hands, it became the Holy Roman Empire"

"Let me get this straight," said Sofia. "As of the 8th century, two different empires competed for the same Roman imperial title and mandate: the original surviving eastern half and the newly revived western half."

"Yes, and a love-hate relationship between the two followed until the Byzantine Empire finally fell to the Ottoman Empire in 1453, leaving only the Holy Roman Empire standing." Antonio armored his lopsided grin.

"Which you'd think would resolve the imperial title conflict, except the eastern title lived on through its latest heir, Andreas Palaiologos, who, ironically, lived in exile in Rome."

Sofia laughed. "I'm sorry, you have to admit it's crazy."

"I do, and it gets even crazier, because Andreas lived in Rome supported by exiled Byzantines who wanted to restore his empire in addition to a small pension from the pope."

"Meaning, that deep down, the pope must have felt Andreas' imperial title was the real-deal or, at the minimum, worth something."

"Indeed, it was worth something, more than you think. I'll get to that in a moment. For now, know that Andreas spent his life travelling Europe attempting to rally help to restore his empire, offering his title to the highest bidder as enticement. Unfortunately for him, the few attempts carried out to help him failed, so Andreas died unsuccessful in 1502, with no descendants. He was buried in St. Peter's Basilica, in the Vatican ..." Antonio left the last sentence hanging as an invitation for Sofia to finish it.

"... confirming, once again, the title's worth, since only rulers of the Church are buried there." Sofia furrowed. "How does Spain come into play, again?"

"Because, as a final act of hope for his lost empire, Andreas left the imperial title in his testament to the Spanish monarchs Queen Isabella and King Ferdinand, and their descendants, that is, the united Spanish Crown."

Sofia was stunned by the twist. "You can do that?"

"You can under Roman Law."

"But why them? It's almost counterintuitive. Even if Spain once was an integral part of the Roman Empire, these monarchs ruled in the far west, a long way from Rome, not to mention Byzantine."

"There were several good reasons. Bear in mind that the Spanish monarchs had recently triumphed against Islam on the Iberian Peninsula completing the Christian Reconquista, while in the East the Crusaders had failed. At the same time, they were also battling the Ottomans successfully in the Mediterranean because of Ferdinand's holdings in Italy. That's why they were awarded the honorific title 'Catholics'. It's not a nickname because they were very religious. It's a veritable recognition from the pope exclusively transmitted through the Spanish Crown for successfully protecting Christian Europe. Added to that, King Ferdinand also happened to hold the title King of Jerusalem and Isabella's queenship had just extended to a whole new world. For Andreas, the Catholic Monarchs seem the reasonable choice to assume the guardianship of the Universal Christian Faith."

"Wait, does the king of Spain, today, still have all these titles?"

"Yes, along with a long string of thirty others, including King of the Islands and Continental Lands of the Ocean Sea, meaning, the Americas. Few of them sustain practical value anymore, but symbolically and historically speaking they are noteworthy."

This gave Sofia pause. She remembered that the statue of Queen Isabella in the Heart of Washington D.C read on her pedestal: *Isabella I the Catholic, Queen of Castille, of Aragon, of the Islands and Continental Lands of the Ocean Sea.* Meaning that she stood in front of the Organization of the American States acknowledged as the Queen of the Americas.

Antonio continued. "Now, in addition to theological considerations, there was also a powerful political reason that may have been definitive: Isabella and Ferdinand had married their daughter, the heir to the Spanish Crown, to the potential heir of the Holy Roman Empire, explaining why Andreas specifically mentioned their descendants in his will."

"What do you mean by potential heir?"

"The Holy Roman title was elective, not hereditary. Despite this, it had a way of staying within the same family; there was little risk in betting who'd be next."

Sofia was truly impressed. "So, by giving Isabella and Ferdinand his imperial title, Andreas aimed at recreating the unified Roman Empire through their grandson.

"Charles V, the Holy Roman Emperor," confirmed Antonio.

"Why is he only known by his western title, then?"

"Because he didn't formerly inherit from his mother until much later in life. But he exercised from early on as her co-regent. Consequently, in practice, he concentrated enormous theological and political control over half of Europe and large portions of the Americas, which became a massive problem. Not everyone was happy under the broad rule so, once more, those wanting to break away politically galvanized their population around religion. Several German princes backed Luther's Protestant movement, adopting it for their state religion, and Henry VIII soon followed with Anglicanism. In the end, instead of a reunited empire, another sad period of Christians pitted against Christians for political interests ensued, leading Charles V to make a tough decision: He split his empire up again. He abdicated his Spanish Crown in favor of his son and handed the Holy Roman title to his brother. Then he retired to a monastery in Spain."

Sofia nodded softly. "Alright, I see how Charles III inherited the Roman imperial title and its attached mandate, but how does any of this help me understand the king better with regards to his pact with Washington?" asked Sofia.

"In truth, it helps understand both, Charles and Washington. You see, there is a whole other side to this story that goes to the heart of the imperial title's true worth." Antonio shifted a little in his chair. "To be clear, Charles III's core concern was the integrity of his aging empire and Washington's was securing a solid foothold for his emerging one. So faced with common foes, and strictly from a political viewpoint, it made sense for them to team up. At the same time, there was a long-standing belief in Europe that the Rule of an Empire—in the sense of its strength and prosperity—was transferred in a lineal progression westward by Providence. It's known as *translatio imperii.*"

"You're losing me," said Sofia. "Are you saying they believed there was some kind of magical Rule passed along like a baton from one empire to the next under the eagle eye of Providence?"

"As strange as it may sound, yes. And I would add *literally* yes, if by eagle you mean the Roman eagle."

"But how, why?"

"For legitimacy purposes. It goes back to the poet Virgil in the 1st century B.C. In trying to justify Augustus becoming an emperor, he asserted that the Roman Republic was simply receiving the preordained Imperial Rule as it progressed from Mesopotamia to Athens to Rome. In the Middle Ages, this idea was resurrected to justify Charlemagne's legitimacy to the Roman title, since he and his empire were west of Rome, contrary to Byzantine. And later, to strengthen its 'Holy' aspect, it was attached to one of Daniel's Biblical prophecies; one that referenced a succession of empires, according to which the heir to the Roman Rule would be in office at the time of the Messiah's return." Antonio paused. "In short, it became a question of political empowerment and religious fate to be associated with the Roman Imperial title, a sentiment that was very much alive and well in the 18th century. In fact, as recently as the 19th century, Napoleon was still after it. That's why he adopted the Roman Royal Eagle for his emblem. But to prevent him from getting his hands on it, Francis II, the Holy Roman Emperor at the time, had the empire and its title dissolved. Napolean then turned his attention to the Spanish Crown."

Sofia sat back in her chair. She needed a moment to digest it all. Slowly, the pieces came together. Daniel's prophecy, the Eye of Providence, the Rotunda and the naming of the *Capitol,* the obsession with Queen Isabella, her emblems ... and all the ceremony. It made sense now. The Founding Fathers saw the United States as the preordained rising empire next in line to receive the Rule as it progressed west through Isabella's queenship of the Americas. And Washington—the Freemason—sought to harness its blessings. She looked at Antonio. "Is that what the secret pact was all about? Creating a New Order that shared in the benefits of the Imperial Rule?"

Antonio's facial expression tightened. "Only in part, because Providence does not grant the benefits without conditions. When these are neglected, the Rule moves on. Queen Isabella grasped this. What she did to fulfill those conditions was her legacy and the true backbone of the pact."

His intensity surprised Sofia. "You talk of the Rule as if it were real. You don't seriously believe it is, do you?"

"You tell me. Remember Theodosius I?"

"Yes," she said, tentatively, "he was the Roman emperor who defined the universal Christian faith and attached it to the imperial title."

Antonio drew her attention to the map.

She saw he was pointing to the cross that was labelled *Coca.*

"Theodosius was also the last emperor to rule over the unified Roman Empire. He was born here in this little town in Spain. It sits on Mary's Line just before the town of Madrigal de las Altas Torres where Queen Isabella was born. Almost as if a visual representation of the lineal transfer of the Imperial Rule straight from him to her."

Sofia stared at the map, incredulous. "That is a hell of a visual coincidence."

"It's not the only one."

CHAPTER 32

"Treat said Indians very well and lovingly, and abstain from doing them any injury, arranging that both peoples should hold much conversation and intimacy, each serving the other to the best of their abilities."

—*Queen Isabella's orders to Columbus, 1493*

The lines that kept on giving ...

Finally, Sofia knew the precise reason she was there. But it bothered her. She got up and went to the kitchenette for water. "Michael told me you are associated with ... well, just that, an association that is ... something like the human hand behind Providence. So please don't mess with me. You probably know more about those lines than I do."

"I know a lot about how events have aligned through the ages to get us where we are. What I don't know is how or why they are literally reflected on lines."

Sofia had started to lean down to open the mini fridge door. She stopped and turned to look at him. "You're not behind them?"

"Not the lines. And I'd like to know who is."

"If that's the case, why bring me along for the ride? Lily is the Catholic historian. She is better suited to help you."

"In the big scheme of things, this has nothing to do with any one religion. I need a clear head."

"Why not just tell me from the start?"

"Because, as you can see, it's complicated and you only know half of it. Look, we have two things going on here. One is the Knights and the fundamental danger they pose as they attempt to eliminate or corrupt the truth about the pact. The other is how two crucial elements of that secret pact are reflected on your line. So, while Michael and I collaborate to tackle the first, I have a personal interest in trying to understand the second." Antonio lingered his gaze on Sofia. "I have been watching you for some time. I knew I had to pique your curiosity if I was to convince you to help me."

Convince, she repeated to herself. The common denominator for everyone that sought her out. Sofia turned back to the mini fridge, grabbed a bottle, and waved it at him to ask if he wanted one. He shook his head. She closed the door, straightened up and removed the cap. Then she took slow sips, buying time to think. Since the published essay, her reputation for seeking the truth had further strengthened thanks to her persistence in questioning her own work. So, anyone claiming a miracle aimed to convince her as a measure of validation. The problem was that most of the arguments employed to see divinity in the unexplained, with the best of intentions, boiled down to the usual rational short-cuts: confirmation bias, cherry-picking, and a long etcetera of mental tricks that did not stand up to serious scrutiny. For her, they missed the mark. The breathtaking dance of a flock of starlings at sunset or the sunset itself were examples of true miracles, for they survived the scrutiny of science. For Sofia, divinity wasn't in the unexplained, it was in what inspired awe despite their reasonable explanation.

She examined Antonio. He sat there patiently waiting with his legs crossed and his hands clasped, resting on his lap. Talk about enigmas that required explaining. He was clearly an intelligent man, proficient in research, who had proven impressively resourceful and capable. He had to know better, so how could he fall for the spell of the lines?

She asked him. "Why is this personal to you?"

"The pact was the result of a promise made long before, and I'm the latest in a long list of men and women chosen to see that promise through. So, I have a responsibility to understand why it is linked to your line. That's all I can say for now."

"You're asking for my help. I'm going to need more than that."

"In due time."

"Can you tell me at least your opinion about the nature of the lines?"

He responded with a subtle shrug. "I really don't know what to make of them." He motioned at the map. "When I tell you about that second cross, you'll see that its placement on the line can hardly be explained by chance ... or a human hand." He drew a slow smile. "And I can't think of anyone better suited than the gifted rational mind behind the line's discovery to help me figure it out."

Of course, his answer was masterfully vague, while doused with just the right amount of charm and flattery. His ability to keep her curiosity hooked was uncanny. "Okay," she said and returned to her seat, "if you are going to put it that way. What else do you have?"

Antonio uncrossed his legs and leaned forward to place his forearms on the table. He became so serious that Sofia's throat went dry again. She drank some water as she listened.

"Queen Isabella was a genuine believer. For her, the inheritance of the Imperial Rule in 1502 was more than just about power and prosperity, it was about honoring its mandate. Therefore, it was very present on her mind two years later, on the 12th of October of 1504, when she wrote her final testament."

Sofia picked up on the date. "She wrote it on the anniversary of the discovery of America. I imagine that wasn't coincidental."

"Not at all." Antonio's gaze softened. "Isabella was very sick, probably with cancer, and tormented by two unresolved issues. She made them the crux of her will. One was the power struggle she foresaw following her death. Her daughter Joanna, the heir, did not display the desirable grit to take hold of the reins, and Isabella worried that her son-in-law would take control; a man she doubted had the best interest of her realm or subjects at heart. Consequently, she declared her daughter universal heir, while including a provision stating that, should she be unable or unwilling to rule, King Ferdinand was to take charge as regent until their grandson came of age. It's important to understand that Isabella and Ferdinand were independent ruling monarchs. Neither one had any real power over the kingdom of their spouse, meaning that Isabella was the sole true ruling queen of the Americas. Anyway, as she suspected, when she passed away, her son-in-law grabbed the reigns, but in an interesting twist of fate, died less than two years later. And, per her will, King Ferdinand became regent until their grandson Charles took charge."

Antonio paused to emphasize. "What few people realize is that her daughter Joanna lived well into her seventies retaining all her rights, so Isabella's grandson, Charles V, only exercised as co-regent of Castille and Leon and the American territories for most of his life. This is extremely important, because the fact that Joanna was the rightful queen in the eyes of the law, but unable or unwilling to rule, meant that Queen Isabella's testament remained in force during her daughter's life, ensuring that Ferdinand and Charles were both bound by its terms."

"Brilliant," acknowledged Sofia.

"Vitally so," said Antonio, piercing Sofia with his eyes, "because keeping her testament active was central to dealing with her other concern: The treatment of her native subjects in America. Isabella was displeased with Columbus' behavior and had issued ordinances declaring the natives of the new lands equal subjects to her European ones hoping they'd be respected as such, but the bad news about their treatment kept coming."

The conversation took on a personal taint for Sofia. "When we researched those lines," she said, pointing to them on the map, "my sister told me how Isabella had given Columbus express orders to establish a relationship of mutual respect with the natives and to refrain from harming them. When he disobeyed, she had him arrested and brought back in chains. However, the fact remains that much harm still followed."

"Yes, it did, as with every other expansion in history. But the one thing Spain did that no one else did—thanks to Queen Isabella—was to prohibit the abuse of the conquered by law, because in her mind they weren't being conquered, they were being saved."

Sofia understood. "She believed it was her sacred duty to protect and spread the Christian Faith."

Antonio nodded. "The testament of a monarch was law, and in her testament, she asked her descendants to ensure that her American subjects were justly treated in the spirit of her apostolic mandate, establishing guidelines to that effect. Since it remained active, it couldn't be ignored. Her wish resulted in a body of laws that were unprecedented in history and trailblazing even by today's standards. Unfortunately, it coincided with the Protestant breakaway. So, what is truly sad, is that rather than being celebrated and adopted by the other Christian conquering powers as well, the laws were instead used against Catholic Spain in malicious political propaganda: Since only Spain had laws criminalizing such abuse, only in Spain such abuse was acknowledged, decried and prosecuted, with the result that the legal cases were grossly exaggerated and exploited to make Catholic Spain the poster child of brutal conquest."

Sofia crossed her arms. "Now you are going to tell me these amazing laws were linked to the lines."

Antonio smiled. "That's right, but not only the lines. They are also connected to the US Declaration of Independence in a very fundamental way, bringing it all together."

* * *

Aaron flinched as he ended the conversation. He handed his cellphone back to his house assistant, waved him away, and returned to the meeting.

The nine stern faces sitting around the oval conference table turned to watch him enter the room and approach his seat at the head. They were all family members to one degree or another. No outsiders, staff, or devices were allowed in the room.

His grandson, who sat to his left, got up to help Aaron with the chair, took custody of his cane, and sat back down.

"Still looking," he announced tersely once accommodated.

"We should go public with what we have," settled his brother from across the table. He forcefully tapped the two sheets of paper in front of him as if wanting to stab them. "This alliance was a betrayal of everything the Revolution stood for. It's even worse than we thought. Washington committed treason and it is time we make things right."

A wave of *ayes* was heard around the room.

Aaron stood firm. "I don't want them public. I agree we should reveal the pact's existence. It's to our advantage. But we'll do it carefully scripted in a manifesto. It keeps us in control."

His son, sitting to his right, objected. "There's no need to control anything. The image talks for itself. If we play our cards right, it could boost my candidacy and consolidate my election. But it must be done now. We can't keep stalling."

Aaron was torn. His default inclination was resistance to change. Like his ancestors, he feared that, however abominable the image, truth had a pesky way of backfiring, so it was best to erase it from existence and craft a convenient story. On the other hand, times had changed despite personal inclinations, and with the resources currently at their disposal, if used correctly, the dreadful image could help more than harm.

He swept the room with his eyes. The eagerness to act that he saw in the younger generations was invigorating. It reminded him of his own angry youth and thirst for action, as it did of the short time he had left to see the fight through to its completion.

"I agree," he half-surrendered. "The moment is propitious for your candidacy. We'll share the image. But I insist we hold off just a little longer. The conclusions of our analyst prove I was correct about the meteor," he said. "We are closer than ever to getting our hands on the other half. It's an auspicious sign. Let's give it a chance."

His son rolled his eyes. "Who cares about the other half. We have what we need. And quite frankly, I'm tired of that meteor nonsense. This is the real world, father. It's time to act."

Aaron shot a commanding look at him. "I will not tolerate anyone questioning my beliefs or methods, least of them you. Everything you have or have ever accomplished is thanks to me and my name. Don't you ever forget that. And it will do you good to also remember that without a well-fed army, hot and ready to rise, you are nothing."

"In that case, I suggest we don't hold them back. We've been cautious long enough. Let them rise."

His son had not backed down. He rarely did, anymore.

Aaron weaved his fingers together, resting his hands on the table, and took a deep breath. He was losing his grip, and maybe even conviction. He realized that the long-awaited moment had arrived, yet when faced with it, the oddest thing was happening: an uncomfortable sense of apprehension crippled his resolve. Or was it guilt? Either way, in his world, a weakness.

He warded it off and gave the order. "Start phase one."

CHAPTER 33

"Per the pope's concession of the islands and continental lands of the ocean sea discovered and yet to be discovered, it was my intension to procure, persuade and attract its peoples to the Catholic faith [...] Furthermore, I affectionately beg [my heirs] that you diligently see to it and not consent that their inhabitants receive harm in their persons or belongings, rather the contrary, that they are justly treated in the spirit of these apostolic concessions."

—*Queen Isabella's testament, 1504*

Antonio's gaze was focused. "Here's how it went down," he started. "Leaving aside the obvious geopolitical and economic reasons to settle the Americas, in Isabella's mind, the overarching justification was evangelization, which required, according to Christian core tenets, respect for the evangelized. And the wording she employed in her testament to express it was momentous. She specifically establishes *justice* as the governing spirit of her realms' expansion." Antonio, once again, radiated intensity as if what he shared was personal. "Its importance cannot be emphasized enough, because her testament empowered Spanish missionaries to denounce the maltreatment of natives. When their complaints reached Spain, her husband King Ferdinand, who was acting as regent per the terms of her will, commissioned a group of theologians and jurists to create a legal framework for the *just treatment of the Indigenous People*. This group, composed of Dominican scholars, met in Burgos in 1512 where they debated the human nature of American natives and the rights that derived from it. The result was a legal body of 35 laws, known as the Laws of Burgos, which literally set the basis for universal human rights."

Sofia blinked. Several items were clashing in her mind. One was the mention of Burgos, which she recognized as one of John Adams stops. Another was the mention of Dominican scholars, who were also connected to Mary's Line through the birthplace of their founder, St. Dominque, in Caleruega. But third, and more consuming momentarily, was personal. "Universal human rights? That's a serious claim for a code of laws that I, an interested party, have never heard of."

228

"It's quite unfortunate you haven't," said Antonio with a teasing grin, "because these laws recognized you as fully human, congratulations."

"Well, thank you. How nice of them to notice."

Antonio chuckled. "Seriously, think about it. It's thanks to the humanity recognized in you, the Native Americans, that today the rest of us enjoy Human Rights."

Put that way, it gave her pause. Why, indeed, had she not heard of these laws?

"What's more," continued Antonio, "the rights acknowledged were in some instances more than most Spaniards got. Though required to serve the crown for two years and attend religious education, natives were recognized as free people entitled to private property, and as such, no force or abuse could be employed to make them serve. After that time, they were free to go if they wished."

Sofia was about to complain.

Antonio interrupted. "I know, they were required to serve two years. I never said the laws were perfect, only an honorable first attempt. Please remember, they were adopted over 500 years ago, idleness was considered a vice, and it wasn't personal, natives were considered equal subjects with the same obligations, as much as rights, as any other Spaniard. We were all expected to work hard and pay taxes." He then quickly added. "That said, the temptation to abuse was certainly there, so the laws also prohibited segregation and called for humane living conditions, fair pay, and labor rights such as limited daily shifts and vacation time off. They protected pregnant women from heavy labor and the right to nurse their child for three years away from the mines. Children under fourteen were prohibited from working in the mines or performing any other adult task."

Sofia raised her eyebrows. "I guess that's not half bad for 500-year-old laws," and graciously added, "especially considering not even most natives were sensitive to such matters. How serious were these laws taken?"

"They faced the expected challenges and opposition by the usual unscrupulous souls, and several amendments followed to deal with it. But to answer your question, in general, they were taken very seriously. Every effort was made to implement them with the means available at the time." Antonio paused. "But it was only the beginning. Out of Burgos, rose

Francisco de Vitoria who took the theological and judicial discussions to the nearby University of Salamanca, where he began a revolutionary intellectual movement known as the *School of Salamanca*. At one point, this group of jurists had Charles V pause the settlement of America to debate his legitimacy to do it."

"Are you serious? They questioned the emperor's 'universal' power to his face?"

"Not universal enough yet. He was still only a regent ruler in half of Spain, and in honor of his grandmother, Queen Isabella, he really had no option but to welcome it. I'm telling you, her will was taken very seriously. The result was an updated body of laws appropriately named 'The New Laws of 1545'. Though chiefly focused on the Americas, they seeped through how he, the emperor, ruled over the rest of his empire, challenging from an ethical standpoint his whole range of powers: religious, political, and economic. As a result, they gave rise to International Law in the name of natural law, inalienable rights, freedom of thought, and human dignity." Antonio narrowed his gaze on Sofia. "Some of their acclaimed premises may sound familiar to you. For instance: the right of the people to rebel against tyranny, no taxation without representation, or ... that all men are created equal with the right to life and liberty."

Antonio let that sink in, then continued. "Many of the Founding Fathers were familiar with this school of thought through John Locke and quite a few owned a book of one of the group's most prominent exponents, Juan de Mariana. Thomas Jefferson was one of them."

Sofia was stunned. "So that was her legacy. Queen Isabella's request for the just treatment of her subjects in America led to Human Rights, International Law, and perhaps one of the most consequential sentences in history."

"Yes, and Charles III was bound to uphold and protect that legacy," confirmed Antonio. "There can be no doubt it was on his mind. In 1785, he founded the General Archives of the Indies in Seville to collect the 80 million pages of documents and eight thousand maps and drawings that bore witness to Spain's administration and scientific endeavors over the preceding three hundred years, as guided by the spirit of these laws. Today, anyone in the world can consult the archive online."

"1785 was the same year Gardoqui and Casanave arrived in the US," recalled Sofia. She leaned back in awe. "In order for the New Order to share in the Rule, that legacy had to be adopted from pole to pole ...."

Antonio smiled satisfied like the master who sees his student is ready. He gestured toward the map. "Look at the second cross mark."

Sofia slowly leaned forward to see.

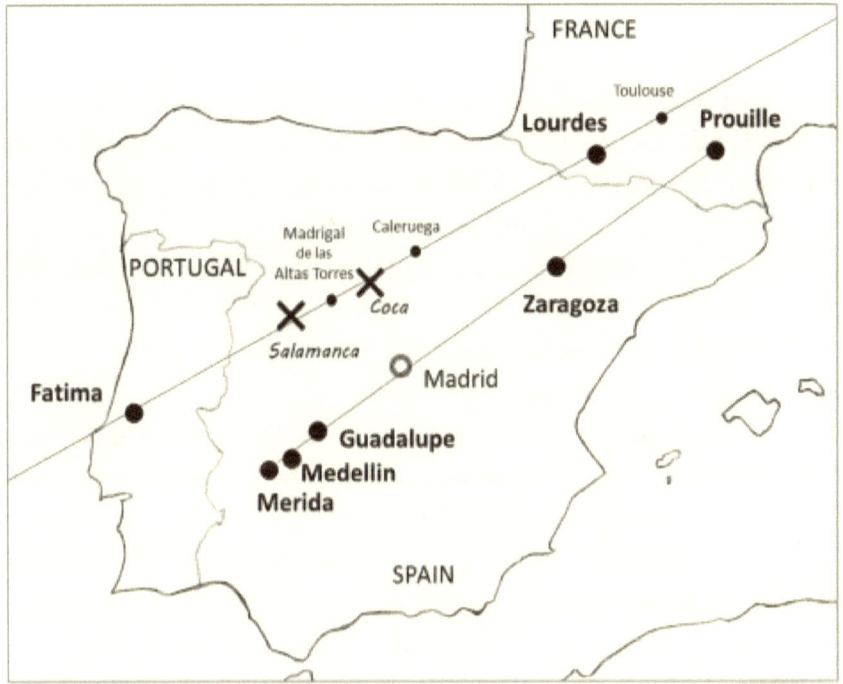

She released a soft gasp. *Salamanca* .... How was that possible? It was almost creepy. Four consequential birthplaces in a row: *Caleruega*, the birthplace of St. Dominic, whose order developed the basis for Human Rights upon its foundational concept of justice. *Coca*, the birthplace of Theodosios I who linked the Universal Christian faith to the Roman Imperial Rule. *Madrigal de las Alta Torres*, birthplace of Queen Isabella, who'd inherit that Rule over a thousand years later, grasping the true spirit of its mandate. And *Salamanca*, the birthplace of International Law founded on the understanding that *all men are created equal with the right to life and liberty.*

CHAPTER 34

"We the People of the United States, in Order to form a more perfect Union, establish Justice, insure domestic Tranquility, provide for the common defence, promote the general Welfare, and secure the Blessings of Liberty to ourselves and our Posterity, do ordain and establish this Constitution for the United States of America."

—*The Preamble of the Constitution of the United States of America*

The man in the dark suit handed the money to the kid with the skateboard. It was a handsome pay for a minor task. All he was required to do was spray-paint the word "ENSLAVER" in red with a blood-dripping effect on the statue of George Washington located on the steps of Federal Hall in New York; the spot where he took the oath of office as first President of the United States.

If the kid was smart, he'd cover his face, do his job discreetly before dawn, and quickly disappear as instructed.

As for the vandalism, it was harmless. It could be easily scrubbed clean, so the authorities, overburdened by the city's more pressing crimes, would dismiss it as a minor mischief. Many more would follow, too small to warrant a crackdown but persistent enough to get a convenient conversation going.

For the Knights, it was the first step in crushing national pride.

It was as easy as psychology 101: One's identity, self-worth or sense of security was intimately attached to one's tribe, be that one's political affiliation, religion, race, country, or alma mater football team. Basically, any social construct that satisfied one's sense of belonging. And social architects, politicians, and marketers were masters at exploiting it, as was any devious mass manipulator.

Washington was the national ideal of a patriot. The brave general in war; the consensus builder of the Constitution; the levelled-party-neutral president, the man of integrity who stepped down from power when it was time. Soiling his image would crush the little piece of him everyone wished to see in themselves, leading to a sense of vulnerability and anger. And these two states of mind were dangerously ripe for manipulation.

232

How to do it?

War Strategy 101: By dehumanizing the enemy so that any action taken against them, however morally questionable, was fair game when not applauded. In this case, the enemy was an untouchable hero, so it was first necessary to make him touchable. Thus, the need to soil his image. The idea was to bring Washington's lesser heroic attributes to the forefront to get a conversation going. It wasn't a new one for sure, but it had always been a moderate one. Washington's evolution from slave owner to understanding the institution wrong to becoming the only Founding Father to free his slaves, had made it possible to forgive the imperfect man, praise his growth, and admire the hero for his accomplishments. The Knight's goal, therefore, was to restart the conversation, only this time radicalize it by strategically flooding social media with outrageous commentary that incensed emotions to the extreme, blurring reality until the idealized hero was no more, and only a monster remained.

That's when Candidate Jackson, supported by his army of patriotic Knights, would swiftly step in to nail the coffin. He'd present himself as the new unifier around what "true" national pride should look like; the first steppingstone on the path to eroding George Washington's legacy, the Constitution.

* * *

Lily rubbed her eyes. She felt tired and cranky.

Despite sleeping as well as could be expected on an overnight flight, the drain from the past few days had caught up, and the lack of traction in her research had her flustered. During the waking hours of the trip, she had invested precious time without success looking into why Judith would be next to Queen Isabella on the facade of Saint Mark's. She had no doubt they were there for her, trying to tell her something, but if not to indicate that the convent guarded the lost fair copy of the Declaration, then what?

She had started by taking another look at Adams' diary to contrast it with his autobiography, hoping hindsight might offer up a slip. As it turned out, it did. John Adam's autobiography, in general, was a cleaned-up version of his diary with few changes, save one interesting exception: Leon.

Why would Adams feel the need to be extra thorough with that entry 25 years later? It beckoned a closer look with the inevitable result that every observation for January 6th became a suspicious hint, starting with the first sentence that mentioned the city the night before.

The phrase was simple enough:

"Leon, which We entered in the Night, has the Appearance of a large ~~River~~ *City."*

Alas, it contained an odd error. Who mistakes a *city* for a *river*? Was he that tired or was it code for something? Lily consulted a map and found that travelling from Astorga to Leon, Adams indeed crossed a river to enter the city, and its medieval bridge led smack into the Convent of Saint Mark. It was the first thing he would have seen and there was no missing it. The building was huge. Its facade was 328 feet wide, literally wider than the river; an awesome sight with its towers, porticos, medallions, and other architectural details lit up by flickering oil lampposts. Yet, Adams didn't mention it until the next day, inserting a casual comment out of sequence and merely referring to it as a school:

"There is a School of Saint Mark here as it is called, an Institution for the Education of the noble Youths here in Mathematicks and Philosophy."

Lily confirmed that at the time the building housed an institution of higher learning, but Adams might as well have referred to a little schoolhouse on the prairie. Playing her sister, Lily deduced that he was probably downplaying the structure for diversion purposes, and the word-jumble in the first sentence was a subconscious slip betraying his intention to do it. Most telling of all, Adams had used the adverb "here" twice in reference to the convent. This tickled her with excitement, because could it be any more obvious? He was blatantly indicating: *"here* is where I dropped it off".

Meteor validated.

If only she had stopped there.

Excitement quickly wore off as she moved through the rest of the entry. She had read it several times before, but now that she scrutinized it for clues, it was amazing how many odd details popped out that had gone unnoticed.

Case in point: Adams had attended the mass of the Epiphany at the cathedral boasting proudly how he had refused to kneel to the bishop. In his autobiography, he came back to express his misunderstanding and regret. Then he casually stated that he had been "conducted" to the bishop's council chamber. While Adams goes on to describe the chamber, Lily wondered: why would he be escorted there? Had he held a private meeting with the bishop? If so, again, why? Adams was in Spain by accident trying to get to Paris as fast as possible. How was it that he was treated with such courtesy on an unplanned trip across a foreign country?

Lily looked up the bishop. Several historical sources remembered Bishop Cuadrillero Mota as an enlightened man, assigned to the post two years earlier by Charles III. In line with the king's religious reformation project, the bishop had renovated seminary studies to improve professionalism and curtail corruption. He was also commended for widely improving social services for orphans, the elderly, and the destitute. For all appearances, he was a good man and must have been trusted by the king, which made the cathedral look more promising as the drop off site.

Again, if she had left it there.

After leaving Leon, and describing his visit to the next town, Adams cramped a list of religious buildings from Leon to the inside of his diary's back cover. Aside from its strange placement, what caught Lily's attention was that it was eliminated from the autobiography. If the list was important enough to be added after leaving Leon, why dismiss it later? But stranger yet, it consisted of an awkward sequence of sentences with strange blank spaces that made no sense. What was that about?

By this point, Lily realized she was in over her head. Discouraged, she decided to leave the psychological analytics to the expert—her sister—and sit back to wait for a sign from heaven. Decoding these seemed to come easier to her.

She sighed and looked out the car window. It wasn't just the lack of progress that had her down. Michael, Gabriel, and she had landed in Madrid and were on their way to an undisclosed location downtown. Michael wanted to check-in with someone about something before heading north and Lily had given up on asking him who about what. His opaque front was starting to really bother her. They were friends. If his withdrawn attitude had to do with a personal rivalry with Antonio over Sofia, he should know to confide in her. If it had to do with the current mission, considering how involved she was, he owed her more than silence.

Lily slid a narrow look at him through the corner of her eye. She was sitting behind Gabriel, who was at the wheel of the rental car they picked up at the airport. Through her diagonal view of Michael, she noticed that his air of vulnerability had vanished. He appeared back to his usual self: focused and in control.

Good, she consoled herself. At least one thing seemed to be going the right way.

Lily turned back to the window. They were driving south along a street she could tell was in an upscale part of the city due to the concentration of luxury brand stores, alternating with museums and nice restaurants. According to a namesake hotel nearby, the district's name was Salamanca.

She recognized the name from the 12th century university. Colleagues of hers associated with it liked to brag in good spirits about how it was one of the oldest of its kind in the world.

A little ahead on the right, a building caught her attention for looking at odds with the rest of the more typical European architecture; a vertical rectangular prism enveloped in white limestone with the entire side covered in windows. It wasn't particularly graceful but apparently important in view of its weaponized soldiers standing guard in front. The seal by the entrance door explained why. It was the US Embassy.

Nice location, she thought, concluding that's where they were going.

Gabriel never slowed down and drove right by it.

Confused, Lily's eyes remained fixed on the building, turning her head back to see it disappear. If not the embassy, where?

Further ahead, just before the National Archaeological Museum, a large open recreational space opened to the right. Since the morning was cloudy and wet, it wasn't very crowded. Gabriel turned toward it and drove along its north side, which led to a roundabout embellished in its center with a statue of Christopher Columbus atop a Gothic revival pedestal. Gabriel circled it to the left, turning south into the right flank of a wide avenue, coming to a stop just before another sizeable roundabout.

"Pick me up in 30 minutes," said Michael releasing his seatbelt. He stepped out of the vehicle, without even a nod at Lily. She watched him approach a black iron fence. Beyond it was a lush green garden replete with tall trees that functioned as an effective green barrier. She could barely make out the contour of the reddish brick building in the background. Despite several large gates around the perimeter of the fence, Michael approached the least welcoming one, a small entrance tucked to the side. He opened it and walked in.

Lily pressed her lips annoyed. They were in the heart of downtown Madrid, meaning it could hardly be a secret what this place was. So, why wasn't she being told anything? Did she really have to look it up online herself? Lily had been asked to leave her cellphone and other personal devices behind but was provided with a secure laptop.

She was tempted to start it up, when a car honked behind them, impatient with their obstruction of the lane. Gabriel rolled slowly toward the roundabout, probably debating where to go. There were no parking spaces anywhere in sight and traffic was heavy. That's when she saw it. Just around the corner, the main gate to the gardens displayed large, gilded words that read in capital letters "CUARTEL GENERAL DEL EJERCITO".

Lily required a double take to understand, not because of the language, which she spoke to a decent degree, but because of what it meant.

It was the Spanish Army Headquarters.

She was baffled. What in the world did an American NSA agent have to discuss with Spanish Military? Lily's blood began to boil. That was it. Michael had some serious explaining to do.

On second thought, why wait. "Stop the car," she called out to Gabriel.

Gabriel wavered. "Is something wrong?"

"Please, stop. Now!"

That was easier said than done. They had just entered the sizable square and traffic was coming from every which way across half a dozen lanes. Gabriel saw that the bus stop area ahead offered an opening. He awkwardly gunned for it, while several cars honked at him disapprovingly.

As soon as he parked, Lily jumped out.

He followed. "What is it?"

She pointed across the traffic. "The army headquarters? What's going on, Gabriel? Are you really NSA?"

Gabriel's youthful features did what they always did when matters got serious. They gained an eerie maturity. "We're many things."

"For heaven's sake, spare me the riddle. Who are you?"

"We've never lied to you, Lily, but please understand, we've sworn an oath of secrecy."

"Really? You've never lied? With due respect, since I've known you and Michael, you've told me you are journalists, bodyguards, secret agents codenamed Mary's Angels, and now apparently, maybe even soldiers. What gives? Does your oath to that enigmatic association of yours include deceiving friends?"

"Please don't say that. We may not reveal the whole truth, but we don't lie to you, Lily." Gabriel showed genuine concern. "Look, I'm not a soldier, though I do exercise as a personal guardian when necessary. Michael, however, is one."

"Michael is military?" Lily was in disbelief. "What kind?"

"The highest-ranking kind."

"When I met him in Afghanistan, he said he was a journalist."

"Technically speaking, he was. He published for real."

"But it was a cover, meaning, he *technically* lied to me." Lily was fuming. "Then at my parents, when he revealed he was NSA, *technically*, that was another lie."

"Not exactly. Listen, I'm just the messenger. You need to discuss this with him."

"Sure, like that's worked for me." Lily released her anger wrapped in a painful sigh when she suddenly froze. She would have sworn Gabriel gave off an odd glow. She then realized his back was to the sun and a cloud had just moved out of the way, releasing its rays. That must have been it.

"Please don't be upset with Michael," he said. "He has good reasons for what he does. I promise you he truly appreciates your friendship." Gabriel then drew a soothing smile. "How about this? Since we are here, I suggest you take a look at your surroundings."

What? Why?

Lily slowly turned her head following the direction of the traffic counterclockwise. The ample roundabout sat at the junction of two main avenues and showcased the capital's imperial architecture at its prime under Charles III. From where she stood, the first building across from the army headquarters to the left was an elegant eclectic structure, decorated with columns, statues, medallions, and iron-laced massive doors. The Bank of Spain. Her eyes continued circling left across the treed boulevard that divided the grand avenue, coming to rest on a captivating building, the City Hall. Its extravagant combination of turrets and elaborate parapets gave it the whimsical appearance of a fantasy castle. It was beautiful. The fourth corner, too, was occupied by a palatial building home to Casa de America, a cultural institution that fostered closer relationships between Spain and the Americas. Lily's eyes barely made it there, though. She got distracted by the majestic fountain in the middle of the roundabout that obstructed its view. In the center, as if throned upon a boulder, a goddess of commanding presence rode a chariot.

Lily stared at it in utter shock, and anyone familiar with her previous quest would have as well.

Gabriel whispered into her ear: "It's the Fountain of Cibeles."

"Cibeles ..." muttered Lily. She turned wide-eyed toward him. "As in the Goddess Cybele, the ultimate mother of gods?"

He nodded. "She is Madrid's most emblematic symbol."

Lily turned back to appraise the fountain more closely. Cybele was, archaeologically speaking, the oldest identifiable divinity in the world. Worshiped in Anatolia as far back as nine thousand years, if not more, she was the Goddess of Creation and Mankind much like the Hopi Great Spirit. Later, in Greek and Roman times, she'd pick up other functions—and some misled worship—but in essence, she was the goddess from whom all other goddesses in the Middle East and the Mediterranean derived, including—her sister would argue—Mother Mary."

Lily was perplexed. How had she missed this fountain during their quest in search of the prophecy? At the time, Lily had noticed that Madrid touched the Spanish Line, but nothing in her research warranted a closer look. Now, she stood in front of this fountain, shocked to discover that Madrid's emblematic symbol was a monumental reproduction of Prophecy

Rock—the boulder back home that contained the prophecy disguised in the form of a goddess and her chariot.

If she had missed this on the Spanish Line, what else had she missed?

Maybe the lines held more secrets.

Maybe their quest was incomplete.

CHAPTER 35

"The Spanish Nation, desiring to establish justice, liberty, and security, and promote the well-being of all its members, in the exercise of its sovereignty, proclaims its will to:] ... [Collaborate in the strengthening of peaceful relations and effective cooperation among all peoples of the world."

— *The Preamble of the Constitution of Spain*

It was early afternoon, and despite the bright sun's best efforts, its warm rays were no match for the autumn chill. Sofia left her gloves on for the short walk from where they had parked the motorcycle to their destination, located on a popular pedestrian street.

They were in Leon.

Antonio had received updates on Aaron's men and knew they were still tied up searching in Saint Mark's archives. Caution was exercised, nonetheless. Aaron could have more men in the city, whose lower profiles might have slipped under the radar. Antonio suggested meeting Michael and the rest on the other side of the old quarter by the cathedral, and true to his polished ways, the meeting spot was a fine restaurant with a convenient private room.

They were the first to arrive, and as soon as they entered the establishment, the smell of its more popular local dish, Cocido Maragato, had Sofia's stomach juices dancing. She could not believe that after stuffing herself with churros and chocolate for breakfast, her appetite could be so easily aroused. It probably helped they had delayed lunch in favor of riding into Leon.

Antonio had warned her. As the afternoon temperatures fell, the rich chickpea-based stew would become hard to resist. Besides, it was a tourist pleaser. The stew was served as a three-course meal in a fun reverse kind of way: First the meat, then the chickpeas and vegetables, lastly the stock as a noodle soup.

Sofia had a personal interest in it. It was named after a local group of people whose origin was unknown, but who had retained a distinct ethnic identity well into the 19th century. Their main activity had been the long-distance muleteer trade with a legendary reputation for reliability.

John Adams, who enjoyed the privilege of travelling assisted by a personal secretary, a dedicated teacher for his two sons, and a half a dozen helpers, criticized the aspect of the hard-working Maragato women with an unfortunate remark.

"Saw Numbers of the Marragato Woman, as fine as Squaws and a great deal more nasty."

It was difficult to tell if the comparison was meant as a compliment to American female Indians, since the term *squaw*, meaning "indian woman", was often employed loaded. Be as it may, Sofia was determined to do her little part to support the memory of those "nasty" women, whose industrious habits prevented them from having pretty nails and tasteful hairdos to delight Adams eyes, by enjoying one of their signature dishes.

The restaurant was quiet as it prepared for the dinner rush, while some locals and tourists strolled into the bar area for a coffee break. Sofia and Antonio were directed to their room and within ten minutes the rest of the party arrived. Lily stormed in, then paused, wavering momentarily on who to greet first.

Antonio's smile won out.

"My, you are so tall," she observed, raising her gaze as she approached him. She offered her hand. "Such a pleasure to meet you in person."

"The pleasure is mine. I trust you had a comfortable journey?"

Sofia fluttered her eyelashes mockingly at her sister and turned to Michael who stepped in with Gabriel in tow.

He seemed genuinely happy to see her.

To her own surprise, so was she to see him. Sofia stepped forward and hugged him. "I'm glad you came." Suddenly she felt awkward about it, so turned rapidly to Gabriel and hugged him tight, as well.

Both seemed okay with it.

Lily and Antonio joined them.

"Michael," said Antonio, offering his hand with an angled grin.

"Antonio," replied Michael, accepting it with a solid stare.

The wealth of subliminal messaging communicated in that exchange, only they knew.

Antonio turned to greet Gabriel, and then while the three men engaged in an exchange of last-minute intelligence, Lily took Sofia aside. "We have to talk."

"I know."

"Now."

"Bathroom."

Lily nodded and turned for the door. "Gentlemen, excuse us. We are going to freshen up."

Sofia was relieved to see the bathroom was empty. They walked over to the back wall away from the door.

Lily arduously maintained a whisper. "You are not going to believe what I saw this morning."

"Wait until I tell you about what I've learned."

"No, you don't understand. We were wrong. Prophecy Rock was not the end of our journey."

"I know."

Lily pulled back. "You do?"

"Yes, the Declaration and the pact are linked to Mary's Line," revealed Sofia. "Can you believe it?"

"They are?"

"Yes! Antonio uncovered two more significant locations on it. It's a long story. I'll explain it later. The point is that if we can also find a connection to the Spanish Line, it could mean the Declaration is the bearer of another hidden message."

Lily felt knocked off balance. She paused to think. "It might tie into what I saw this morning ... well, sort of ... I'm not sure."

"Just tell me."

"Do you know what Madrid's iconic symbol is?"

"No idea."

"A goddess riding a chariot on a boulder."

"You're kidding. Really?"

"And not just any goddess. The oldest known mother of gods, Cybele. And get this: She was worshiped for the longest time as a fallen meteorite by the Phrygians in Anatolia. You know, the bearers of the liberty cap."

"Why do they care for her in Madrid?"

"Oddly, there is a Roman connection. In the 3rd century B.C., the Romans were fighting their Second Punic War with the Carthaginians for dominance over the Iberian Peninsula. This campaign delivered a crushing defeat to Rome. So, shortly afterwards, when Rome was also struck by a meteor shower, it added up to forebode doom. They ran to consult their prophetic texts, the Sibylline Books, and these suggested bringing Cybele's meteorite stone to Rome for good luck. Apparently, it worked. Things turned around, the Romans took Hispania and went on to become the empire we all know from there."

Gee-whiz, thought Sofia, *all roads truly do lead to Rome.* "What happened to her stone?"

"No one knows, but what matters to us is that today she is portrayed as a monumental Lady-Chariot in the heart of Madrid, placed there by Charles III. That has to mean something."

Sofia frowned. "I don't know, Lily. Lady-Chariots were popular in Spain around the 5th century B.C., long before Cybele's stone was even taken to Rome. They were a thing here. It's natural that, one way or another, there would be a monument to one. And just because she was commissioned under Charles III, it doesn't connect her to the Declaration or the secret pact."

"If you remember, Lady-Chariots were forgotten in Spanish history until their statues started popping up again in archaeological sites in the late 19th century. The monument I'm talking about is a fountain designed in 1782 as part of Charles III's beautification of the city. The king would not have known about her ancient worship here. What are the odds he'd choose a Lady-Chariot as one of the city's centerpieces? And did I mention that Madrid touches the Spanish Line?"

Sofia started to shake her head.

"I realize Madrid only barely touches the line," Lily added quickly, "but before you dismiss it, know that all the Lady-Chariots we learned about, including the Lady of Elche and the Lady of Baza, are in the National Archaeology Museum in Madrid, steps away from the fountain. That's one serious concentration of Lady-Chariots in one place. Just saying."

"Can I talk now?"

"You may."

"I'm with you. I don't deny its compelling and may even mean something, but I'm not seeing the connection. Again, just because she was built during Charles III's reign doesn't cut it. You know how this works. The link has to be meaningful, solid."

"Fine. I'll keep digging. There's something else."

"What?"

The reason I know about the fountain is because Michael had a meeting in the Spanish army headquarters located on its square." Lily could see her sister narrow her eyes with intrigue. "Gabriel confessed Michael is military, the highest ranking."

Her eyes narrowed further. "What the heck?"

"Exactly."

"It's never ending with these guys!"

Lily sighed. "I'm pretty fed up with it myself."

"What kind of highest ranking would he be, anyway?" continued Sofia. "It can't be the commander-in-chief, unless he is also secretly the President, which who knows anymore."

"How about the Archangel Michael, the commander of the angels? It doesn't get any higher than that, and as things are going, it's the simplest explanation."

"This is serious, Lily. I don't think I told you, but Antonio's plane was parked at Joint Base Andrews. We were allowed to access the base without so much as showing our faces. We didn't have to stop, remove our helmets, provide a name, show IDs. Nothing."

"Well, that's scary." Lily collapsed against the wall. "This implies we have two ... what, generals? ... from different countries, working undercover together, and apparently with an exceptionally generous license to roam freely, probably thanks to their ties with an enigmatic association that looks over the fate of the world." *Gabriel wasn't kidding when he said the world was in a bad place and the stakes were high*, she thought.

"*That's* what's scary to you?" said Sofia. "Our lines are involved, we are neck-deep in this, and we have those two high-ranking, over-qualified, whoever-they-are serving as our personal bodyguards."

The two sisters exchanged troubled looks.

Lily straightened up. "Whatever. I'm not walking away from our lines, no matter how scary."

"I thought you'd say that." Sofia turned for the door. "Let's head back. I have some ideas I'd like to bounce off you."

* * *

Aaron watched the news satisfied. Major networks were hyping up the act of vandalism for their respective ratings with headlines like: *The War on American Values* versus *Is it Time to Reckon with American Legends?* History experts and other guests provided their two cents of wisdom, while the web lit up with racist comments eliciting the pertinent outcries.

What a bunch of fools, rejoiced Aaron. It was so easy.

He wasn't alone.

Aaron and his brother sat in matching leather armchairs, separated by an antique side table in front of the large split screen.

"The noose was a nice touch," complimented Aaron.

"I wish I could take the credit. That was all them," clarified his brother, watching a handful of young men on screen throwing objects at the police.

Give them a lit match and they'll burn the building down for you, thought Aaron.

"I'll have preparations for phase two get underway."

"One thing at a time," cautioned Aaron. "This phase must run its course."

"This phase is running better than expected. Let's not squander the opportunity to provide the public with a glimpse of his treason while we still have their attention. We could lose it to a UFO sighting tomorrow."

Aaron would have chuckled at the quip if he weren't so disgusted with human stupidity. He shifted in his chair. "We'll regret it. It's best to feed their imagination than supply facts they can contrast and argue."

His brother, several years younger, released a frustrated breath. "We've gone through this, Aaron. The council has decided. Keeping the alliance secret has done nothing for our cause. Times have changed, as have the tools at our disposal. The alliance will be leaked as it suits us, and by the time we are done, either this country looks like it was always meant to or it's war for real."

The breaking news of riot scenes and confrontations between supremacists and activists in front of Washington's statue filled both halves on the screen. One of the journalists was expressing his shock at how fast social media had galvanized people to the site in a question of hours.

Aaron felt contempt for the young man. The fool was raised in the age of social media. How could he be surprised by its power. And if he was half the professional one should be to report on cable television, he ought to know there was always an interest group behind these timely outbursts. A handful of the rioters were paid recruits to get things rolling by breaking windows and throwing objects, while the rest happily pitched in after answering strategically placed Internet rally cries. Nothing like good drama to attract the cameras.

Then again, perhaps the young man did know. Nothing like good *shocking* drama to keep the audience's eyeballs stuck to the screen.

In any case, the young reporter would be busy for a while. It was merely one of several well-planned skirmishes to come.

"Brother," started Aaron matter-of-factly, "the war has already begun."

CHAPTER 36

"Canonigos
Cassa de San Isi one, one Cassa de San
Marcus Nine Parish Churches, including the Cathedral."

—*John Adams' Diary, 6 January 1780*

When the sisters returned to the dining room, they found Antonio was gone and a somber mood occupied his place.

"What's happened?" asked Lily.

"Washington's statue in New York was vandalized this morning at the break of dawn," explained Michael. "Some disturbance followed through the morning, and just as things were calming down, a masked individual was seen climbing the statue to tie a noose around Washington's neck. Web chatter is fueling the escalation. The city has brought in riot police reinforcements. The National Guard is on standby."

Sofia understood. "It's coordinated. The Knights?"

"Their opening salvo," he confirmed. "We are running out of time."

She swept the room with her eyes and brought them back inquisitively to Michael.

"In view of how things are quickly escalating," he explained, "Antonio went to personally check on the two at Saint Mark's."

"Is he going to have them apprehended?" asked Lily.

Gabriel answered. "There's no cause for it. They haven't committed any crime, at least, not here, not yet."

"Regardless," added Michael, "it's in your best interest that the Knights are kept busy searching for the Declaration, thinking they are ahead."

"What if they are ahead and find it while they're at it?" asked Lily.

"Without you, I highly doubt it." He winked at her. "And in the very unlikely scenario they did, they'd have to get through Antonio with it." This last bit he said with a side look at Sofia.

For Lily, Michael's complimentary wink was like a warm hug. Her friend was back.

Sofia was not amused. She felt the urge to protest Antonio's absence, not sure on what grounds. She then wondered if he had quietly planned all day to hand her care back over to Michael and take off to do his own thing again. She reminded herself he had been up front about it. The mission came first.

Still, it hurt.

The sisters caught up on each other's findings during dinner. For a believer like Lily, to learn the details of the two additions to Mary's Line and the consequential grouping they belonged to, produced more than a thrill; it was pure religious ecstasy. If it had been the 16th century, she'd be levitating.

As the dessert plates were removed and coffee served, Gabriel took his cup and stepped outside the room, Michael checked his phone for the latest on the evolving events back in the States, and Lily sat across from her sister displaying a broad satisfied smile.

Sofia overtly ignored it and took charge. As if pounding a gavel for attention, she said: "I've been thinking ..."

Michael put his phone away and looked up.

"We should consider the possibility that we are looking for multiple sites."

"Really? Why?" asked Lily.

"Well ... we know two Spaniards arrived in the US in 1785. One, a high-profile diplomat, Gardoqui, and the other, Casanave, an anonymous immigrant under the protection of Washington. And both presided over the ceremonies of the laying of foundational stones for iconic buildings. Jay and Adams display a similar profile. Consequently, I wonder if we should be looking for two sites in Spain symbolically equivalent to St. Peter's and the White House."

"I'm confused," admitted Lily. "That totals four sites. Are you saying there may be three copies of the pact in addition to the original? Seems like a lot."

Sofia shrugged. "I don't know how many copies there are, if any. I'm simply stating that the pageantry around this whole affair requires we don't neglect the pattern."

"Fair enough," accepted Lily. "In that case, the pattern tells us one of the sites should be in Madrid. And the other, well, either it's here in Leon or ..." Lily furrowed, "more likely Burgos from what you've told us about those laws. We're in the wrong place."

"That's what I initially thought," said Sofia.

"But?"

"But we have a problem. I looked it up. The building where the Human Rights Laws were drawn up, the Convent of Saint Paul, no longer stands. It was ransacked by Napoleon's troops and fell into disrepair until it was torn down in the 19th century. The Museum of Human Evolution stands in its place now."

Lily whistled. "That's not good. If a copy was ever there, it was either captured or moved somewhere else, which makes it as good as lost."

"You said it. *If* it ever was there."

"All these ifs are giving me a headache," said Lily.

"Tell me about it. You know how I love to work with nothing but speculation."

Lily narrowed her gaze on her sister. "Which beckons the question: why are you doing so well with it?"

"Let's just say I'm trying to stay positive."

"You? Positive? Sure. Fess up. What is it? You know something."

Sofia grinned. "Okay, let's call it a hunch, but I just don't see the level of vital unease in Adams during his visit to Burgos as I see in his visit to Leon."

"Are we working off the same diary?" said Lily. "From what I read, his stress levels were off the charts in Burgos. He almost lost it there. He declared the trip the worse experience in his life and told everyone off."

"Yes, that's the point. Too intense to be fake. It comes across as a genuine fatigue-related breakdown. I get the impression he had completed his mission by the time he made it to Burgos, was exhausted, and ready for the trip to be over."

Lily leaned back in her chair, redrawing her taunting smile. "You realize that leaves us with Leon, where a meteor pointed us to from the beginning, and Madrid, where the ultimate Lady-Chariot, who was worshiped as a meteorite, happens to be."

"Cute. Or ....," emphasized Sofia, exaggerating her cynical tone, "Leon, where the entry in Adams' diary is overtly suspect, and Madrid because John Jay was stationed there."

"Your version is boring."

"Explaining why poor Plato was obliged to employ *mythos* to help enlighten people like you with his revolutionary *logos*. God forbid—pun intended—that thinkers like me bore you with simple reasoning."

Michael cleared his throat loudly. "Any idea where you'd like to start looking in Leon? The sooner we can discard a site, the sooner we can move on to the next."

Sofia stared him down for a second, then dug under the map for her diary folder and extracted a sheet of paper. She placed it on the table. "I would suggest we focus on this last entry in the journal. That's not to say I'm ready to discard the Convent of Saint Mark or the cathedral. Lily's observations are valid."

"Well, thank you," said Lily, surprised.

"You're pretty good at boring reasoning. You should try it more often," teased Sofia, launching a defiant look at Michael.

He lifted a peace palm.

She continued. "Adams' downplay of Saint Mark's; the use of the word *here* twice, and then referring to the convent yet again on the last page, betrays an odd attachment to the place. Clearly, something about that convent is important to him.

"On the other hand," she continued, "being escorted to the bishop's council chamber in the cathedral is also interesting, as is his detailed description of the room. Unlike with Saint Mark's, he doesn't downplay it, yet he stops short of admitting a meeting took place."

Sofia tapped the scanned copy with her finger. "Then, again, this last part of the entry for January 6th is particularly strange for several reasons. First, the way it was done. Adams had already left Leon and moved on to comment about the next town. But then, he suddenly leaves the last sentence unfinished and awkwardly adds this section to the back cover in reference to Leon. On the surface, it's an innocuous list of religious buildings plus an off-the-cuff comment about the proprietor of the region, a count by the name, Conde Luna. I looked him up. Not much there."

She pointed to a word. "However, look at this. Adams wrote the word *Canonigos* centered on a line all by itself for no apparent reason."

That's where Lily had given up. "I noticed that. *Canonigos* is Spanish for 'canons', priests who assist a bishop and work in a cathedral. Adams makes one other mention of them when describing his visit to the council chamber. He indicates the bishop meets with the canons there." She glanced at Sofia. "It could be Adams' subtle way of confirming he met the bishop."

"Good point," said Sofia. "But look at the next sentence." She read it.

> *"Cassa de San Isi—space—one—space—one Cassa de San Marcus—space—Nine Parish Churches, including the Cathedral."*

She looked up. "I have not seen him leave blank spaces between words like this anywhere else in the diary. Two of them are placed on either side of Saint Mark's as if trying to isolate it from the rest of the sentence. Have it stand out, maybe?"

Lily reread the sentence quietly a couple of times. "Actually, if you pay close attention, it reads as if he is checking off a list: *one* drop-off at San Isi, whatever that is, and *one* drop-off at Saint Mark's. And it's interesting he refers to both as *Cassa*."

"That's 'house' in Spanish, right?"

"When written with one 's'. He misspelled it. Either way, it can also mean 'home'. I don't know about the *Isi* place, but the convent is no mere *house*. You could fit a neighborhood in it. So, I'd be more inclined to understand it as code for 'becoming a *home* for something'."

"Okay, but why two homes in the same city?"

Both sisters fell silent, giving it some thought.

"Didn't you say he attempted to travel to Madrid but was warned against it?" asked Lily.

Sofia nodded. "At least, twice."

"Pardon my *if*," said Lily, "but what if it was determined unsafe for Jay to carry a copy with him, much less the original, during his risky two-month distraction detour at sea. Adams may have been charged with carrying both. It might explain his stress levels and attempts to reach Madrid. He was supposed to deliver one there, but in the end, deterred from going, he was forced to leave both in Leon. His meeting with the bishop could have been to let him know where. I read that the king assigned the bishop to the position a couple of years earlier. He must have been a trusted man and tasked with arranging to get the Declaration to the king at a safer date."

Sofia winced. It sounded awfully convoluted, but then again, the whole thing had been ridiculously convoluted from the beginning.

"You have to admit Saint Mark's is looking pretty good," said Lily. "Adams keeps on coming back to it. The original fair copy could still be there, after all."

Sofia looked down reflexively at Adams' odd entry. "You might be correct about the two documents being dropped off in Leon. I can see Adams being a nervous wreck for failing to deliver one to Madrid." She then looked up again. "But the one left in Saint Mark's, if it was left there, was not the original."

"You seem sure about it."

"Knowing what I know about Washington and Charles III now, there is a more suitable *home* for their pact; one we have not discussed yet."

Lily listened surprised. "Go on."

Sofia tapped the diary's scanned page with her finger. "*Cassa Isi___.* The blank space leaves the name incomplete, and it's a clue if I ever saw one."

Lily stared at it, trying to understand. "Why? Adams might not have known how to spell it and didn't think the place was important enough to ask."

Sofia drew one of her smart aleck grins. "Oh, it's important, alright. I looked it up."

"You sure did a lot of looking up today. When did you find the time?"

"While we waited for you. Antonio wouldn't let me leave the suite. Nothing better to do."

"You were stuck in a hotel suite with a hunk and found nothing better to do? So sad."

Sofia's cheeks blushed neon red, while Michael reinforced his poker face.

Lily chuckled, delighted she had wiped the grin off her sister's face. "Sorry, you were saying?"

Her triumph was short lived.

"It's the Basilica of San Isidoro; definitely not a mere *house*, but rather the most important historical building in the city, if not the whole Kingdom of Leon," revealed Sofia.

"The basilica is more important than the convent and the cathedral?" asked Lily.

"A great deal more." Sofia intently redrew her angled grin. "And its name, *Isidoro,* is rooted in Greek. Adams knew very well what he was doing when he broke it up the way he did."

CHAPTER 37

"I am all that has been, that is, and will be. My veil no mortal has yet raised."

—*Inscription on the statue of the Goddess Neith-Isis according to Plutarch*

Lily lowered her eyes as she pondered. She had a basic understanding of Greek, hopefully good enough to see what her sister had noticed.

Isidoro.

"Isidore" in English.

The etymological construction of the word—its original meaning—was not all that uncommon. In fact, it didn't require an extensive knowledge of the Greek language to understand, at least, not for someone immersed in religious academia like her. Adams had dropped the *doro,* which derived from *doron,* "gift". Lily knew this from the name Theodore, meaning "Gift of God". Consequently, Isidore, or in Spanish, *Isidoro,* had to mean "Gift of Isi ...".

Who was Isi?

It hit her quickly. Lily raised her wide eyes. "*Isidoro* means 'Gift of Isis."

Sofia smiled. "That's right. Isis, the Egyptian goddess."

Lily appeared lost. "I still don't get it. What was Adams trying to say by removing *gift*?"

"It's a wink to Freemasonry. And the intent was to veil *gift*, not remove it. Long story short, in Egypt, the original Goddess of Creation, Neith, was said to be represented in her temple covered in a veil as a metaphor for creation's impenetrable secrets. Over time, Neith was assimilated with Isis, the Goddess of Wisdom, Magic and Secrets, and the Veil of Neith became the Veil of Isis. Isis's cult was adopted in Greece and Rome, which functioned like a mystery rite. Worshipers were initiated through secret rituals with the promise of spiritual growth and access to mystical knowledge and a blissful afterlife. Sound familiar?"

"Freemasons."

"Right. So, while for Freemasons lifting the veil of Isis symbolizes access to the ultimate spiritual secret or truth, for the Enlightenment at large, lifting the veil of Isis was adopted as an allegory for unveiling nature's secrets through scientific discovery and learning. Either way, the 'gift' was knowledge."

Lily turned reflexive as she remembered something. "In his later years, when asked about the Revolutionary War, Adams' response was quite cryptic. He said there was a part of its history that would never be told and referred to it as the Secret of Secrets."

"It makes sense," said Sofia. She spared a moment to admire the clue. "So simple, yet so effective. *Cassa de San Isi* .... He is telling us that a veiled gift, the Secret of Secrets, was delivered there to the Basilica of Saint Isidore."

"You have to hand it to Adams, that clue is pretty nifty."

"More than you think," said Sofia. "Name-games aside, the building itself contains something particularly precious for Freemasons, maybe explaining partly why it was chosen in the first place. The basilica was built upon the church of Saint John the Baptist and claims to *house* one of his relics. St. John the Baptist, together with St. John the Evangelist, is the patron saint of Freemasonry. They are referred to as the Holy Saints' John, and the Freemasons hold their two prime celebrations on the two saints' feast days. Further, the first official Grand Lodge of Freemasons was formed in London on St. Johns the Baptist day, in 1717; such is his importance to them."

"So that's it, then: thanks to the basilica's name and the relic it houses, the basilica makes the most sensible choice for a Freemason like Washington."

Sofia shook her head. "No."

"What do you mean, no? You literally just laid out why yes."

"I laid out why Adams' clue makes sense, if it is one. But knowing Washington, I think his motivation to choose a site was beyond Freemasonry and more in line with the ideals of the Enlightenment. Especially as it pertained to government. That's why he took personal interest in the laying of the Capitol cornerstone. He sought to establish a strong symbolic foundation for the new form of government he foresaw for America: The New Experiment. So, if Washington chose the Basilica of San Isidoro to deposit the fair copy, the basilica must have some kind of strong connection with the Enlightenment, and more specifically, the New

Experiment." Sofia suddenly paused and rubbed her face, reflecting mental fatigue. "And how in the world does a 10th century basilica in Leon fulfill a requirement like that?"

Lily froze in thought. She looked at her sister spooked. "Back up a moment. Is there any chance this basilica gets its name from Isidore of Seville?"

"Yes, why?"

Lily released a nervous chuckle. "I can't talk for the New Experiment, but if there is anyone in history who embodies Enlightenment, that would be him."

* * *

Elvira Conde Luna was distracted. She was carefully turning the pages of an exquisite 16th century manuscript. This was the highlight of her day. She was a digital archivist proficient in the latest programming languages, database management, computer forensic tools and a long list of software applications for the storing and maintenance of historical documents and materials. Her job, day-in and day-out, submerged her into a stolid computer environment, which she happily endured in exchange for the privilege of working with the priceless historical artifacts she digitalized. For her, each piece had its own unique soul, and their touch was the closest thing to experiencing history in one's own flesh.

Elvira truly derived joy from holding these wonders in her hands, and it was a good thing she did, for it was also her family's sworn duty to protect them.

A male voice greeted her as his steps could be heard approaching. It startled her a little. Elvira raised her large green eyes and quickly drew a broad smile. "Hi, Antonio. I was wondering when you'd show up."

"I've been a little busy."

"So, I've heard. Quite some excitement you had in Washington."

Antonio brushed it off with a shrug. "Just part of the job."

"Sure, I have bullets flying at me every day at work as well."

"Like anyone in their right mind would dare aim at you after what happened this summer."

Elvira drew a mischievous grin. "If you are referring to that rumor circulating about the guy who wouldn't keep his hands to himself and now might never have kids, all true. He had it coming."

Antonio chuckled. "So how is it going here?"

She pouted playfully. "Typical you. Straight to business." Elvira closed the manuscript and gently put it back on the shelf. Then she walked over to her makeshift station. "Your two American friends are downstairs. They've been here all day going through every room, nook, and crevice. I swear they've even looked under the rugs." She reached for a small stack of papers that were stapled together and handed them to Antonio. "That's the paperwork granting them access. It's pretty generous."

"Did they give you any trouble?" he asked, looking through it.

"Not really, I guess."

He looked up. "What do you mean?"

"I don't like the way they go about their search. It's a little rough. It makes me nervous. They're going to damage something. And they won't let up on their obsession with concealed storge spaces. I've tried to explain that most of the pieces have been moved offsite to the museum, but they keep insisting. I dread they'll start hammering the walls." She leaned in and whispered. "Besides, the big guy looks at me funny. I've caught him staring at my nose piercing and tattoo several times. I think he disapproves."

Antonio raised an eyebrow. "I'm inclined to think the opposite."

"Really?" she smiled. "You think so?"

"He clearly has an appreciation for beautiful things."

"You like to torment me, don't you? You are aware that celibacy is no longer a requirement of my legacy, right?"

"Was it ever?"

Elvira laughed and then tilted her head as she played with a blond lock of hair. "So, are you going to tell me what is going on with those two?"

"Nice try. You know I can't. I have my secrets, you have yours."

"Come on, Antonio. You owe me."

"I do and I am forever in your debt."

"In that case, dinner?"

The phone rang.

Elvira scoffed at the interruption. She looked at the screen. "Talking about your buddies ...." She answered. "Yes, how may I help you?" Her smiling green eyes suddenly darkened. "I've already told you, sir, we do not have any undisclosed storage." She listened. "Yes sir, I am aware you come with full access, and I have provided it." Elvira rolled her eyes at Antonio to indicate her annoyance. "Yes, sir, I'll be right there." She cut the communication.

Antonio dropped the documents back on the table. "Why do they want you downstairs?"

"Who knows," she shrugged. "I'm supposed to assist them again tomorrow at the city museum. I don't know if I can take another day of this."

Antonio didn't like it. "Is there anyone else around?"

"No, everyone went home. I'm the only one left. But don't worry, I can take care of myself."

"I know you can." He locked eyes with hers. "But the time has come."

Elvira's body tensed and, inadvertently, she caressed the tattoo on her wrist with her thumb. She, and many before her, had been expecting this moment.

"While you go and get things ready," said Antonio, "I'll encourage those two to wrap things up here."

"I understand," she said with a solemn tilt of her head.

Elvira quickly collected her things and left.

CHAPTER 38

"The Treasures of knowledge acquired by the labors of Philosophers, Sages and Legislature, through a long succession of years, are laid open for our use, and their collected wisdom may be happily applied in the Establishment of our forms of Government."

—*George Washington, Farewell letter upon disbanding the army, 8 June 1783*

Lily shook her head. "The irony ...." And shook her head again in disbelief. "So ... we are considering the Basilica of San Isidoro as the deposit site, because Adams played with the etymology of its name to provide a clue; a clue designed for a Freemason. Good so far?"

Sofia nodded.

"But not content with that, you also expect the basilica, itself, to meet the two requisites that would have made the site worthy in Washington's eyes: a strong association with the Enlightenment and the New Experiment. Correct?"

"Correct."

"Well, as I said, I can't talk for the New Experiment, but I can assure you the basilica is strongly associated with Enlightenment through the bearer of the name." Lily wrinkled her forehead to organize her thoughts. "Saint Isidore was the Archbishop of Seville, a city in the south of Spain, in the 600s. I know of him because he is one of only thirty-seven Doctors of the Church. The title is awarded to scholars who have contributed significantly to theology or church doctrine, and his written corpus was very influential in Western Europe during the Middle Ages and most of the Renaissance. So, in my world, he's big," she said, and added, "but, historically speaking, outside of my world he is even bigger. You see, Isidore believed that education transcended religion and took it upon himself to compile and preserve *all human knowledge* no matter if Catholic or not, with a particular interest in saving the Greco-Roman classics. So, Isidore is credited with assembling the earliest and most comprehensive encyclopedia in the world. Organized in twenty massive tomes, it covered everything, and when I say everything, I mean everything: grammar, rhetoric, mathematics, medicine, law, buildings, minerology, agriculture, war, games, ships, clothing, kitchenware, you name it. Each item was listed alphabetically within its relevant topic and volume. And, by the way, he systemized the use of the period, coma, and colon as we know them today."

"Very impressive, but I don't quite get the irony," said Sofia.

Lily smiled. "The irony is in the title and method Isidore used for his encyclopedia: *Etymologies*. Isidore shared in the longstanding belief that studying the origin and evolution of a word provided a fuller comprehension of the thing it named and, through it, the world at large. As he put it, and I'm paraphrasing here: *one's insight into anything is enhanced when the etymology of its name is known*."

Sofia held her confused frown.

Lily explained. "Let's take the word 'awesome' for instance; it's a modern term but it will do the trick. Originally, 'awe+some' meant *to cause fear* as in *to stand in awe of God*. But over time, we went from fearing God to admiring God, so 'awesome' evolved to mean *to cause admiration*. Therefore, its etymology not only explains its original meaning and construction, but also how the evolution of its meaning mirrored the evolving world around it and vice versa."

"Talk about living up to a name," said Sofia. "So, Adams used the etymology of the basilica's name as a clue, not only because the meaning of the name itself worked for his audience, a Freemason, but also because *ironically* it fit the working method employed by the man who names the basilica." Her eyes flickered as she processed the information. "Adams must have been more of a genius than we thought."

"At the risk of setting a dangerous precedent I'm sure to regret," said Lily, "there is a simple rational explanation to why he was so smart about it."

Sofia listened intently.

"As I just said, Isidore of Seville was enormously renowned. He singlehandedly saved Greco-Roman classical works that otherwise would have been lost forever. His encyclopedia was the most widely consulted textbook in Europe for over a thousand years, and its reproduction was up there with the Bible. But he also produced dictionaries, history books, and science books in addition to theological writings. His body of work garnered him epithets such as 'The Schoolmaster of the Middle Ages' or the

'Last of the Latin Scholars'. I mean, even today, Isidore has been proposed as the patron saint of the Internet. The man has been huge forever, but more importantly ..." Lily paused, "... his sage status was consecrated to the highest level by Alighieri Dante, in his Divine Comedy, when he placed Isidore in the Sun's sphere of Enlightenment in Paradise. Isidore was *literally* seen as the embodiment of Enlightenment. Adams was well-read, the clue would have been a no brainer."

Sofia went silent while looking at her sister with an eerie stare.

"You are scaring me," said Lily. "What is it?"

"It's funning how you keep saying he was the embodiment of Enlightenment. Did I mention that the basilica is named after him because his *body* is literally there? His remains are kept in a silver urn in the altar."

"Holy Mary Mother of Jesus, are you serious? His body is physically there?" Lily was wide-eyed by the implication. "If this is how the basilica meets the Enlightenment requirement, I can't wait to see how it meets the New Experiment one."

"Neither can I." Sofia jumped to her feet. "Let's go find out."

* * *

Antonio quickly checked the adjacent rooms to be sure no one had lingered behind without Elvira knowing. Satisfied the place was empty, he positioned himself on alert, at the top of the stairs, tucked into a door recess. He had heard the phone at Elvira's station ring, so expected one of the men to come up and see why she wasn't answering.

Oddly, no one did.

He waited an instant more.

It was suspiciously silent.

Antonio leaned slightly forward and looked down the stairs through the corner of his eyes. They must have realized something was up. He would have.

Antonio reassessed. He knew there was no exit in the basement. The men would have to make their way up eventually.

How long would that be?

He had no appetite to wait. If this were a dire situation, he wouldn't think twice about rushing down. But it wasn't, and he much preferred to resolve situations cleanly.

Antonio walked over to Elvira's station. He picked up the phone and dialed the basement.

An unfriendly voice answered. "Del Mar, let's not waste time. You have two options: You get out of the way, or we burn this place down and then go find lovely Elvira."

The threat to hurt Elvira didn't faze Antonio. God help the enforcer if he tried. He'd better pray she didn't hear about it. Instead, Antonio focused on the threat to burn the convent down. There was no worse offence to a Spaniard than threatening a national treasure. He had to think fast. They must have planned for it.

Antonio bought time. "A threat like that, out of the gate without even a *hello*, is very rude," he responded as he ran his eyes around the open space. They wouldn't choose to start a fire in the basement, because the walls were made from stone. The incendiary device must have been planted on the main floor; one liable to be activated remotely at short range. It would be small for stealth purposes and placed in the spot most conducive to maximizing the damage rapidly, while away from the stairs, their only way out.

"You have ten seconds to leave through the back door," he heard.

Antonio pivoted to gauge the distance. The back door was further away from the stairs than the front one. It would allow them to get away before he'd have time to come back around to block their escape.

He measured his words. "We have intercepted an interesting message sent to your partner's phone. From its content, I get the strong feeling you are not aware of it." Meanwhile, he fixed his eyes on the magnificent beam in the middle of the room that sustained the elaborate wood ceiling. That would be his pick. He swiftly approached it and looked behind the palm tree at its base. There it was.

"Your attempt to distract me is pathetic. Five seconds."

Antonio ripped the device from the beam, placed it on the floor and smashed it with his heel. But there would be more. One alone on the massive beam would make the process too slow. Antonio continued looking for the secondary devices. He studied the two sizeable free-standing bookcases that flanked the beam, placed there as space dividers. They were tall and stacked with files, several consulting books, and precious manuscripts like the one Elvira was working on. A fire on either one would burn quickly, and its flames engulf the beam to reach the ceiling fast.

Casually, Antonio attended the call as he examined under the shelves: "Your partner has been ordered to return home alone."

The tangible hesitation he perceived through the phone was almost as loud as the faint *click* he heard coming from one of the shelves. It had been activated. He rapidly reached under, located the device, and pulled it out, launching it to a nearby bin. He didn't have time to destroy it, since he simultaneously heard another one *click* on the other bookcase. This one had the extra split second necessary to burst into flames. A file caught fire. Antonio leaped over, smacked the file off the shelf with his bare hand and stomped on it. Then, he pulled the sleeve of his jacket over his hand to remove the hot device. That one he did smash.

"I smell smoke," he heard. A pause followed. "Don't bother with the extinguishers. They've been disabled."

Extinguishers? scoffed Antonio to himself. Obviously, tattooed man was guessing what was going on. "Good news," he replied, "we won't be needing them." He approached the water cooler, filled a cup, and calmly returned to extinguish the small fire in the bin. Then he spared an instant to examine the damage on the sleeve of his leather jacket. This one was one of his favorites.

Antonio winced and continued. "Now the bad news: your friend has been ordered to put a bullet in your head at twenty-two hundred hours today. It would appear you have a scheduled call at that time to report on your progress. Am I correct?" He only heard silence, so he continued. "Your boss must have a morbid desire to hear you drop dead while you update him." Again, only silence. Antonio switched to a persuasive tone. "I know what you are thinking. I recommend you don't get messy. Let your partner walk. If we successfully follow him back to your delightful master, not only do you get to live, but you may even receive beneficial treatment for your kind collaboration in bringing him down."

Antonio proceeded back to his initial position on alert at the top of the stairs. Suddenly, he heard an unpleasant shot. Its sound waves reverberated up the railing. He closed his eyes momentarily and sighed. As he opened them up again, he saw tattooed man walking up with his hands up.

When he reached the top, tattooed man said: "I'm not stupid. If you are going to follow someone, it's going to be me."

CHAPTER 39

"Mother," he [Perceval] asked. "What's a [...] monastery?"

"A beautiful, sacred building that houses treasures and dead saints, and where we consecrate the sacrifice of Jesus [...]"

— Perceval, The Story of the Grail by Chretien de Troyes, 12th century

The basilica was a five-minute walk from the restaurant, but it was taking them an eternity to get there. At least, that's what the sisters felt asked to slow their pace and linger behind with Michael while Gabriel scouted the route. Apparently, the narrow empty street ahead was of more concern than the open area awash with tourists in front of the cathedral where they stood now. When they impatiently asked Michael about it, he telegraphed: Narrow equals ambush. Crowds equal shield. And space equals maneuverability.

Sofia's urge to proceed was partly fueled by the guilt clamping her chest since Dan's death. He had died solely to deliver her a strong warning. Her only hope for some measure of peace was to help locate the Declaration and foil the Knights' plans with it. It would avail Dan's death and, maybe, allow her to amass enough courage to face his daughter and grandson.

In Lily's case, her impatience resulted from reenergized conviction. She had been struggling with her faith for some time. Nothing new. Afterall, doubt was the backbone of faith. For Lily, however, faith was more than a Sunday morning errand, it was her life. And her job, teaching the history of religion—with all its good and much bad—perpetually challenged it, submerging her too often into a fog. When she discovered the two lines, they became her guiding rails through it, and the Lady-Chariot she saw that morning was like a little extra reassuring boost.

"What's taking him so long?" complained Sofia.

Lily distracted herself by admiring the cathedral's rose window. "I wish we had time to go inside."

266

"I'm good. Saw two of them yesterday. That's plenty for me." Sofia turned to Michael and tapped her wrist as if to say *time is running*. He shrugged back to indicate the obvious, he was still waiting to hear from Gabriel.

"It's stunning," persisted Lily. She examined the facade. During her many trips to Europe, she had seen her fair share of cathedrals and never tired of them. Her understanding of their architecture and art provided a sensory experience beyond the purely spiritual.

"Did you know this facade is unique in that its towers are separated from the central nave? Usually, facades are designed as one solid, continuous front. Here, it's an illusion. It all comes together beautifully thanks to those robust flying buttresses."

"Fascinating." Sofia's attention was on the street they were supposed to be heading to.

"It also has the highest concentration of stained-glass windows for its size, making it one of the finest examples of Gothic architecture. That was the goal, you know. Gothic architecture sought to maximize elevation and the amount of light coming in while conserving the sturdiness of the structure. Adams said he liked the cathedral of Astorga more than this one. I wonder if he knew it was modeled after this one." Lily turned to Sofia. "You saw it. What do you think?"

Sofia responded absently. "I don't know. They look the same to me."

"That's what I just said ...forget it." Lily eyed her sister askance. "You okay?"

"Yes, why?"

"Less than twenty-four hours ago you were giggly like a fifteen-year-old. Now you're Grumpy and Droopy rolled into one. Did something happen with Antonio?"

Sofia's eyes were downcast as she pushed a pebble around with the tip of her boot. "Nothing," she brooded, "that's what happened." Sofia looked up. "I don't get it. He seemed interested in me, but then suddenly, after the video conference, he went cold."

"Did you ask him why?"

"I tried. He was elusive. Said something about honoring Michael's concern for us and that he had to reset his priorities, focus on the mission."

Sofia waved her hand as if to shrug it off. "Whatever. It's probably better this way."

Lily observed her sister briefly. "Sof, I love you, but for all your analytical brilliance, you are so clueless sometimes."

Sofia looked confused.

"Don't you see?" started Lily. "You *are* the mission. Michael tried to tell you; we are the kings on the chessboard. Why do you think we have two free-roaming-super-generals watching over us? It's possible Antonio was under the impression you were an accessory to finding the Declaration until Michael's concern for you made him realize you were central to it."

Lily checked on Michael and judged he was out of earshot. She lowered her voice, anyway. "Look, at first, I too was confused with the dynamics going on. I noticed Michael was distraught about you and Antonio. I thought he was jealous. And, quite frankly, it upset me how disengaged he had become from me while at it. But then Gabriel explained that Michael was consumed by the global extent of the threat that the Knights posed. And when he pointed me to the fountain of a lady-chariot, it reminded me of our crucial role in neutralizing threats like them."

"Right, we're back to that again," said Sofia. "We are the chosen ones. Our mission is to reveal divine messages of Peace to the world. Got it." Sofia noticed Michael nodding. Hopefully he was hearing from Gabriel.

Lily despaired. "After everything we've been through, how can you still fight it?"

"Because that's how my brain works, Lily. I can't help it. It short-circuits when something doesn't make sense. Think about what you just said: Two high-ranking generals protect us because we are chosen to spread divine messages. You might be able to sustain that thought in your mind without any effort, but my brain is stuck churning as it tries to visualize the faces in the US and Spanish army control centers when they got an email from God asking for bodyguards." Sofia smacked her forehead. "Oops sorry, I forgot, God sent a meteor. An email would have been too *boring*."

"You know, you can mock me all you want, but even you can't deny that we indeed found a message and that the two lines led us to it. And you can question if the lines are divine or not from here to kingdom come, but they are, once again, leading us to another message, while overqualified escorts are very-much-in-fact protecting us." Lily's tone had taken on an uncharacteristic severity. "You need to step out of your square digital brain for a second and face the reality of what that makes us."

"O-u-c-h ..." Sofia stared at her sister vexed for a moment. Then she exhaled. "Fine. I'm sorry. Tell me, what does it make us?"

"One message makes us the chosen ones; two messages make us prophets. Like it or not, Sof, we are prophets." Lily stood strong waiting for Sofia to explode.

She didn't. Instead, Sofia calmly said: "You mean it makes us prophetesses ..." She paused as if to untangle her tongue. "Well, that's a mouthful. Okay, I see why you prefer prophets."

"Seriously?"

"Yes, look it up in the dictionary."

"No, I mean: that's all you have to say? Let me repeat: We. Are. Prophets."

Sofia inhaled a deep slow breath. "I heard you the first time. As you can imagine, I'm trying very hard to let you be you and just go with it. In exchange, be so kind to let me be me. Besides, if anyone is a prophet that would be you. You are the one who sees the signs, not me."

"You interpret them, meaning we both qualify according to the dictionary. Which, by the way, I did consult. And you know what? It's annoyingly sexist. *Prophet* gets a page-long description, while all *prophetess* gets is three words: 'a female prophet'. The dictionary does not have the courtesy of providing us with our own definition. We are no more than an appendix like the *fe* to a male or the *wo* to a man."

Sofia looked at Lily for a split second and then broke out laughing.

"What?" said Lily.

"Nothing. I love you, too."

A little later, the attendant at the ticket counter shook his head. "I'm sorry, we can't arrange for a private guide unless you are a group of 25 or more. You may join the next tour, though." He pointed to a group of people waiting to the side. "It's not too crowded. The guide should have no trouble answering all your questions. It starts in 15 minutes. Otherwise, we also have self-guided tours if you prefer."

"Thanks, I'll consult with my friends." Sofia stepped away from the window and assessed the people waiting. The man was right, there was only a family of five and a couple. They could easily hog the tour guide. Still, she puckered her face. This was turning out to be the easiest search ever. If they had been cuddled this far, surely, they weren't about to be abandoned now.

"Where's Antonio when you need him," remarked Lily, reading her mind.

"Good question." Sofia looked at Michael and Gabriel. "Have you heard from him?"

Michael spoke. "He's tied up at Saint Mark's. He knows we are here." His eyes suddenly narrowed on a tall, blonde woman in her late twenties who was approaching the group from behind the sisters. She was difficult to miss. Aside from being stunning, she wore tailored jeans that hugged her long slim legs, combined with a sparkly purple cardigan matching her metallic lipstick and hair tips.

"Excuse me," she called. "Are you Drs. Sofia and Lily Auru-Soto?"

Voila, thought Sofia as she turned. Her eyes went straight to the woman's nose piercing. She had nothing against facial jewelry but couldn't help feeling an instant of pain when she saw one. She averted the stare as fast as she could.

"Who are you?" asked Michael.

The woman offered him her hand. "My name is Elvira Conde Luna. I work for the city's cultural department. Professor Del Mar sent me a text moments ago asking me if I didn't mind assisting you." Elvira drew a broad smile as she finished greeting Gabriel and turned to Sofia and Lily. "Who can say no to Antonio, am-I-right?"

Sofia was lethargic in her response, distracted as she was now by the woman's surname. *Conde Luna*. Sofia had learned that, like her mother, in Spain women kept their family name after marriage and passed them on to their children as well. That's why Hispanic surnames doubled up like hers did. In this case, *Conde* and *Luna*, separately, were quite common surnames, but together they translated suspiciously to "Count Luna", the title of the count Adams referenced in the last paragraph of his clue-riddled entry for January 6th. She recalled it in her mind:

The Grandee who is the Proprietor of the Land in and about Leon is the Comte de Luna, a Descendant from the ancient Kings of Leon.

Sofia was beyond coincidence right about now. What was going on here?

"It's very kind of you to accept with such short notice," said Lily, reaching for her hand. "I hope it's not an inconvenience."

"Not at all. To be fair, Antonio stepped in for me in a sticky situation at Saint Mark's. It's the least I could do." Elvira rolled her large green eyes. "Believe me, I much prefer to be here."

"Sticky?" asked Sofia, the last one to shake hands. Why, what happened?"

"Oh, nothing. It's been a long day. I was at the convent and a couple of gentlemen visiting there became a little overbearing. Antonio was sweet and volunteered to take over." Elvira suddenly paused to study the group. "I hope I wasn't rude. They're not friends of yours, are they? They are American like you."

"No," settled Michael. He then signaled something to Gabriel who excused himself and stepped outside.

Elvira did not hide her interest in their reactions. "Wonderful. In that case," she said, showing the way, "shall we?" As they walked in front of the ticket window, she addressed the attendant, "*José, vienen conmigo.*"

Jose acknowledged with a nod that they were with her and waved them in.

Elvira led them through a short hallway and stopped under an arch that opened to a rectangular cloister. "Are you interested in a general tour of the whole complex or something in particular?"

"Not sure," admitted Sofia. "Can you give us a snapshot of the tour?"

"Of course. It starts here on the ground floor and proceeds around the cloister. The first stop is the Royal Treasure with some very interesting pieces like the original urns of St. John and St. Isidore, the oldest bell in Spain, a mysterious rooster weathervane from the 7th century, or a unique Viking miniature box. Unfortunately, Napoleon troops didn't leave much else when they looted the building."

They were here as well? thought Sofia. *That was not good,*

Elvira must have read her face. "Still, there is much to discover. The basilica is much more than a church. It also had a monastery with the royal residence attached, and a visit to the Royal Pantheon is a must if you like art. Its arches and ceiling contain some of Europe's most exquisite and best-preserved Romanesque paintings. Then, the cloister, where the monarchs held council, is a compulsory stop to learn about the kingdom's proudest historical moments. Leon was one of Europe's greatest Christian kingdoms during the Middle Ages, and this royal collegiate, for being the royal residence, was intimately intertwined with its history."

Lily showed surprise. "I'm sorry, did you say this basilica is a collegiate?"

"Yes, a royal collegiate."

Sofia looked at Lily confused. "Meaning what?"

"A collegiate is like a cathedral but without the bishop. It is run by a self-governing college of canons as in *independent canonigos.*" Lily made sure to drag out the last two words.

Sofia understood. That must have been what Adams was hinting at when he placed the word *Canonigos* centered on a line all by itself. He was attempting to bring attention to the basilica as opposed to the cathedral.

Elvira further explained. "This complex was envisioned as the symbol of the Christian north when the city of Leon became the seat of the kingdom. It was the time of the Crusades, and while most of Europe was tied up in the East, the Iberian Christian kingdoms were holding the fort in the West. At one point, the kingdom grew to be one of the largest and strongest, and to showcase it, an important number of relics and treasures were brought to this royal complex to enhance its prestige, such as those of St. Isidore." Elvira's tone then gained a hint of mystery. "However, a few of the items were so valuable they were kept *secret*, requiring special protection. To that effect, a unique institution run by the royal women was created and later a chapter of canons brought in to help, thus, royal collegiate."

Sofia's heart almost stopped. Had she understood correctly? "If we were to be interested in the *secret treasures*, where would we find *them*?" she asked.

"In the tower." Elvira swept her open hand across the cloister to the opposite corner where the tower could be seen. In the process, she pulled on the sleeve of her cardigan. That's when Sofia noticed the tattoo on her wrist: a bowl-like semicircle with a red sword inside and a candle on top.

"The basilica was built attached to the Roman wall," continued Elvira, "and its robust tower provides access to it. For this reason, it served as a vault when not as an escape route to carry the more valuable items off to safety when needed. To this day, it continues to safeguard Lady Urraca's Chalice and the Renaissance Library." She paused to emphasize, "Do not be misled by their names. The library, for instance, holds a magnificent collection of manuscripts, priceless bibles, and rare books from as far back as the Middle Ages—along with other *priceless documents*."

It was clear to Sofia this woman was trying to tell them something. "I say we start there."

"Excellent choice," celebrated Elvira. She led the way toward the tower as the green in her eyes glowed shrewdly. "You should know I have spent hours in the library archives scanning and cataloging. If there is a special manuscript, book, or document you are looking for, don't commit Perceval's mistake. Just ask. I'm sure I can satisfy your curiosity."

The hint was so obvious, it rendered Sofia breathless. Perceval was the name of the knight who searched for the Grail. According to the original story, he could have avoided the quest altogether if he had simply asked about it when he first saw it.

Apparently, Lily recognized the reference, as well. "Since you mention it, you don't happen to have seen the American Holy Grail around here somewhere, have you?"

Michael launched a disapproving stare at her.

Lily shrugged and whispered: "She told us to ask, so I asked."

Elvira stopped sharply at the foot of a stairway and turned around to look at Lily with a pointed stare. "American? It was delivered through legitimate channels to us and has since been in our custody. We have no intention of relinquishing it." Though polite, her tone came across like the growl of a lioness protecting her cubs.

Lily was taken back, not sure where that came from, while Sofia couldn't believe Elvira had just admitted to the fair copy being there. "Can we see it?" she eagerly asked.

Slowly, Elvira initiated her climb. "Please, follow me. It's kept in its own room adjacent to the library," and added, "closely guarded."

Michael's phone rang. He looked at the screen troubled. "I must take this. You go ahead."

The sisters hurried to catch up with Elvira.

CHAPTER 40

"The boy saw that wonderous sight, the night he arrived there, but kept himself from asking what it might mean [...] A servant entered the hall carrying a white lance [...] and everyone saw [...] the drop of blood that rolled slowly down. [...] And then two other servants entered, carrying golden candleholders [...] A girl entered with them, holding a grail in both her hands — a beautiful girl, elegant, extremely well dressed [...] The grail that led the procession, was made of the purest gold, studded with jewels of every kind."

—Perceval, The Story of the Grail by Chretien de Troyes, 12th century

Lily was astonished. "So, you weren't kidding. You really do have the Holy Grail here."

"Professionally speaking, I cannot confirm that." Elvira said this, sharing an enigmatic look with Sofia. "Off the record ... yes, it's here alright."

Sofia acknowledged her hint with a discrete nod and examined the display. It contained a Eucharistic cup formally known as Lady Urraca's Chalice, which in recent years, according to Elvira's introduction moments earlier, had made the headlines around the world when two local historians realized it could be the legendary Holy Grail. Due to the increased visitor traffic that followed, it was moved to its own room in the tower and now stood solitary, glowing under converging beams of light in a large cubic glass-display roughly measuring three feet per side. The rest of the dim-lit room was empty with no decorations or other items to distract, just the four ancient stone walls sustaining a vaulted ceiling, all under the watchful eye of the guard standing on alert at the entrance. The effect was imposing while dignified for a cup suspected of being the one Jesus Christ drank from during the Last Supper.

One of Sofia's first assignments working for Dan had been precisely the Holy Grail. It had also been one of the easiest legends to rationalize. The whole thing started with a French poet, Chretien de Troyes, who in the 12th century wrote *Perceval, The Story of the Grail*. He was the latest, in a long string of storytellers, adding his personal touch to the legend of King Arthur. He wouldn't be the last, but his personal contribution, the *grail*—without the *holy* yet—would offshoot into a phenomenon of its own. The story described the grail as a bowl encased in jewel-studded gold. The Eucharistic cup here did a good job of matching that description because it was exactly that, a bowl converted into a cup by a gold casing studded with jewels. But De Troyes' story also said that Perceval's grail had the power to cure, and that magical element was what inspired another French storyteller, Robert de Boron, to link Perceval's grail to Christ's Chalice, becoming thereafter one and the same in literature and popular imagination.

At some other time, Sofia would have found this situation amusing. In trying to track down the American Holy Grail they had inadvertently ended up finding the actual Holy Grail, or one claimed to be.

But this was not the time to clarify myths. Something else was happening and it was giving Sofia the chills. Upon pronouncing the words *off the record*, Elvira had discreetly tapped the pedestal that sustained the display with the knuckle of her index finger. The pedestal was cubed like the glass-display on top and of equal dimensions but opaque. Having grasped that Elvira was trying to carry two conversations at the same time, it could only mean that she was indicating the lost Declaration was right there, hidden in the pedestal.

It was poetic, really. The fair copy was guarded by Christ's Chalice giving "Under God" a whole new meaning.

Naturally, Lily was captivated by the cup. "This makes two Holy Chalices in Spain, then. This one and the one in Valencia."

Elvira explained. "Both vessels have in common that their dating and characteristics are consistent with a 1st century Jewish ritual bowl. Their background stories are very different, however. The Chalice in Valencia has a long oral tradition linked back to St. Peter who, according to the legend, brought it with him to Rome from Jerusalem. From there, it made its way to Spain through St. Lawrence, to eventually end up in Valencia. It's connection to St. Peter makes it particularly popular with the popes." Elvira pointed. "This one, on the other hand, is attached to a paper trail that came to light in 2010."

While they stood there, a slow trickle of visitors circulated through the room. Many could be heard questioning the bowl's authenticity as they approached walking down the hall, but all invariably quieted down in reverence as soon as they stood before it. In their hearts, they wished it to be true.

An elderly couple strolled in. In his excitement, the man forgot the rules and raised his phone to take a picture.

The guard politely called out to stop him. "*Señor, no se permite hacer fotos.*"

A little embarrassed, the man apologized and joined his wife to admire the piece.

Elvira lowered her voice. She started by looking at Lily. "In 2010, two local historians, Torres and Ortega, realized that some of the 11th century Islamic artifacts in the Royal Treasure had been erroneously classified as trade goods from the Islamic south, when in reality they were from Cairo, Egypt. Since one of my jobs is to catalogue and digitize city archives, I was brought in to search for any document that may reveal a possible trade or political relationship with Egypt at that time." She turned to Sofia. "In the process, I recovered other interesting documents," and swiftly returned to Lily, "but found nothing in relation to Egypt."

The senior couple continued to the library as a boy and a girl entered the room running raucously. The guard asked them to calm down. They giggled, took a quick look at the display, and moved on. A medium-aged couple, no doubt the parents, followed in, though were quick to leave with worried faces when they heard the children fight over something in the library.

The room fell momentarily silent.

Lily was consumed with curiosity. "So, what happened? How did you realize you had the Holy Grail?"

"In a very unexpected way. For us, the scholars in Leon, the possibility of having a direct relationship with distant Egypt in the 11th century was an exciting prospect. Since we found nothing here to substantiate it, one of my colleagues was sent to Cairo to check their historical archives. To our pleasant surprise, two different parchments that mentioned King Fernando the Great of Leon were discovered. One explained that a severe famine had swept Egypt, and the ruler had sent out a request across Islam for help. The emir of Denia, a city on the east coast of Spain, responded very generously by sending boats full of provisions. Grateful, the ruler of Cairo wished to repay with equal kindness by sending back gifts and inquired if there was something in particular the ruler of Denia desired. There was." Elvira leaned into Lily. "The parchment reveals that the emir of Denia specifically asked for the chalice worshiped as that of Christ in Jerusalem. He explains that the Christian king of Leon had become very powerful, so the ruler of Denia hoped to appease him by offering something as precious as Christ's cup." Elvira straightened up. "Unfortunately, the document breaks off there, but it helped explain why we had the rich collection of items from Egypt. They were gifts."

Lily's eyes shot wide-open. "That's the understatement of the century. I can only imagine the shock. It also inferred the Holy Chalice was among those gifts."

Elvira chuckled. "Yes, there was a generalized shock indeed, because we did in fact have a valuable chalice among the basilica's treasures dating back to that time." She tilted her head at the display. "This Eucharistic cup had always been somewhat of a mystery. All that was known about it was that Lady Urraca, who happened to be the daughter of the king mentioned in the Egyptian parchments, had donated her personal jewels to make the casing you see. That's why it carries her name, the Chalice of Lady Urraca. "Elvira's eyes twinkled as she slid them toward Sofia." But she was no ordinary lady. She was the head of the *Infantado*."

While Sofia raised an eyebrow, Lily asked: "What's the *Infantado*?"

"It's the name of the female order led by the royal women of Leon charged with the patronage and care of the kingdom's religious buildings and possessions, especially their sacred items. I don't think there is a name for it in English. It was quite unique."

"As in royal maidens?" ask Sofia, reminded of the well-dressed girl in the castle that paraded the grail according to De Troyes' story.

"More like very powerful royal maidens," clarified Elvira. "Some of them were unwed daughters of the king, like Lady Urraca. She chose voluntarily to stay single. Others were ruling queens when they held the office. To put it in modern terms, they were the Grand Masters of an order that oversaw a rich network of monasteries that controlled large tracks of land and people."

Sofia felt a dizzy spell. Elvira had just revealed who she was. Adams had referred to Count Luna as a Grandee descendant from the ancient kings of Leon, meaning that the count was the highest-ranking aristocrat in the kingdom. Since Leon was no longer a kingdom with its own monarch, that made Elvira heir to that female order. She was confessing to being the Grand Master and custodian of the two grails, the Holy one on display and the American one hidden in the pedestal.

No wonder she was so protective.

Meanwhile, Elvira continued to explain to Lily. "According to the Egyptian parchments, the Holy Chalice would have arrived here around the year 1054 when Lady Urraca headed the order. Knowing what we now know about the bowl, it explains why she converted it into a Eucharist cup and why since then this basilica has had the exclusive right to display the Sacred Sacrament permanently. It also explains other historical oddities like why the pilgrimage path of St. James was rerouted to pass along the front of the basilica or why the Order of the Knights of the Sword was founded here in Leon, instead of in Santiago where St. James was buried."

"The Knights of the Sword? You mean the Knights of St. James, right?"

"Same thing. Their insignia was a red cross depicted in the form of a sword on their white capes. It was red for the blood of St. James who was decapitated with one."

Sofia's eyes dropped to Elvira's tattoo. It was interesting how every new detail surrounding Lady Urraca's Chalice matched Chretien de Troyes' description: A royal monastery housing a precious grail in the custody of a royal maidan and protected by bleeding swords. The only thing missing from the parade scene where Perceval sees the grail for the first time were the candles.

The equivalences gave her the excuse to ask something else on her mind. "*Off the record*," started Sofia cautiously, "what's your personal opinion? Would you say this one here," she tapped the pedestal, "is the *original*?"

Two couples holding hands entered the room and stood around the display. The men looked related, maybe brothers. One of the ladies had placed herself next to Elvira. Elvira stepped to the side to give her some space and then responded. "I have no doubt it's the original." This she said looking at both Sofia and Lily.

Sofia's chest swelled.

"I should warn you," added Elvira quickly, "part of it is missing."

Lily exhaled. "It's damaged?"

"Not badly," reassured Elvira, looking only at Lily. "Besides, thanks to its missing fragment we were able to confirm this was the chalice the Egyptian parchments referred to."

Lily looked closer at it. "How so?"

"According to the second parchment, the emir of Egypt believed the cup of Christ had healing properties. Before sending it to Denia, he had a fragment broken off and kept it in Cairo."

Healing properties? What the ...? Sofia's knee-jerk reaction was to call Dan and tell him they should revisit the Holy Grail myth. It might not have been totally made up after all. The one here could have been the inspiration for Chretien's story. Sorrow soon followed.

The two couples continued their visit to the next room. Lily walked around the display examining the chalice. "Where is the piece missing from? I don't see it?"

"Look at the top rim over here," pointed Elvira. "It's barely visible under the gold band. As you can imagine, everyone was a nervous wreck when the encasing was removed to confirm the piece was indeed missing, confirming this was the bowl the parchment referred to."

"Unbelievable. Right here, in front of your eyes all this time," marveled Lily. "Why don't you refer to it as the Holy Grail in your promotional materials?"

"We are scholars. We don't have a sample of Jesus's DNA to confirm he drank from it. Short of that, we are greatly in debt to Lady Urraca for the graceful way in which she hid the bowl in plain sight to protect it. It's only fitting the Eucharist cup should continue to carry her name."

The tour group they had considered joining earlier just now entered the room. The guide directed the family of five and the couple to stand around the display on the other side. It got tight.

"Can you tell us why it was kept secret?" asked Sofia. "I mean, it would defy its purpose. Items of such importance would have been highly publicized."

"That was the intent, but the unrest that followed soon after its arrival put it in grave danger. This building has endured tremendous hardships; it has been raided repeatedly through the centuries." Elvira's eyes gained a dark hue. "The last time was in 1808 when Napoleon troops occupied the basilica and looted most of the treasures. The more valuable items," she said, waving her hand vertically up from the pedestal to the display, "were successfully hidden thanks to how few knew of their existence, or that they were here. We have good reasons to believe Napoleon came personally to this front during the war looking for it. His troops searched in Astorga, Leon and Burgos. One can only shudder to think what would have happened if he had captured it."

Sofia was struck by that last comment. What exactly did she mean by it? How could the terms of a pact between Washington and Charles III be dangerous in the hands of Napolean?

She asked: "Any chance you can remove it from the display so we can take a closer look?"

"I'm afraid not. It's very delicate."

"We've come a long way to see it. Surely a brief look can't harm it."

The lioness in Elvira resurfaced, shutting down any further conversation on the matter. "There is a reason it has survived this long. No exceptions."

Sofia was puzzled. Why admit to the pact being there if they couldn't see it? Had she missed something in the intricate double-layered conversation? Or was it triple? She had lost count. She found herself looking around the room wondering if there were cameras or hearing devices that justified such extreme caution. Naturally, there was. A security camera aimed directly at the Holy Grail.

Think, she told herself. If this royal maiden was open to confessing the pact was there under her guardianship, why not go somewhere safe to talk about it? ... Elvira was turning out to be as frustrating as Antonio ... But then, she was sent by him ... Was she a member of the association as well? ... Why so much mystery? ... *Ugh!*

Whatever, she resolved. If this was how it had to be, she could play this game better than anyone. How to ask about the pact's content in Holy Grail talk? *The New Order ... the New Experiment ...* she had it!

Sofia faced Elvira. "This has been fascinating. I'm curious now, where do you keep the Round Table?"

Elvira morphed back to her sparky self and drew a broad smile. "Let me show you."

* * *

Michael waited outside with Gabriel. They saw Antonio approach.

"How did it go?" asked Michael.

"He's on route back to the States and willing to collaborate. He will be handed over as agreed." Antonio shook his head displeased. "Stay vigilant. We suspect they have more men in the city, and they'll get more desperate as we corner them."

Gabriel nodded. "We will. We're counting on that."

"Good. How's it going in there?" asked Antonio.

"According to plan. Fate is doing her job."

Antonio scoffed. "With due respect, you leave little space for Fate to do anything."

"We just follow orders from higher up, as do you," said Gabriel.

"You know well I follow no orders. My allegiance is to a promise."

"Spoken like a true honorable Spanish knight. Throw in a platonic love and Quixote would be jealous of you," teased Gabriel.

Antonio was not amused. "I should have been alerted to who she was."

"There is a lot at stake," said Michael. "Last on our minds were your feelings."

"Don't insult me, Mike. It's beneath you. It's not about me. *Her* feelings matter."

"That's your problem, Antonio. You get too involved."

"*I* get too involved?" challenged Antonio. "And what exactly are *you* doing here?"

"Ensuring that your weakness doesn't jeopardize the greater good. You should not have stepped in to protect the two civilians in Washington. As hard as it may be, we can't be everywhere all the time, and it puts the mission at risk. As agreed, from here on, you will stand back until we take care of the Knights. Then we'll get out of your way, understood?"

Antonio reinforced his combatant gaze. "Let me make this clear: I don't care what you think about my weaknesses. I will step in when and where I consider I must. Therefore, be grateful it is in Sofia's best interest that I stand back."

Michael released a breath. "You're right, we care about the sisters as much as you do. It's the reason we are here. I give you my word no harm will come to her."

"That's all I ask."

"What will you do in the meantime?" asked Gabriel.

Antonio directed his dark eyes toward the basilica as if x-raying its thick walls to see inside. "I'll collect my things and be on my way."

CHAPTER 41

King Arthur: The Lady of the Lake, her arm clad in the purest shimmering samite, held aloft Excalibur from the bosom of the water, signifying by divine providence that I, Arthur, was to carry Excalibur. That is why I am your king.

Dennis, the peasant: Listen. Strange women lying in ponds distributing swords is no basis for a system of government. Supreme executive power derives from a mandate from the masses, not from some farcical aquatic ceremony.

—Monty Python and the Holy Grail

They had descended to the ground floor. Sofia and Lily followed Elvira through the archway into the cloister. The corner where the tower stood high, crowned with the rooster weathervane, seemed popular with the visitors, who lined up to have their pictures taken there. Lily surmised the reason was it made a photogenic backdrop.

Elvira led them to a quiet spot not far from it, and with a mischievous grin, swept her hand across the cloister's open space to announce: "I present you the Round Table."

Silently, Sofia assessed the gallery of ancient arches that framed the patio, while Lily voiced her confusion.

"Okay, I'll bite," she started. "Where? Mind you, I wasn't really expecting the legendary table, but nothing here is round, not even the columns."

"Trust me, there is a Round Table here, the real historical one. You will soon see it. But first, I must tell you a story and, as with most Spanish stories, it starts with a miracle." Elvira took a small, yet severe breath. "In the year 1158, a drought devastated the kingdom and, naturally, the peasants turned to St. Isidore for help. With the Grand Master's blessing—at the time Queen Sancha Raimundez—his urn was removed from the altar and carried in a procession. This displeased Isidore. The further away they transported his urn, the heavier it got, until it became too heavy to bear. As

284

soon as it was deposited on the ground, the miracle occurred: it started to rain."

"Let me guess," interrupted Sofia, "they built a chapel there."

"No." Elvira's response was sharp. "Isidore was an enlightened man, he was trying to make a point."

Feeling scolded by the teacher, Sofia thought it wise to restrain her commentary.

Elvira continued. "The peasants attempted to return St. Isidore's urn back to the church, but the urn would not move. Concerned, they reported it to the queen. She ran to the site, prayed, and promised Isidore to never move his remains again. Since then, they've laid in peace in the altar."

Elvira paused.

While Sofia scratched her head, wondering what the point was, Lily observed: "I've noticed women held high power here in the Middle Ages; Grand Masters, ruling queens ..."

"Yes, and all of them forces to be reckoned with. In fact, the mother of Queen Sancha Raimundez was also a ruling queen, the first one in Europe to do it in her own right. Her name was Urraca. She was the niece of Lady Urraca." Elvira's grin hinted there was an epic story behind these women, itching to be told, but left it at that. "Anyway, going back to our miracle, Queen Sancha Raimundez brought in the charter of *canonigos* to refortify the protection of the kingdom's treasures. Unfortunately, the fresh-new canons, in their zeal, attempted to take ownership of St. Isidore's miracle and concluded it warranted the obligation of an annual tribute from the peasants. Having understood Isidore's displeasure at being paraded, the peasants along with the queen had a strong hunch he'd like being monetized even less. So, they agreed to show their gratitude by presenting St. Isidore with a voluntary gift in the form of a candle, the symbol of his Enlightenment."

There it was, thought Sofia, the missing item from De Troyes' parade: the candle.

"The dispute between the canons and the people," continued Elvira, "led to an annual tradition known as *Foro u Oferta*, meaning 'Obligation or Gift'. Every year, the peasants selected a representative to deliver their candle and argue on their behalf that the gift was voluntary. The canons would then accept it, while disputing in turn that it was an obligation. That tradition continues to this day." Elvira pointed to the corner where visitors were taking their pictures. "Every April, the two sides meet here, in this cloister, to continue the debate. And to be clear, it is not a mock recreation performed by actors. The real city mayor and town hall representatives meet with the real abbot and canons."

"Seriously?" said Lily. "The real leaders of the city have been performing the ceremony for 900 years?"

"That's right. They form a circle in this cloister and present their arguments in a battle of oratory skills. It always ends in a tie, and the debate is then postponed to the following year. Today, the ceremony is better known as *Las Cabezadas* or 'The Noddings', because, upon departure, and despite their disagreement, both sides bow to each other three times in an exaggerated manner to express their mutual respect. Most visitors find it quite colorful and entertaining." The green in Elvira's large eyes intensified into a dark olive shade. "I trust you see the moral of the story?"

"I'll give it a try," said Lily. "In the Arthurian tales, the Round Table was meant to infer that the knights sitting around it, along with the king, were all equals. In this story, the clergy and the people also meet in a circle of equals with the right to present their arguments and respectfully disagree."

Elvira bowed to Lily. "I applaud your insight. I should clarify that the monarchs are also symbolically present by this setting, the cloister, where they convened their councils."

For Sofia, something about this story was off. Why would the real leaders of the city, both secular and religious, agree to subject themselves to the awkward caricature of exaggerated bows or mock debates for almost a millennium? Not even a miracle could accomplish that. There had to be a powerful reason driving it.

Elvira observed her struggle. "Is there a problem? You seem conflicted."

Sofia hesitated. She worried Elvira, the lioness, might bite her for doubting a local tradition. She braved her thoughts, anyway. "I don't understand why the disagreement is remembered at all. I find it odd. It's not my intention to belittle the importance of a popular celebration in your city, but a mere disagreement over a tribute does not carry enough weight to justify its celebration for almost 900 years with the direct involvement of the town leaders. And I'm pretty sure they don't do it to entertain visitors. At its core, there must be the memory of something extremely important."

Slowly, Elvira curtsied at Sofia. "You make Isidore proud. As he did with words, ceremonies and people, too, require a closer look under the surface to gain a more comprehensive understanding of them. You are correct. The colorful reenactment of *Las Cabezadas* is like the bejeweled golden encasing of our precious Chalice, a smokescreen of sorts that protects the true treasure hidden within. In this case, the memory of an extraordinary historical event the people of the kingdom refused to forget."

The two sisters exchanged expectant gazes.

"Let me explain," said Elvira. "The European feudal system of the Middle Ages limited freedom of movement and individual rights. People were generally born into the service of a feudal master for life, as were their descendants. However, here in Spain, circumstances were a little different. During the Middle Ages, we were fighting the *Reconquista* and as the Christian north pushed south gaining the control of new territories, monarchs needed their subjects free to move and willing to settle on the dangerous frontier. To lure them, our monarchs developed the habit of offering exclusive individual rights and guaranties known as *Fueros*. Basically, they were bills of rights that granted freedom of movement, protection from the abuse of authority, the protection of private property and inviolability of the home, special protections and rights to women, procedural guarantees, and so on. The practice over time normalized the understanding that our monarch's power was largely in the hands of their subjects. An exquisite example of this, is how our neighbors, the people of the Kingdom of Aragon, swore in their kings:

> 'We, who are worth as much as you, but together more than you, declare you Principal, King and Master among equals, so long you guard our laws and freedoms; otherwise, no.'"

Master among equals... Lily was impressed. "I get it. The throne was a voluntary gift handed to the king by his equals in exchange for protection, not an obligation. That's what your annual enactment celebrates."

Elvira met her gaze with an odd expression of satisfaction. "That's right, and there is a true historical event behind the enactment. You see, it was here in Leon, in this cloister precisely, where in 1188 the first documented example of parliamentarism in the world occurred."

Lily and Sofia turned to each other to share the same thought: *The New Experiment* ...

"Believe it or not," continued Elvira, "it was thanks to a boy, a 17-year-old king named Alfonso IX. His rivals were not the Muslims in the south but his own relatives in neighboring Christian kingdoms. They disputed his right to the throne. War lurked, as usual, as did the need to collect taxes for it, which strained the new king's approval ratings. So, he convened the *Cortes de Leon of 1188,* inviting representatives from the nobility and clergy, and, for the first time, the people. The three powers met right here," Elvira swept her hand across the cloister, "at a round negotiating table where they all had equal *voice and vote.* It is difficult to state how historically transcendental it was. For the first time in feudal Europe, the people had a formal say in their government and legislation. Put in modern terms, out of this congress, the resulting constitution promised to respect the existing bill of rights which, approved in 1017, were trailblazing in their own right, and to establish checks and balances on the powers of the king via the power of the purse."

Sofia and Lily were numb to shock anymore, still they looked at each other shaking their heads with amazement. The New Experiment with a Constitution and Bill of Rights, the whole package.

Elvira cleared her throat, her gaze turned solemn, her posture regal. "May our history serve as a cautionary tale. Never take your rights and freedoms for granted. Time can be cruel. Rulers come and go, wars ravage, empires rise and fall, and power can switch from reasonable hands to tyrannical ones in the blink of an eye."

Sofia nodded as it dawned on her that maybe Lily was right. Maybe they were prophets of sorts. Like the people of Leon, who preserved the memory of their early sovereignty in an annual reenactment, so the memory of the pact's true spirit had to be preserved. To this end, in virtue of the pact's connection to their lines, she and Lily were being recruited to tell its story before the Knights corrupted its memory or had the truth erased.

"Come," said Elvira. "Before we wrap up, there is one more thing I'd like to show you."

Lily braced herself. What else could possibly be left?

Elvira led the twins into the Royal Pantheon.

Lily raised her eyes. The crypt's arches and vaulted ceilings were decorated in rich colors displaying diverse scenes from everyday life mixed with biblical ones. "They're stunning," she admired. "I believe you said they were Romanesque. Your restauration efforts are masterful. They look like new."

"These frescos have never been touched."

"You're kidding. Those bright colors are original?"

Elvira nodded. "These paintings were commissioned by Lady Urraca." She drew Lily's attention to the scene of the Last Supper. "Notice something missing from the table?"

"Yes, everyone has a cup except for Jesus. His chalice is missing."

"Think about it," said Elvira, "Lady Urraca donated her own jewelry to convert the chalice you saw upstairs into a Eucharist cup, yet, in these paintings, which she personally commissioned, it's missing from the table."

"I see it," said Lily. She pointed to the top left corner of the scene. "The cupbearer is holding it in his hand. It's just the bowl without the encasing." She paused to draw a broad smile. "His eyes—they're looking straight at Jesus."

"That's right," celebrated Elvira. "Lady Urraca had left us a clue about the true nature of her Eucharist cup. Right there, in plain view, all this time."

Elvira took a deep breath. "The tour ends here. I hope I succeeded in fulfilling your curiosity." She slid her eyes deliberately from one sister to the other. "On your way out, in front of the church, I recommend you stop to see the sculpture dedicated to our *colorful* tradition, *Las Cabezadas*. I'm certain you will find it very interesting."

Sofia and Lily stepped outside. The exit led them to the backside of the church. The breeze had cooled considerably. They welcomed it to clear their minds.

"Was that intense or what?" exclaimed Lily. "I feel like Dorothy, transported by a tornado to Camelot instead of Oz, and then chewed up and spit out. My head is still spinning."

Michael and Gabriel approached them.

"Are you two okay?" asked Michael. "You look dazzled."

"To say the least," admitted Sofia. Her temples pulsed as she tried to keep the different layers of information straight. She was desperate for paper and a pencil to write it all down in columns of perfectly ordered bullet points. But it would have to wait. First, she turned right and started walking.

"Where are we going?" asked Michael, as he followed.

"There is something we have to see."

Lily fell in step with Michael and shared a look of wild disbelief with him. "You won't believe what we learned. The original Declaration, I mean the real-deal fair copy is in there, and they use the real-deal Holy Grail as its paperweight. It's crazy!"

"You picked up on that?" said Sofia surprised.

"Of course, I did. After the way you all played me last time, I pay close attention to everything that is said."

They reached the front of the church and scanned the plaza for the sculpture.

"I don't see it," said Lily. "Where is it?"

Sofia tapped her shoulder and pointed. "Over there."

They approached it. People walked by it obliviously. The reason was it stood inconspicuous at the corner of a restaurant's patio flanked by tables, giving the impression it was the restaurant's corner marker rather than a city statue.

The piece consisted of a light-colored stone pedestal with a plaque attached to one side, explaining the bronze scene it sustained on top: the moment a representative of the people handed an oversized candle, which looked more like a poster tube, to the abbot of the *canonigos*.

Just when they thought they were numb to any more surprises. Sofia and Lily looked at it in a state of stupor for several long seconds.

"Un-believable," exclaimed Lily, finally.

Sofia swallowed. "Right there, in plain view, all this time ... John Adams delivering the secret pact."

* * *

Antonio stood quietly in the dim-lit room, sparing a moment to show his respect for the Holy Chalice.

Elvira came in, carrying a large portfolio in her hand. She stopped and addressed the guard. "*Nestor, espere fuera, gracias.*"

The guard studied both briefly, then nodded and stepped outside as instructed.

She approached Antonio. "I did my best to disclose what I could. I think they understood."

"Thank you. I owe you again."

"No, this one is on me. This day was long awaited. It was my pleasure to be part of it. I do have to say, though, they weren't what I expected."

"Don't underestimate them."

"I don't. I noticed they fit their respective roles well." She angled a mischievous grin. "I tested *her*."

Antonio narrowed his gaze on Elvira. "What did you do, Elvira?"

She threw her head back and laughed. "Don't fret, I was relatively well behaved. Besides, she stood her ground. I like her."

Antonio shook his head, failing to hide his smile. "We should get on with this. I need to get going."

Elvira grew concerned. "Are you sure it is a good idea? It would be my honor to continue watching over it."

"It's no longer safe here. More will come searching, especially once it becomes public, and you have your hands full as it is." Antonio inclined his head at the Chalice."

"The four deposit sites were chosen for a reason," insisted Elvira. "This part is the only one that remains in its original site. Won't their vital force be broken if you remove it?"

"Not where it's going, I assure you."

Elvira studied Antonio's handsome features. She was burning to know where that could be, but she restrained herself from asking. If anyone understood the vow of silence, it was her.

Diligently, she crouched and laid the portfolio flat on the floor. She then pressed her hand against the pedestal's panel. Its integrated nano-scanner identified the size, shape, prints and lines of her hand, clicking the panel open. She reached in and gently pulled out the tray containing the two large parchments in their protective sealed envelopes. For their preservation, they could no longer be rolled up.

Elvira took one last look at them. It was endearing to see them so fragile and pale, while containing something so remarkable. Hopefully, if the twins lived up to the expectation, its content would inspire. Otherwise, it could spell disaster.

Carefully, she slid them into the reinforced portfolio, zipped it, and stood up.

In a discreet underwhelming ceremony, Elvira transferred custody of the sealed promise back to the knight sworn to protect it.

CHAPTER 42

"The colours of the pales are those used in the flag of the United States of America; White, signifies purity and innocence, Red, hardiness & valour, and Blue, the colour of the Chief signifies vigilance, perseverance & justice."

—*Charles Thomson, Remarks and Explanation on the Great Seal, 20 June 1782*

Following the visit to San Isidoro, the sisters felt adrift on how to proceed. For good reason. While in possession of a fabulous story to tell, they had no concrete evidence to back any of it up.

This was particularly challenging for Sofia. She couldn't function this way. Sure, the trove of symbolic and historical anecdotes collected were fascinating, but they were held together by a thin string. That was not good enough for her standards, not by a long shot. And, in the end, what was it they really had? Maybe-maybe not a secret alliance that maybe-maybe not revolved around the creation of a league of empires founded on maybe-maybe not some well-intended ideals that never came to fruition. Seeing how it all went to hell afterwards—Europe continued with its endless conflicts akin to perpetual civil wars; Spanish America fell into an actual pit of shattering civil wars, and the United States went onto a land rush frenzy at the expense of slaves, natives, and neighbors that inevitably led to its own civil war—so much for Strength in Unity and all the ceremonial dancing around it. In sum, how could she "reasonably" make the case for an inspirational covenant or "reasonably" link it to a line that called for Peace—of all things—if the only evidentiary proof was a document that she was not allowed even a quick glimpse at to verify its existence. It was killing her to know it was right there at the reach of her hand but to have to walk away.

Lily didn't require the ultimate piece of evidence to function. No doubt the historian in her wished she had it, but the believer in her sought elsewhere. Her lines kept on giving and a meteor had guided her to a city where a building housed the personification of Enlightenment, the birthplace of the New Experiment, the Holy Grail, and a formidable pact, all in one place. It was surprising the basilica didn't glow at night. And there was the problem. It was all too much to not really have anything at all, particularly when contrasting it with their previous quest. Completing Mary's Line to its destination had revealed a visual, tangible miracle: the reproduction of the Hopi *Straight Path of Peace* on a planetary scale. As far as Lily was concerned, the word "Peace" written with neon stars in the sky and signed "God" would not have been more powerful. Consequently, if a fireball was going to direct her to Leon where the secret covenant was apparently guarded by the Holy Grail, nonetheless, Lily expected to walk away with something a little more substantial than literally *nothing*.

So, from opposing perspectives, the twins shared the same frustration: they remained empty-handed.

The unsettled mood extended to Michael and Gabriel, who, for their part, contended with growing dangers. The decapitation of the Knights was bound to happen within the next 48 hours, leaving a headless scorpion furiously swinging its unpredictable stinger. It was difficult to discern if it was best to run home for cover or stay as far away as possible.

Eventually, an interesting Solomonic decision was taken. Since it was late, rather than heading to Madrid straightaway on dark, lonely roads to catch an early flight the next day, they'd spend the night in Leon in the one place that still held some potential to give them clarity.

When researching the Convent of Saint Mark, Lily learned that its 18th century addition had been converted into a *parador*, that is, a state-owned luxury hotel. The elevated number of historical buildings in Spain that required hefty upkeep was taxing on her economy, so many were converted into self-sustaining tourist accommodations to secure their preservation. The establishments were generally located in spectacular settings or significant spots, and Saint Mark's was a nice balance of both.

That's where they were headed.

A solid, cold draft met them as they turned the corner into the expansive plaza that preceded the convent. Coming from the old quarter, they had arrived on its east side by way of a narrow street. While expected, the sight of the sprawling building, with its beautiful plateresque facade illuminated against the backdrop of the starry night, took their breath away.

The Convent of Saint Mark consisted of three major structures attached behind one continuous front. On the right of the main entrance stood the 16th century church and the old convent, both built upon the 12th century pilgrim hospital. Then, while several smaller touches were performed throughout the years, the largest and final addition was seamlessly attached to the left in the 18th century and was now the *parador* with its tower overlooking the river and medieval bridge.

Sofia and Lily knew immediately they had made the right decision to come here. It was difficult to fathom that two centuries and a half earlier, Adams would not have been equally impacted. Yet he made no mention of the place in his diary until the next day with the conspicuous absence of descriptors, an eccentricity for a man with no shortage of adjectives in his vocabulary.

Gabriel had reported their plans to Antonio who secured the two best connecting suites in the establishment. But Sofia and Lily were in no hurry to retire for the evening, for Adams' suspicious silence had imbued them with a strong sense of inevitability. They slowed down their pace to examine the varied decorative elements that adorned the facade on their way to the entrance.

Michael asked Gabriel to run ahead, check in, inspect the rooms, and arrange for special parking. Their rental car was stationed back by the restaurant, and he wanted to bring it closer. Meanwhile, he scouted the wide-open grid-like plaza in front of the convent drawing a scowl in anticipation of his verdict. "We are sitting ducks. Let's not linger outside more than necessary, okay?"

The sisters didn't hear him. Their bodies stood rigidly as each one gawked at a different section of the front, mesmerized by what they had already spotted.

Sofia was first to stop in front of the church while Lily wandered ahead. A stone-carved relief on the outer jamb of the portal had captured her attention. The image was of a considerable size, placed in a predominant position, and repeated symmetrically at eye level on each side of the entrance. It was hard to miss. She walked through the gate and approached the one on the left. Gently, she ran her fingers over its fletching.

Remarkable, she thought. It was a bundle of arrows tied together by a ribbon. But this bundle was special, because, in its uniqueness, it was also evidence that Adams must have stood in that same spot.

While at the National Archives, Lily had shown Sofia illustrations of Queen Isabella's bundle of arrows as they appeared on her Spanish coat of arms and coins. They were invariably depicted fanned out much like you see them on the current US seal. Here, however, the relief represented the bundle in a rare format: the arrows were aligned vertically and parallel to each other like Roman fasces, in the same manner Charles Thomson had sketched them for the Great Seal in his proposal to congress. It could not be a coincidence. Roman fasces were never depicted as arrows, always wooden rods, and symbolized authority, the Imperial Rule. Combined with arrows, Sofia realized it signified: *Strength of the Rule through Unity.* There was only one way Thomson would have known to reproduce this distinctive take on Queen Isabella's bundle, and she was looking at it. One more example of Adams' fixation with this building.

Meanwhile, closer to the main entrance, Lily, too, had made a discovery. She had gone looking for the two architectural medallions that contained the portraits of Queen Isabella and Judith. There was a total of thirty-eight medallions lined across the facade with images of mythical, biblical, and historical figures, but only three portrayed women, and the three had been placed together in a panel of their own. Now, standing in front of them, framed as they were, Lily realized she had made a terrible mistake: she had neglected the third lady.

Lily closed her eyes to scold herself as a good Catholic nun would. Then she called for Sofia and Michael, "You need to see this."

"Whatever it is, can we discuss it inside?" said Michael. "Raphael says he's picking up chatter that something is coming down. We might not have 48 hours after all."

"This is important."

"You should see what I found," said Sofia. "Adams was really struck by this place."

"Yes, and I know why. Get over here!"

Sofia peeled away from the arrows and joined her sister. "Okay, what is it?" she asked, looking at the wall.

Lily shook her head as she waved her hand at the three medallions. "I can't believe I missed her yesterday."

Sofia examined the three ladies. Time had severely eroded their faces. If it weren't for their breasts, it would have been difficult to tell they were ladies at all. It helped that their names were included in the frame of the medallion, if you knew Latin that was.

"These three figures are the only women on the facade," started Lily. She pointed. "The one on the right is Judith and the one in the middle is Queen Isabella."

"I remember," said Sofia. "You thought it was proof the meteor was guiding you here."

Lily's finger slid left toward the third lady. "Yes, but I neglected to consider her."

Sofia squinted. Only the woman's right eye and mouth remained. "Who is she?"

"Lucretia."

Sofia tried to place the name. It yielded nothing. "Never heard of her."

"No, but you should have. Lucretia is the link we were looking for. By being here on this panel with Isabella and Judith, she connects the Declaration and its pact to both lines." Lily was visibly distraught. "Sof, you're right, faith blinds. As soon as I discovered that Judith and Isabella were here together, confirming my miraculous meteor, I looked no further. She was right there, next to them. But I didn't care to see."

Sofia considered her sister briefly. "No, Lily, only blind faith blinds. It's human to make mistakes. That's why it is important to acknowledge that we can make mistakes even in Faith. Only then we'll be open to identifying errors when they happen—because they will happen—so we can correct the course. And that's what you just did like a pro. It's a very hard thing to do." Sofia then shrugged. "Who knows, maybe because you acknowledged your mistake you will discover the miracle is even greater than you originally thought."

Lily softly chuckled. "I can't believe you just said that, even if only to make me feel better."

"Did it work?"

"More than you think. The miracle *is* greater. That's why I'm upset."

"Oh boy. Go on. Who is this mysterious woman?"

Lily redirected her attention to the third medallion. "Lucretia was a noblewoman who lived in ancient Rome when it was still a monarchy in the 6th century B.C. She was notorious for her virtue, reason enough for the son of the king to want her. So, he raped her. The next day, she disclosed the attack to her family and then committed suicide. Her husband, her father, and a sympathetic member of the king's family, Brutus, pained by the monarchy's tyrannical ways, formed a revolutionary committee to overthrow the king. Led by Brutus, they discussed the best form of government to replace the monarchical system, choosing a republic, and then circulated a document with a list of grievances that justified the revolution, hoping to persuade the king's army to support their cause."

Sofia was in disbelief. "Talk about history repeating itself. Was Brutus' middle name George?"

"It's a myth," clarified Lily. "There may be a kernel of truth in it, but it's largely the legendary foundation of the Roman Republic. It was believed true for a long time, though, and inspired poems and plays by the likes of Chaucer, Dante, Shakespeare—and Voltaire. Voltaire wrote his tragedy 'Brutus', in London, in 1729, which later saw a surge of success in Paris while Franklin and Adams were there. The three men met in 1778, generating great expectation because, as you see, the legendary foundation of the Roman Republic served as the blueprint for the foundation of the United States' Republic."

"So, it was planned from the outset ..." Sofia slid her eyes to look at Queen Isabella's bundle of arrows. "... All designed to channel the strength and prosperity of the Rule."

"It's more than that, Sof. It was predicted on this wall."

"What do you mean it was predicted?"

"That's the greater miracle. By being on this wall to the left of Queen Isabella, Lucretia is predicting the American Revolution." Lily took a few steps back to appraise the facade better. "Look at the medallions. They are a succession of characters receiving the Rule from east to west." Lily pointed.

"From Alexander the Great, Greece, to Augustus, Rome, to Charlemagne, France, to Queen Isabella, Spain. That's why Adams was so impressed by this wall. When he saw Lucretia on it, positioned to the left of Queen Isabella in a panel of their own, he must have seen it as a sign that Providence favored his mission."

Sofia sighed. Fatigue was taking hold. "Lily, please, be serious. She's just a secondary character from a legend that happened to inspire the Founders."

"I am serious. That's the point. The fact that she, Lucrecia, a secondary character, is on this wall instead of Brutus is proof."

"Lily, it's been a long day—"

"Just hear me out," insisted Lily. "This wall is all about *translatio imperii* as evidenced by the succession of characters on it. Consequently, Queen Isabella's presence makes sense; she literally inherited the Rule straight from the source. But Judith and Lucrecia have nothing to do with it at all, so why are they here? Further, why isn't Brutus? His legendary election as magistrate of Rome following their revolution set the stage for how emperors were elected. He symbolizes the legitimacy of the Imperial Rule better than anyone. So, again, why isn't *he* on this wall? The only explanation is that Brutus would never have stood out, while Lucrecia does. She was placed here as symbol of the Revolutionary War and its Declaration next to Queen Isabella and Judith to capture our attention and connect the secret pact to our lines."

For the life of her, Sofia could not get used to her sister's reasoning. "Let me repeat what you just said: A legendary character from over two millennia ago was placed on this 16th century panel, akin to a flashing beacon, to predict the American Revolution that would not happen until two centuries later, for the sole purpose of capturing our attention five centuries later, just to let us know the pact is connected to our two lines."

"Correction: to let us and everyone know. It's the visual proof we needed."

Sofia rubbed her face. "Or here's a crazy thought: Have you considered that these three lovely ladies were chosen for their traditional gender role in art as symbolic virtues? Judith is, no doubt, *Bravery*. Lucretia must represent *Purity* or *Innocence*. And both flank Isabella, who ... well ... called for *Justice*."

Lily slowly angled a grin. "You mean as in Red, White, and Blue? Or is that just another coincidence, as well?"

CHAPTER 43

"[...] this is the point in your political fortress against which the batteries of internal and external enemies will be most constantly and actively (though often covertly & insidiously) directed, it is of infinite moment, that you should properly estimate the immense value of your national Union."

—*George Washington, Farewell Address, 19 September 1796*

Aaron's halfhearted grin reflected his bittersweet sense of victory.

It was done.

One page of the alliance, the one with the image, had been attached to their manifesto and *leaked* through the appropriate channels. The more serious news agencies were submerged in shock, gasping for air as they verified their sources before exploding with the breaking news. The rest had not bothered to contrast anything and were plastering their broadcasts with the image.

That was good.

On the flip side, his men in Spain had failed and he was informed that the consequence of it was on route headed his way.

That was bad, relatively speaking.

He had the money, the right contacts, and an army of lawyers on his side. By the time something was proven against him, if it ever was, he'd be long gone. The tricky part was to isolate his family from the shakedown so that the fight could go on. Luckily, the solution was easy, he alone would take the full blame proudly like a badge of honor.

Yet pride was not what he felt.

On balance he felt old, the kind of old where you realize life is passing you by and you can no longer keep up. And worse, you see judgement close and find yourself sporadically looking back to second-guess your actions.

Aaron rushed to block those thoughts from his mind. He sat in his armchair with his throbbing knee stretched out on a cushioned ottoman. The screen on the wall was split as usual, turned to his two preferred networks. Not out of loyalty, but for practical reasons. Between them, they held the largest quota of viewership from both sides of the aisle, and he had invested generously in both.

But like himself, their days were numbered, as well.

Aaron rolled his eyes around the room. His brother, who was only a few years younger, was at the desk working on his laptop somehow able to savor every *like* or *share* the leak was generating across several social platforms. Meanwhile, his grandson paced in front of the window with a joyous bounce, mumbling something about *tiks*. Or was it *toks*?

Lastly, by his side was his son exchanging messages and virtual currency on a private forum. Aaron wouldn't be caught dead trusting invisible money.

In any event, if he had understood correctly, their news release had successfully filtered from the Internet's underground to mainstream where it was spreading like wildfire, and all he could think was how he dreaded what was becoming of the modern world.

The Jacksons had arranged for the news to break during their weekly family dinner. While the women watched the children with the help of the nannies, and the uniformed help prepared the meal, the men enjoyed their aperitif discussing important business. The ideal world in Aaron's mind. Everyone in their place as it always had been and always should be.

His son tried explaining how they were working the modern platforms to get their message out.

"Things have changed, father. Younger people choose to follow someone they recognize and relate to; they are referred to as influencers."

And that was the problem, thought Aaron as he listened. Youth in his day listened to pastors and read the Bible. Now they were at the mercy of just about any fool filling their heads with dangerous nonsense on a handheld device. He made sure to express as much, and his son chose to forego pointing out the irony of how they were benefiting precisely from doing just that.

"What about the bottom line?" argued Aaron. "How many so-called influencers do we need to buy in order to match the reach and impact of a single major news network?"

His son had rolled his eyes in response. "No one watches cable anymore, father. Least the ground army that matters to us. And how many times do I have to explain that you don't buy influencers, you feed them."

"What are they, zoo animals?" snapped Aaron.

His son laughed. "You could say that. And they eat up anything they believe will go viral."

"How do they know what is going to go viral?"

"Because it's their job to make it go viral taking advantage of their large following. That's why they are called influencers and get priority access to so-called *leaks*. Technology companies do it all the time. They are perpetually *leaking* the features of their latest product to their industry-leading influencers so these can impress their followers with exclusive reviews on what's in the pipeline. By the time the product is released, people are lined up outside the door to buy it. In our case, our target influencers are conspiracy vampires. All we need to do is label our leak something like 'What they don't want you to know—"

"Conspiracy what?" interrupted Aaron.

"Conspiracy vampires," repeated his grandson from across the room. "I coined it myself. They are idiots who live off sucking the life out of the latest loony conspiracy and quickly move on to distract with the next one before anyone realizes how ridiculous and unfounded the first one was."

"No!" Aaron punched the arm of his chair with his fist. "How dare you associate our fight with that rubbish? The threat is very real. Our values are being eroded and our population replaced by all that mixed rabble at our borders invading our country supported by hippies who believe in participation trophies—"

"Dad, I hear you," said his son, weary of having to endure the diatribe again. If the word *hippy* was any indication, he had been suffering it for a long time.

"Don't you *hear me*." Aaron despised that turn of phrase. He found it condescending when waiters used it on him every time he complained. "Our family has been fighting this travesty for centuries. We've received a sign. It's now or never."

His son exchanged a conniving look with his uncle. "Relax, father. Indeed, the time is now, and we will prevail."

In another time, that would have appeased Aaron. But facing death as he was, the strangest thing was happening. A dreadful sense of guilt was setting in.

CHAPTER 44

"We hold these Truths to be self-evident, that all Men are created equal, that they are endowed by the Creator with certain unalienable Rights, that among these are Life, Liberty, and the Pursuit of Happiness."

—*The Declaration of Independence, 4 July 1776*

Lily glanced around to secure her footing and retreated for a broader view of the rest of the convent's facade. She didn't want to repeat the mistake of not checking the rest of the medallions for additional clues.

Thanks to the small lights embedded in the corners of the pavement's grid, visibility was enabled just enough for her to notice the silhouette of a solitary stone-cross a few yards away. It was set upon a pedestal in the form of a three-stepped pyramid. Suddenly, she was startled by the sight of a man quietly sitting there on the top step facing Saint Mark's. It took her about half a second to realize it was a statue. Lily approached it. From the statute's attire, she could tell it portrayed a life-size pilgrim taking a break. He had removed his sandals, laid them by his side, and leaned his head against the cross with eyes shut. It was uncanny how real he looked in the semidarkness.

Lily grinned. Not surprisingly, of all places, the cross was placed right in front of the three ladies, far enough for a full panoramic view of the building, while not so far that you lost sight of the important details. "I bet this is the best seat in the house."

Sofia turned to check for herself. Of course, it was. She took a seat next to the pilgrim. "I'll never look at urban sculptures the same way again," she remarked.

Making herself comfortable on the other side, Lily simply smiled. She was in bliss overdrive and not even the cold from the stone that filtered through her clothing troubled her.

Michael withheld his protests. Oddly, an ominous alert from Raphael put him at ease: *All operatives have been called back to base.* Translation: The Knights' membership had been summoned in preparation for an offensive move. Further translation: The twins, for now, had slipped to the bottom of their priorities.

Sofia asked Lily to share with her the rundown on the rest of the medallions. She had not bought into the whole prediction thing, but was aware that Adams could have, making Saint Mark's a strong candidate to harbor a copy of the pact, or provide clues to its whereabouts. With a few exceptions, beyond emperors, the remaining figures were household names such as Hercules, David, El Cid, King Ferdinand, and a long list of grand masters of the Order of St. James. For Sofia, it was a nagging downer. All she saw was a lineup of mythological, biblical, and historical characters defined by their brutal strength or war and conquer at the heart of their greatness. As a psychologist, she understood their legendary deeds or victories encapsulated heroism or national pride, but, as a mere mortal, she was also aware it came at the expense of sheer brutality too often for the sole benefit of the few at the top.

It occurred to her how the same could be said for Washington and King Charles III as the idea of 'conquer' hit home. Nothing personal against natives; both had also fought other Europeans or whoever it took, just like natives had fought natives. It was the cruel reality of human history; everyone had fought everyone; everyone had conquered and been conquered. But in her case, it beckoned the question, why was she, a Hopi, being asked to tell the story of their imperial alliance?

Sofia's roaming thoughts were interrupted when Lily called her attention to the tower at the end of the building by the river. "Sof, take a look at that relief over there."

Centered on the tower's front, was a carved image visible thanks to the beam of light directed at it. It was the iconic sword-like cross of the Order of St. James placed standing vertically over the saint's scallop shell at the top and a lion at the bottom. Sofia observed that the lion was not rampant as it profusely appeared in the kingdom's coat of arms. Instead, it was on all fours looking more like a docile pet dog.

"What about it?" she asked.

"Did you know that most US Presidents used coat of arms during their presidencies? John Adams inherited his from his mother and started using it as a diplomat in Europe."

"So?"

"His coat of arms consisted of crosses in the form of a sword and lions. That relief on the tower would have been the first thing he would have seen after crossing the bridge. Further reason for him to see this wall as a providential sign and his mission blessed."

"You're probably right."

"You don't seem impressed. It's a pretty interesting coincidence."

"No, Lily, you're a historian, you know better. Swords and lions were prevalent in the Middle Ages. Half of European royals and aristocrats carried them in their arms because they symbolized the values of knighthood. And this building was the headquarters of a knighthood. In fact, Chretien de Troyes, the French poet who wrote about the Grail, penned a poem around it. Its original French title was *Yvain or The Knight in Leon*. It's the story of a knight who saves a lion from a dragon, so the lion—symbolic of chivalry—follows the knight around loyally like a pet dog."

Sofia abruptly fell silent.

"What is it, Sof?"

"I'm struggling. All this symbolic nonsense, I'm tired of it. Chivalry is supposed to encompass the ideals of loyalty, honor, charity, and unconditional love. Do you know of any real-life leader or hero who has ever truly met that standard?"

"I'm a Christian sister. I devote my life to one."

"You know what I mean. We're battling a supremacist group calling themselves *Knights,* for crying out loud. It's always been an illusion. Not even the knights in Chretien's stories stand up to expectations. The same applies to these men." Sofia swiped her hand across the facade. "They are considered heroes or hailed *Great*, but they are far from it. I mean, Hercules? Really? The guy killed his wife and children in a spout of madness. And what about David? He sent a loyal soldier off to the front lines to die because he lusted for the poor guy's wife. If you can't fake true greatness for legendary characters, what hope is there for real men? So, don't get me started on any of those emperors."

Sofia paused. "I guess what I'm trying to say is that whatever noble values the secret alliance was purportedly built upon, it apparently had the same effect in the lives of real people as those espoused by the Declaration, that is, none. It was only a few decades ago that unalienable rights were legally recognized and implemented for everyone. We are being asked to sell an invisible product that has left behind no observable dent for over two hundred years. All we have is the potential good intention of two men, who, quite frankly, I'm not sure I'm ready to champion, either."

Lily considered her sister with sympathy. "Neither am I. Nor do I think the lines want us to. It's not about them."

Sofia drew a puzzled gaze.

"Look, let's start with Queen Isabella. All in all, she was pretty *great* if you ask me, but definitely not perfect. Regardless, it was her request for *Justice* that set a major ball rolling. In Burgos, a group of jurists took that request and laid out a body of laws that sprouted over time into today's Human Rights. Upon them, Francisco de Vitoria, formulated the universal natural rights of all men to life and liberty, which his School of Salamanca spread across Europe and the Ocean. Then, Jefferson, a man far from great, stamped them on a fateful document, which later Lincoln—much greater—embraced to spur a stronger unified country more prone to implementing them. Even then, it would still take time, but today they inspire a large part of the world; a world that is much better off thanks to it. Sure, there is a lot yet to be done, but we are getting there, and we need to make sure we stay on track to get there." Lily paused. "The makers of history may be flawed, some more than others, but we can't get bitterly stuck in their bad, because it's not about them. Our lines represent Peace and Justice, and if there is any chance the alliance contains the promise of Peace and Justice—"

Sofia waved her off with a smile. "Fine. Got it. Our mission is to keep the ball rolling forward. *That* I can get behind." She stared at her sister with admiration. "Lily, you make an outstanding prophet, and you'd make an even better minister. Heck, you'd make an extraordinary pope."

Lily curtsied. "Well, thank you. And I think your inner struggle goes to prove that true knights do exist, and you are an extraordinary example of one."

"Well, thank *you.*"

"It's time," came Michael's booming voice.

"Time for what?" asked Lily.

"For the two of you to do your extraordinary part. The Knights have released a page of the pact along with their manifesto. It's bad."

CHAPTER 45

"Sub umbra alarum tuarum protege nos."
[Protect us under the shadow of your wings]

—*Motto adopted by Queen Isabella for her emblematic eagle*

It felt like the news channels were tripping over their own attention span, unable to decide if they wanted to focus on the shocking discovery of the lost Declaration's fate, the startling image on the back of one of its pages, or the outrageous manifesto released along with it.

Sofia held the remote in her hand struggling with the same indecision, switching from one news program to the next, trying to gauge the situation.

She froze her thumb.

She had landed on a report displaying the image full screen, while an expert commented on it in the background. His credentials in the top corner under his name indicated he was a US history professor and author. Sofia identified raw emotion in his voice. It was apparent he was in the throes of deep denial, negating what everyone was seeing.

"It's absolute baloney. My ten-year-old son can design a fake composition better than this."

Sofia frowned. Too visceral. Too personal. This expert was going to offer little in the way of objective information.

"Suffice to say our Founding Fathers would never have subjected themselves to committing such a travesty."

Travesty ...? Sofia studied the image. True it was surprising, maybe even unsettling a little, but only because it differed from what was learned in school. Other than that, it was difficult to judge it in terms of good or bad. It consisted of five coats of arms placed around Queen Isabella's bundle of arrows under a guiding star. The title banner read *United Empires of America*. One of the armorials was that of the United States, as rendered in 1782. The other four belonged to the Spanish-American viceroyalties at the time of US independence. Therefore, whether the union was a good

310

or bad thing depended on the terms of the alliance, which the Knights had conveniently withheld. What they had done successfully instead was to anticipate their strongest condemnation for what the terms purportedly established, while presenting the image as an abhorrent example of George Washington's treason. The expert was being reckless. He was reacting to the conditioning of a hostile group without any real knowledge of the facts.

Sofia couldn't help but feel sorry for the man. She surmised he was probably in panic mode fearing for his reputation because, regardless of the Knights' maneuver, the truth was that the five coats of arms reflected a reality that he, the expert, had failed to address in his books: they all presented the same pattern.

She moved on to the next channel hoping to find someone less rattled. The scene was similar to the previous one, only the image shared the screen with the concerned face of the host while he listened to the expert on the phone.

"I can't talk to the authenticity of the document. All we have is a scanned copy of an image claimed to be on the reverse of one of its pages."

Wonderful, thought Sofia. She paused to listen. At least this expert was humble about her limited information, and subsequently cautious.

The host posed a question.

"In your own words, you have scavenged through the papers of the Revolutionary War for decades. What is the likelihood Washington could get away with a secret pact no one knew about without leaving a trail?"

"The likelihood is laughable. None. Period. Let's be serious. How do you veil an alliance of this magnitude? Besides, Washington always made it crystal clear he did not want to be tied to anyone."

"But that image is difficult to deny. The Knights claim, and I quote: 'The Great Seal of the United States clearly replicates the same heraldry pattern of the armorial of the four Spanish-American viceroyalties. This is an unequivocal proof of George Washington's allegiance to the tyrannical Spanish Crown', end of quote. You must admit they do look very similar."

"I'm afraid you'll have to consult an expert on heraldry. All I can say is that when it comes to European-style blazons, they all look the same to me."

As the host and the expert broke into a nervous laugh, Sofia exasperated. *Well, that was worthless.*

She took a moment to review the image once again.

Indeed, the pattern was hard to deny. They all contained eagles. But what did it mean? Was it that difficult to find an expert who could calmly clarify it?

She reminded herself that denial was a natural reaction. Since the image was uncomfortable—for what it implied—it was preferrable to center the debate around the authenticity of the document, hoping to prove it a forgery and call the Knights' bluff to make it go away.

Unfortunately, Sofia suspected that was exactly what the Knights wanted. They had crafted a false association with its own gravitational pull. If you sided with their world view, you rejected the alliance and everything it represented. On the other hand, if you rejected what the Knights stood for, inevitably you also rejected their claim. Either way, regardless of the true spirit of the alliance, it was set up for rejection.

Sofia broke away from the screen to look around. Gabriel had commandeered the printer from the hotel's business center and stood by it, waiting for Raphael to send over information on the history and symbolism of each armorial. She had requested it.

Meanwhile, Michael was glued to his cellphone. His concern was the manifesto and its ramifications for the safety of the sisters. As if matters were not bad enough, the Knights had sequestered Mary's Line for themselves. They had renamed it Providence Line and presented it as proof that a higher power had chosen the United States as the promised land for the superior race to create a New Order in their image. Therefore, they argued, it was their duty to rise and take the country back to its original purpose, which they claimed the Hopi sisters sanctioned through their line.

This put Sofia and Lily in a dangerous spot, because the Knights would surely try to prevent them from contradicting their claim. So, they were on lockdown again, in their elegant suite, while every text message Michael received seemed to elicit a tense follow-up call.

Lily sat next to Sofia in front of the television with her leg jerking in a nervous tick. It bounced up and down in pace with Sofia's thumb on the remote. Personal safety aside, both were dismayed that their line, which called for Peace, was in the spotlight promoting anything but.

The laptop rocked on Lily's unstable lap as she performed her own online research. "So rude," she said.

"What?" asked Sofia, blinking each time the TV screen changed. She was grateful for the wealth of channels the establishment offered from around the world.

"No one has anything to say about us or our line, as if the Knights never mentioned it. It's all about the Declaration and that image."

Sofia smiled at her sister's characteristic attempt to lighten up the atmosphere. "Give them time. It's coming." She suddenly retained her thumb hovering over the remote's abused button. On the current channel, a brave soul was addressing the heraldry pattern.

About time.

She listened.

"Let me first clarify the terminology," he started. *"In heraldry, the coat of arms refers to the elements displayed on the shield alone. In the case of the US, the shield contains a blue horizontal bar—or chief—at the top that represents Congress, and vertical red and white strips—or pales—that cover the rest of the shield. As Charles Thomson aptly put it in his proposal: 'The pales in the arms are kept closely united by the Chief and the Chief depends on that union & strength resulting from it for its support'."*

"Would you say the shield is the most important element?" asked the host.

"Most certainly. Everything else around the shield is symbolic dressing. For instance, in our Great Seal the bundle of arrows reinforces the idea of strength in union, as it relates to war, while the olive branch represents the preference for peace."

"What about the eagle, then? The manifesto suggests that the eagle represents the Spanish Crown, therefore, implying submission to it."

The expert waved his hand dismissively. *"In the case of the US seal, the eagle is what we call the 'support' of the shield. The majestic eagle represents power and strength. That's why several empires have displayed it prominently in their standards going back thousands of years, among them the Roman Empire. Those countries claiming to be their heir, which between you and me is pretty much everyone in Europe, Russia and the Middle East,"* he chuckled, *"displays an eagle in their armorial. It is a very common fixture."*

"I see the appeal. Power & Strength. It's a reasonable choice and, accordingly, a logical coincidence."

"Yes. Now, to be fair, I should point out that Spain has a special relationship with the eagle. Though the country's history is intimately rooted in the Roman Empire, the rise of its own empire coincided with Queen Isabella, who had embraced St. John the Evangelist's eagle as her emblem while still a princess. To her it also represented 'protection' and therefore was later adopted as the guardian for the united kingdoms of Spain following her marriage to King Ferdinand. In this vein, the Spanish viceroyalties did indeed display her eagle as part of their arms to symbolize the Crown as protector of that union. In fact, as you can see, their arms contain a crown, either worn by the eagle itself or placed upon the shield to reflect this."

"But that is not the case of the United States. Our armorial contains the bald eagle, and it certainly does not wear a crown."

"That's right. No crown. No Roman Empire connection. If anything, the choice of the bald eagle comes to affirm our country's exceptionality. The bird is unique to North America. Again, Charles Thomson put it best: 'The Escutcheon is born on the breast of an American Eagle without any other supporters to denote that the United States of America ought to rely on their own Virtue.'"

The host chuckled with apparent relief. "Well, that settles it. The American Eagle is as uniquely American as it gets."

Lily frowned. "I wished the so-called experts did their homework. They're making my profession look incompetent."

"I suspect he did. I get the sense that in his mind he truly believes the Founding Fathers chose the American Bald Eagle for its uniqueness and saw the bundle of arrows for its purely symbolic meaning: strength in unity. Considering the reigning consternation right now, he figured it was better not to mention the *minor* detail that the arrows, for their part, were uniquely Spanish." Sofia shook her head. "The poor guy has no idea he just played right into the Knights' hands."

* * *

The meal was superb. Aaron was still licking his lips. He felt reenergized and in a much better mood. He sat back in his chair savoring every tormented expert wiggle and squiggle through their shame and ignorance. He snickered. "God bless the fools." He swirled what was left of his after-dinner drink in his glass. The rest of it had mixed in his stomach with his evening pills, making his knee throb noticeably less and his spirits float higher. In this instance, life was good.

"Shoot those arrows," he ordered, laughing as if it were an ingenious joke.

"Loaded, pointed and released," reported his grandson, who was on his third double. "Images of Spanish coins and Continental currency containing identical bundle of arrows are circulating and gaining speed. We will be vindicated one viral arrow at a time."

They both broke out laughing.

Meanwhile, Aaron's son sat at the desk stabbing the computer screen with his eyes in preparation for his next move. His first and only drink remained untouched. He needed to focus. Each male member of the family had been assigned several tasks and he had botched one of his. He clenched his hand into a fist thinking about it. Not the failure, but the task itself. It was moronic, in his opinion, to incorporate the ridiculous line in their strategy. The old man's messianic complex was becoming a problem. The initial plan was to *persuade* the twins for their support. Now they no longer cared for it, leaving him stuck neutralizing them; a waste of effort and resources he could have done without. The screen flickered as he ordered the latest anonymous leak. The sooner he flushed them out from under whatever rock they were hiding, the sooner he could get rid of the stupid distraction and focus on the endgame.

CHAPTER 46

"May the kingdoms of Peru and New Spain be governed and ruled by viceroys, who represent my royal person, and hold the upper government, to do and administer justice equally for all our subjects, and attend to all which will lend greater calm, tranquility, dignity and peace to those provinces."

—*Charles V (I of Spain) & Holy Roman Emperor, 20 November 1542*

Gabriel walked over with a stack of prints. It contained a summary report for each of the four armorials of the Spanish viceroyalties. He dealt one to Sofia and another to Lily and then checked on Michael. Seeing he was tied up on the phone, Gabriel kept the two remaining reports for himself.

Close by, there was a desk against the wall. He grabbed the chair and spun it around. As he fell into it, he explained: "This is what Raphael has dug up so far. He'll let us know if he finds anything else."

Lily gave her restless leg a break and leaned forward to place the laptop on the coffee table. She gestured toward Michael as she asked Gabriel: "How is it going?"

"Not good. The risk level has increased. Despite the call for all-hands-on-deck in the States, the word is the Knights are sparing resources to look for you here. Mike is talking with Antonio; they are arranging safe transportation. We need to get you to safety."

"But why waste time and resources on us?"

Gabriel spoke softly. "To neutralize you. They have no other option. The Knights made a big mistake dragging you into this. The moment they proclaimed that one of your lines sanctions their actions, they gave you an audience. Your opinion has tremendous weight, and the press is interested in it. They are searching for you as well."

"And we must take advantage of that audience while we can," added Sofia. "Washington's legacy was an independent United States. The Knights are spinning the armorial image to question it."

"Can't we just say that? You know, alert people to be wary of the Knights' agenda?"

"It's not that simple. Conditioning works even when you're aware of it. Publicity is a good example. We all know popular athletes are paid to wear a certain brand, yet the positive association sells. More so if you fancy the product already. Anyone remotely sympathetic with all or part of the Knights' ideology will be predisposed to buy it."

"Right, but that leaves us having to prove that the alliance was a good thing. Quite a tall order considering we never got our hands on it. The fact remains we don't really know that to be true."

"First," said Sofia, "stop talking like me. It's disturbing. Second, if the terms of the alliance were clear-cut-bad, the Knights would have released them. So, while we might not be able to prove anything positively, we can establish reasonable doubt by finding the cracks in their claim with what we have: the armorial image."

Lily remained unconvinced. "Sorry, I just don't see how. Let's face it, Queen Isabella's eagle functioned as a territorial marker. That's how royal armorials work. There is no way around that."

"Exactly, which plays in our favor," stressed Sofia. "Look, the Knights assert that the Great Seal, which also functions as the US's coat of arms, was granted by Charles III in time for the peace treaty to showcase his grip on the colonies as they were released from Great Britain. If that were the case, the king would have granted his personal emblem, not those of his long-distant ancestor. The fact that Queen Isabella's emblems were adopted instead goes to show that the union wasn't about territorial possession, but rather about something more transcendental like sharing in her legacy. Make sense?"

"Actually, it does. Very smart, sis."

"There is a caveat, though," warned Sofia. "The Knights carefully crafted their entire manifesto around decrying the armorial image. This kind of investment means there is more to milk. We need to find out what that is."

Lily nodded. "Okay. Where do you want to start?"

"Let me," said Gabriel. "I have the information for the viceroyalty of New Spain. Its coat of arms was the earliest and sets the stage for the rest. But before I start, just to be clear, a viceroyalty was simply a state, and it was governed by a viceroy, a stand-in man for the king. He had them in Spain and Europe as well. In America, due to the great distance, viceroys enjoyed a little more freedom, but were controlled by limited terms, renewable once." He looked down at his sheet. "New Spain was huge. At its maximum extension, it reached north as far as Alaska, covering two thirds of current US, all Mexico, Central America, Venezuela, the Caribbean and some islands in the Pacific such as Guam and the Philippines. It was very prosperous for being the trade nexus between Asia and Europe, aside from its rich resources. The capital was Mexico City, and since the city itself was founded before the viceroyalty, its coat of arms was adopted for the viceroyalty at large. The same would be true for the other three." Gabriel looked up. "Here is an interesting detail: Mexico City was established and, therefore, granted its coat of arms on the 4th of July 1523."

Both twins surveyed the image with raised eyebrows, as Gabriel went on to describe it.

"Initially, the king granted the city an armorial containing a castle and rampant lion to link it back to the mother kingdom of Castille and Leon. The locals, supported by Hernan Cortes, rejected it in favor of a customized design that observed the legendary foundation of the city. It worked nicely because it revolved around an eagle. According to tradition, the wondering Mexicas had been instructed by God to be on the lookout for an eagle perched on a prickly pear cactus for a place to settle. That site was Tenochtitlan upon which Mexico City was built. Therefore, the Spanish Crown's eagle—as denoted by the crown on top of the shield—was included in the shield as the eagle sighted by the Mexicas to symbolize the union of cultures. The border reads 'Kingdom of Mexico Tenochtitlan.'"

Gabriel signaled that was it.

"4th of July—customized eagle—sets the stage for the rest," murmured Lily. "These details can be twisted to infer that the United States was created in the image of Spain's earliest viceroyalty."

Sofia shrugged it off. If that was all they found, it was too much of a stretch. "What about Peru?" she asked.

"More of the same," said Gabriel. "The viceroyalty of Peru was created to administer all Spanish South America, except for Venezuela. It too prospered thanks to its extensive trade network between Europe and Asia, and rich resources."

He checked his notes. "Its capital, Lima, was initially called City of the Kings because it was founded by Francisco Pizarro on January 6th, 1535, the day of the Epiphany. That's why the shield contains the three crowns of the Three Kings or Magi and the guiding star of Bethlehem hovering over them. The border reads 'This is the Real Sign of the Kings' in reference to Jesus Christ being the guiding star for the Spanish Crown. As for the support, it's two Spanish royal eagles, not to be confused with the double-headed eagle of the Holy Roman Empire." Gabriel looked up. "To make this distinction the smaller star was added at the top to symbolize St. John's halo. And the reason there are two eagles is because one stands for Queen Joanna I, the legal queen at the time—she had adopted her mother's eagle—while the other stands for her son Charles V in his role as co-regent."

Again, Gabriel signaled he was done.

And, again, Lily summarized the tricky items. "Lima's armorial confirms that, when in doubt, the halo establishes the eagle as that of the Spanish Crown. There is a halo in the US seal. Then, not sure if there is a connection, but the armorial image released by the Knights contains a guiding star as well."

This time, Sofia winced. The halo troubled her. It could be a problem in combination with the image she held in her hand.

She was up next. "I have the viceroyalty of New Granada. It was created much later in 1717. Britain had become aggressive at attacking Spanish ports, especially in the Caribbean, so Spain carved New Granada out of the two original viceroyalties to make the region's protection and administration more manageable. It included current Colombia, Venezuela, Ecuador, Panama and Guyana. Its capital, Santa Fe, was established back in 1548, on the 12th of October, coinciding with the anniversary of the discovery."

She paused to study its coat of arms.

It required little explaining. The entirety of it was Isabella's eagle displayed in identical manner to the US eagle, only more than 200 years older.

"What is it holding in its talons?" asked Lily.

Sofia checked her notes. "Pomegranates. I guess that's what *Granada*, the name of the viceroyalty, means in Spanish. According to this, it goes back to Queen Isabella and King Ferdinand completing the *Reconquista* with the capture of the Muslim kingdom of Granada in 1492. It took them ten years. During that time, their military camp's name was Santa Fe, and that victory freed up the resources that sponsored Columbus. He set sail seven months later."

Sofia bit her lip. This armorial, whose eagle looked the most like the US one, specifically symbolized the continued expansion of Spain's united kingdoms from the Iberian Peninsula to the Americas. It was easy to see the Knights exploiting it as their banner.

Still, that was nothing.

Lily released a long exhale. She had skimmed ahead through her report, and saw it held all the ammunition the Knights could hope for and more. "Guess when the Viceroyalty of Rio de la Plata was created?"

Sofia braced herself.

"In August of 1776, at the same time the Founding Fathers were formally "creating" the United States by signing the engrossed copy of the Declaration. Portugal had been pushing Brazil's border into Spanish territory, so Charles III created the Viceroyalty of Rio de la Plata on a temporary basis to deal with their land grabs. It encompassed Argentina, Paraguay, Uruguay, Bolivia, part of Peru ... and Equatorial Guinea in Africa." Lily paused briefly at that oddity to check she had read it correctly. "Anyway, the king put a trusted military leader at the helm, who performed exceptionally well, proving the administrative division was efficient, so he made the viceroyalty permanent. That commander was promoted to viceroy."

Lily looked up at Sofia with great concern in her eyes. "It was all coordinated by the king's right-hand man in the Americas, Jose de Galvez. That is the same guy who was at the same time directing Spanish support for Washington. And once the Portuguese conflict was resolved in 1779, his full attention turned to the US Revolutionary War. It was one of the reasons Spain delayed in committing."

Sofia began to massage her temples.

"As for the shield," continued Lily, "Buenos Aires was chosen as capital. The city's armorial was that of its founder, Juan de Garay, which was granted to him in 1591. It displays the Spanish crowned eagle holding the cross of the Order of Calatrava—I imagine he belonged to it—and four eaglets at its talons representing the other four cities he founded in the name of the Crown."

Lily concluded with a despondent sigh, which Sofia picked up as she listed the damning parallels.

"In that same vein, the capital of the United States carries the name of its founder and his coat of arms for its flag; the same founder who, supported by Spain, was the commander during the war and likewise "promoted" to President thanks to his success, with the Spanish ambassador standing by his side and a Spanish warship firing the salvos. And that same founder and President designed the capital after the town where Spain committed to the war in 1779, reserving a spot in its heart for Queen Isabella, the owner of the ubiquitous haloed eagle."

A moment of silence ensued. With a little creativity and a lot of malicious intent, the Knights could use the combined pattern of the five armorials to establish the US as the fifth viceroyalty and George Washington as its viceroy.

Finding cracks would not be sufficient. Without the terms of the alliance to prove otherwise, it would be close to impossible to effectively counter their narrative.

CHAPTER 47

"The foundation of our Empire was not laid in the gloomy age of Ignorance and Superstition, but at an Epoch when the rights of mankind were better understood and more clearly defined, than at any former period."

—George Washington, Farewell letter to the States, 8 June 1783

Michael approached the group. He signaled Sofia for the remote. She handed it to him, and he switched through the channels until he landed on an American cable news network.

Sofia and Lily gasped when they saw their faces on the screen. The picture had been taken at one of their talks three months earlier. The bottom banner read: Do Hopi Sisters Claim the United States part of Great Spirit's Plan?

The host was interviewing a political guest who declared himself sympathetic with the Knights.

"Here's what the manifesto says," started the host. *"Our children are being indoctrinated to believe that Manifest Destiny was a vile excuse to brutally take land that was not ours. Now, these two courageous ladies have come forward to vindicate the truth: that the Lord had destined the land for us."* The host looked up. *"Do you agree with this statement?"*

"Look, I'm not saying it was done right. Some atrocities happened and maybe things could have been handled differently. But we did bring civilization, liberty, democracy, and prosperity. No one can deny that."

The host insisted. *"But to state that two Hopi women preach the righteousness of it is going a little too far, wouldn't you say?"*

"We must surrender to the fact that it was God's will. Providence Line clearly shows that a Divine Hand chose the United States specifically to create a New Order based on our traditional Christian values, and our Founding Fathers acknowledged this on the back of the Great Seal. The real question is: What was George Washington thinking? Why would he betray Providence's will and sell us out?"

Michael moved to the next channel. A televangelist could be seen pacing a lit-up stage enveloped by an auditorium big enough to hold ten thousand attendants. The sign hanging overhead read: Stand and Fight for what is Right.

"*As one of our greatest military leaders Eisenhower once said: 'Under God reaffirms the transcendence of religious faith in America's heritage and future; in this way we shall constantly strengthen those spiritual weapons which forever will be our country's most powerful resource in peace and war'. And I add,*" continued the preacher, lifting a threatening fist, "*the Lord guided our chosen brethren to this land and abominable forces of evil have been undermining our mission since. Providence Line tells us to stand and fight until our last drop of blood for our Faith, our traditional Values, and our righteous Way of Life.*"

Despair washed over the sisters.

"No, no, no," said Lily, "That's not what it tells us at all. Peace. It wants Peace. Only Peace. No blood. Just Peace."

Michael changed to another channel.

A perfectly groomed man waved a Mormon bible in his hand.

"*Providence Line points to Salt Lake City. Not the Vatican. Not the Mecca. Not any other religious center. There is no greater sign from the Lord that His plan for you is with us. Come meet with the missionaries. We'll pray, read the scriptures, and discuss the teachings of Jesus Christ with you.*"

Michael pointed the remote to the screen one more time.

The focused gaze of a news anchor took up the screen as she listened to a Religious Studies professor from an Ivy League school on a phone connection. The headline asked: Providence or Superstition?

The professor's voice was tempered by his drawl: "*...Providence Line is just another version of a Ley Line. Ley Lines became popular in the 20th century. They promote the idea that ancient societies erected sacred centers or structures along straight paths and large distances to connect an imaginary network of magnetic, divine, or psychic nods. There's even the occasional collection of alien beacons. Take your pick. We are wired to see patterns, and a straight line is the simplest of them all. In the end, anyone can construct one that suits their needs and people will see what they want to see in them...*"

Sofia rubbed her face. "Well, he is right about that."

A painful breath escaped Lily. "What if that's what we are doing, Sof? Maybe we just see what we want to see in ours."

"Of course, we do, Lily. You see Mother Mary begging for Peace in the world, and I see an interesting enigma. And we'll argue our case as everyone else has the right to argue theirs. But, hell, if we are going to let anyone claim we condone Manifest Destiny."

Michael silenced the TV and stood facing the sisters. "Your straight lines are going to be stretched, twisted, bent and curled until you don't recognize them anymore. I suggest you get used to it. For now, we have something more pressing to worry about. A reward for your location was launched online an hour ago. The challenge states you are on the hunt for your next prophetic message. That's why your line is so hot right now. And it's turning into a mad rush to see who can find you first. There is already a rumor circulating that you have been spotted here in Leon. We're just moments away from a hotel guest or a member of the staff claiming the prize money and their five minutes of social media fame."

His phone beeped.

As he took a quick side look at its screen, Lily shared her shock with Sofia. "One hour. That's all it took to find us. Holy Mary Mother—"

"Let's go," said Michael. "Our helicopter is 15 minutes out. That's about the time it will take us to get to the airport."

Just then a knock was heard at the door. "Room service."

Everyone's immediate reaction was to look at each other wondering who had ordered.

No one had.

Michael signaled Gabriel to take the twins into the adjoining room. He had no intention of opening the door but took the precaution as a matter of course.

"Let's sneak out this other door," suggested Lily.

Gabriel shook his head. "Not yet. Both rooms were booked under diplomatic code names. Since it looks like they know you're in that one, this one might be compromised as well."

Michael waited for the twins to be out of sight. He looked through the peephole. "Wrong room. I didn't order anything."

Sofia felt a shiver as she donned her coat and grabbed her backpack. She couldn't see Michael from where she stood, but the deep rumble in his voice would have brought down the walls of Jericho. It was sure to cower a casual treasure hunter.

"I'm pretty certain it's the right room, mate."

Well, that was scary. Instead of deterred, the person at the door came back cocky.

Gabriel picked up the room's phone handset and punched the front desk button. "Ma'am, a fight has broken out in the hall on the second floor. Please send someone to check it out ... yes, of course, I'll remain in my room. Just, please, hurry."

Sofia was further mystified. Despite his open lie, Gabriel's pupils had not dilated a micro of an inch. That was some high-level training.

Soon enough, muffled voices were heard out in the hall and the sound of several pairs of running feet pounding the floor followed. There must have been more than one person outside.

Michael appeared at the connecting door. "Time to go. Stay close to me. Gabriel last."

The sisters nodded.

The hallway appeared clear. The rooms were disposed around an open central area, overlooking the cafeteria on the ground floor. They stepped out into the hall and steered toward the stairwell, hugging the wall away from the railing.

Once on the ground floor, Michael had them wait while he stepped out into the lobby. It was busy considering the late evening hours but not overwhelming. Nonetheless, the hotel personnel could be seen exchanging uneasy looks. He flinched. That confirmed the twins' exact location had been divulged and they expected problems. He relayed the situation into his communication piece.

Quietly, he then led the way toward the main entry hall, hoping they could still sneak out unnoticed. The entry hall was separated from the reception area by an arched doorway to the left; an elegant sitting room on the right, and a stone stairway dominating the welcome area in the center. He slowed down when he saw a guard block access to the reception area and route people to the welcome partition. The situation was getting worse by the second.

Michael asked Sofia and Lily to step behind the arch for a moment while he checked things out ahead. He soon located the hotel manager, who was scrutinizing the growing crowd. It was clear from her tense demeanor and sharp gaze she was entertaining a complete closedown of the establishment.

Micheal got a glimpse of her name tag as he approached her. "Ms. Nájera," he called.

Her eyes flickered when she recognized him. "I was about to contact you to discuss the situation. Are the sisters alright?"

"Yes, but we think it might be better if we left." He gestured with his head back at the archway to the reception area, where they could be seen discreetly waiting.

She nodded. It didn't show, but she was grateful.

"Could you create a diversion?" asked Michael.

"Certainly." Nájera turned toward the stone stairway, which snaked first to the right and then left before heading straight up to the first floor. It had been cordoned off. She made her way through the cord and climbed to its second elbow to look over the stone railing into the room as though elevated on a pulpit. With a powerful clap of her hands, she drew everyone's attention to herself.

Michael was impressed. No hesitation or objections. Just immediate results. He was ready to recruit her on the spot.

He returned to the archway but stopped momentarily to listen to his earpiece. He *Rogered* what was transmitted and looked at the sisters. "Be ready to run if necessary. Though these people are harmless tourists and locals responding to an online challenge, the reward has been doubled. Do not stop or talk to anyone. Keep moving forward no matter what. I don't want the crowd blocking our exit. Ready?"

Sofia and Lily nodded.

Michael checked once more. Nájera was kindly reminding everyone that while they were all welcome to enjoy the public facilities and services the establishment had to offer, they should also remember it was a home away from home for its guests and asked that they respected their peace and privacy.

Gabriel took the lead this time. Sofia and Lily slipped out close behind. Michael followed last, relaying everything into his earpiece as they went along. They barely made it halfway. A wandering teenager, who cared little about what the hotel manager had to say about anything, spotted them. He raised his phone and called their names, hoping to get a clear frame of their faces. He was pushed to the side by a bruiser wearing a Keep Calm shirt who rushed forward hoping to beat him to it.

As instructed, Sofia and Lily continued moving with heads down and an extra kick in their step.

While the hotel security guard stepped in front of the bruiser and the teenager, a squirmy individual wiggled through with his phone camera ready in one hand and grabbing Lily's arm with the other to turn her around. Michael, whose biceps almost matched the width of the tourist's waistline, gripped the guy's arm and squeezed it until he let go with a squirm. No words were required.

Sofia stuck with Gabriel, pushing through the doors out into the plaza. She momentarily paused. Maybe it was just that the situation was a little unnerving, but when she looked up, she saw the grid-like open space spotted with shadowy figures approaching the hotel like zombies converging for an attack. She felt her heart race and sped up after Gabriel. He had rushed ahead to start the car. It was stationed in front of the church under a no-parking sign. They had received special diplomatic authorization with the promise they would leave early the next morning.

Gabriel reached the vehicle and noticed the tires had been slashed. He knew instantly it was not the act of a random challenge-taker. There were professionals hidden among the growing mob. He quickly scanned his surroundings, but it was difficult to discern much in the semi darkness. He signaled Michael, who could be seen concentrated, trying to hear what was being transmitted to him.

Sofia and Lily came close together, hiding their faces as people gathered around them. The crowd was still subdued enough to respect personal space, but their competing calls asking them to look up were slowly getting more agitated. Gabriel shielded them, demanding from Michael what to do.

Michael finally displayed a gesture of relief and instructed them to move toward the center of the plaza.

Sofia and Lily were puzzled. That hardly seemed the safest place. Their natural instincts told them it was best to retrace their steps back into the establishment. Then, suddenly, they understood. The thumping of helicopter blades could be heard approaching fast. People turned their heads up toward the sound, surprised. The helicopter had no identification logo, name, or numbers. It was just black. If not for its blinding beam of light, it would have been difficult to see. The swirl of wind generated made the crowd disperse away from its landing spot.

As it maneuvered to touch down, keeping everyone's attention, a rough looking guy from the crowd launched forward toward the twins with something in his hand. Gabriel reacted swiftly and blocked the attacker's weapon with his left arm, followed by a swift punch to the jaw with his right fist.

Michael watched on alert for others and detected a man prowling closer from behind a group of onlookers. He refrained from using his gun due to the concentration of innocent people, some children. Instead, he simply caught up with the guy and took care of him from there.

Meanwhile, the pilot signaled to Sofia and Lily it was okay to approach. As they moved forward, a third man intercepted them. He never got a chance to raise his weapon, much less point it. Sofia had hooked her leg behind one of his knees as Lily pushed him back. The pivot maneuver made the attacker collapse to the ground before he could register what happened. Sofia and Lily didn't stop to explain. Sofia kicked his weapon out of his hand toward Gabriel and then dashed for the helicopter with Lily close behind.

A fourth and last man tried to make his move but was blocked by the crowd, who seeing the sisters were getting away, started to shove each other with phones raised flashing. Luckily, the parents of the young children retained the presence of mind to keep them back. The rest had stopped thinking and were recklessly putting themselves in harm's way getting too close to the helicopter and its blades. Once the sisters were safe on board,

Michael finally resorted to reaching under his coat for his gun. He aimed in a 45-degree angle to clear the blades and shot once into the air. It startled everyone long enough for Gabriel to jump in the back, while he took the front seat next to the pilot.

The helicopter rose rapidly, leaving behind a furious burst of camera flashes, soon reduced to a sea of blinking fireflies.

Sofia slumped back into her seat and took her first full breath since stepping out of the hotel room. She then noticed the pilot had turned to look at her.

Only his smile was visible under the helmet's large visor.

It was Antonio.

CHAPTER 48

"To serve God our Lord and the good of the people in our kingdoms it is advisable that our vassals, subjects and naturals, have in them universities and general studies where they can be instructed and graduated in all the sciences and faculties, and by the much love and will that we have to honor and favor our Indies, and banish from them the shadows of ignorance, we create, found and constitute in the city of Lima in the Kingdom of Peru, and in the city of Mexico of New Spain, universities and general studies, and agree to grant them [...] the freedoms and rights enjoyed by the graduates of the university and studies of Salamanca."

—Decrees of 1551 as compiled in the Laws of the Kingdoms of the Indies, 1681

The sudden descent motion stirred Sofia awake. She opened her eyes and looked around. Like her, Lily and Gabriel had dosed off and were twitching back to life. She didn't know about Michael. All she saw was the back of his solid chair. Antonio was focused on the landing maneuver.

Sofia wondered how long they had been in the air. She straightened up and combed her hair with her fingers hoping she had not looked silly while asleep. At the start of the trip, she had found herself frequently sneaking side-looks at Antonio and on several occasions caught him looking back. Her heart leaped each time despite all she could see of him was his chiseled jaw.

It was official: she had a crush on him.

She sighed helplessly and looked out the window. With a man like him, so alluring to the senses while private and individualistic, she was in for a heartbreak regardless of something happening between them or not.

Town lights came into view and two sparsely dotted strings—one red and the other white, moving in opposite directions—revealed a throughway below. Other than that, the flight had been over dark extensions of land that might as well have been a body of water for what she could tell.

In contrast, the helicopter's interior was designed in light colors. It was nicely appointed with comfortable leather seating, arm rests with cupholders and some other nice touches like ambient lighting. And it wasn't as loud as she had expected. It clearly had state-of-the-art noise-control features.

Sofia felt a nudge on her arm. It was Lily. Her sister had switched seats with Gabriel to have access to the other window, leaving him stuck in the middle. Her face radiated excitement as she tapped the glass on her side and pointed to something below. Sofia turned back to her window to look but couldn't see anything other than the light residue spilling over from what Lily had spotted on her side. She shrugged with her hands open asking for clarification.

Lily curled a mischievous smile and rolled her eyes around the cabin pantomiming she couldn't say out loud.

Why not? wondered Sofia.

When they landed, she could tell it was at the foot of a large structure but couldn't see what from her position. And apparently it was in the middle of nowhere due to the absence of urban lights as far as her eyes could see. She waited impatiently for someone to signal it was okay to disembark. Her sister continued to taunt her with teasing looks Antonio's way. He was busy shutting down systems, so Michael was first to exit the aircraft. He came back to Sofia's door and opened it. Sofia thanked him and quickly walked around the front of the helicopter to see.

She looked up and froze.

Lily joined her. "I told you!" she said with a restrained shriek. "He owns a castle!"

Sofia blinked several times to make sure she was truly awake. The beams of light shooting up from the ground focused on its robust towers to enhance the solid stone architecture. This was no delicate Cinderella palace. It appeared to have been around forever and fought in some mighty battles. The scars were there to prove it as seen in the mixture of styles employed to patch it up over time. One tower was square, another rounded. One was covered with a conical roof, another flat. And yet another one was open at the top simply rimmed with embattlements. The windows varied as well. Some were of a simple arched design, while a couple displayed curvy morish lines. But, overall, the castle was imposing, probably the point.

Sofia could only imagine if it appeared this impressive from the back what the front might look like. She took a few steps to the side with Lily for a quick peek, not daring to divert too far from the lit path in the dark, while they waited for Antonio to finish up.

A few minutes later, he was done and headed up the slope toward a gate, signaling everyone to follow him.

Lily took Sofia's hand and pulled like a ten-year-old excited to see inside. They rushed by Michael and Gabriel and caught up with Antonio. Lily fell in step with him, while Sofia lagged awkwardly half a step behind, trying to look less eager.

"Thank you so much for getting us out," said Lily.

"Always happy to help," he said.

"So, where did you bring us? Is this castle yours?"

"It belongs to a private entity."

"And they just let you use it?"

"It pays to have the right contacts, especially if they are family."

"Quite some family you must have. Do you get to come often? It's huge. I imagine you don't come *alone*?"

Antonio chuckled. "I wish I could enjoy it more than I do. But you're right, it's too big for one person. Besides, during good weather it's leased out for weddings or corporate events. Since it's now vacant, I thought it would be a safe place to bring you while we decide our next step." Antonio turned to look at Sofia. "I can't take my eyes off you for five minutes, can I?"

Sofia blushed. What did he mean by that? Was he referring to their exchange of looks in the helicopter. Or was it about having to rescue her again? Perhaps a play on words for both? Neither? She chastised herself. Why was she making such a big deal over a sentence?

They reached the gate. He opened it and politely let everyone go through first. It led to a patio. From there, Antonio guided them to the private residence wing, tucked to one side away from the public area and sealed off with signs restricting access. When they stepped inside, there was a stark difference in style to suit modern comforts without losing too much of its medieval atmosphere.

Antonio offered everyone something to eat or drink, which they all declined. It had been a long day, they were tired. He showed them to their rooms.

Lily and Sofia became reenergized as soon as they were left alone. They ran around checking each other's rooms and exchanging impressions. Then, when they determined it was quiet, they sneaked out to inspect the rest of the place. Sofia found the decor surprisingly modest for her idea of a castle. Lily reminded her that most functioned as forts, not fancy entertainment halls. Still, it was quite austere. Tall, whitewashed walls, some covered with huge tapestries displaying medieval battle scenes, contrasted with the dark wood that framed doors and windows. Sofia saw little in the way of architectural accents other than a coffered ceiling here or there, though she was impressed with the oversized walk-in fireplaces and wrought iron chandeliers. All in all, her final verdict was positive. Sofia decided she liked the practical minimalist design that had been pulled off with a touch of casual elegance.

But one thing caught the sisters' interest over everything else. The large painted portraits. Their aristocratic figures shared an undeniable familial resemblance with Antonio. One in particular left no space for doubt. It rested over a massive fireplace in the main grand room, indicating that the stately knight pictured in it was the great-great-plus patriarch of the family. Dressed in armor with a gilded brocade cloak draped over his shoulders, his large dark eyes glanced unwaveringly at the observer, while his defined lips drew a soft debonair grin. His hair was shoulder-long, and his left hand rested on his sword at waist level. If not for his early 16th century attire, he could easily have been mistaken for Antonio's father. The sisters were mystified. Why would Antonio be secretive about his lineage? It would seem to them there was a lot of history to share with pride within these walls.

The next morning, a warm ray of sunshine caressed Sofia's face. She stretched leisurely, feeling rested despite the late night. She threw back the covers, slipped into her shoes and grabbed her coat from the ornate armoire to step out onto a small lookout balcony. The sun was already halfway to noon, making her realize she had slept in. She inhaled the fresh air and lowered her gaze to the tall trees below. Beyond, an expanse of dormant fields and rolling hills extended as far as the eye could see.

The scenery was simply beautiful.

Back in the room, she heard a single knock followed by the swoosh of her bedroom door opening. Sofia didn't bother to turn. It was obvious from the animated stomping who it was.

"Isn't this place crazy?" she heard Lily say. "Last night, I was disappointed we weren't staying at Saint Mark's, but this castle totally makes up for it. Did you know Queen Isabella was hosted here once? Antonio's family must be connected to her somehow."

Lily said all that in one breath.

Someone should cut back on her morning expresso, thought Sofia and asked: "How do you know?"

Lily joined her on the balcony. "From an informational booklet I found in one of my drawers. According to its history, the castle is almost 1,200 years old and was handed down through a high-ranking noble family. It doesn't provide the name, just says that a private corporation took over about fifteen years ago." She switched to a whisper. "That must be how Antonio hides his identity." Then she squinted in thought. "That portrait of the knight we saw in the great room has been bugging me. I know I've seen him somewhere." She shook her head and moved on. "Anyway, come, I have something to show you. You are going to flip out."

Sofia followed her in. "Has your Mother superior ever commented on your expressions?"

"No, why?"

"Nothing."

Lily approached the bed where she had dropped her laptop on her way to the balcony and perched on its edge.

Sofia closed the balcony's glass doors and rubbed her cold hands as she sat next to Lily. "What is it?"

Before showing her the screen, Lily explained. "I was very upset yesterday to see everyone appropriating Mary's Line to suit their personal needs. Yes, I know, where is it written it belongs only to us ... but its message of Peace was being completely neglected. All anyone cared about was where it pointed to or how to exploit it to their advantage."

"To be fair, Lily, you did all the legwork to find it. You are entitled to some ownership. That said, what's new? Wasn't that the purpose of the line in the first place? You concluded Mary designed it as a path back to her son and *his* message because the world had diverted from it. The sad irony is that the line is falling victim to the crime it was denouncing."

"And that's why I suggest we rename the lines Peace and Justice to make their purpose clear," said Lily.

"Sounds good."

"But it also got me thinking. Once we constructed the Peace Line, we thought that was it. We never extended the Spanish Li—Justice Line across the Atlantic to see where *it* pointed to."

Sofia widened her gaze with interest. "Okay ... what did you find?"

Lily turned the laptop screen to show her. It displayed one of their working maps. The one that spanned the Atlantic Ocean to show parts of Europe and Africa on the right and part of the Americas on the left. It contained the Peace Line rendered complete, but Lily had also prolonged the Justice Line through the south of Portugal, across the ocean and Brazil, to finally end in...

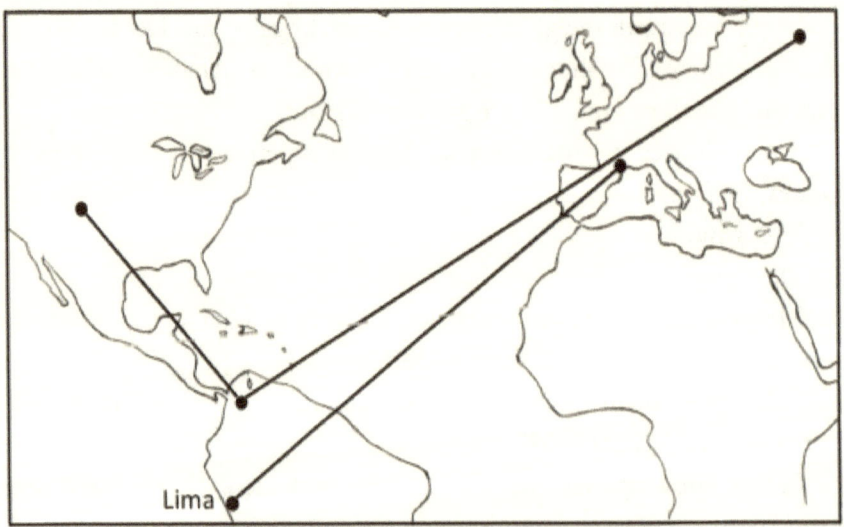

"Lima, Peru," murmured Sofia. She stared at it for a moment. "Why does it lead there? Do you know?"

"I think I do, but I'm going to need you to restrain yourself."

Sofia playfully crossed her heart, though she was genuinely curious. The coincidence that it led to one of the coats of arms seen in the image of the alliance was intriguing, to say the least.

Lily went there, precisely. "Yesterday, we learned that Lima was founded on January 6th. And we know John Adams was in Leon dropping off the alliance on January 6th. I don't know if that date is meant to tell us something else, but on the Christian calendar, it is the date of the Epiphany. Consequently, Lima's coat of arms contains a guiding star, which also appears on the image of the five-empire alliance. And let's just throw in there that a meteor guided me to Leon. So: guiding star—January 6—secret pact—Leon—Lima, all connected. You follow, so far?"

Sofia nodded despite her strong objection. Leon was not on any line and its only loose connection to the rest was a date. She listened quietly.

"Then, Lima's coat of arms reads 'The Real Sign of the Kings' to clarify that Jesus Christ was the guiding star for the Spanish monarchs. And this is exactly what Mary's Line is all about. It's the path back to her son and his message of Peace. So once more, the Spanish Line, by pointing to Lima in Peru, complements the Peace Line. And it makes perfect sense. There can only be Peace with Justice, and Justice with Peace."

Sofia began to draw a doubtful frown.

"Hold your horses. I'm merely warming up," said Lily.

"Fine but settle on one name for the lines, will you."

Lily brushed her off. "Just listen. It's getting interesting. I looked into the city of Lima and found another connection with Leon. In 1550, the locals wanted a university in the city because it was too expensive to send their kids to Spain for higher education. So, they selected two representatives, one civil and the other religious, to make their case before the king."

"Why?"

"Why what?"

"Why ask the king? Couldn't they just build one?"

"Yes, but they weren't interested in just any random university. The people of Lima wanted the same privileges, freedoms, rights, curriculum, and title recognition for their school as those held by none other than the prestigious University of Salamanca. You know, the one promoting natural unalienable rights for all humans."

"Really? That *is* interesting."

"You can say that again, because the king gave them his stamp of approval and a few months later decreed another university for Mexico City under the same terms. Thereafter, over a dozen universities followed all over Spanish America almost surpassing the number of universities in all of Europe." Lily paused and looked straight at her sister to tease a revelation was coming. "That university in Lima continues to function today. It's the oldest running university in all of the Americas and they named it ... Saint Mark."

Normally, Sofia would have ignored a simple name coincidence, but Adams' odd repetition of the adverb *here* scrolled through her mind as if trying to say: *there is a school here and another one over here.*

"That means," continued Lily, pointing to the map, "that this University of Saint Mark in Lima at the end of the Justice Line and oldest in America, mirrors the University of Salamanca, which is on the Peace Line, and is the oldest in Spain."

"Okay, but—" started Sofia.

"Hold on, there's one more thing. Guess who founded the University of Salamanca in 1218?"

"I can't imagine."

"The same king who celebrated the first parliamentary round table in Leon in 1188, Alfonso IX. Sof, you see what's happening here. Unalienable Rights and the New Experiment, as connected through the same king, are reflected on both lines and spread through sister universities on both sides of the Atlantic."

Sofia stood up to think. While her mind denounced the stretched out, convenient associations, her heart embraced the powerful message it conjured. "Peace, Justice, Human Rights and Sovereignty melded into one ball rolling forward through education, the ultimate equalizer ...."

"Yes, *but* ...," volunteered Lily, "the connection is loose at best. I know."

"Actually, I think you might be onto something."

Lily jumped to her feet. "I knew it!"

Sofia cautioned. "The message is consistent with the lines *but,* precisely because of that, a loose connection won't cut it. The link must be strong, powerful. The lines have been consistent about that as well."

"Okay, so, what do we do?"

"The only thing we can do."

"What?"

"Find it."

CHAPTER 49

"However our present interests may restrain us within our own limits, it is impossible not to look forward to distant times, when our rapid multiplication will expand itself beyond those limits, & cover the whole northern, if not the southern continent, with a people speaking the same language, governed in similar forms, & by similar laws; nor can we contemplate with satisfaction either blot or mixture on that surface."

—*Thomas Jefferson to James Monroe, 24 November 1801*

A van from a nearby town arrived with lunch. Antonio had called his favorite restaurant and asked them to prepare an assortment of their more popular dishes. The owner, who had the wise habit of handling Antonio's requests with discretion, considered her prized garlic soup a good heartwarming starter, followed by a variety of cold and hot tapas sure to satisfy most tastes. Additionally, bread fresh out of the oven was included, along with a nice selection of local pastries. To wash it down, Antonio visited the castle's wine cellar and chose a soft red produced on site that went well with the mix of flavors they were about to enjoy.

For Sofia, the star ingredient was the setting. Lunch was served in the four seasons room overlooking the small vineyard rimmed at the bottom of the incline by a meandering river. Somehow, she ended up seated next to Antonio who at that moment was refilling her wineglass.

Michael was bringing them up to date on the latest events back in the States. Tattooed man had delivered. His boss, retired Senator Aaron Jackson, was arrested overnight on high crimes and misdemeanors at his home in the presence of his family. Rumors circulated that he'd soon be charged with a list of unspecified conspiracies. While cable news showed images of the family denouncing it as a political ploy by his enemies who wanted to destroy America, the web was flooded with comical memes and videos of America's highest representatives of both sides accusing the other side of scheming to bring down democracy.

Lily passed him the salad. "I must be missing something. You cited a long list of crimes the retired senator will be charged with except for one: his involvement with the Knights."

Michael passed the salad along and lunged for the sirloin bites in Port wine sauce. "We have to tread carefully there. The Knights of Destiny is a family affair. We may have enough to bring down the current head, but his son has declared his intent to run for president. That makes him untouchable unless we have something solid to implicate him as well."

"So, nothing has changed," said Sofia. "The king is dead, long live the king. Only the new king may soon be even more powerful than the previous one."

"I'm afraid so. But don't worry, it is also the first time we've been able to get our hands on someone in the family. It may take time, but we'll find a way to drag them all down."

"And meanwhile what?" said Lily. "We let the heirs to the Knights spread divisive misinformation and incite violence?"

Her concern was valid. Matters had heated up since the publication of the manifesto. It's title—One People, One Language, One Religion —was geared toward stirring up the worse side of tribal instincts. Internet bots and innumerable false social media accounts targeted everyday hardworking folks who, feeling they did their part, channeled their personal frustrations and angers toward anything redolent of disloyalty, now personified by Washington. Some of his private communications were being published out of context, adding to a very unfavorable picture, and his statues around the country, particularly his memorial in D.C., were being sprayed with words such as "traitor" or "coward" to further aggravate the mood against him.

However, by association, anything Spanish—or Hispanic, in general—was faring worse. The Knights didn't even have to do anything. Isolated incidents were voluntarily popping up across the nation as a precursor to how things could get really ugly, really fast. Especially after the absurd assault on the bust of Cervantes, author of Don Quixote, in San Francisco, which was sprayed with the word "bastard" for no other reason than being Spanish. The burning of several Floridian flags had been rapidly mirrored in Alabama because both contained the red Cross of

Burgundy, a legacy of Spain's rule. This had Arizona and New Mexico on alert fearing something similar could happen there. And attacks on statues and plaques remembering Spanish historical figures had escalated beyond spray paint. Several had been beheaded or toppled all together. So, cities like St. Augustine, Los Angeles, and a long list of others in the south and west were on high alert paying close attention to evolving events.

Yet, these for now *anecdotical* incidents were soon to be overshadowed. The three men at the lunch table received a notification at the same time. Antonio suggested everyone moved to the private living room. There he turned on the large-screen television. A chaotic scene appeared in which police, dressed in riot gear, surrounded the statue of Queen Isabella in Washington D.C. as a sizeable group of rioters threw objects at it. Ironically—if not sadly—a large, bright red target had been sprayed on her chest just above the peace dove that was carved into the pomegranate she held in her hands.

This caught Sofia's attention for a couple of reasons. "Why do the police care to protect this statue?"

"It's not about the statue. Look at the rioters," said Michael. "They are organized and uniformed. They are wearing matching camouflage pants and display their rallying cry on their shirts. It's a bold move by the Knights to telegraph they fancy themselves an army and are on standby to carry out an offensive. Basically, they're recruiting."

"The location is no coincidence either," added Antonio.

Sofia nodded. "The Organization of American States," she said. Sofia squinted to read the text on the shirts, but the camera angle framed a broad scene showing the police trying to disperse the agitators, making it difficult to see. Abruptly, the camera zoomed in on a masked individual aggressively attempting to break through the police shields. The text came into view.

NO BLOT OR MIXTURE

Sofia felt her heart sink. She knew well what that meant.

It was little known that the man widely celebrated for crafting the sentence that summarized American values, had diligently worked behind the scenes to undermine them. Thomas Jefferson, like his fellow Founding Fathers, saw the United States as a rising empire, but he was particularly ambitious about it. Jefferson foresaw a future in which the United States overtook the whole continent, North, South and everything in between until, that is, a slave by the name of Gabriel planned an uprise in Virginia in 1800. He was purportedly plotting to take control of the Virginia State Capitol and hold Governor James Monroe hostage as he negotiated freedom for himself and his peers. The plot was thwarted and Gabriel along with his brothers and 23 slaves were hung, but it was source of much fear among plantation owners, because it came on the heels of another slave uprise taking place in neighboring Haiti. That one had been successful.

Thomas Jefferson was elected third president of the United States in its mist. In discussing how to deal with the growing unrest among the black population—both free and enslaved—with Monroe—the fifth president—he cautioned about the optics abroad of mass hanging the instigators, and several alternatives were debated. Jefferson didn't like the idea of relocating problematic slaves within the US out of concern they would persist in creating disruption. He didn't want them expelled to neighboring countries, since the plan was for the United States to expand into them. That left sending them back to Africa.

However, this only resolved part of the colored problem. While Native Americans were displaced west and isolated in reservations, interracial marriage had been accepted, legal and even encouraged for centuries in Spanish America and therefore *Blot and Mixture* was widespread in its population. Jefferson's growing dread for other races had him switch from aspiring to spread throughout the whole continent to establishing limits toward the south beyond Cuba. In a letter to his successor James Madison—the fourth president—in 1809, Jefferson advised:

> *"He [Napoleon], will consent to our receiving Cuba into our union to prevent our aid to Mexico & the other provinces. That would be a price, & I would immediately erect a column on the Southernmost limit of Cuba & inscribe on it a Ne plus ultra as to us in that direction. We should then have only to include the North [Canada] in our confederacy."*

It was Jefferson who reinforced the obstacles to emancipation, flared animosity towards the southern neighbors, and laid the pavestones for every trail of tears that followed, slowing down the advance of unalienable rights almost to a freeze, until Lincoln infused them with new life.

And from what Sofia was seeing on the television, a frigid storm hovered over them again.

Yet, she smiled.

"I know that look," said Lily. "You've picked up on something."

Sofia pointed to the television screen. It displayed a close-up of Queen Isabella's statue. "That target, placed like that on her heart, is disturbingly personal."

"What's disturbing is you smiling about it," said Lily. "She represents the bundle of arrows prominently displayed in the center of the five coats of arms. A target on her is a strong statement of rejection for the alliance. It makes sense."

"On the surface, maybe so. But on a subconscious level it's like when a serial killer leaves clues behind, hoping to be caught. It would be a different story if the target had been placed on the forehead. That would have been cold, detached. On the heart, it conveys guilt. And I think I know why." Sofia looked around at the men. "Do any of you have a copy of the armorial image?"

She noticed Antonio didn't move. He simply stood staring at her. Pleased.

Michael reached for his cellphone. "Hold on. I'll get it for you." When he had it on screen, he handed it over to Sofia.

She turned the image for everyone to see as she pointed to the phone's screen. "Let's ignore the five coats of arms for a moment," she said. "This image contains two other elements. One is the bundle of arrows. It's located in the center of the composition. The other is the guiding star. It, too, is centered but placed in a higher position, presiding over the composition." She addressed her sister. "We know that great pains were taken to deposit the secret pact ceremoniously in equivalent sites in the US and Spain. Therefore, if like her arrows, Isabella stands in the center of the US capital, it follows that the personification of the Guiding Star stands somewhere high in Madrid."

"Of course," said Lily, "a statue of Jesus."

Sofia nodded. "Thus, the guilt. Senator Jackson must have known that targeting the queen's statue was tantamount to attacking her symbolic counterpart Jesus Christ."

Lily suddenly paled. "And he had the target placed on her heart ... I know what statue it is ... Unbelievable!" She excused herself and ran back to her room to fetch her laptop.

Sofia trailed her sister, her gesture reflexive. When Lily had left the room, she slowly turned to Antonio. "I gather I've passed some kind of test?"

Antonio exchanged a look with Michael and Gabriel to indicate he was taking over. Both responded with a single nod. He then approached Sofia as he motioned toward the door behind her. "Please, come with me."

CHAPTER 50

"[...] considering the diffused population of these states—the consequent difficulty of drawing together its resources—the composition and temper of a part of its inhabitants—the want of a sufficient stock of national wealth as a foundation for Revenue and the almost total extinction of commerce—the efforts we have been compelled to make for carrying on the war have exceeded the natural abilities of this country and by degrees brought it to a crisis, which render immediate and efficacious succors from abroad indispensable to its safety."

—George Washington on the state of American affairs, 15 January 1781

Antonio guided Sofia down the hall.

"Where are we going?" she asked.

"The library."

"I heard you have an impressive archive. Is that where you keep it?"

"One of them."

Sofia slowed her pace. "Stop."

Antonio turned a couple of steps ahead. They stood in a stoned wall vestibule, a sort of transitional space between the renovated private residence and an older part of the castle.

"Enough with the terse replies. Enough with your games. You have no right to keep treating me like this," she said.

Antonio took a step closer to her and craned his head to look down. His broad shoulders almost spanned her field of vision. He was wearing a white shirt unbuttoned at the collar and, as he clasped his hands behind his back, it opened just enough to hint sculptured pectorals underneath. "I have every right, Sofia," he said firmly. "I inherited an extremely delicate responsibility and have sworn to carry it out to the best of my ability. You have been identified as a new associate. I will not apologize for taking every precaution to make sure you are right for the job."

"With due respect to you and your responsibilities, *I* decide if *I* want to be a candidate."

"You will. If you come with me, I'll explain, and you'll be able to make an informed decision," he said.

There he was again, asking her to follow him without clarification. She had never been one to follow blindly, and he was getting away with far more leeway than she was used to granting, because she liked him. A lot. But it was becoming a question of self-worth by this point.

She took a step back.

"Please," he said in a softer tone. He released his clasp and motioned toward a robust double-wooden door decorated with carvings of draping ivy. "The answers to your questions are behind those doors. I promise."

"*All* of them?" she demanded.

"As they pertain to you, yes. With time, more."

"Antonio, it better be worth my weight in gold to walk through those doors. This is the last time I concede without further information."

"Trust me, you won't regret it."

She closed her eyes. Then, without a word, she led the way.

The doors opened into a moderately large room. The window shutters were closed. Antonio turned on the lights, which he kept at a low dim level. It took Sofia a second to adjust her vision. When it finally sharpened, she saw the expected walls covered floor-to-ceiling with shelves containing an interesting variety of old books in different sizes and binding styles, mixed in with rolls of documents and manuscripts. No cobwebs, crackling fireplace, or leather armchairs, though. Just a well-organized and well-maintained corpus of invaluable historical materials housed in one of the castle's towers.

A large mahogany table took up most of the center of the room. She observed Antonio going to it and standing ceremoniously at one end. That's when she realized what lay spread across it.

Her heart skipped a beat.

Could it be...?

Sofia held her breath as she approached the aged parchments. She took a broad sweep of the four sheets. They looked so fragile, sealed in their protective sleeves. Most of the text had paled, and large sections were impossible to read with the naked eye, but its defining elements were unmistakable. She noticed the hasty annotations on the margins, words crossed out here and there, and others added. In essence, a collection of rushed last-minute amendments that provided a precious glimpse into the working minds of the Founders at a decisive moment for the new nation and themselves.

But two words stood out at the top of the first sheet miraculously well-preserved erasing any glimpse of doubt:

... created equal ...

Sofia shot a look at Antonio to share her awe. She was standing before the original fair copy of the Declaration of Independence of the United States of America.

He simply smiled, giving her the time and space to enjoy the moment.

Sofia leaned forward and resumed her survey of the rest, which contained the expected list of grievances that had justified independence, concluding with the members of Congress pledging their lives, fortunes, and sacred honor with a firm reliance on the protection of divine Providence.

Having reached the bottom, she grinned. Two signatures authenticated the document, and one was huge. She judged it was even larger than its equivalent on the engrossed copy. John Hancock really wanted to leave his mark. Charles Thompson's was notably more modest.

She straightened up, took another sweeping look to soak it all in, and, satisfied, signaled her wish to see the back.

Antonio circled the table to the opposite side and helped her turn the sheets over. She was nervous enough to have to wipe her hands dry on her jeans in the process. On the reverse of the first one, Sofia recognized the heraldic image that had monopolized the airwaves during the last 24 hours. But then, she did a double take.

"This title is in Spanish."

"The pact was written in Spanish and English," explained Antonio. "These two first parchments contain the Spanish version. The other two contain the English one." He suggested with his hand to finish turning them over so she could see.

As they proceeded, this time Sofia did see the English image that had been the source of tension on the reverse of parchment number three. That left the entire agreement reduced to one page per language. Quite scant for a union of five empires. She was going to comment on it when she also noticed something missing.

"There's no signature." She leaned in for a closer inspection and found no residue or faint evidence there ever was one.

"No," said Antonio.

She looked up quizzically at him.

"It's complicated," he said.

Sofia began to raise a stern eyebrow.

Antonio gestured for clemency. "I was about to explain." He reached for a miniature jewelry box that sat on a shelf close by. On its lid were two gilded initials, G and W.

He opened it and handed it to her. "The union of empires was a long-term aspiration. This document is a statement of intent agreed to by Charles III and Washington upon an honor system. Not an official treaty. What you have in your hand is the closest thing to a handshake."

Sofia looked inside. "A lock of hair?"

"It was common practice to give a lock of hair as a personal memento. More so for George Washington than my king. I believe there are more than fifty samples of his hair preserved in Mount Vernon alone. In this case, it establishes his physical presence to support his word. Charles III corresponded in kind."

"I'm confused. I remember Dan telling me you had asserted there was a signature."

"A reporter misinterpreted my words. What I said was that Washington sealed the pact, not that he signed it. During the war, each side held on to their half of the agreement on a conditional basis. When the war was won, they proceeded to seal it with the exchange of locks and consign their covenant to emblematic deposit sites."

Sofia shook her head amazed and wondered if that was the real reason why the Knights had withheld the terms. No signature meant no proof Washington had agreed to anything.

However, he *had* agreed to something.

She turned her attention to the last parchment. Four modest paragraphs constituted the entirety of the commitment. "So, what exactly did they shake hands on?"

Antonio lingered his response. He lowered his eyes to the parchments, showing a rare instance of emotion; one of loss for what could have been. Slowly, he raised them again to meet Sofia's gaze. "A peaceful and prosperous league of empires united around the promise of mutual respect, defense and shared values."

Sofia remained silent.

"Let me draw you the picture. I'll start with Spain. At the time of agreeing to this pact, like his empire, Charles III felt old and exhausted. When he wasn't fighting wars to protect his territories, he was fighting them for the family. And if external hostilities were not draining enough, the internal battles were almost worse. The administrative, commercial and defense restructuring he had undertaken across his territories was not well received by many. Reports began to arrive from America suggesting that he grant broader autonomy to his territories to avert disaster. Then, in 1779, while in the midst of growing external aggression and internal pushback, and having just wrapped up a war with Portugal, Charles III was faced with having to choose between joining France in support of thirteen rebel colonies who were guaranteed to become a monumental threat on his doorstep or risk letting Britain take over North America.

"George Washington was just as exhausted if not more. He had been fighting for four years in grueling conditions with a demoralized and penniless army, while enduring desertions, rebellions, conspiracies, personal death threats, and treason by some of his closest men. Add to this that support for the cause waned rapidly as the colonies fell into total ruin, and that it was becoming abundantly clear France alone could not deliver victory. But worst of all, there was no loyalty among the colonies. The threat of going their own way was tossed around at the first sign of discord, foreboding a formidable challenge to stabilization, reconstruction and the sustainability of a united front."

Sofia grasped the dire situation. "They were two desperate men in desperate times and haunted by a bleak horizon."

Antonio nodded. "In this juncture, they made a promise to unite and support each other."

"It seems reasonable considering the circumstances."

"More like idealistic. That's why amongst themselves they called it the Quixote Pact and went largely unwritten. The pact was sure to antagonize the powerful aristocracy of both sides, who were bound to lose some of their privileges, because it was only viable so long as each side matched the relevant freedoms of the other. For the rising United States, it implied extending equal citizenship and rights to all its population." Antonio pointed to the first article and read.

> *"There shall forever subsist an inviolable and universal Peace & Friendship between his Catholic Majesty & the United States, and the Subjects and Citizens of both.*

"For Spain it implied relaxing her trade restrictions while enabling political autonomy for her territories." He slid his finger to the next article.

> *"Every privilege, exemption and favor with respect to commerce and political freedoms which now are or hereafter may be granted to one, be also granted to all."*

Antonio looked up. "They were lofty goals, though ultimately contingent on point three." He looked down and read.

> *"The United States shall guarantee to his Catholic Majesty all his Dominions in America as his Catholic Majesty shall guarantee to the United States all their respective Territories."*

Sofia nodded her understanding. "How many people knew about it?"

"Initially only a handful of trusted men in Spain, Spanish America and the US. There was no point in ruffling feathers if the war was not won first. So, Spain agreed to join the conflict and went on to battle Britain in Europe, Central America, and in the Gulf of Mexico, draining British resources from the Revolutionary War. In May of 1781, Bernardo de Galvez, the Governor of Louisiana, took control of Pensacola, closing Britain off from the Gulf and the Mississippi and opening the opportunity to land the decisive blow in Yorktown. Seeing the end near, on September 22, Congress approved a formal treaty proposal for Spain that incorporated these three articles. Meanwhile, Spain collected the necessary funds and backup so that DeGrass could add his naval forces to those of Rochambeau. The battle of Yorktown was won." Antonio pointed to the jewelry box. "That winter, Washington stayed in the house of Spain's envoy, Francisco Rendon, in Philadelphia hosted by the king to discuss the next step."

Antonio released a soft sigh. "Charles III died in December of 1788 distraught by the death of his son Gabriel one month earlier. He was a man who truly loved his family, and the prince was a highly gifted young man. His surviving brother, the heir, not so much. Washington honored the pact until his own death eleven years later. By then the world was a very different place."

"As where the men who took over," said Sofia, grasping why it went wayward.

"Charles III and Washington weren't naïve," said Antonio. "They knew it would be a long, rocky road ahead. When they placed one half under the protection of the Holy Grail and buried the other half in the White House cornerstone, it was hoping the spirit of their covenant would survive." Antonio directed her attention to the pact's closing sentiment.

> "Upon the pillars of Peace and Justice to all and with the blessing of Providence, may a New Order thrive for the Ages."

He slid his deep gaze from the parchment to her and concluded. "We must not let that spirit wane."

Sofia cocked her head. "Was your family asked by the king to see it through?"

"My family's oath goes back much further. If you accept my offer, and at the appropriate time, I'll tell you about it. You'll understand then my need for caution."

"What's the offer?"

"Your lines, they bring our missions together ..." He paused, "... but they're not the only ones. This is not limited to Europe and the Americas."

"You think there are more lines?"

"I know there are. I've already located one, and I'm certain there are more. Maybe they even have their own associated chosen ones like you and your sister. If you join me, I'll put my resources at your disposal to find them."

Sofia stared at Antonio as a truckload of questions dumped into her brain. If there were more lines, where? Why convert global ideals of Peace, Justice, Education, and whatnot into a puzzle that required deciphering and discovering? If there were others like Lily and herself, did that mean she belonged to a worldwide club of chosen ones? Chosen by who? And who was he, Antonio? How did he know the things he knew? What kind of oath did his family swear? To whom?

There was only one way to find out.

"Two conditions," she said. "One: I want complete freedom to question everything and follow the research wherever it takes us."

"Of course."

"Two: My sister comes with me."

He flinched. "I like Lily, but she is a Catholic sister. These lines are not restricted to any one faith, nation or any other identity or social construct."

"Lily and I are at our best when we work together. We are Hopi: Balance and Harmony guide us."

Antonio drew a broad smile and offered his hand. "Deal."

CHAPTER 51

"All these storms we endure are signs that the weather should soon be temperate and good things will happen to us. For it is not possible that neither evil nor good last forever; and so it follows that evil having lasted a long time, good must now be close at hand."

—*Don Quixote by Miguel de Cervantes Saavedra, 1605*

Short of two hours had passed. Antonio told Sofia about the new line he had discovered and was giving her a general outline of what the idea was going forward, when his cellphone signaled an alert at the same time that Lily was heard in the vestibule calling for her.

Sofia stepped out. "What is it?"

"There you are. I've been looking all over for you. Come, you won't believe what is happening."

Lily led her sister and Antonio back to the living room and waved her hand at the television screen. Gabriel was already there. Michael walked in from the next room, putting his phone away in the thigh pocket of his pants. The wide smile on his face made him almost unrecognizable.

The news broadcast was still transmitting from the heart of the District; its cameras trained on the statue of Queen Isabella. But the scene had changed drastically. Instead of an unruly group of rioters, Sofia saw dozens of people clustered peacefully around the sculpture, as if a shield to protect it. They stood silent, replicating her posture, holding a lit candle in their hands.

The camera receded for a wider frame to capture the flow of more people with candles approaching from all directions, while the rioters were being displaced to the fringes without putting up resistance. Sofia surmised they had probably received orders to stand down. She imagined that hurting peaceful Americans was not the visual the Knights were going for. The few loose cannons who persisted in provoking trouble were effortlessly bounced on by the police.

"What is going on?" she asked.

Lily radiated joy. "It turns out that *We the People* are smarter than we give ourselves credit for."

Sofia questioned Lily about what she meant with her gaze.

"Alright, so here's what happened. When you suggested the queen's statue likely had a counterpart in Madrid, as in a statue of Christ somewhere centered and elevated, I remembered reading about this curious monument." Lily leaned over the coffee table, picked up her laptop, and showed her a scenic picture of a hill covered in pine trees, parks, and a stream at its skirt. "The monument is at the top of this hill, but get this, the hill, which is oddly in an area that is otherwise flat, is literally the geographic center of the Iberian Peninsula. It's called the Hill of the Angels."

Sofia noticed Michael and Gabriel widening their smiles.

"Look, Sof," said Lily, zooming in on another image, "At night it's illuminated like a Guiding Star. It's the monument to the Sacred Heart of Jesus."

The Sacred *Heart* of Jesus ... Sofia grinned. Thus, the target on the queen's chest, the senator's guilty giveaway.

She examined the monument. It was a 38-foot statue of Jesus Christ with open arms standing upon an 85-foot pedestal, which in turn stood on a 2,000-foot-high hill above sea level with fantastic panoramic views of the capital.

"How did you know?" asked Lily.

Sofia shrugged. "I knew there would be a statue of Jesus in Madrid. It is Spain after all. Though, I admit I was thinking more of a prominent church tower in the center of the city. I had no idea it would stand on a hill in the exact geographic center of the whole peninsula overlooking the city."

"No," said Lily. "What I meant was how did you know it stands on the Spanish Line? I mean, the Justice Line?"

"It does?" Sofia was shocked. "Are you saying that that monument—on that hill—in the geographic center—sits on the Justice line?"

"Squarely. Look."

Lily switched to her map of Spain. It was updated with Antonio's findings. In its center she had added a large star.

"Sof, this is the same line that reaches Lima, where their coat of arms contains Jesus as the Guiding Star, as well. You can't deny it this time. It's the connection we were looking for. It has to be—"

Sofia was bewildered. She raised her hand in surrender. "Agreed."

Lily smiled with a bounce of excitement. "Well, in discovering this, I came back to tell you about it, but you were gone. Not wanting to disturb," she said, sliding a grin at Antonio, "I went ahead on my own and signed into our media account. I wanted to share this finding as a segue to reclaiming our Peace Line. To my surprise, I found thousands and thousands of comments expressing disgust for the Knights' attempt at corrupting it. It turns out people aren't buying their narrative. Instead, they support our work. They get the true message of the line, they really do."

Sofia felt a rush of emotion. Their last year had not been futile after all. She cast a look at the television screen. The number of people holding candles around Queen Isabella continued to increase. "But how is this happening? Who's guiding them there like that?" she asked.

"We are," said Lily. "I summarized the best I could how on the armorial image she symbolizes Justice, and the Guiding Star symbolizes Peace, and how they connect back to our lines. Then, I took the opportunity to suggest the new names for the lines and added that from *our humble perspective* ...." Lily paused. "Hope you don't mind me including you?"

"There goes my reputation."

"You're welcome. As I was saying, from our humble perspective, the Peace Line shows us the path back to Jesus' message as the Justice Line tells us it comes from His Heart."

"Very poetic."

"Then I shared the story about Leon's celebration of respectful disagreement to highlight the importance of being united around core values regardless of our superficial differences, and then signed it with a candle emoji, you know, like the candle of enlightenment that is at the center of their annual debate."

"Nice touch."

"The next thing I know, the post is going viral, and this starts to happen." Lily motioned to the television.

Just then, *Breaking News* flashed on the large screen as it switched to another live stream several thousand miles away. Sofia and Lily exchanged wide gazes when they recognized the hill. Hundreds of Spaniards were converging at the foot of Christ's monument with candles in their hands to show respect and support for their American friends who were shielding Queen Isabella. It was only the beginning. A drone backed away to transmit a broad arial view of the procession of vehicles trying to access the hill.

Lily got emotional. Her eyes welled. "We did it, Sof. Our message is finally spreading."

The television screen split in two halves to display the live streams from both sides of the Atlantic side-by-side. Despite the background difference, the scenes appeared to merge into one united sea of flickering candle lights.

"No, Lily," started Sofia, "you're getting the credit for this one. All of it. You broke the spell. While the Knights tried to stir up anger and hatred by resorting to the usual bitter and divisive tactics, you offered an alternative vision, one of unity and respect. Clearly, *the people* much prefer to keep the ball of Peace and Justice rolling forward."

Lily happily accepted the acknowledgement, as the good spirit continued to spread on screen. Even the news anchors could be heard shifting to an upbeat tone, celebrating the gratifying turn of events.

"So...," said Lily suddenly, her impish eyes switching back and forth between Sofia and Antonio. "While I saved the world, what were you two doing?"

EPILOGUE

Early the next morning, Antonio flew everyone to Madrid. They landed on the grounds of his stately residence on the outskirts of the capital, where two vehicles waited fueled and ready to go. They lost no time there. Their first order of business was to split up again and safely deliver each half of the pact to its new deposit site. In due time, they would be exhibited for the public's benefit, but emotions were still volatile and swindled by conspiratorialists and interest groups.

The plan was to get a grip on the situation, let things calm down, and meanwhile design an educational campaign to tell the true story behind the pact. That job was assigned to Lily. In addition to her professional qualifications, the public had fallen in love with the wit and genuine heart she had displayed online the previous day, though it's very likely the allure of her mysterious magical lines also helped. In any case, she was a natural for the social media platforms and her fan following had skyrocketed overnight providing her with an audience she was all too happy to engage.

At this moment, Lily stood with Sofia and Gabriel in front of the Bank of Spain, holding a nondescript art portfolio in her hand, and admiring the Fountain of Cibeles. The sisters hid behind sunglasses, grateful that the hectic life in the big city had everyone walking by them too busy to realize who they were.

Once again, Lily was in awe of the monument but for a very different reason this time. "Unbelievable," she said.

"Isn't it funny how you are the one always using that word?" observed Sofia.

"I use it to describe you. How are you not blown away by this? What are the odds that the two most secure places on the planet to keep the fair copy safe happen to be watched over by lady-chariots? That's like the mother of all coincidences. Pun intended."

"You're exaggerating."

"Am I? The Great Spirit of Prophecy Rock has guarded you-know-what for centuries back home. And you read the article about this bank's underground vault." Lily pointed over her shoulder. "Not only is it the most secure in the world, but it also just-so-happens that, if the vault is in jeopardy, she, Cybele, the Mother of all the Gods, is designed to literally dump millions of liters of water within minutes to flood the preceding chambers. That makes two Great Spirits depicted as lady-chariots protecting vitally important treasures. There's no way that's random, Sof."

"Agreed. Nothing is random. Everything has a reasonable explanation behind it. We just have to find it."

Lily elbowed Gabriel. "What do you say? Reasonable explanation or mysterious ways?"

Just then, Michael approached, saving his cousin. He had stopped by the military headquarters across the street to wrap up a few things. While at it, he arranged for safe passage on a military plane to transport their priceless artifact back home. Antonio had offered his plane, but Michael did not see the need to waste another day travelling back to A Coruña, where his aircraft was still parked, when they could hitch a secure ride from the military base near Madrid. So, Antonio transferred temporary custody of the American half of the pact to Lily, who was then charged with delivering it to the Hopi elders in Oraibi, Arizona. Their mother Sakwa had been notified and was getting things ready.

"Settled," said Michael, addressing Lily. "We have a plane waiting for us at the base." He then motioned Gabriel to go get the car.

"Good," celebrated Lily. "I have so much to do. As soon as I'm done in Oraibi, I need to get back to Phoenix. I have interviews to set up and a bunch of causes to plug in. I heard from Sister Genevieve this morning. She is heading to Afghanistan. Things are really bad for women there and only getting worse."

Sofia shook her head, smiling. Her sister's fans had no idea what they had signed up for. She then turned to check on the main entrance to the bank. Antonio had not been gone all that long, but she wished she had been allowed to go down to the vault with him. Having read the article about it, she was intrigued. At that moment, Antonio stepped out escorted by the bank's president. She knew who he was, because he was waiting on that same spot to receive Antonio when they arrived. Sofia found the level of reverence exhibited by everyone toward him, in the face of his extreme privacy, difficult to process.

She saw them shake hands and exchange farewells.

"That didn't take long," she remarked when he approached.

"They like to hurry things along when it comes to opening the vault."

"I read online there are other juicy secret artifacts down there. Is it true?" asked Lily.

"Sorry, can't say." He angled a teasing grin. "But you have no idea."

Lily smacked him on the shoulder. "You're mean."

He chuckled as he turned to consult with Sofia. "Ready? We should get going if we want to make it before nightfall."

She nodded and the goodbyes began.

Antonio offered his hand to Michael. "Don't be a stranger."

"I won't. And don't you forget, I'm watching," said Michael. "You take good care of her."

Sofia rolled her eyes playfully at him. "I'll remind you I am a black belt. I can take care of myself." She then stepped forward to hug him goodbye. "But I appreciate your caring. Thank you." She brought her lips closer to his earpiece and whispered. "And you too, Raphael. Thank you for everything. I'm looking forward to meeting you in person someday."

As she stepped back, Michael drew his tender smile. "He says he does, too. Hopefully, soon."

A sudden cacophony of angry, honking drivers announced Gabriel's arrival. He had cut through the busy traffic in the roundabout and parked the sedan haphazardly with two tires on the curb in a prohibited spot. He jumped out and motioned them to hurry.

Sofia rushed to hug him. "Thanks for everything, Gabriel. Please keep an eye on Lily while I'm away. Don't let the limelight get to her head."

"I can hear you," said Lily. She leaned into Antonio. "And you, make sure to tune-up her skills during your training. She says she is a black belt but hasn't whopped a backside on her own in decades."

"If I recall, the last time I did, it was yours," said Sofia.

"As I said, decades. We were at a warrior's summer camp learning survival skills while communing with nature and its spirits. You can imagine how that went with her. Had to let her win; give her a little something, you know what I mean?"

Lily turned to Sofia. They stood looking at each other for a few seconds, and then slowly hugged, holding it tight.

"Love you," said Sofia.

"Love you, too," said Lily.

They let go.

"Say hi to mom and dad. Tell them I'll see them sometime in the Spring," said Sofia.

She walked over to Antonio. He was now waiting beside his motorcycle, which was parked on the sidewalk. A different one. Not surprisingly, he had a whole collection. This one was a long-distance touring motorcycle designed with comfort in mind. He handed her a helmet. She took it and instantly swung her leg over the bike to sit in front. "I'm driving."

Antonio stood momentarily stunned though soon enough surrendered with an accommodating smile. "As you wish." He took his place behind Sofia, showing some initial signs of awkwardness, which rapidly disappeared as soon as he held on to her. That he seemed more comfortable with.

Sofia made sure to take off with a roar.

Michael grunted as he trailed them with his eyes. "Let's go. The plane is waiting." He turned to the car and got in the passenger seat.

Lily held Gabriel back. "There are a couple of questions I never got an answer to. One: why does only she get to receive training?"

"In your new mission, she is going to be more exposed out on the field."

"Exposed to what?"

"To whatever comes her way. That's the point of the training. To be ready for the unexpected."

"And why does the training begin on the north coast?"

"You heard Antonio. He thinks it's best for Sofia to hit the ground running. Train on the job. They're going to follow up on a lead there before heading back to A Coruña to fetch his plane."

"Right, and they named it 'Mission Seafood and Cider'. Sound fishy to you?"

Gabriel laughed. "Talking about mysterious ways, that's the *Gran Capitán* for you. It's what makes Michael nervous about him."

Lily froze. "What did you call him?"

"The Great Captain. His nickname among his Spanish agents."

That was it. Lily now remembered why Antonio's ancestor looked familiar to her. "Gabriel, we have to drive north on this avenue, *Paseo de la Castellana*, on our way to the base, right?"

"Yes. Why?"

"There is a quick stop I'd like to make."

Fifteen minutes later, Gabriel parked in front of the National Museum of Natural Sciences.

"Make it quick," said Michael.

"I will." Lily jumped out and turned away from the museum toward its gardens in front. At the end of a short, winding path, there was a pond-like fountain with four decorative waterjets shooting up. And overlooking the water, upon a white pedestal, rose the bronze sculpture of a woman riding a horse.

It was the Monument to Queen Isabella the Catholic.

At first, it might strike as unusual to have the queen's monument placed in front of a natural science museum, but Isabella, as if she had not done enough in her life, was also credited with promoting women's education. She lamented often having received very little herself and ensured that her daughters did not suffer the same fate. In preparing them to be queens, they were instructed in all the sciences, languages, and skills afforded to any man of their time aspiring to become a leader.

Lily came around the monument to its front and rested her hands on the hip-high railing that edged the pond's curvy silhouette. She looked up. The artist had done the queen justice. She looked commanding, her eyes set firmly on the horizon, while escorted by two men afoot. On her right was her trusted counsellor and administrator, Cardenal Mendoza, and on her left was the young knight who Lily was interested in. He appeared confident, guiding her horse as he held its reins in one hand and his sword ready in the other.

El Gran Capitán, she whispered to herself. She knew of the Great Captain due to his special relationship with Isabella. Not romantic, but one of mutual loyalty. It was quite inspiring, and Lily harbored plans of writing about it someday. Isabella referred to him as the *prince of all the knights,* and rightfully so. As young as seventeen, Gonzalo—that was his name—already displayed innate qualities of chivalry, when he alone one night confronted three men on a dark street to save a woman from being kidnapped. He came from a noble family, and by this time had been in the royal service for four years as a page to Isabella's younger brother, Alfonso. She was sixteen when they met, and the three teenagers hung out together, developing a close friendship and affection.

Alfonso's early passing brought them even closer, a bond that became the source of much jealousy for Ferdinand. As a woman, Isabella had to concede much for her husband, but never gave in on Gonzalo. He was untouchable. And he corresponded with the same loyalty on a personal level as much as on the battlefield, for though Gonzalo was legendary for his chivalry, he was more so for his military genius.

Lily shook her head amazed as she recalled that his skills were in full display for the first time during the precise battle that secured the throne for Isabella. And that battle took place in the small town of La Albuera, linking him to the Justice Line and the meteor. She remembered mentioning it at one point. How had she not made the connection with the painting sooner?

To be fair, no portrait of the Great Captain was known to survive, and Lily did not like most renditions made up of him. They failed to meet the highly complementary descriptions supplied by those who had met Gonzalo in person. Until now. The large painting she had seen in the castle was more in line with what she expected, and if she had to guess, that portrait was behind the young version of the Great Captain she was looking at.

That young knight would go on to become the commander of the queen's army and hand Isabella her most cherished gift, the Kingdom of Granada. Then, per her request, he took to Europe to defend Ferdinand's interests in Italy against France, developing the tactics of modern warfare that made him undefeatable and widely studied in military academies around the world to this day. And it was there, in Italy, where his allies and foes alike, out of admiration for his prowess in battle and magnanimity toward the losing enemy, nickname him *The Great Captain*. It was not lost on Lily that his reputation led the pope to recruit him to lead a coalition of Christian forces against the Ottomans, and his victory on Christmas Eve of 1500 settled Andreas Palaiologos' decision to leave his Imperial Roman Title to the Spanish monarchs. Antonio's ancestor had been there for Queen Isabella's every critical and fateful milestone.

Ferdinand would not be kind to him when Isabella died, but history would. In Spain, Gonzalo's memory as the measure of a true knight was honored with the ultimate tribute: The aspiring heirs to the Spanish throne were required to swear their oath of loyalty to the laws of the land and the rights of its people on his sword. Even Cervantes, who famously mocked the stories of knighthood through his world-famous parody "Don Quixote", spared Gonzalo with kind praise in his novel.

Lily could not understand why Antonio kept his ties to the Great Captain quiet. Then a strange thought crossed her mind. Gonzalo was buried in Granada less than half a mile from Isabella, her loyal guardian even in death. Was it he who swore the family promise? And what promise could that be? The protection of her legacy? Or something else?

Lily grinned. An enthralling mystery to uncover in due time. For now, what mattered was that, should it run in the family, Sofia had found herself a true knight.

You go, sis.

A WORD FROM THE AUTHOR

History is the story of us, written by us; and there is so much to tell that we have no option but to pick and choose what to tell. Inevitably, it will always be subjective. Always. Even the most professional historian, with the best of intentions, is forced to choose from among the enormous amount of data to fit a particular focus. That focus can range from a kind curated collection of historical facts for the education of young minds, to decrying horrible wrongs of the past so they don't repeat or rejoicing in the epic events and heroes of a collective. Of course, there is also the corrupted malicious type, but let's not sour the moment.

In my case, my intent with this novel was to share with my children the richness of their mixed heritage. They are half American thanks to their father and half Spanish thanks to me, and that is one explosive combination with a whole lot to be proud of.

As a playful wink to this, I named my new mysterious hero *Antonio del Mar Valiente*. Sounds like the dashing lead in a telenovela, and rightfully so, because *Antonio* was the name of their Spanish grandfather and *Del Mar* (Delmar) was the name of their American one, and both, like true heroes, were genuinely beautiful and brave (thus *Valiente*). It takes great courage to stay wholesome in a world where integrity is perpetually challenged.

Of course, their grandmothers are also present. In fact, their graceful and loving spirits spill over into this story from "Mary's Apostles". So, I trust that their names, *Mary* and *María de los Angeles*, are self-explanatory.

Last, but not least, there is also Thai in our family-mix, and that very-much-loved part is celebrated through the brilliant Sofia.

Thank you for choosing to read "The Quixote Pact". I hope you liked it. If you have a moment, please share your thoughts about it in a review. I always look forward to them, and it helps other readers choose their next adventure.

OTHER BOOKS BY THE AUTHOR

VictoriaCaro.com[1]

TRAPPED IN A DREAM

Thirty years ago, two infants were rescued from a secret project. To ensure their survival, they were separated and never told of the other or what was done to them. Under the watchful eyes of their guardians, both grow up showing no signs of anything out of the ordinary. Today, Faith Fernandez is a schoolteacher in Los Angeles dedicated to her community, and Dr. Christian Luxford "Chris" has made a name for himself in Maryland as a neurologist specialized in sleeping disorders.

All appears good ...

But it's not.

What their guardians don't know is that Faith and Chris have been keeping a troubling secret of their own: they can sense each other. The perception is faint while they are awake, but at night, in their dreams, it gains exceptional strength. While growing up, it was a source of fun and games, and during their teens, an alluring encounter. Unfortunately, adulthood soured the experience. They came to understand there was something very wrong about it. So, while Faith chose to downplay Chris as a product of her overactive imagination, Chris worried that Faith's ghostly presence portended mental illness and made his strange condition the secret focus of his work.

When the opportunity to advance his research in Los Angeles presents itself, a place he was always drawn to by Faith's pull, Chris quickly accepts. Shortly after arriving, as he struggles with her increased intensity during waking hours, the unexpected happens: Faith is brutally attacked and left in an odd state of sleep she can't wake up from. He, the expert, is assigned to her case. As soon as he recognizes her, his world comes crushing down. She is real. Flesh and blood real. How is that possible?

---

1. http://www.victoriacaro.com

A desperate race will follow. Chris must unravel the mystery behind their telepathic connection to work out Faith's cure, as her window of recovery closes fast and her attacker lurks to finish the job.

ESSENCE

At the end of *Trapped in a Dream*, Faith and Chris barely survive the cover-up of an illegal experiment that gave them telepathic abilities.

Now, in *Essence*, while on vacation in Barcelona, Spain, and as they come to terms with their new reality, Faith inadvertently connects with another experimental subject, who she witnesses committing a murder. Horrified, all she is able to discern from it, is that the subject is a woman, and the act occurred in some kind of laboratory.

Unable to go to the authorities, Faith and Chris are teamed up with a local trusted, though unpredictable agent, Professor Xavier Vall, whose loyalties are not always clear, but who apparently is uniquely qualified for undisclosed reasons to keep them safe.

So, once again, Faith and Chris find themselves in the middle of an unfathomable conspiracy in pursuit of a sinister woman, unaware she has extraordinary skills far more advanced than their own, and willing to stop at nothing to protect a shocking secret.

MARY'S APOSTLES

Fifteen years ago, Sofia Auru-Soto survived a traumatic event that everyone around her celebrated as a divine miracle.

Today, Sofia is a psychologist running from her past and dedicated to discrediting irrational phenomena. Her life will take an unexpected turn when her estranged sister, Lily, a History Professor, shows up without warning accompanied by an enigmatic journalist, Michael Amir, asking for her help. She claims to have discovered a hidden message in a papal homily that reveals the existence of a surprising alignment of Marian shrines as if a divine path of sorts. Convinced it guides to a prophetic secret; Lily seeks Sofia's analytical genius to decipher its ultimate destination. But they must hurry; dark forces trail Lily and have already attempted to thwart her investigation.

For Sofia, an innate skeptic, the request makes her uncomfortable for obvious reasons, but worried about her sister's nonsensical claim and suspicious of the sinister influence the charming Michael seems to have over her, she agrees to collaborate. The next 48 hours unfold into a race through the most intriguing miracles, legends, archaeology and lost relics in history in search of the clues that complete *Mary's Path* to its final revelation.